Book one of The Kings of Pendar

The Remnants

Troy A. Skog

DEDICATION

I have been blessed with the best parents a person could want, a wife who loves me, two beautiful children that think their dad is crazy for writing books about dwarves and trolls, they may be right. Family I consider to be friends, and friends I consider family. Thank you one and all for your support.

.

Welcome to Pendar!

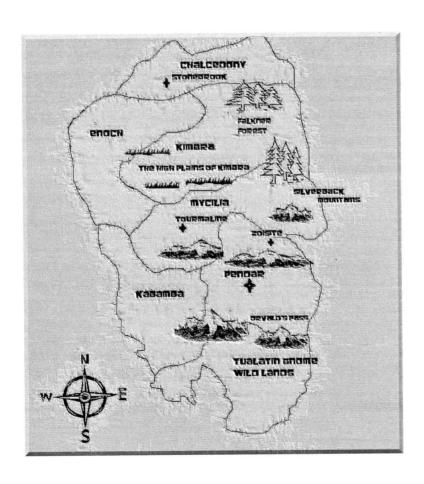

Troy A. Skog

Prologue

The horns from the city gate blasted out their call, the citizens of Pendar spilling out into the streets to see what terrible event had befallen their army. The young dwarf Relysis stood atop the wall next to his mother waiting for the soldiers to enter the gate. They were at the gate visiting his father, a captain of the home guard assigned to securing the portcullis. Peering between the battlements, Relysis could see the army approaching. The dwarves all had the hoods of their cloaks pulled up, their faces hidden as they crossed the bridge below him. At the center of the detail, they bore with them a litter, the body covered with a simple non-ornate blanket. Following along, immediately behind, was the pony of the dwarf king, Orvald Karan, its saddle empty.

Relysis tried to run to the inner wall but his mother, sobbing, held him fast to keep him out from underfoot. Men scrambled to their posts along the wall and messengers were sent to alert King Rommel Ellingstone. Relysis finally pulled away from his mother's grasp when the way was clear, running across to see the dwarves. Hoods cast, they were forming up in the courtyard, lining the roadway to receive their fallen king into the city. Upon seeing the body of the king pass below him in the courtyard, Relysis instinctively moved to pull his hood over his head, struck by the moment and vowing to someday bring justice to the gnomes who had slain his king.

The funeral lasted a week, as was dwarf custom. Throughout the entire city, men and dwarf alike were in mourning. Shortly after Orvald Karan was laid to rest with his ancestors in the tombs of the ancient mountain city of Zoisite, the dwarf council met with King Rommel to determine the ascension to the dwarf half of the shared throne of Pendar. Orvald was without an heir so the council voted against elevating one of their own in exchange for the highest cabinet position on the council, and so it became that the two races combined to be one.

Pendar remained strong and united for the next hundred plus years without being threatened ... until now....

Troy A. Skog

The Remnants

Chapter One

Samuel Ellingstone, King of Pendar, studied the valley from the back of his horse. General Relysis sat next to him astride his pony. The day had dawned shrouded in fog, and now it settled down into the valley, effectively hiding the horde of gnome soldiers preparing to attack his army. Samuel knew the gnomes were there for it had been the same every day since he led his army out from behind the protective walls of Pendar and into the mountains to meet Orgle's gnomes in battle.

"I've made the decision to evacuate the city. We need to give the people enough time to escape beyond the reach of our enemy. How did it come to this?" Samuel spoke the rhetorical question through gritted teeth, his jaw clenched in frustration. He was unconcerned that those around him listened in on his musings as he searched desperately for answers.

Nothing seemed to add up for him as he replayed the events in his mind without taking his eyes from the fog covered valley. The soldiers in his army had trained in these hills and lived on this land their entire lives. Yet now, with few successes on the battlefield and casualties mounting daily, he had no other option than to begin the organized retreat back towards Pendar.

"Let's get to the command post. There is much to discuss before we begin."

Shaking his head, he pried his eyes from the fog that threatened to consume him, and looked to his most trusted friend. Together, they turned their steeds and headed off to meet the commanders of his army.

"Good morning, gentlemen," he began the meeting looking around the room, noting with a sinking heart the absence of a number of close friends. "I'm glad the fates of war have not robbed me of all my most trusted advisors."

Each of the officers at the table realized that as important figures in a country at war, any day could be their last. But, like the soldiers they led into battle, they were men and dwarves of honor and would never want more than to support their king and country. Samuel allowed only a moment for those in attendance to dwell on their fallen before continuing.

"I spent considerable time during my sleepless night deliberating the answer to one question: Why does Orgle bring his army to a halt without fail each night? Gnomes see as well in the dark as our soldiers and he has enough troops he does not need to rest to keep them fresh. During the daylight hours he has complete control of the battlefield, countering our moves as soon as we consider them." He paused before going on. "It is as if he has access to our plans and strategies."

The room burst into cries of dismay as they shouted down the possibility of spies in their camp. Not a one thought it possible that any of their men, those with the knowledge of the plans that were developed in this very tent, could be a traitor. The men and dwarves leading the divisions on the battlefield were above reproach in the eyes of their commanders, and Samuel reassured them all of his belief in his army.

"Fear not, I have the utmost trust and confidence in all of you and the officers you command. I also feel that none possess the ability to infiltrate our camp without detection." He knew that statement wasn't entirely accurate but hurried on, disallowing any from questioning his false assurance.

"However it is becoming evident that we face greater numbers of an army that fights as one. We all grew up hearing tell of magical talismans and devices that grant great power to their bearers." His eyes scanned his rapt audience finding no naysayers among them. "I believe Orgle to be in possession of some sort of talisman of considerable power; a magical instrument that gives him insight into our movements, and allows him complete control over his soldiers. Though every magical tool has its limitations. I believe Orgle's talisman only works during the light of day. However, in this, I can only theorize..." he trailed off, letting the hint of uncertainty bring his men to want to believe in the soundness of his theory.

Samuel spoke of impending defeat, words that had never been considered in the long history of their nation. At no other time had an invading force so tested the army of Pendar. Never had such a large force invaded so deeply into their homeland. It was a tide that needed turned if Samuel hoped to have an army left to push back the gnome horde. It was with this urgency pushing them that the assembled leaders began to formulate their plan to strike back, to try to tip the balance back in their favor. Time was short to plot out the details. Messages were quickly put to paper so that couriers could get out of camp before the gnomes gave chase. Soon the call went out that the sun was breaking the horizon and that all should prepare for imminent attack. Battle plan decided, Samuel and Relysis mounted up and headed back to the front lines, uncertain whether it would be enough to slow the gnomes for another day.

"The messengers with my orders for my brother are riding back to Pendar at this very moment, but Stephen needs time to coordinate the evacuation of the city and avoid a panic. The elderly, the women, and children will take time to mobilize and gather supplies. It will take several days to organize such a task and longer yet to travel to safety." Samuel felt the toll of his office, but wanting to be strong for his commanders, straightened his back and lifted his chin. "I am confident Stephen will be able to muster those in the city for the evacuation."

Relysis's words were gruff. "We will give those in the city the time they need to travel to the mountains to Zoisite. If the gnomes breach Pendar's walls, hopefully the prospect of laying siege to yet another city will be enough to dissuade them from pursuing." He bristled behind his graying beard at the bleak outlook facing his king.

Samuel was a man of considerable strength, both in character and physical presence, and Relysis could see that it pained him to speak of evacuation and defeat. He also knew the men and dwarves in his army respected him for his courage and cunning on the battlefield as well as for his fair and knowledgeable rule. The decision to evacuate the city wouldn't be questioned, just as the decision to bring the battle to the gnomes wasn't.

The most recent buildup of troops by the Tualatin Empire had been witnessed by scouts observing the border and immediately reported to the king and his council. The call had immediately gone out to the soldiers of the Pendar kingdom to defend their borders. When all the available warriors had been assembled, five thousand broad shouldered dwarves armed with double-bladed battleaxes and protected by thick leather armor marching side by side with three times that many men with bows and swords, had gone to turn back the invasion. Samuel and his elite cavalry were at the front with spears pointing skyward and shields gleaming in the sunlight. With his army staged in the mountains along the approach the gnomes would travel, scouts hidden deep behind the gnome front lines continued to report the movements of the gnome army and its immense size. Undaunted by the sheer numbers facing them, Samuel and his commanders had few doubts that the outcome would be in their favor and engaged the gnomes in battle with confidence.

Samuel's army fought admirably and yet now, ten days later, they had been forced back through the mountains towards Pendar, regardless of their tactics or superior use of the familiar terrain. Too many times they had the canyon narrows well defended allowing only a small portion of the enemy to bring its weight to bear. With arrows raining amongst their numbers from above felling a gnome for each arrow let fly, yet they pressed forward. The mighty bearded dwarves swung their battleaxes at the point of attack, but the gnome army scratching, clawing, and biting with their teeth filed to points when their blades failed.

The armies of Pendar were unaccustomed to these results on the battlefield, yet they held to their belief that their king would see them through to victory. Even now, as the army was briefed by their field commanders on the plan for a fighting retreat, the troops accepted their orders without argument. Exactly as Relysis predicted.

Ear splitting war cries drifted up out of the fog, signaling to Samuel and his army that the attack they expected would not be long in coming. All along the line the army tensed for the rush. Their energy was steadily being drained with every attack and Samuel knew that soon their concentration would begin to waver from fatigue. They were better trained when compared to the gnomes they faced, but for every gnome that fell three would take his place. It had become a war of numbers and Samuel was undermanned.

Faintly, through the fog, the outlines of the first wave of gnomes could be seen rushing up the canyon, their thin lanky bodies loping up the rise, their crudely constructed weapons waving overhead as they whipped themselves into a battle frenzy. Samuel's archers began loosing their arrows, trying to break the momentum of the rush. The gnomes kept moving forward, trampling the fallen, knowing that they would most likely suffer the same fate as those now underfoot. Yet they remained undeterred, and when the distance between the armies was gone, they threw themselves against the cold steel of axe and sword. More behind them willing to do the same.

The men and dwarves held against the initial thrust, though when the number of gnomes they were fending off heavily outnumbered their own, they were forced back. They fought the onslaught as they inched backward, always trying to strike down another foe before giving ground to the two or three willing to take his place. The day continued on, the army of Pendar regrouping and counterattacking, answering the call of the field commanders to press forward whenever the enemy's attack faltered even for a moment. With every surge Samuel's army would regain precious ground to be fought over once again when the gnomes would regroup. Samuel was devastated, watching his soldiers fall around him in great numbers while across the field of battle, Orgle pushed his army without regard.

Only as dusk fell did Orgle call off the attack, as he did every night. King Orgle was a gnome like those he ruled, though his rule was not by birthright as was Samuel's. He had laid claim to the throne by force and deception and he ruled with a singular passion that galvanized his army under him.

Orgle felt that to destroy and enslave the city of Pendar, the sworn enemy of every gnome, would transform him into a legend, revered for all times. Every gnome's attitude towards their neighboring nation was one of malice and hatred, for reasons both real and perceived. It had been that way for so many generations that most had forgotten the reason, but their leaders fueled the passion through their misguided religious rituals of human sacrifice and other such acts. Orgle knew that harnessing this passion would enable him to accomplish his personal mission to conquer his sworn enemy. Their leaders whipped them into a hateful frenzy by making a spectacle of killing any prisoners they captured during small border skirmishes. Though many times, unknown to the population, the "prisoner" had been a gnome dressed to deceive the population when no Pendarian could be found. It was this impassioned army that now, many years after Orgle's rise to power, threw themselves onto the blades of Samuel's soldiers seemingly willingly.

Tonight the respite for Samuel's army came as the sun set on the battlefield. The men and dwarves had come to expect the nightly ceasefire and tonight the stoppage came when the Pendarian army needed it most. In all truth it could have come sooner. They had been pushed beyond even their worst-case projections for the day. Samuel's plan for tonight was predicated on his army controlling the ravine they had just been pushed from an hour past. Runners were sent out to the field commanders with orders for what was needed. When all was ready, the signal was given and his tired and beaten army pulled themselves up and charged into the front lines of the gnomes' army as it began settling in for the night. The surprise attack accomplished what they hoped and the enemy retreated a little further. They had gained the leading edge of a short cliff with their last rush.

The day had been tough, though they had won back the bit of ground they needed. Tonight they would set into motion the plan they had formulated in the meeting that very morning. This would be the night that would decide the fate of Samuel's reign. Would it be enough to turn the tide?

The troops began laying out their camp and dug defensive positions. Meals were delivered to the men on the front line, for they dared not leave it undefended. As the hours passed and the sky darkened to moonless black, the men and dwarves quietly began to assemble into squads ready to carry out their commanders' orders. While they waited for the signal calling them to action, the army took the time to take a guarded rest. They were exhausted.

It was a single arrow, set aflame and sent soaring into the night sky, that brought the front lines of Samuel's army up and out of their positions. No longer silent, but roaring battle cries as they poured into the sleeping gnome army, the Pendarians blazed a path through the ranks of disoriented gnomes. They cut as deeply as they could towards the very heart of the beast that they had battled for so many days without success. The battle lust washed away their fatigue and pain they experienced the first taste of victory on the battlefield since this war began.

The stout dwarves spearheaded the point of attack, their mighty war axes cutting down the enemy as the gnomes scrambled out of their holes. The men followed, loosing arrows over the heads of their shorter dwarf brethren, breaking up the defenses as the gnomes tried to organize into fighting squads. The rout continued uncontested for nearly an hour with the gnome losses piling up at the feet of their attackers.

Orgle was only aware of the frontal assault, although it was a two-pronged attack being implemented this night. He screamed out his orders, venting his frustration with his sword to the ultimate dismay of anyone that was in his vicinity, all the while gripping his enchanted blue stone close to his chest. With the chaos threatening to consume his army, he stormed back into his tent, followed reluctantly by his remaining commanders.

While the wedge of dwarves and men battled deep into the enemy camp, two other forces carried out their assignments. The first group retreated back into the mountains to prepare defensive positions. The other, a small squad, moved out and quickly skirted the chaos in the middle of the camp, circumnavigating the army as they stealthily bypassed the outposts and made for Orgle's tent.

Captain Alex Kern led his squad south from the main army, keeping clear of any gnome outposts that might have maintained their positions despite the havoc in camp. The young captain couldn't afford any delays on this mission. This was possibly the most important task of his military career, a career that included numerous forays into gnome territory to scout the happenings in the enemy's homeland. Tonight he led a small squad selected for speed. They all carried swords for protection but they weren't equipped to fend off an attack from a patrol of much size. Theirs was an information-gathering mission with orders to refrain from engaging the enemy.

After clearing the last gnome outpost Alex led them south and began to run parallel to the main battle. They were cautious, but confident, that all eyes would be turned towards the battle and thus made good progress. Alex kept himself on point, expecting at any time to run into enemy forces as they strove for the rear of the camp. It had been mentioned during the planning phase that Orgle might be able to *see* this assault with the aid of his talisman and have a division in position to intercept the squad. However, as they approached, there were no signs that Orgle knew they were coming. Still, Alex and his men remained alert, constantly scanning the surrounding landscape for potential ambushes. They had traveled for nearly two hours and hadn't yet rounded the backside of the camp, seeing firsthand the size of the army that they faced. Alex began to doubt whether any intelligence reporting could change the outcome for the king. Thankfully it wasn't much longer before they could finally start circling back towards where Orgle's tent had been erected.

Alex brought his men to a halt, ordering them to gather round and take a knee. He wanted to go over again the purpose of the mission. He stressed that they were to avoid engaging the enemy if possible for Samuel needed to know what Orgle possessed to control his army. The king had given Alex authority, only if it was deemed possible and the plan infallible, to obtain the talisman from the gnome leader or, in an even bolder move that would decapitate the enemy, to assassinate Orgle. That decision was to be left to the captain based on what he encountered on the ground. Though he kept his doubts to himself, after seeing the immense size of this army he began to think it might be the best option. All of his men nodded in agreement, they had served under Captain Kern on many missions and trusted his judgment. Alex had a history of bringing his men home alive.

After their duties had been passed out to all eight of his men they retrieved ragged dirt covered cloaks from their packs and pulled them on, followed by rubbing handfuls of dirt on any exposed skin. Although it was a simple disguise, it would hopefully gain them some concealment amongst the gnomes, who were known to never be clean, while they penetrated the chaos that was now the gnome encampment.

Alex led his men directly to the tent of the gnome leader. He couldn't afford to spend time disguising the direction of his squad by circling or scurrying about. They met no resistance, as they approached from behind; there was no rear guard. It was either due to all the soldiers heading for the main battle, or misguided arrogance on the part of Orgle. The men spread out, taking cover where available as they neared the tent. Only Alex, accompanied by his lieutenant, settled on the ground immediately behind the tent. Alex leaned forward listening intently, trying to discern how many gnomes were in attendance for Orgle's ravings. Clearly their leader was enraged by Samuel's bold night attack. It was also apparent that Orgle did not have the same control of his army now as during the day. Alex needed to see what was happening inside so he pulled his dagger from his boot sheath and made a small cut in the side of the tent.

Orgle had returned his sword to his scabbard and the commanders now milled about, wary. Several of their comrades lay on the ground outside the tent, their lifeblood soaking into the ground. The slain had not been so cautious when Orgle was initially informed of the attack. This was the first setback his army had experienced and he demanded that his commanders stop the attack and turn the opposing army back. Orgle held his hand up high, waving it about frantically; obviously distressed. Alex knew some gnomish words and phrases, those he'd picked up from captured scouts in the past. He could make out more than a few curses coming from the tent, along with references to the time of night and how long it would be before the sun would rise. Most of his anger was directed at what Orgle held aloft in his hand. It was a blue crystal that looked very ordinary at the moment but from the way he was carrying on, it was obviously the source of Orgle's power. Alex sat back, thinking. He knew he must make his decision on how to proceed, and if his assessment was correct, he needed to do it soon. There were maybe a couple of hours at most before the sun would rise and Orgle would be back in control. He backed away from the tent, motioning his men to gather around.

"We are up against an opponent who is obviously out of control," he began in a hushed whisper. "He has a blue crystal in his possession. I cannot tell how he uses this magical stone, although I feel it is dormant at the moment."

"Orgle is surrounded by ten officers. You can thank him for reducing his ranks for us with his own sword." Alex's statement took the men aback; they had never experienced that type of insanity by any of their own commanders.

"Our choices are two as I see them. Our first is that we take what information we have gathered and return with great speed to report to our king. The second, and the one I favor, is that we storm the tent and take the stone by force. We may even get an opportunity to slay Orgle along with some of his commanders." He looked each man in the eye, knowing they agreed with him without needing them to speak a word.

Alex took only a brief moment to outline the plan and assign positions. His men shifted to their hastily assigned positions; their mission now stood on the brink. If they succeeded and beheaded Orgle's army, they would be remembered in legends long past their days, even if this one was to be their last. Alex dared not think about the possibility of failing. He had no one to spare to relay the information gained to this point. If they weren't successful, this knowledge would die with them. His plan was a gamble and it seemed the future of his country the wager. Alex was less worried about his own wellbeing than the mission. He'd been in precarious positions before and his men had always carried the day.

He glanced towards the east to gauge how much time he had before sunrise. A few hours yet. The men moved closer to the tent. Chaos still ruled the camp and no one challenged them as they assembled with Alex. He unsheathed his sword and raised it, poised to strike the blow Alex hoped would turn the tide of the battle. He glanced at the men around him to make sure they were ready, and then he let his arm descend. The decision had been made; instincts and training were the only required tools now. With a battle cry to honor Samuel, Alex and his men rushed through the gash in the wall, swords drawn and determination showing through their dirt covered faces. Orgle and his commanders were frozen in place as the squad followed their captain into the tent.

Alex and his men used the element of surprise to their advantage, cutting down five of Orgle's top commanders before any opposition could be mounted. The gnomes were ill-equipped to counter this bold surprise attack of the command post. They fumbled with their swords, unaccustomed to the feel of the hilt in their hands, a result of the neglect of their skills as they rose in rank in Orgle's army. Alex, and two others assigned to secure the crystal, drove to the blue stone as the bulk of the squad sought to disrupt those seeking to aid Orgle. Alex and his companions easily dispatched the two officers positioned between the gash in the tent wall and Orgle. Carrying their momentum, they crashed into the gnome leader himself, knocking him down and dislodging the blue stone from his grasp. Fumbling the stone actually saved Orgle's life, for Alex and his men redirected their energies to obtaining the crystal and what they thought would be the key to victory.

Alex's first lieutenant was the first to reach the stone, scooping it up and clutching it to his body as Alex silently cheered the good fortune of his squad. He had risked the mission for this very opportunity and now they had succeeded. Immediately, Alex called for his men to disengage and fall back. It was well that they did, for Orgle's elite squad of bodyguards finally responded to the sounds of battle in the tent and came pouring in through the front flap. The operation had taken no more than a minute, but the toll was obvious as Alex accounted for his men before following those that remained out the hole in the back wall of the tent. Many of Orgle's officers would never lead battalions to war, but neither would two of Alex's squad see the war shift in favor of King Ellingstone now that they possessed Orgle's magical blue stone. With silent thanks to the fallen for their sacrifice he disappeared into the dark night with the remaining squad members, intent on making Orgle pay for those left behind. As Alex led his men through the camp it was Orgle's voice that replayed in his mind. The rage that had been directed at him as he slipped from the tent made him question his decision to fall back after securing the stone, leaving Orgle among the living.

Troy A. Skog

Chapter Two

The guards at the main gate blew their horns as soon as they recognized the messengers thundering up the road on lathered and worn steeds. They had ridden all night, trading off tired horses with those trailing on leads, keeping them as fresh as possible while still covering ground at a pace that would get the message they carried from the king to his brother, the prince, to the castle by dawn. It was still an hour before sunrise, but the men and their uniforms couldn't be mistaken for any other than the messengers of the king even in the muted light of predawn. The guards manning the portcullis threw the levers opening the gates, timing it so that the horses slowed only slightly as they crossed the wooden planks of the bridge and through the open gate. Archers high on the city walls trained their bows on the road, protecting the messengers from pursuit. As the weary soldiers wrung the last bit of energy from their mounts, driving them on through the city streets, sleepy-eyed citizens peeked out shuttered windows to see what the horns heralded.

Prince Stephen's solitude was interrupted as he walked the castle grounds when he heard the horns from the gate. He hurried towards the castle entrance, both eager and apprehensive for the news delivered by the messengers. The previous messages received hadn't been encouraging, and his brother Samuel had stated he worried things were likely to get worse in the near future. As Stephen came into the courtyard, he saw the messengers dismounting amongst a throng of castle guards asking questions of the tired riders, all of them curious about how the war was going. Grooms rushed out and gathered the horses, leading them away to be walked, rubbed down, and watered. The messengers attempted to straighten their uniforms as best they could after a long day and night in the saddle, while trying to field as many questions as possible.

As Stephen walked out of the shadows to greet the messengers, one of the castle guards called the group to attention. The highest ranking messenger bowed as Stephen approached, straightening as he handed Stephen the sealed message pouch.

"The Kingdom of Pendar thanks you for your service. I pray you had a safe journey?" Stephen continued after receiving a confirming nod. "Please, take the time you need to clean up and get some rest."

With the message pouch in hand, he fought the urge to open it where he stood. Proper court etiquette required that he assemble the council members and read it with them present, involving them in the decision making process. He would do what was required of him, as his father had taught him.

It didn't take more than a few minutes to assemble the required members of the court. They had all heard the herald as the messenger entered the city and were making their way to the king's meeting room when he sent his summons. Stephen paced back and forth at the head of the room, impatiently awaiting the last of the members' arrival. He would follow the required procedures, but he didn't have to enjoy the wait. When the last member came through the door, Stephen called the meeting to order. The other members rushed to find seats, and with the exception of a chair or two sliding on the wooden floor, the room was silent.

"We have received another message from my brother, excuse me, King Samuel," his anticipation distracted him causing the slip, but none in the royal meeting room appeared to have noticed. "I will read the message exactly as King Samuel has written so that we may all hear his words as intended and without interpretation." He passed the letter to the court steward to verify the seal and received it back with an approving nod, assuring the rest of the members that indeed the seal was authentic. There could be no matters of politics in times of war when quick action was tantamount.

"Dear Members of the Council," Stephen began to read. "I will not give you any false hope. The tide of the battle continues against us. It forces us back with great loss of life to dwarf and man alike. Every day we are pushed farther back, bringing us closer to the city we are trying to defend. It looks as though within the week we will have retreated to within the city walls. Tonight will be a pivotal night for the defense of our country; much will be decided." The room was silent, the council members had no knowledge what the king had planned, but it would have taken place last night as the messenger carried this very letter to them.

"It is feared that," Stephen continued to read his brother's note, "it will be necessary to move the women, children, and those unable to wield a weapon to Zoisite." This brought an eruption of emotions from those in the audience.

"This cannot be true," howled councilmember Sigmund, louder than those around him. He was a well-respected dwarf, a former member of the home guard, and vocal in his belief that the city walls could turn back any force. "This city was built with taller, thicker walls than any other. Dwarven built, I might add," he cried proudly, pounding his fist on the table, rattling cups and writing tablets for emphasis. "We have the best defenses in place, why would he order us to abandon the city?" He looked around the room at the others, all nodding and murmuring similar sentiments.

"Now that I have everyone's attention, I ask the question of you: why haven't we heard from our neighbors? Do they not respond to our requests for aid? Do they not remember all the years we have protected them from the Tualatin gnomes?"

"Quiet please," Stephen raised his hand to regain their attention. "There is more to the letter. I think we should hear the rest before we make any decisions. Samuel has always led with the peoples' best interests at heart. Please let me read the rest without interruption, we will have time then to discuss what we must do after." He didn't outwardly disagree with those in the room, though he doubted his brother would order the withdrawal from the city if it was unwarranted.

"If you begin preparations now the city should be emptied by the time the army returns, which I estimate will be no more than five days from the receipt of this message. Pack only what is needed to survive at the mountain fortress: food, clothing, and basic supplies. Enough for an extended siege should the main army be pushed from Pendar. I also implore you to be sure Marie and Edward lead the caravan to Zoisite." Stephen paused, shocked. This wasn't the news he'd expected. He felt his brother was being overly cautious in removing the civilians from the city, and now he spoke plainly of losing the city entirely. There were no interruptions this time as the council sat in stunned silence, waiting for him to continue. He looked up from the letter and studied the faces around the table, trying to read their thoughts.

"Our losses are continuing to take their toll on our effectiveness. I am fighting an organized retreat, saving as much of my army as possible to defend our city walls when we reach it. If those walls should fall, we will join you at the mountain stronghold. I would like to report more encouraging news, however, I would not mislead those of the council. The force we face is vast and the willingness of their leader to sacrifice them to our blades is disheartening. Please repeat our calls for assistance to our neighbors to the north. Let their kings know that any help they could spare could be the difference between our city standing, or falling. We will buy as much time as we can for you to evacuate. Be swift to pack and do not tarry in your journey. May the army be successful tonight and the evacuation for naught. I hope this letter finds you well. Your King, Samuel Ellingstone."

That was it then, Stephen thought, as he placed the letter on the table in front of him. They were abandoning the city. He looked to the faces around the table. How were they going to react to this latest message? Would they argue about the king's directive to evacuate? Mostly the faces were downcast. Even Sigmund was speechless, a feat in and of itself. It was Stephen's time to lead and he knew the moment for action was now, but it was then that he looked at the open doorway and saw her standing there.

The king's wife, Marie, stood staring at him, apparently having heard at least the majority of the message. There was nothing to do about it now and maybe his chore would be easier since she heard it firsthand. The council remained quiet, waiting for someone to break the silence that held the room, knowing this wasn't just a bad dream that would end with them waking in a cold sweat.

"There are procedures in place for evacuation, gentlemen. You know what needs to happen in the next few days. Please take charge of your assigned areas within the city. Do not tarry. Samuel wrote of trying to give us five days. We know not what last night's events entailed, nor their success. Five days may be wishful thinking; assume three and we will err on the side of caution. Try to remain calm and convey the need for expediency

16

to the people without causing panic. I will pen another round of messages to be delivered at once to our northern neighbors asking yet again for help." Making sure to make eye contact with Sigmund even if in his own mind he knew it was a waste of ink and messenger. He finished with a nod to each of the members. Excused, they hustled from the room, frightened into quiet compliance. Dealing with the queen was going to be more difficult by far.

"What is this talk of evacuating the city?" she asked in a harsh whisper. "How can you order the withdrawal from the city without consulting me first?" She paused, hearing the selfishness of her statement and amending it as well as her tone, elevating it beyond a whisper. "The council didn't even attempt to discuss our available options. What are Edward and I to do? Do you expect the queen and the heir to the throne to be whisked away to hide like frightened children in the mountains? What does that say to the army returning to the city? It is important for the army to see the heir awaiting them. They need to know there is a future to fight for." Her features hardened. "It is my decision that Edward and I remain behind awaiting the king's return." Her statement left little room for negotiation. Her volume had continued to rise as she came to the conclusion.

"Marie, please don't be so hasty in your decision," Stephen implored. "Samuel will be displeased should he return and find his family has not escaped to the safety of the mountain stronghold."

"No! I have made up my mind, we shall not abandon the city in the face of this vile threat!" Marie hissed. "We shall stand with the city's defenses until the king returns with his army. Only with them shall we depart."

Stephen knew she wasn't thinking clearly and spoke softly. "Marie, Samuel is thinking about the welfare of both of you in giving this order. He is also guaranteeing the royal bloodline is preserved if something were to happen." He knew immediately that he should not have said that last and Marie's response confirmed it.

"This is the way it will be, do not press this matter," she held up her hand, cutting off Stephen from saying anymore. "I am Queen while the king is away I have the final say in my kingdom. Edward and I will be here, awaiting the return of my husband!"

Stephen stared at her, measuring the queen's conviction. He knew without a doubt that she would not be swayed from her decision. He slowly nodded in agreement, picked up his papers, and walked past her without another word. Stephen continued on his path towards his chambers rethinking the plans that had been made for just such an emergency and how they would have to be altered now that the royal family would not be accompanying the evacuees. His brother would have to be informed. That message was going to take some time to formulate, in part because Samuel would not appreciate that Stephen had bowed to the queen's wishes.

By midday, Stephen had dispatched a handful of messengers. They could be seen leaving through the main gate of the city, some headed north to call on their neighbors, others for the battlefield. Stephen had written the messages with his own hand so that no detail would be forgotten and especially so with the message to his brother. He'd taken the opportunity to voice his displeasure over the queen's decision to stay behind, hoping it could be kept between the two men.

With his messages safely on their way, he headed toward the dining hall to get a quick meal and hopefully catch up to a councilmember or two to inform them of the queen's decision. When he arrived at the hall the room was empty save for some members of the home guard taking a quick meal before returning to sentry duty. Stephen filled a bowl of soup for himself waving away the kitchen staff, uncomfortable with their desire to wait on him. With his soup in one hand and a partial loaf of bread in the other, he found an out of the way table and took advantage of the rare solitude it presented him. The quiet lasted only moments before Councilman Sigmund came in with his assistant to grab a quick lunch as they continued evacuation preparations. Stephen got their attention, waving them over after they had each filled a bowl of their own.

"Well met," he began as they found seats on the bench opposite his own. "I'm not sure if the news has reached your ears yet, so let me tell you before you begin eating." He frowned. "I would hate to have you choke on your bread," Stephen's frustration seeped into his comment. "The queen has determined that young Prince Edward and she will not be accompanying the other evacuees when they leave for Zoisite."

"Do you think that is the wisest thing to do considering the risk to their lives?" Sigmund asked, his displeasure matching Stephen's.

"You are correct to question the wisdom, but you were not in the room when the queen told me of her choice. She will not change her mind. Frankly, I doubt anyone would get a word or two in before they were dismissed." He paused, wondering silently if even his brother would be able to persuade her otherwise. Stephen felt he had already overstepped his bounds by saying as much as he had and let it go. Stephen's pause told the dwarf sitting across from him as much, and he nodded knowingly at Stephen.

"Your message to the king informed him of this development I can assume?" Sigmund asked, noting Stephen's quiet nod. "Then we must put together an explanation to give the people. I have a mind to make *her* tell them," he muttered. "That might get her to change her position, though it's unlikely. I'll get with some of the other council members and I'm sure a diplomatic statement can be drafted. I'll make sure you see the statement before we circulate it to the citizens." Feeling the pressure compounding with the gravity of his duties, Sigmund hurriedly began eating his soup, trying to keep his beard from catching most of it.

Stephen felt guilty for burdening Sigmund with another task when the dwarf's plate was full with all the preparations for evacuation. Stephen had to admit it might be an easier task for someone not quite as close to the queen as himself. He decided he would stop in and visit Maria and Edward. He couldn't afford to alienate her now, and any line of communication that he maintained would be invaluable in the days to come.

He arrived at Edward's playroom after looking in several other places he thought Prince Edward and his best friend Bernard could be spending time. He was relieved when his search finally resulted in two squealing boys. The two were always together when Bernard's mother was working in the kitchen during the day. It was a good arrangement for their mothers, as it kept the boys both entertained and from being constantly underfoot. The boys were five years old and, while playing together was advantageous, it didn't mean they never found ways to get into trouble. It was no secret that two little boys with mischievous minds could always think of more things to do together than one could alone.

Marie was with them sitting by the window, staring out towards the distant plains, her despair plain in her profile.

"Uncle Stephen!" both boys chirped in unison, clambering to their feet when he walked into the room. Bernard was so used to hearing Edward calling him Uncle Stephen that he'd adopted the title without knowing otherwise. Stephen never corrected him because he found it endearing to be thought of as family by the boy.

"How are the queen's bodyguards today? Is she safe from the Black Knight?" Stephen asked them. It had become a ritual for Stephen to ask the boys since the day Stephen told them a fable about a knight who lived in the nearby forest. The purpose of the tale was actually to discourage the pair from wandering off into the woods after a particularly distressing incident last spring.

Both boys ran over to stand in front of him as he entered the room. They made their best attempt to imitate the salute of the royal guard and reported, "All is in order and secure, Uncle Stephen!" Their enthusiasm was contagious, so much so it even brought a smile to the queen's drawn face.

Stephen returned the salute, "Your service to the crown is much appreciated. The kingdom is in your debt for the continued fine work you are doing. As your reward you may report to the kitchen and each request one pastry of your choosing from the cook." Neither boy waited a second longer before they ran from the room, down the hall towards the kitchen. Stephen watched them depart then turned, walking slowly towards the window where Marie was sitting. If only he knew what he should say to her, something that would make her reconsider her impulsive decision.

"Marie, I'm sorry to intrude upon your vigil," he began gently. "I think we need to discuss some of the issues that relate to Samuel's orders."

"I'm sorry too, Stephen," she said, without looking away from the window. "I know this isn't the best way to handle the evacuation, and probably will make it more difficult than if

Edward and I were to leave with the others. It's just that I have a feeling deep down within me that something terrible is going to happen. If Edward and I stay behind, in the city, maybe whatever it is can be prevented." She paused, taking a shaky breath to collect herself. "I don't know," she continued, "It's probably just nerves talking, trying to rationalize my wanting to stay, but this feeling can't be denied. If I found out later I could have made a difference by staying, I wouldn't be able to live with myself." She dabbed at a tear forming at the corner of her eye as she finished, never taking her eyes off the distant plains, watching for the return of the army.

Stephen knew there would be no further discussion today. He stepped over to her and laid his hand upon her shoulder, reassuring.

"I know this has not been easy for you, Marie, knowing Samuel is in constant danger and alone without his family. You having to hide your emotions and go about your day as if everything is fine, in an effort to give hope to the people. I know how you feel, Marie, because I share the same burden. Everyone is looking to me for strength, and all the while I'm trying to emulate the decisions I believe Samuel would make were he here." He moved to look out the window, shaking his head.

"He is a hard one to replace. The citizens love and respect him, and await his triumphant return. Yet he comes with the enemy at his heels and the losses of many of his army weighing him down." She shook her head then sniffed. "It will still be good to have him home, though his work won't be finished. It will only be beginning in earnest as he fights to put his city back to rights, and we will be here to support him however we can. Once he's back and acclimated we'll discuss again the possibility of moving the royal family to safety."

Marie nodded silently at her own declaration, and Stephen felt that he had at least accomplished his goal of communicating to her at some level his desire for her and Edward to leave the city. He had said all that he could for now so he excused himself and left her alone to her self-appointed sentry duty. He headed towards his private chambers, hoping that the other members of the council were experiencing better results than he had. At the moment, he simply wanted some privacy to sort out the details of the defense of the city. He knew it was wrong, but he'd been ignoring even considering the plans since the beginning of the campaign, hoping it would be a victorious army returning instead of one in full retreat. He arrived at his room and immediately went to his desk where a map of the city lay rolled in its protective casing. He sat down as he spread it out on the desktop. Time slipped away quickly as he immersed himself in the configuration of their defenses, wondering as he looked upon the map, if these walls could indeed withstand the assault that was surely coming.

Later that evening when he took a break to get a bite to eat, Stephen found Marie and Edward standing at the balcony, gazing out over the castle walls. Together, they watched the horizon for any messengers who might be maybe carrying news of recent events on the battlefield. Everyone held out hope that the plans to evacuate could be avoided. Stephen and Marie would speak to the city leaders tonight after dinner from atop these walls, reminding them of the importance of keeping up their morale during these trying times. It would not be an easy speech. Rumors were already sweeping through the city, and the citizens were getting anxious. They were a proud nation and had never before been in danger of being pushed from their homes. The queen and her son waited quietly together, but no messengers came. When they were informed that dinner was nearly done being served, they left the wall and walked in silence to the dining hall.

Dinner passed with nothing more than small talk being made at the table. Stephen, preoccupied with his defenses, had too much on his mind. Although several members of the council ate nearby, little of the day's activities were discussed. Before they all dispersed, the council members arranged to meet prior Prince Stephen's speech tonight so they could brief him on what they had accomplished, and also to pass along their observations regarding the mood of the city. As they were milling about, Marie excused herself and took Edward to their chambers to put him to bed.

Edward talked of the day's adventures with his little friend, Bernard, and all that he'd done. His mother listened, enjoying the innocence of her young son. He missed his father and had no concept of the danger Samuel faced fighting for their country. That he was better off for his ignorance was undeniable and she found no need to try to explain to him what was happening in the bigger world outside the city walls. At least he would sleep well this night. Someone in the castle should, she thought. Marie tucked him into his bed and kissed him on the forehead.

"Sleep well, my little prince. Daddy loves you and he will be home soon." He smiled up at her and quickly turned his head and shut his eyes. It was enough to make her smile, if only for a moment. She headed out of his room, down the hall, and towards the balcony atop the wall where Stephen had called the city leaders to gather. She would be there with him to show support, though her heart was no longer behind the campaign.

Chapter Three

Orgle recognized the danger as soon as the men began rushing through the slit in the back of the tent, but not soon enough to call for aid. Before he knew it, he'd been bowled over and the Starrock sent skittering across the tent floor. His elite team of gnomes followed the criminals turned thieves into the night, pursuing them through the camp and following the trail of chaos. Orgle's rage burned uncontrollably. An hour later, his squad returned with the blue stone in hand along with several prisoners, unlucky enough to have been captured alive. Now, as he sat on his makeshift throne, he thought back to the day his fortunes changed, turning him from commoner to the most powerful gnome in the history of the Tualatins.

It was neither brains nor brawn that had shifted his fortune. It was something he had lucked upon during his scavenging of the old troll caves near the place where he had grown up. The fact that he was down in the cave that day when all the others refused to enter spoke something of his nature. He wasn't one to let others tell him what he could or couldn't do.

There had been some mysterious disappearances and the elders decided it was less trouble to ban the exploration because those few who came back carried no treasure. So the elders of his tribe had schooled the population, telling them the troll caves were guarded by ghosts of their long departed occupants. It was the lure of treasure that usually motivated the greedy gnomes, but they often times could be dissuaded through fear. The stories created to invoke fear hadn't worked on Orgle; he'd gone further into the labyrinth of the troll caves than those before him. He'd been rewarded with the treasure that lifted him up to where he was today. That treasure was known as the Starrock.

The Starrock had been left behind by the race of trolls when they abandoned the caves, and as far as anyone could tell, the trolls had vanished completely. The Starrock was a nondescript blue crystal of average size mounted on an ornate gold chain. The gold chain was what had caught Orgle's eye. He'd located it amongst several other items that looked ceremonial in nature, in a room that appeared to have been a temple of the trolls. It

25

was the gold that Orgle was initially attracted to, knowing that it would have trading value, so he hung the chain about his neck and continued to search the remnants of the room in search of more gold. It was as he crossed the room and a thin beam of the sun shining through a shaft cut in the mountainside struck the crystal, momentarily illuminating the room in a brilliant burst of blue light before returning to its normal torch lit shadowy state.

Orgle stopped in his tracks, startled and unsure of what had happened. It took him only a moment to make the connection to the blue crystal that swung against his chest as the origin of this color change in the room. He turned and stepped back to the beam of light and carefully dipped the crystal into the edge of the beam. The color burst forth from the crystal, bathing the room with its brilliance until Orgle withdrew it from the sunbeam. Orgle thought this time he noticed something else, aside from the change in the color of the room, a hint of a figure hovering at the edge of his sight. Once again he dipped the crystal into the light, but this time Orgle left the crystal within the beam of light; the now familiar flash of light no longer shocking. Now he looked deeper into the light where something moved within the glow. It wasn't easily discernible until the ghostly figure of a troll walked toward him and bowed. He wasn't sure what it was yet he instinctively knew it contained a power greater than anything in his world. Removing the gem from the light he tucked it within his tunic, causing the light to blink out, taking the troll with it. He wasn't sure how, but he determined right then that he would master the secrets that would bring out the power within the crystal, and that he now had the tool that would make him the most powerful gnome to have ever lived. His thoughts swirled as he made his way out of the cave and by the time he reached the surface, he already had a target for his wrath: the city of Pendar.

Then he spent the next twenty years perfecting the use of the stone, manipulating the gnome high council to do his bidding until at last he'd taken control and disposed of each member. Tonight he'd been dealt a blow. He would recover with some losses to his army, but that was to be expected. His army would regroup at dawn when the sun once again powered his crystal and he would issue his commands telepathically to attack King Ellingstone's hated army.

The question before him now was what to do with his prisoners before he killed them. They would serve another purpose with their deaths, although that would be later. Could they be forced to talk? To divulge enemy plans? Probably not. They had rolled the dice with the daring night attack with, Orgle had to admit, fairly good results. He motioned to one of the guards.

"Bring that one to me," he pointed to Alex, who was grabbed roughly by his arms, bound together behind his back.

"He would like to tell me something that will save his life," Orgle said through clenched teeth, the anger of the bold attack still burning deep within. The guard grinned, knowing that nothing would save the doomed prisoner, not even if he told Orgle every detail of the war plan. He quickly dragged Alex over to the floor in front of Orgle, pushing him down until he lay prostrate on the floor.

"I will tell you nothing of my king's plans," Alex stated before Orgle had a chance to ask a single question. He remained loyal and defiant, though his face was being pushed into the dirt floor, and the guard's foot rested on the back of his head.

"You might as well kill me now and be done with it. My men know nothing beyond tonight's raid, so you can release them to their king that they may avenge the deaths of our squad." It was a bold statement, issued from a position of little strength. It had been a long night. From the time they escaped through the back of the tent, nothing had gone according to plan. It had not taken Orgle's guards long to catch up with them. It was as if they could track the stone regardless of dark or distance. It hadn't made sense at the time and he still couldn't get his mind around it. His men had fought bravely but in the end the numbers against them made the difference. Only three of them remained alive, and they were still under his command and his responsibility.

"Oh, fear not brave soldier, you will be killed; have no doubt. They too will be used in the days to come," Orgle spoke as he gestured to the others sitting, also bound, off to the side of the large tent.

"But right now I need to know what else your King Ellingstone has planned. I have a schedule to keep and this feeble attempt tonight has cost me precious time. So please, spare yourself and your men some rather hideous torture and tell me all that you know. The longer it takes to get the information from you, know that I will do the same and worse to your men when it is their time. Take a moment and reflect upon their fates. It is all up to you." Orgle leaned back in his throne, gauging the man's mettle. Would he take the easy way out to hopefully save his men from some cruel fate, or would his sense of loyalty to a doomed nation provide Orgle with some extra fun? "Take your time. I have a few minutes before dawn and then I will need your decision." He motioned to the guard to help Alex to his knees so that he could look him in the eye.

Alex thought it through as best he could and, surprisingly, came to a similar conclusion to that which Orgle proposed. He and his men had been basically, no actually, assured of death at the hands of this evil tyrant. What was there to gain by giving him any information? Well, Alex supposed, his men need not suffer any greater harm than death itself. But to what end? Delaying that which was promised? Or rather quickening the process and therefore making it less painful? Then it came to him.

"Good gnome," he said, "I apologize. I know not your proper title, but I think there may be a scenario that spares us, my men and me, from your hideous designs and provides you with a steady stream of intelligence in regards to the movements of my king and his army." It wasn't much of an argument to keep his men alive, he realized now that he had spoken it aloud.

"Hear me out Orgle! I think that it may surprise you what knowledge I hold concerning the rest of the campaign." Hopefully that sounded more impressive, not that he could possibly know details beyond his part in the raid last night, but his bluff might have bought them some time.

"You think to fool Orgle!" Orgle shouted back at him, getting up from his throne and squatting in front of Alex. "What could you possibly know to justify dragging you and your men along with my army? You may have noticed that there are no others of your kind, or your short allies. I keep no prisoners! You are either a use to me now or you are discarded. Do not think that you will be treated otherwise." How could this puny man think to manipulate him like that? Orgle was insulted and would not be thought foolish. The slight would cost the man dearly. He would learn to respect Orgle's power! The slightest gesture to one of the guards standing watch over his prisoners brought the guard's sword into motion.

Alex twisted around as the look passed between the two gnomes, turning in time to see the sword tip burst through the chest of Sergeant Tripleton. There was only enough time to lock eyes with Tripleton, the latter knowing that his fate had been decided before his head dropped and he crumpled to the ground. Alex shouted out for Orgle to stop, to spare his men, when Orgle grabbed him by his hair and yanked his attention back to him.

"You knew not who you dealt with and your man paid the price. Do not mistake me for one of your soft commanders! In my army, there is no such thing as disobedience! Those who don't follow orders are eliminated." Turning now to his guards, he motioned them to pick up the fallen man.

"Do not waste his life force or one of you will take his place feeding the stone this morning." Several gnomes rushed forward, picking up the limp man and carrying him towards the table that held the blue stone.

"You will bear witness to the events that will destroy your pitiful nation," he said to Alex. "Watch and learn that there will be no other outcome than the enslavement of your nation and the total annihilation of the royal family. There can be no survivors of the Ellingstone blood line, and I will be the rightful king." He turned and headed for the table that now held the slain man. The guards forced Alex and the two remaining captives to watch Orgle perform the ceremony that brought the blue stone to life. As the three men looked on, they all knew that Samuel and his commanders were not equipped to fight this enemy.

It was at that same moment that Samuel stepped from his tent and witnessed a beam of blazing blue light streak up, into the morning sky. It was captivating in its brilliance, so much so he could hardly turn away. He felt it was calling to him, searching for him. He closed his eyes and shook the feeling out of his head. Surely he had only imagined the connection. The light lasted only a moment and then was gone, along with the feeling of intimacy of its touch.

He looked back across the battlefield. The gnomes were beginning to stir, but not in their usual frenetic bloodthirsty attack that typically greeted Samuel's army at dawn. Samuel felt confident his men had surely disrupted the gnome army, and he hoped that just maybe it had bought them the time they needed to regroup.

It was a needed respite for his army. They had been busy most of the night following the attacks, erecting barriers and constructing stake pits along the route of their retreat. The natural surroundings had lent a hand and the ground recaptured the night before had been put to good use. It would take even Orgle's unstoppable army of gnomes the full day to clear a path to Samuel's army and he intended to take full advantage of any time they were given.

Samuel's army was up at dawn and prepared for the assault, but quickly realized that the enemy was in no condition to go on the offensive after last night's counterattack. If the gnomes took time and regrouped like any other conventional army, Samuel's army too would have time to catch their breath.

Mercifully, the morning passed without an attack and the men and dwarves used the time to shift their positions and build additional defenses. Midday passed and they waited as Orgle and his gnomes struggled to clear the barricades set up during the nighttime retreat. They continued to keep archers at forward positions to harass the gnomes, taking turns within each squad between resting and repairing their weapons of war. After the dinner hour passed and the sun began to set behind the mountains to the west, Samuel knew that last night's raid had been a nearly complete success. It had bought his army a full day of rest and preparation.

The missing squad had been troubling Samuel's mind all day. Their absence spoke volumes. They were some of his best scouts; more adept at eluding capture than any other squad in his army. They were experienced and had made many sojourns into enemy territory before with great success. However, infiltrating the enemy's camp with the leader's tent as your goal was probably asking too much. They should return tonight if they were free and still breathed. Possibly they were hiding behind enemy lines while the sun plodded its way across the sky.

Scouting reports began to come in, confirming Samuel's suspicion that Orgle was dispatching large squads, apparently to guard against another night like the last. He wished he was able to press the attack again tonight, but Samuel's army had spent the day recovering from the constant pressure of the previous week's relentless assaults. The rest would be needed as tomorrow would surely be another day of throwing back the gnome army. Samuel turned towards his tent. He needed rest too.

It was just about dawn when Samuel roused himself from his slumber. He didn't give the bugler the signal to wake the camp, knowing that he had time before the enemy attacked. The question that always plagued him in the morning hours was 'How much time?' Samuel needed to know the progress of the gnomes. As a matter of course, fresh scouting patrols would be dispatched to relieve those that had spent the night watching Orgle's army. Maybe those returning would have the answers he needed so it was just a matter of being patient now.

It was a given that Orgle would push the attack today, and if Samuel had to guess, it would take until at least midday to clear the remaining obstacles that Samuel's dwarven companies had instituted during the retreat. This valley had been chosen for its natural attributes, a series of natural steps leading up to a plateau where the army now camped. They had made formidable barriers in a very short time, collapsing some of the access points and building additional obstacles. Their construction, even in haste, was impressive.

Samuel pushed aside the tent flap and stepped out, looking up at the clear blue sky. His thoughts drifted homeward, wondering what his family was doing on this day. Thinking how nice it would be to spend the day with them, wandering the many gardens and courtyards that surrounded the castle and then considered how much different that would be compared to the day on the battlefield that faced him and his men. The city would be a bustle of activity; people would be packing their belongings and making the last preparations to evacuate the city and strike out for the mountain stronghold. Samuel hoped to provide them with at least a week's time to climb the mountain pass and find security within the walls of Zoisite. The ancient dwarven fortress had not been used in recent times except by soldiers on training missions. Though it probably wasn't in the most livable condition, being dwarven built it would be

31

structurally sound and a safe haven. If Samuel's army of men and dwarves could stop Orgle at the walls of Pendar, those people migrating now wouldn't have to spend more than a month before returning home. His thoughts were interrupted as he looked up and saw a message detail coming into camp from the castle.

The commanders were called to council after they ate a quick breakfast, giving the riders a moment to refresh themselves after their strenuous ride from the castle. Samuel knew the messengers had not borne dire news because they were not wearing a black scarf tied about the upper arm, a simple enough system to help expedite messages that carried more weight and could not await a full assembly of Samuel's commanders. Today's meeting was ready to get under way when Samuel arrived at the command tent. All of his staff was present, along with the ranking member of the message detail.

"Good morning gentlemen," Samuel began. "Today will bring us an opportunity to regain command of this war. Orgle has pushed us back for nearly two weeks, but that is in the past. I'm confident that from here on out we will bring his army to a halt." His staff cheered and pounded the table, tired of being driven ever backward. The bravado was welcome and Samuel hoped to change the mood of the meeting from desperation to one of confidence. Samuel continued when the cheers began to settle.

"We have positioned our front lines at the entrance of the Red Rock canyon, with its sheer walls and the uphill climb to where we are dug in now. Orgle won't be able to bring his army of superior numbers to bear in the confines of this canyon where the walls narrow and will funnel his gnomes into our front lines. The walls are tighter than any other so far at only one hundred paces wide. His poorly trained soldiers will not be able to swarm our lines and our soldiers will be able to fight one on one and effectively control the line," Samuel spoke confidently.

"Nor will Orgle be able to circumvent the canyon without marching his army north to Orvald's pass, the next navigable gap in the mountains. That would take him a full seven days and tire his army while we rest and regroup." Samuel paused to receive some sign of affirmation from those gathered in front of him, receiving nods indicating agreement at his sound thinking.

They had been through this scenario in their military training. It made sense and left them in a favorable position relative to what they'd faced in the past.

"Our goal as I see it," he took care to project the utmost confidence, "is to hold Orgle in this canyon for at least five days before falling back to the city walls. The march back to the city at a controlled retreat will take at least two days, thus giving the inhabitants of the city the time necessary to gain the safety of the mountain fortress Zoisite.

"Gentlemen, we're all aware of the needs of our nation and I would ask you to think of possible tactics we can use to stop Orgle and his rabble of an army. While you ponder the options, I must attend to some matters of the city."

With that, he motioned for the guard to bring in the messenger from outside the tent. The messenger stepped inside and proceeded directly to his king, stopped and saluted, holding out the message in its sealed pouch. Samuel accepted the pouch and dismissed the man, instructing him to get some much needed rest. He broke open the seal, noting before he did that it was his brother Stephen's personal seal and not that of the city council.

Samuel read the message, stopping halfway though at the point that Stephen revealed to him the queen's decision to stay behind at the castle. The commanders stopped their discussions as they looked on at their exasperated king, mumbling to himself about his challenging wife. Samuel noticed the silence in the room around him and looked up from the letter.

"I apologize for interrupting your deliberations."

"Has there been an incident with your wife?" asked Commander Relysis, his concern evident on his face.

"No, it isn't anything serious, but the ramifications could possibly be bigger than the battle we fight now." Samuel responded, noting alarm on the faces of those around him. "The queen has decided she will remain behind with our son Edward and my brother Stephen to welcome the army back into the city."

"Your Highness, this means potentially that the entire Ellingstone family will be trapped within the walls of a city under siege. If the gnomes breach the walls the entire

Ellingstone lineage will most certainly be lost," Relysis growled.

Samuel raised a hand to interrupt his most valuable commander and confidant. "Your perception of the situation is correct, Relysis, and yes, the future of the Ellingstone family would be in jeopardy. However, if we stop this army where they stand we will render the queen's declaration meaningless. I would implore you to put this matter out of your minds for now; we can do nothing to control it. It is nothing that can be dealt with until we return safely to the city. What we can control now is in this canyon, and I need to know how we can dissuade Orgle from continuing his assault."

Having directed his commanders, yet again, to continue planning, he stood and excused himself so that he could contemplate the developments at the castle.

As directed and was their strength, the commanders planned. Orders were sent to the troops. The morning passed and midday came and went, with still no word of Orgle's movements as the troops anxiously awaited battle. Samuel too was anxious and began to wonder if the advance scouts had been set upon and eliminated without being able to send word of the enemy's position. He dismissed that almost immediately on the grounds that the scouting squad was a full forty strong and would be spread out to cover more territory making it impossible to eliminate all members of the scout group.

The only other option for Orgle was to bypass the well-defended Red Rock Canyon, where Samuel's army currently waited, and take an alternate route, marching his army around to the north and through Orvald's Pass. If Orgle did divert his army to take Orvald's pass, it would take a whole week for him to make it. Orgle was impatient, and would rather inflict casualties on Samuel's army no matter the cost to his own.

Samuel mounted up and started out toward the front lines, having assured himself that Orgle would have to bring his troops though this canyon. He stopped and spoke with a number of regiments and various individuals along the way, trying to bolster the morale of both the men and dwarves. By mid-afternoon Samuel had made his way to the front line defenders. Dismounting from his horse, he received a salute from the regiment's lieutenant.

"Put your men at ease, Lieutenant. I'm not conducting any inspections today." Samuel paused to allow the lieutenant to issue the command, but it was at that moment that a forward observer sounded the alarm. Men on horseback were coming in at a full gallop from the south. The lieutenant responded immediately, barking out orders as men scurried to their assigned positions. Samuel, surrounded by his security force, remounted and waited as the horsemen drew ever closer. When they were still some distance off they were identified as members of the forward scouts. The army began to stir as the news of the scouts' return swept back through the ranks. Nobody knew yet what news they carried, though they figured Orgle's army wouldn't be too far behind.

The scouts skidded to a halt, the horses lathered and winded. Dismounting, the captain of the squad quickly identified the king and led his mount to him.

"Your Highness, Captain Highfield reporting."

"Please Captain, report the message you have brought with such obvious haste," Samuel intoned.

"As you wish, your Highness," the captain began. "It was just midday, and the men had taken lunch from their provisions, eating in shifts so that vigilance was maintained." He paused to catch his breath and gathered his composure before continuing. "It was then that the easternmost stationed pair was set upon by a gnome force that had crept up on them without being noticed. The alarm was raised down the line, everyone to the last rallying to their aide. The gnome force was larger than we expected, though it didn't number enough to give us a good fight had we all been formed up to fight as a unit from the outset. Instead, the first arrivals were swept under with those initially engaged by the gnomes. Only after we had formed up as a squad did we turn them back, and once they had fully fallen back we were able to count our losses at fifteen men lost." He paused, letting the assembled men digest the losses of yet more of their brothers in arms.

"The gnome army was moving into our field of view by this time so we decided there was naught to be done but gather our fallen and return back with this message." Captain Highfield stood before his king, visibly shaken by the fact that a full third of his squad had been lost, awaiting his king's questions.

Samuel recognized the pain his officer was in, knowing that even though losses were expected in war, they were never easy to deal with. He did, however, need certain information and had to ask. "How far away is the main body of the gnome army and when would you project that they will come upon us?"

"Your Highness, we were fully two miles forward of our front lines when we were attacked by their scout unit. At the pace they were traveling, taking into account the obstacles they had to cross," Captain Highfield paused momentarily, doing the calculations in his head. "I would figure them to be only two hours behind, although I fear it may be sooner."

"Thank you, Captain, your efforts are appreciated. Now take your squad to the rear to regroup." Samuel turned to the lieutenant, still present and awaiting his command.

"I need a messenger squad dispatched immediately to all corners of the army, telling one and all that the enemy approaches and will engage us within the hour."

King Samuel remounted, wheeled his horse about, and headed in the direction of the cavalry unit he knew would be assembling at the western edge of the canyon. The gnomes wouldn't be able to use their strength of numbers within the confines of the canyon and the cavalry would serve as a disruptive force to break apart Orgle's initial attack, scattering his phalanx. The men and dwarves, more maneuverable and more skilled with weapons, would be able to turn back the gnome horde with equal numbers fighting on both sides of the line. Samuel and his commanders counted on this when they devised their plan. The terrain in this canyon would allow the cavalry to break up any momentum that the opposing army might achieve along the front line. It was imperative for the Pendarian army to maintain control of the front line. A few small pockets of incursions could be repelled with a few losses, but a full-scale breakdown here would be catastrophic for his army. Samuel knew there was no room for error and had therefore decided he would lead the cavalry in these harassing charges against the enemy with strategic and deadly accuracy.

When he arrived at the staging area, four groups of men numbering three hundred each were busily checking and rechecking equipment on their horses, looking for anything that might hamper their effectiveness once on the battlefield. After the initial inspection was complete, the subsequent checks were more to work through the nervous energy that filled the troops, knowing that the battle they'd been waiting for all morning would be joined within the hour. A few adjustments were made to the waiting horses' tack here and there as needed.

The waiting had started at dawn, but the news of the gnome army's position no more than a couple miles away left the men feeling unprepared for the battle to come. The doubts were there, even though they all knew the formations they would employ today; they were not new to any of them in the cavalry. They had been practicing them since selection into the elite corps. The reality was that they had come to this war with a confidence instilled in them from prior skirmishes. Yet, every day, they had swept through the enemy's ranks with little effect. Their self-doubt was palpable, visible on a face here or there. And while the unit as a whole remained confident, it would come down to individuals doing their duty despite their doubts.

Samuel recognized the questioning look in the eyes of too many of his troops. He would have to provide them with an example of courage that could not be denied.

Orgle's army appeared down the valley just short of the two hours predicted by the scouts. They positioned themselves barely outside the range of the archers then waited as the ranks behind them filled the valley. They stood shoulder to shoulder across the entire valley with more coming in behind. From the elevated position at the top of the slope the men and dwarves could clearly see the numbers poised to meet them. The ranks, as far as the eye could see, continued to funnel in indicating that still more moved into the valley.

Samuel's hopes began to slip as the gnomes poured in through the far end of the valley. It didn't take a military strategist to calculate the way this battle would play out. Orgle had enough soldiers to keep pushing forward from the rear no matter the toll. Those who fell along the front line would merely be crushed by the masses coming from behind. Experience showed that they did not seem to care about the wellbeing of their comrades. This day would end badly for the army of Pendar. Even within the confines of the valley they chose for this stand, his soldiers could not hold back the flood about to be released against them. Need pressed him and his mind raced to save his kingdom.

It was a rash move, he knew. It reeked of desperation, but he needed to disrupt Orgle before his entire army was in place. Samuel called his commanders together and informed them of his plan. They were to prepare to charge immediately knowing that something, anything, needed to be done before the enemy army gathered for its attack. They agreed. His front lines would stay dug in while the cavalry smashed into their front lines. There were going to be casualties, but there was no helping that. To let Orgle organize a full charge would be disastrous. The units formed up as soon as the call was sounded, positioning their war horses in lines forty horsemen wide, everyone gripping their spears tightly. His horse, sensing the excitement in the air, danced beneath him, gathering itself for the battle to come. All eyes were on Samuel as he moved to the front of the cavalry. Everyone anticipated his signal.

Samuel looked back at his men, knowing that some or all would surely be lost. There was no guarantee of even his own safety in the heat of the battle. He took a moment, staring into the eyes of those comprising his front ranks. They would take the brunt of the punishment, but the men knew he would be there with them. Slowly he raised his sword in a clenched fist above his head, his horse spinning about beneath him to face the horde. Shouting out a battle cry, he dropped his sword and kicked his steed into motion. Behind him, the ranks leaped forward, not letting their king out ride them. Lances were lowered into a ready position as they began to close the gap.

The downhill charge got the attention of the gnomes immediately, creating the distraction Samuel had hoped for. Orgle's level of control was evident when many gnome soldiers, going against instinct, stepped out on foot to meet the mounted men. Others shrank back, only to be stopped by those behind. Samuel looked down at the wavering wall of soldiers as his horsemen closed the gap. The indecision shown by some was a boon for his cavalry; gaps in the line would yield to his charge more than a unified front.

The impact when they came together was brutal for both sides. Men were unhorsed when their mounts took spears through protective leather breastplates. Any gnomes in the path of destruction were run down, trampled beneath hooves of horses trained to fight; a soldier on four legs lashing out with steel shod hooves. Gnomes that remained standing along the margins of the attack immediately jumped in and began hacking at the fallen cavalrymen, heedless of the next wave of riders bearing down on them. The riders rolled through the horde, slashing with their swords once they were forced to drop their spears. All the while the gnomes clamored to pull them from their saddles.

Samuel, surrounded by his men, fought those few gnomes that came within sword length. Most were cut down before they got close enough to endanger the king. He let the attack continue for only a few minutes, long enough for the whole of their force to engage the gnome army briefly, before he called for a retreat. The cavalry spun about upon his command and retraced their path, back through the gnomes who had converged upon them, back to their own ranks. The gap between the armies closed as Samuel's men raced back through the chaos to the open valley floor between the two armies. The gnomes took up the chase, angered at the rashness of their foe, and seeking to catch any human stragglers. Samuel had counted on the gnomes they'd engaged giving chase. As his men feigned a full retreat, the gnomes left the safety of the main army and stretched out across the valley floor.

The cavalry was ready and wheeled about, sweeping back along the path of their retreat and cutting down the exposed gnomes who, without the advantage of overwhelming numbers, fell easily to Samuel's mounted army.

When the gnomes finally regrouped and scurried back to the safety of the front lines, Samuel once again changed his tactics. The cavalry galloped back in an arc, bringing them parallel to Orgle's front line, running down any who dared step out onto the battlefield. They were able to make several passes, spacing themselves to lure out more of the gnomes and creating a deadly zone that no proper thinking gnome would dare cross. Yet under Orgle's control, they continued to trickle out onto the field. It wasn't until the trickle turned into a flood that Samuel called for a full retreat back up the hill to the safety of his own ranks.

Emboldened by the retreating cavalry, the gnomes surged across the gap, sending up a battle cry of their own as they rushed to engage the foe. Samuel watched as they flowed towards him, slowly being funneled between the walls as they closed in, jostling for position. They were a tide of destruction, moving forward to break against his wall of men and dwarves. He had one more surprise for the enemy before the armies met. He gave the signal for the archers to release the first of many volleys to rain a thousand arrows down amongst the advancing gnomes.

The archers had time to loose several volleys before the gnomes engaged Samuel's front line manned by dwarves wielding axes and men with spears and swords. Then they turned their bows to helping repel pockets of gnomes as they pushed through the line of men and dwarves. The cavalry helped where they could, charging through the gnomes whenever they showed signs of gaining momentum. The gnomes' attack wavered and finally began to retreat when Orgle realized he wouldn't be able to push the army out of the valley as easily as anticipated. Many more of Orgle's army fell from arrows as they retreated back beyond bow range. There, Orgle's commanders regrouped their regiments, establishing new lines and settled back, awaiting Orgle's instructions.

Orgle didn't believe Samuel could possibly think he could hold him off in this canyon for long. He reasoned that Samuel must be trying to stall the army, hoping to buy time for the evacuation of his precious city. His knowledge of the evacuation was just another benefit of the powerful stone that he kept in his possession. He also felt confident that the evacuation wouldn't be completed in time and within two days he would be sitting on the throne of the once powerful Pendar. The entire lineage of the Ellingstone family would be eliminated and he would have an uncontested claim to the throne.

Orgle checked the position of the sun, grimacing. Soon daylight would be gone. This close to his goal, he wanted to continue pressing his enemy. In a moment of confidence, he made his decision. It wasn't his usual tactic and he would have to motivate his troops without the Starrock, but he would push his troops to fight through the night. Samuel's army would be anticipating the usual nightly reprieve; it would take them by surprise. Granted, they were more rested than his own troops, but they couldn't withstand the weight of his numbers for long and would tire quickly if his army fought through to dawn. Without daylight, Samuel's archers would be virtually useless bringing the battle down to numbers. Orgle liked his odds as he called for his commanders.

Samuel gathered his commanders too. It was apparent to him, and those now seated with him in the war tent, that this valley wasn't going to be held for the five days he'd hoped. The discussions going on around him reflected his fears. The new projection was three days, if even that.

"We need to make plans for the upcoming days," Samuel stated, his tone commanding to reach them over the din. "The cavalry will not be able to work as well now that Orgle has closed upon us. Right now Orgle's army has marched all day and should be requiring some rest. What can we do to keep them from getting the rest they need without compromising our troops?"

General Relysis, as was usually the case, spoke first.

"Your Highness, we can press them through the night if we can use the cavalry for diversions while the archery corps move out onto the battlefield and into bow range. If we reduce the divisions down to squad size fighting units, they would be able to move quickly and respond faster than the standard cavalry divisions we're using now."

"What about the lack of light?" Samuel countered. "Won't that reduce their accuracy and put our own army in danger? What will they be shooting at exactly?"

"Dwarves don't use bows, so I understand your doubt, but today I witnessed the deadly use of the arrow by simply letting them fall amongst the enemy ranks. No specific target, still deadly. I believe that the same tactic would work at night. Possibly even with better results, due to the terror of an unseen, silent killer falling amongst the gnomes." Relysis continued to lay out his strategy, encouraged that he had the attention of those gathered.

"Use the cavalry to help mark the zone by lobbing torches above the gnomes' ranks, giving the archers a target to shoot towards. Or better yet, toss small pots of burning oil. The oil would spread fire about when it landed. Anyway, just make sure the riders don't linger after they make their throws. This should keep the gnomes off balance while we rest and watch from behind our front lines." He finished detailing his plan and sat down, waiting for questions or even suggestions to improve the plan. He heard nothing.

"If there are no objections, we will go ahead with this strategy then. Please dispatch runners to the supply tents so they can begin preparation of the clay pots. Let the cavalry riders and archers know that they will be pulling another shift tonight. Make sure they are completely clear on the plan so they can work in unison and not stumble over themselves in the dark."

The commanders took their leave and Samuel was left standing alone in the tent doorway looking around at the army preparing for the night ahead. The sun was about to set again, throwing the valley into the blackness of night. No campfires would burn tonight; the only fires would come from clay pots this night. Tonight would tell him much about his army; if they could hurt Orgle's army while not taking casualties, it could be the turning point they so desperately needed. He stepped out of the war tent and headed for his own, knowing that even a short rest could help revitalize him so that he could help later when the fighting renewed. The men about him, as he crossed through the camp, were busy with preparations and paid no heed to his passing. He hardly noticed them either, lost in thoughts that concerned those who were miles away at the castle. Thoughts he could push from his mind during the day when he fought alongside his men only to rush back into his mind when the world around him got quiet.

He entered his tent and lay down on his cot, not even bothering to remove his uniform. To relax, he began to quietly sing his Edward's favorite little song that worked so well when putting his son to sleep. It proved to be equally effective for Samuel to catch a few moments of sleep himself and he soon drifted off in mid verse.

It was some time later that a dark-cloaked figure stepped out from Samuel's tent and slipped silently into the night. Even amidst the confusion of a camp at war, the troops guarding the king's tent should have challenged his passing, but they never noticed his departure and there were no alarms raised at his passing. The ability to seemingly disappear while in plain sight, especially when combined with a list of other very specific skills, was what made this individual good at what he did, and very dangerous.

Troy A. Skog

Chapter Four

Stephen watched from his balcony as the first of many wagons laden with possessions and provisions left through the gates of the thick granite walls. Mothers, with their children perched atop the loads, guided teams of oxen in the absence of their husbands. A smaller security detail than Stephen felt comfortable with, was escorting the caravan up into the mountains. It was all the soldiers they could spare while still leaving enough behind to defend the city walls when the gnomes arrived. No news from the front lines had arrived for two days now and he felt it could not be good news that they were being spared. A noise behind him broke his train of thought and he turned just in time to see little Prince Edward scurrying to hide behind the tapestry that hung on the wall of Stephen's chambers.

"What was that?" Stephen pondered aloud for the child's sake. "Could that have been that pesky rat that I saw in the dungeon the other day?" A little giggle from the bulging tapestry confirmed that it was no rat, but rather the self-proclaimed hide-n-seek champion of the palace.

Edward hadn't quite figured out that usually the adults he was hiding from were not really looking for him, or were merely letting him entertain himself. Stephen walked over to the lump in the tapestry and nudged it gently with the toe of his boot.

"Well, it feels like a rat, but it's awfully big. Maybe I should call the castle watch and they can come up here and drag it back down to the dungeon where it belongs." Stephen knew that Edward wasn't particularly fond of the old dungeon, damp and dark as it was. Edward had insisted on following him down there on an occasion or two and had clung to his pant leg afraid of being left behind. It wasn't used in its intended capacity anymore, and had been converted instead into a root cellar to keep stores for the palace kitchen.

"Oh look, it's a little boy!" Stephen exclaimed in mock astonishment as the little prince immediately jumped up from his hiding position.

"Hi, Uncle Stephen. Mommy sent me to fetch you down to breakfast. She says you need to eat so you grow up big like

Daddy." He announced in his most important sounding voice, clearly trying to convey his mother's tone.

"Are you sure she didn't mean that you needed to eat your breakfast so that you could grow up big like your dad and not me?" The innocence of the child gladdened his heart. Edward just stared at him, not sure how his uncle could misunderstand the directions. "Come on Edward, I'm sure breakfast is just the thing for both of us." Stephen scooped the boy up into his arms and threw him across his shoulder like a sack of potatoes as he left his chambers en route to the dining hall. Maybe the queen was right about not leaving the city. He sure would miss this little guy if he was sent off to the mountain fortress.

Stephen's day was filled with meetings followed by more meetings. The first such meeting was immediately after breakfast with the city defense council, followed by one with the troop commander in charge of the next caravan of evacuees scheduled to leave tomorrow. Those meetings took up his morning and after lunch he met with the palace chief of staff to determine the needs of those staying behind after all others had been moved to the mountain fortress. After that, a steady stream of various individuals met with him concerning matters that hadn't even crossed his mind. He understood that people would be looking to him for answers in his brother's absence but it was beginning to wear him down. He never envied Samuel's position on the throne, and a day like this only served to reinforce his contentment at being the younger brother. Thinking of his brother reminded him that no messenger from the battle had arrived today and that could only mean one of two things. A knock at the door brought him back to the task at hand and he invited the caller to enter.

"Your Highness," Eloise curtsied as she addressed Stephen. "The palace staff is gathering for a last meal together before most of us leave in the morning and we would like to request your presence."

"I would love to Eloise. It will probably be one of the last good meals we have once the army chefs take over in the kitchen. I don't believe their pastries will compare favorably to your own. I would also like the opportunity to say 'good-bye' to that little rascal of yours, Bernard. I wish Marie would take

Edward and go with you. Those two little guys are going to miss each other."

"Thank you, Your Highness. We too will miss the Ellingstone family, and believe me your family will be in our thoughts while we are away. I must be to my chores now. Dinner will be ready in twenty minutes." With that said, she curtsied again and left the room, closing the door behind her as she scurried back to the kitchen.

Those twenty minutes, he thought, would give him enough time to straighten the papers on his desk and scribble down a couple of thoughts that he had concerning the cities defenses and items that he wanted to talk about with the committee in the morning.

Dinner was a little more somber than he had anticipated and he couldn't wait to finish the affair. 'Good-byes' were exchanged with all and a few tears shed by the queen and her personal attendants. When Stephen sensed that things were winding down, he stood.

"I want you all to know that I realize that the days ahead will be hard and trying. When you are feeling down, just hold onto the knowledge that Samuel, and our army will turn back the enemy in the end. Then we will all gather again in this hall and celebrate our victory. I want to leave you with that hope to get you through the days to come. I know that everyone has much to do tomorrow so I would suggest that we all get a good night's rest. Good night, keep yourselves safe in the days to come. Like I said, we will meet again in this very hall in a short time." He turned and left the room, afraid someone would notice the tears welling in the corner of his eyes. They needed to see strength and courage from him now, not doubt.

On his way to his chambers, he came across Prince Edward and his friend Bernard playing in the hallway. They were dressed as soldiers with their toy wooden swords strapped about their waists and capes trailing behind. Stephen could tell some plans were being conceived by the pair as they huddled together and whispered. They didn't realize the point of whispering fully and were letting any chance of secrecy evaporate as they talked loud enough for Stephen to hear most of what the plan entailed. As best as he could tell from the portion he overheard, the plan involved sneaking down to the courtyard where they expected to encounter the Black Knight. They planned to swiftly subdue him and bring him to justice and this war to a close. With the war over, Bernard would be able to stay with his friend at the castle and the two wouldn't have to part. Stephen had to admit their plan, in theory, was what needed to be done. If only Orgle and his gnome horde could be dealt with so easily.

He hated to break up this planning session but decided, unless he wanted to be searching the courtyard by torchlight for these two protectors of the kingdom, he better send them along to bed.

"Good evening, Knights of Pendar. I hate to interrupt your plans to rid the world of evil, but it is getting late and the world must wait until tomorrow before it is saved. You both must run along to your own rooms before your mothers find you roaming the halls. They are coming right behind me."

Without a word, only a glance between them, they broke off and each ran off to their own bedchambers. Stephen chuckled to himself. These two who were bold enough to attempt the capture of the dreaded Black Knight, yet felt their mothers were far more dangerous. He watched as they disappeared down the hall and then found his way to his own chambers. He changed into his bedclothes after glancing over a couple reports. Ready for bed, he stepped to the window and looked down at the walls surrounding the castle. The guards were visible as they crossed into areas lit by torches along the walkways atop the walls. Darkness had enveloped the landscape and a quiet calm settled over the city that had been bustling with activity since dawn. His gaze lifted towards the city walls and beyond, looking for any signal that would announce a messenger bringing word from his brother. With a resigned sigh, he turned from the window hoping to find sleep and rest tonight. He just missed the shadowy form that dropped from atop the wall into the castle courtyard below.

Marie found her young son lying atop the sheets of his bed, still wearing his cape and his sword belted about his waist. She moved him enough to get his belt off then tucked him beneath the covers without disturbing his slumber. Leaning the sword next to the bed so he could find it in the morning, she stooped and kissed him lightly on the cheek. His eyes blinked open long enough to return her kiss. After giving her a hug, dropped back into his peaceful sleep. Marie smiled down at her precious little boy and her thoughts went to his father.

Where was Samuel now? How much longer could he hold off the gnome horde? She knew it was futile to try and answer these questions and would only cause her another sleepless night lying awake and imagining the worst; guessing at what was transpiring on the battlefield. She patted the boy on the head and headed for her own room where she ended up lying in bed and forcing herself to think of better times to come. In her mind Samuel was with her and Edward and they spent their days enjoying time together. Edward played, his youthful energy tiring out his parents just by watching him. She drifted off to thoughts of her family and slept peacefully for the first night in days.

The cloaked figure glided from cover to cover. The courtyard was dark now except where torchlight from the wall above illuminated patches on the ground. The small spots of light were spaced about and easily avoided, almost as easily as the guards on the city and castle walls had been. The patrols walking the streets of the city weren't aware they had an unannounced visitor. That was how he felt about himself; someone who could go where he wanted without anyone knowing of his passage; an unannounced visitor. Often, he was neither welcome nor invited, but a visitor nonetheless. He stepped in the shadows as two of the kitchen staff passed on their way home. They noticed nothing out of the ordinary as they passed within arm's length of the late night visitor, their eyes not yet adjusted to the night. They talked together as they passed his hiding place and he learned what he could from their casual conversation. It appeared from what they said that the palace staff was off until morning and that all the residents of the castle had turned in for the night, which meant fewer chances for someone to mark his passing and announce his presence. A smile almost creased his face.

The shadowy figure moved forward now that the courtyard was vacant again. Moving quickly, he stopped with his back pressed against the castle wall. He scanned the area behind him and atop the walls, assuring himself that he remained undetected. Once he was confident his presence was still a secret, he looked up for the window he had deemed the best point of entry. He'd spent a few hours perched atop a building across the square watching the castle, its inhabitants, and their movements. It was a ground floor window, which his experience told him usually wouldn't be used as sleeping quarters, and it had remained dark since he began his silent vigil. He slid along the wall several paces until he found himself crouched below the window. His position, hidden from the sightlines of the guards atop the walls by the many trees that grew in the courtyard, only made his task easier.

It was a deadly mistake to get ahead of oneself and think an assignment easier than it really was. His discipline forged through years of training reasserted itself and he stopped, scanning his surroundings once again for potential resistance. His diligence proved justified as a foot patrol entered the courtyard in route to the kitchen for a late night meal. They traveled the same pathway the kitchen help had just used when they exited the courtyard. They too passed without noticing the visitor. He no longer needed to worry about another patrol entering the courtyard because he knew it was unlikely that more than one patrol would be relieved to eat at the same time. As soon as the patrol disappeared into the castle, he went about getting inside.

A small dagger appeared suddenly in his hand and he used it to pry open the window, quickly levering himself up and through the window with barely a rustle of his cloak. Once inside he crouched low, his back to the wall, and waited for his eyes to adjust to the dark interior of the room. A quick scan of his surrounds revealed that he had found his way into the royal library. There were books on the shelves about the perimeter of the room. Crossing the room, he could see notes still spread out across the nearby table along with several maps. They were the defensive strategies for the city. He shook his head. Those making the plans for the city's defenses had no idea of what was coming; Orgle and his army couldn't be stopped.

He shook his head again. This was not his concern. He moved along to the door. There was no time to contemplate the future of this castle. He knew that time was his enemy tonight, but he also knew that being patient was his only defense against discovery. An alarm now meant almost certain death for him. And although intimately familiar with death, he was not looking forward to his own. Avoidance would be the key to his success and he concentrated intently on the noises that came through the night to his trained ears. The hall outside the library door was quiet and no light showed through at the bottom of the door indicating that the hall was dark and quiet.

He cracked the door open. Sliding into the hall, he found it as empty as he'd assumed it would be. He stole down the hall looking for a stairway to bring him to the upper levels and the sleeping chambers. The castle was large and it took a few minutes to locate a stairway that would serve his purpose. It was sparsely lit with wall-mounted torches that would reveal his presence to any that happened by. He could tell from where he crouched that the kitchen was not far away. The patrol that had passed in the courtyard was still making noise fixing their meal and he suspected, based on the castle layout, that when they were finished in there they would be passing this way when they left to continue their rounds. A quick assessment of the situation had him gliding silently to the top of the stairs on his soft leather soled boots. It would be safer at the top of the stairs should the patrol came out of the kitchen.

He found himself in a dimly lit corridor with a single torch burning at the far end of the hall. It was laid out poorly from his perspective, for it left him vulnerable. His form would be silhouetted should someone come along behind him. This was becoming an increasingly difficult task and time was slipping away from him. The royal staff would be up early to begin the day's chores and the more people moving about made his situation much more precarious. Hurrying down the hall, scanning the doorways he passed, he was keenly aware that at any moment he could be detected in the open hallway with no immediate access to an exit. Suddenly he stopped, placing his hand gently against wood. This was the door he sought.

It was worn in manner to suggest that it was handled roughly, likely kicked open routinely. If it was a room at the tavern, it would go without notice, but this was in the royal palace and that wouldn't be permitted. There was most likely another cause for the wear pattern. It fit the description of his target and he pushed the door open enough to allow entrance and slipped inside. Shutting the door behind him, he stopped to listen for any sound of disturbance from the person sleeping within. The slow steady rhythm continued uninterrupted and he advanced. Noting the window at the head of the bed, he quickly determined that it would be his primary escape route. Letting his highly trained body and mind take over, he strode across the room. His instincts were controlling his thoughts and actions, and stopping to think would only slow his response.

A small sword leaning against the bed nearly proved his undoing. Grabbing the toy as it toppled towards the floor, having felt the weight against his toe as he accidentally nudged it from its resting place. There was no room for error on this job; it demanded absolute secrecy. He was starting to feel uneasy and he forced his mind to refocus. He pulled his dagger from its sheath nestled within the sleeve of his cloak and bent down over the child, who unaware of the cloaked presence looming above him, continued to sleep peacefully.

Chapter Five

The morning was clear and the sun shone down on the battlefield, the scene in front of Samuel was grim and disheartening. Looking at his army, it was easy to calculate their fate. This past night had gone to Orgle's army. The canyon had done little to aid the men and dwarves of Samuel's army and Orgle's gnomes continued to push forward. Samuel's plan to bring the battle to the gnomes failed when Orgle abandoned his normal routine of resting at night and instead sent his gnomes on the attack. The cavalry had been all but annihilated early on. The flaming pots had given the gnomes targets and they concentrated their efforts on clogging the escape routes for the men on horseback. It wasn't long before the cavalry dropped that tactic and fell back to trying to defend the constant push of gnomes.

With the cavalry effectively taken out of the battle the gnome army had free access to roam along the front line, probing for any weakness in the defense. A wedge formation comprised of dwarves armed with their battleaxes had been able to cut through the gnomes' attack, although it had been costly to and hadn't really impacted the gnomes. That tactic, like that of the cavalry, had been abandoned. Soon the archers were forced to conserve arrows out of necessity, whereas earlier in the night they had let them rain from the sky with some success, wounding and killing a great many gnomes.

Now the troops working near Samuel could be seen packing the supply wagons in an attempt to beat Orgle back to the city. A full retreat had been called, barely a day and night after digging into the canyon that should have held off the enemy for days. Samuel met with his staff of commanders and they advised him it was time to retreat while he still had any semblance of an army. It would do no good to get back to the city with none to defend its walls, they reasoned. Samuel had to agree, though it meant he had to admit defeat today. To wait much longer would jeopardize the retreat as they would be unable to defend their flanks and surely the gnome army would overwhelm them in the open.

The injured had already begun moving out of camp in wagons laden with supplies, finding what room they could amongst the boxes. The dead, their numbers being too great, would have to be left behind for now. Someday the army would return to honor those who had fallen in the canyon, but today they had to take care of those who could still raise a weapon in defense of the nation.

And so it began, days before they ever imagined it would, with word being passed throughout their ranks to prepare for yet another fighting retreat. It was the only way to protect the slow moving army while it crawled the twenty miles back to the protection of the city walls. Still, it would be a difficult task to keep the troops organized and the flanks protected as the gnomes kept the pressure on their rear.

As the army fought its way back to the protection of the city walls the men along what had been the front lines now became the rearguard, fighting fiercely, knowing that to be wounded now meant almost certain death. No one could stop and help the injured back to their feet as the gnomes relentlessly pushed forward with little to stop their momentum. Here and there along the line of defense, the gnomes would be stopped and even sometimes forced to retreat, but overall it was a steady surge. The men and dwarves brought the wagons laden with injured and what few supplies remained as much time as they could, striking down any and all gnomes that came against them. The day was long and no one knew what the night would bring.

As Samuel had hoped, the gnomes became somewhat more cautious when the sun set and darkness blanketed the battlefield. He also changed the routine, keeping the gnomes guessing by digging in to fight when the enemy expected them to fall back. The ploy worked and Samuel's army began to gain ground; the army began to flow rearward and closer to home at a greater pace.

Dawn found them still outside the city's protective walls with several miles yet to cross before the gates would open to receive those who made it home. Both armies were beginning to tire from the constant fighting on the run and neither was able to keep troops fresh along the line. The men and dwarves continued to leapfrog over each other's positions as they fell back, trying to catch their breaths before they were once again called upon to stem the advancing tide.

The morning found Samuel's army out on the wide open plains and away from the protective walls of the canyons. The threat of a flanking action from Orgle's gnomes became a worry that Samuel and his commanders had no answer for. The only hope they had now was to outrun the gnomes and get behind the protective city walls with as many soldiers as they could. They ordered the troops to fight less and retreat farther after every engagement, hoping to save energy for their run.

Orgle wanted as few survivors as possible to reach the city and called to his army to keep pushing at greater and greater speeds no matter the cost. Both leaders watched as the distance to the city disappeared.

Both called for more speed from their troops, one to save his army, and the other to destroy the one that stood against them. Faster and faster the armies moved, never disengaging from the fight, always moving.

When the Pendarian army could see the city on the horizon they fought less and ran more. A full rout was on and they knew they would only survive if they made it to the city walls. They'd closed the distance to the city walls to less than a mile when they were met by the reserve forces left to defend the city, charging out to their aide. A cheer erupted from the tired throats of those returning as the reserve cavalry pounded past them, stopping the pursuit of the gnomes who had no answer for the fresh soldiers on horseback. The cavalry, while outnumbered, kept them off balance and harassed the gnomes long enough for the remainder of their brothers to make it through the gates.

The gates remained open only long enough for the survivors to straggle in, immediately followed by the reserve cavalry who had come to their aid. Then they swung shut, sealing the city behind its towering granite walls.

Gnomes that ventured too close in their pursuit were greeted with a shower of arrows and eventually retreated out of range to regroup. On the other side of the walls, Samuel looked around him at the remains of his once proud army, wondering whether he could have done something different that could have turned the battle in his favor. He determined that it had merely been a numbers game until now, and certainly things would turn in his favor now that he was safely behind his walls.

The walls were dwarven built back when the two races combined to form the current nation. They were five paces thick, made of granite hauled down from their mountain domain, and assembled with tight joints that made climbing difficult at best. The walls were tall enough that only with a very long rope attached to a grappling hook could someone hope to reach the top. Scaling the wall was made even more difficult, considering that defensive positions had been built in to protect those on the wall from enemies below while allowing them to remove any hooks that found purchase. Even the gate, which is usually a weak link in a city's chain of defense, was designed to withstand assault by a complex mechanism that enabled them to position large granite slabs behind the doors to reinforce them. It made the gates nearly as solid as the walls and gave confidence to those inside. Men and dwarves were already scrambling to take up positions along the wall.

Samuel's confidence in the wall helped lift his spirits to some degree. He realized that now that they had sealed the gate, it was the time to report back to the castle and get filled in on details concerning his kingdom. He assumed Orgle would resume his assault soon and he would be needed back at the wall, so it was best to hurry. Stephen would have news and city business to talk about, and there would be decisions that needed to be made now that the army was back in the city. He spun his horse and started towards the castle, realizing now that the immediate danger was past, he didn't know what he was going to tell Marie of their future.

Outside the walls, Orgle was beside himself with anger. Samuel's army had eluded his grasp and escaped him only to wall themselves up in the very city he meant to have this day; in his mind it was Orgle's throne that Samuel occupied. He called for his assistant, Notal, to bring in the prisoners for a special ceremony. Notal disappeared out the flap of the hastily erected command post to find the many prisoners dragged along behind the advancing army for just such a purpose as this.

Orgle remained in his tent, contemplating the choices that lay before him. In the end, the Starrock was the one solution that could end this battle today. It would cost him, though not as much as it would his prisoners, and he hesitated at the thought. The other option would be to lay siege to the city and wait them out while he threw his soldiers at the wall, hoping they eventually used up all the arrows Samuel's army possessed. It would take a while and he didn't want to wait. Losing a few thousand more gnomes wasn't the issue. Patience was. It always came back to time with Orgle.

Notal arrived with his three prisoners, roughly pushing them in through the tent flap and knocking them to their knees in front of Orgle. Orgle knew then that today was the day and quickly ordered the necessary arrangements to be made. He was willing to pay the price. The prize was too close to ignore for a moment longer and he assured himself that the years ahead would be sufficient compensation for whatever happened today.

As Orgle left the tent, Notal and his men were gathering the required implements to satisfy his demands. Orgle looked into the bright sun-filled sky and nodded knowingly. The stage was set to bring about the end of the Pendar kingdom. This was to be his crowning achievement and would certainly elevate him above all other gnomes now and forever.

Stephen stepped out of the castle to meet his brother in the courtyard, confused and conflicted. He was glad to see his brother home safe, but so much had gone wrong on the battlefield and now too at home. Words he didn't know how to speak aloud floated through his mind. How could he possibly tell his brother about the nightmare that had played out within the castle this past night? Samuel reined in his big stallion and dismounted, then stopped and looked long into the eyes of his brother.

"What dire news must you tell me, little brother?" Samuel asked from the back of his mount. "You could never hide your emotions from me. I know you entirely too well for that."

Stephen stood motionless, rooted to his spot on the walking path, looking up at his brother, speechless. Still struggling to form the words and speak them, finally he blurted them out, "Edward is gone!" He could have been more tactful, but getting the words out in any form had seemed impossible.

Samuel didn't respond, rather he looked past Stephen towards the castle as if he expected to see the boy coming out the door to greet his father finally home from the war. It was an awkward moment, with Stephen not knowing what his brother would do next. The king's reaction to his awful news could not be predicted. Samuel had just been chased home in defeat by the gnomes, only to be greeted with this. For many, it would be too much and tears or rage would be expected. Instead he dropped his gaze back to his brother and asked, "What have you discovered in your investigation of this matter?"

Stephen hesitated for a moment before he continued, unsure of his brother's lack of a reaction. He was neither shocked nor visibly moved by Stephen's horrifying announcement.

"The boy was missing at breakfast yesterday morning. A maid was sent up to rouse the boy from bed and moments later her cries of distress could be heard throughout the castle." Stephen paused looking deep into Samuel's eyes, again trying to glean some indication of what was going through his mind. Unable to read anything, he pushed on with his narrative.

"The castle guards responded immediately, running to the aide of the girl for she was clearly in some sort of pain. They reportedly came upon her in Edward's room, clutching the torn and bloodied bed sheets from the boy's bed in her hands. The alarm was sounded and a search for him was begun. The ensuing search throughout the castle and surrounding area has revealed nothing that could tell us anything of the boy's whereabouts or the murderous villain who carried out the crime. As of yet, the only thing that is known with any certainty is that the culprit left with the boy's body through the bedroom window, then took Edward with him from the castle grounds.

"I'm so sorry, Samuel. This happened on my watch and I feel personally responsible for this crime. I will seek justice as long as I draw a breath." Stephen stopped, a cauldron of emotions brewing deep in his soul: anger, sorrow, and hatred all directed toward his nephew's killer.

Samuel climbed down from his mount and looked at his brother's face. The pain revealed there was immense. How could he have done this to him? It would have to be set right before the night passed, but first he had to find his wife.

"Stephen, I am sorry to put you through this but I'm going to need your assistance in a very important task. I hope you can trust me even though I cannot tell you more until tonight." Samuel reached out to Stephen to hold him by his shoulders and looked directly into his eyes.

Stephen stepped back, unsure what his brother was saying, not trusting his reaction. "Do you know something about the prince's disappearance that you are not telling me? You show no concern for his wellbeing. At first I thought you were fatigued from battle, and the shock of the news and its impact escaped you. Even now, with all laid out before you, your son apparently murdered and his body carried off, still you do not react. I demand you tell me what you know." Stephen stopped, nearly on the verge of grabbing his brother by the coat and shaking him.

"I ask for your assistance, Stephen, and instead I get demands. What do I need to do to in order for you to believe that I have my faculties about me?" Samuel paused and internally rebuked himself for his quick tongue. It wasn't Stephen he was angry with and he shouldn't make it appear so. Stephen stood unmoving, awaiting a response from his oddly affected brother. Samuel knew him well enough to know that he would not let the matter drop even though he implored him to trust him. Stephen was simply concerned for the young prince and he couldn't be faulted for his devotion.

"I'm sorry for my remark. I can't make excuses for myself, but it has been a long and arduous campaign and obviously things have not gone the way any of us planned. I have made decisions that I now question, and one of those in particular does involve the situation that most concerns you. To answer your question, yes, I do know more of the details surrounding the disappearance of Edward than anyone else in the castle does or should know." He cast his eyes about, making certain they were not overheard. "Please take my word that it must be as such and it is better this way." Samuel had hoped to buy some time with his brother, but the confusion on Stephen's face made it clear an explanation wasn't going to wait.

"Stephen, I need you to swear an oath to me. Not to your brother, but to the King of Pendar. It must be given and accorded all the secrecy required, considering its significance. Dare I say that if circumstances warranted, it would be punishable by death for treason committed against the throne." Samuel looked straight into his brother's eyes, the seriousness of the statement evident on his face as he awaited Stephen's oath.

"Of course, I would not commit treason against the kingdom. As a proud member of the royal family I swear complete and utter silence, until advised otherwise by you." Stephen then raised his fist and placed it over his heart, saluting his king as a show of his respect to his leader.

"Thank you. You should know that it wouldn't be your own life forfeited it would be Edward's. He is alive and has been temporarily removed from the city. He is in capable hands and is in no danger. Right now, that is all I can divulge. For his safety, and those with him, it must be thought that the boy has been indeed slain where he slept." He clasped his hand on Stephen's shoulder, knowing what he must be going through, and then stepped past him, walking in silence towards the castle.

As Samuel walked towards the castle, he wondered if he had erred in even telling Stephen. The fewer individuals who knew the boy's true fate the better, but could Marie be denied the truth? What could he possibly tell her to ease the pain of losing her little prince?

Samuel had walked no further than a dozen steps towards the castle when the call to arms was heard from those at the city walls. He spun on his heel and rushed to leap into the saddle. Mounted, he urged his horse into a gallop, back through the very streets he had just traveled. What could be happening outside the city walls? The gnomes in Orgle's army should be just as weary as his own army, he thought to himself. They couldn't be attacking already.

As he rode away, Samuel glanced back over his shoulder towards the castle where he had been born and raised and where Marie was now awaiting his arrival. He decided that as soon as he returned from this latest crisis she deserved to know her son's fate.

Chapter Six

Samuel arrived at the gate to find men and dwarves scrambling to take up positions along the wall. Many who had just finished the retreat to gain the protection of these walls now had to take up arms to defend them. They were dog tired but dug down deep to find the reserves to help ready the defenses, and they were confident now that their walls would turn back the persistent gnomes. Samuel's confidence and pride grew upon seeing his army gathering arms and readying their positions to repel Orgle's ranks. He spotted Relysis atop the wall and made haste, running up the steps to speak with him.

"What is the cause for the alarm?" Samuel asked, somewhat out of breath from his rush back to the wall. "Are the gnomes already moving to attack? I should think Orgle would call for them to regroup after an extended march. However, our foe isn't known for convention. Regardless, he hasn't had time to build war engines to scale our walls or batter the gates."

Relysis pointed to what appeared to be a sacrificial altar erected on the field stretching away from the city walls. It had been hastily erected just outside bow range and gnomes scurried about, preparing the site.

"We think something big is about to happen out there," he nodded towards the altar. "Orgle obviously has something with significant magical power. We never found out what it was because the detail we dispatched never made it back to camp, but we know his troops are driven and controlled by something beyond our grasp." Again he nodded towards the altar and the activity surrounding it, his face grim. "This has the look of something powerfully evil."

The rest of Orgle's army was agitated. They knew something was about to take place and were definitely unsure of what to expect. As soon as the gnomes preparing the altar finished their work, they scampered back to the front line and melted away from sight. The men on the city's wall got the feeling that those gnomes were running for their lives and became apprehensive as well. Samuel was counted among them.

The field was quiet for a short while until someone spotted movement coming forward through the gnome ranks. It was a small contingent of elaborately dressed gnomes that pressed forward, finally emerging from the rest of the horde and crossing the field towards the altar. A sharp-eyed spotter atop the wall called out that they could make out several men accompanying the delegation. Clearly they were not moving on their own accord, and were fighting to free themselves from the bonds that held them. The guards escorting the prisoners prodded them from behind with sharp, metal tipped spears, drawing blood from their weary bodies with each jab.

"Assemble a recovery force," Samuel called out to his cavalry commander. "We need to save those men." From a fate becoming all too apparent to Samuel. He'd quickly deduced that these were the men under Captain Kern, and maybe Alex himself, who disappeared several nights ago trying to capture Orgle's talisman. Orgle's horde had never been seen taking prisoners on the battlefield, killing any enemy soldier left injured. Samuel knew these men must be saved. They had been on a mission to save their nation and now they were about to give their lives in a ritualistic ceremony; a ceremony most likely intended to embolden Orgle's army while demoralizing his own.

The cavalry members scrambled to mount their horses and head for the main gate while the small group of gnomes leading the men reached the makeshift altar and positioned them so Samuel could easily see the faces of the three men. As suspected, it was the men from his special task force he looked upon now. They stood quietly, bravely resigning themselves to the fate that awaited them. They had done all they could for their king and now knew they would be making the ultimate sacrifice. The party of gnomes standing behind the captives waited. Apparently the time was not right for the grisly ceremony to take place. Orgle was visible behind his lines, unmoving.

Samuel shouted instructions down to his assembly of cavalry riders to make haste that the ceremony was being delayed for some reason and a window of opportunity remained open to them. Samuel discounted any sort of idea that Orgle was trying to draw him out onto the battlefield to attack him in the open. There hadn't been enough time to organize such a ruse. The situation reeked of sorcery and evil magic. Samuel found himself for the first time in this war, truly scared.

The gate's reinforcement panels were drawn aside and the gates opened wide to let the cavalry charge out onto the field. Archers took up positions atop the walls to defend against an offensive should they need to protect the riders' retreat. The cavalry thundered out onto the plain. There was no disguising their intentions. The distance was not too great and speed seemed to be the only option. Orgle called forth several hundred soldiers he'd positioned behind the ceremonial altar, and they charged to intercept. It wasn't an all out attack, but it was just as effective at stopping the hard charging cavalry.

Colonel Welton, the commanding officer of the mounted soldiers, upon seeing Orgle's response, called for the main body of horseman to wheel to the right in an attempt to draw the gnome response away from the intended target. The gap between the forces was closing. Time was running short, but the misdirection worked and the gnome army overcompensated. They were suddenly out of position to prevent a 12 man squad peeling off in an attempt to drive to the altar and rescue the men. It was Welton's only chance and it looked to all those watching from the wall to be a great adjustment on the run. The mounted rescuers closed the gap on the gnomes standing about the altar, and were seen pulling swords from their scabbards, closing the remaining distance to the apparently defenseless gnomes. Suddenly, a supernatural bright blue light flared out from Orgle's hands and enveloped the entire group of riders.

It was such a bright explosion of light that the men and dwarves standing upon the wall of the besieged city reflexively threw their hands up to protect their sight. The men on horseback had no such opportunity and were instantly struck blind by the searing light, suddenly helpless when only moments ago they seemed poised for victory. They tried to control their now blind and terrified mounts with little success and were easily dispatched by the less affected gnomes.

Colonel Welton called for a retreat of the remaining riders back to the city walls, unprepared to combat this new weapon of Orgle's and unwilling to lose more of his riders. The horses' hooves clattered to a stop on the stone paved streets inside the gate. Many of the men wouldn't turn back to face the gate until they were assured the opening was once again sealed shut. The light had unnerved them, and with no protection from its brilliance, the men realized how vulnerable they were without their sight. An entire squad had just been slain without even raising a sword against the enemy. Even during the retreat of the last days, they had always been able to strike back at their enemies. These men, however, hadn't had a chance.

The gnome soldiers that countered the cavalry charge dropped back, not wanting to tempt a bowman into taking a long arcing desperate shot. They settled into an uneasy parade rest, ready to respond to any more charges by the cavalry, awaiting orders from their leader.

Orgle was disgusted by Samuel's attempt to rescue his captured soldiers. He wasn't as weak as Samuel assumed he was and that was why he was going to win the day. Tonight the city would be his, he thought, smiling as he announced that the ceremony would be delayed no longer. He motioned to the guards who promptly brought forth the prisoners and bodily lifted them atop the altar, aligning them so they were positioned face up, next to each other in a row.

Orgle stepped forward once the captives were in position, again pulling the dull blue crystal from beneath his robe. In the other hand he held an ornate knife. He began to chant to the stone as he held it up to the sun, watching in anticipation as it began to glow.

The soldiers of Samuel's army covered their eyes to ward against another possible blinding flash, but they could tell that this time it was different. What was coming was going to prove more terrifying than any mere flash of light, and against this new force there would be no defense.

In ignorance they sat atop the wall and agonized over the fate of the men who lay prone atop the altar, cursing under their breaths, railing against the injustice of being unable to help their friends.

Samuel was no different than the soldiers he stood with, although he was the king and he was expected to have an answer for every situation. Now was no different. He stood atop the wall, staring across the plain, watching the blue stone come to life. He knew of no stone that had a life force, not in this age. It had to be a talisman from an age long gone. His mind raced. There had to be something to counter even this powerful force, something he could bring against Orgle to save his kingdom from the fate that awaited it.

The light grew brighter and he and his men watched helplessly as Orgle began the ceremony that meant the deaths of three more soldiers of their army. They did not turn away, instead letting their anger build, fueled by the injustice they watched unfold before them. The ceremony continued, although the men on the wall couldn't hear the words spoken. Nor would they when Orgle summoned the rightful owners of the stone. Orgle held the now bloody knife aloft letting the blood drip down onto the stone, enough blood to cover the many faceted surfaces. He stopped his incantation and now, in silence, waited.

It wasn't long before a mist began to flow from the stone, swirling and expanding before it merged into a great, hulking form comprised of living tissue, bone, and muscle; the phantom troll that lived within the stone. Orgle did not move nor speak as he looked up at the substantial being standing in front of him. When he decided to call the troll forth, he'd imagined a ghostly apparition emerging from the stone. Now he wasn't sure he was prepared to deal with such an imposing creature. Orgle had used and abused the troll locked in the stone so many times in the past to manipulate the minds of those around him. For the first time, he began to question his own actions. He had to swallow hard to regain his bravado, steeling himself to make the demands that would secure the Pendar nation as his own. Before Orgle could say a word, the troll broke the uneasy silence.

"Who dares call Wilgar from the stone? It couldn't possibly be Orgle, the great and wise gnome leader?" His statement dripped with sarcasm, revealing his true feelings about the holder of the stone. "You should have left me where I was, trapped within the Starrock. There is no sending me back into my prison, my sentence has been fulfilled. Now you have no choice but to do as I have asked of you so many times from within my prison."

"I brought you forth to offer you complete ownership of the Starrock in exchange for one last service to my people." Orgle tried to find the right mixture of confidence and deference, not wanting the troll, with his immense size, to squash him where he stood. It gave him pause that the threat of returning him to the rock seemed to no longer be a threat. "I will give you possession of the stone and allow, no arrange, for your passage home in exchange for the use of one thousand of your troll brethren to bring down the walls of the city of Pendar." There it was, the key to his plan: presenting a freed Wilgar ownership of his prison for a one time use of his people. He knew that even more than Wilgar coveted his release from the stone, he wanted to possess it. To the trolls, the stone was important and it would mean a tremendous amount to their tribe to possess it again.

Wilgar stood looking down at the puny little gnome, barely half his height and a quarter of his weight and considered the proposal. It would be no small feat to call forth the number of warriors Orgle requested. He turned and looked upon the tall granite walls that encircled the city of Pendar and thought through what would take place. Then finally he smiled, confident in the outcome.

Without looking back at Orgle he stated simply, "I will call forth the required warriors as you have requested. We will not, with the exception of defending ourselves, participate in the battle beyond tearing down the walls that protect those within. Once we are done with our task, we will take leave of you and carry with us the Starrock." He paused before proclaiming a firm, "Agreed?"

It was not a statement open for negotiation and Orgle wasn't in a position to barter for more. He was unaware that Wilgar had already used the stone immediately upon his release to summon an army and would, if need be, use it to destroy Orgle's army without hesitation.

Orgle agreed to the terms but began to realize the precarious position he had put himself in. With his one bit of leverage gone, he had given Wilgar everything. He didn't want to seem intimidated though, so he stalled.

"Let me discuss this with my commanders. We want to make sure this is the best use of the stone's power; I may not want to surrender it if this won't guarantee victory for me."

"Let me explain something to you, you pathetic little whelp," Wilgar spat. "Your days of using me and the power of the stone are over." The anger rising in his voice cut through his calm demeanor as he turned to look down upon his former master.

"I am no longer a prisoner of the stone, nor do you possess the power to put me back within it. You may, with great loss to your army, kill me and take the stone back as your own, but know that an army of trolls has already been dispatched to bring the Starrock home. Don't think for a moment that they will be in any mood to show mercy. The walls will come down and the debt for my release will be paid." With that said, he stepped towards Orgle, removing the stone from his grasp before stalking away in the direction of Orgle's personal tent. Pausing momentarily, he turned and tossed a black stone the size of Orgle's fist to the gnome. "This stone is even more powerful than the Starrock, if you're smart enough to figure it out." The slightest crease lined his face, possibly the hint of a knowing smile.

Orgle stood, speechless. Things were beginning to spin out of his control, but Wilgar had promised him the walls would be torn down. He would shift his plan accordingly. His gnomes could overpower the inhabitants of the city even if he didn't control their thoughts with the Starrock. They could be convinced to finish this campaign with the prize so close at hand, especially if they thought they were following a band of trolls into battle.

Samuel and his army looked on with amazement from atop the city walls as the creature materialized in front of them and then watched the exchange between the troll and Orgle. They did not hear the details of the deal struck, but were feeling uneasy about any sort of alliance between the two races. The dwarves had battled trolls in days gone by and had, in fact, lost many warriors to them. Long ago they had even been chased from their city under the mountain far to the east before settling in the mountain stronghold where the evacuees from Pendar were headed now. That thought triggered a memory from a story Samuel had heard as a child from one of the dwarven members of the cabinet. What was it though? His mind was racing. He knew it was important but he couldn't grasp the elusive thought.

"Relysis, keep me informed of happenings in Orgle's camp, especially if that troll makes another appearance. I must return to the castle and find the key to stopping him. There is a story I remember from my youth that until now I thought to be nothing more than fanciful entertainment. It just may be the answer we have been looking for to save our city." He didn't stop to wait for Relysis's answer, and instead headed down the adjacent stairway. It was a mere flicker of hope, but if he could fan the flames and supply more material, it could be transformed into a beacon of hope. He didn't hear Relysis speaking to him as he headed down the stairs but he knew he could be counted on.

Relysis watched the departing man and nodded. Knowing the king as he did, he didn't doubt he was close to solving the problem that faced them. He called after him. "I will send messengers to the castle to update you on the siege, unless, of course, the gnomes begin an assault. Then we would signal you with the horn." He turned back to survey the field. The appearance of the troll had left him feeling uneasy. The dwarves had a long and tumultuous history he couldn't put out of his mind. The trolls had been gone for hundreds of years and it didn't bode well for those in the city that they were back now and possibly joining forces with Orgle's powerful army.

Samuel arrived at the castle in a rush heading directly for the royal library. Running past the castle guards, he called to have Stephen summoned immediately to help him. The guards scrambled immediately to find his brother as Samuel made his way to find the answer to his puzzle. He was standing in the doorway of the library when Stephen arrived, followed closely by a distraught Marie.

Stephen watched his brother stride across the room, pulling old leather bound tomes from the shelves and depositing them on the nearest table. A number of them already formed a pile. Samuel was in a trance and barely noticed them enter the room as he quickly leafed through one after another. "What is it Samuel? You have almost run over more than one guard in your haste. Has the battle begun at the city walls?"

Marie stood quietly beside Stephen, her emotional reserves nearly spent by the events of the past day. She stared at her husband, the father of their child, as he tore through the stack of books in search of something obviously very important. Right now, she needed him more than whatever it was that he searched for. "Edward is gone," she sobbed. It was all she could get out before she burst into tears.

Samuel, finally aware that he was no longer alone in the library, dropped the book he'd been leafing through and rushed to his wife's side. "I must explain my actions to you," he started and then turned to his brother. "Stephen can you please shut the door. No, you can stay," he said, answering his brother's unspoken question. "Marie, please stop crying. Your baby is fine and in safe hands."

This statement brought her back immediately from the dark hole she had fallen into. "Where is Edward? How do you know that he is fine? There was so much blood in his bed, there is no way that he wasn't mortally wounded." Staring hard at her husband, she demanded the answers she needed to put her mind back together.

"When I heard your decision to stay within the city proper instead of evacuating with the rest of the citizens, I realized that I needed to act in order to protect the royal lineage. I called in a favor from the most capable man I know in any situation requiring stealth and secrecy. His name is Kurad. He has been a friend to the throne now for more years than I care to count and has shown nothing but courage in the face of danger. His loyalty is beyond reproach," Samuel stated and then began to tell Kurad's story.

"We met years ago when our father had me traveling about the countryside learning the art of diplomacy, meeting with dignitaries from neighboring countries. I would have to say the most important discovery I made on those journeys was Kurad. The short version of the story is that my escort and I came across a band of miscreants giving Kurad all that they could and yet still he was holding his own, but beginning to tire. With the additional troops accompanying me, the bandits were quickly dispersed."

"Kurad traveled with my escort to Mepolia to the north during which he spoke of his travels and struggles as a young man on his own. Despite our differences we made a connection and have kept in contact ever since. It is a friendship that has helped us both, not to mention the kingdom, whenever he brought information from abroad. In fact, it was Kurad that first reported stirrings among the gnomes and thought it worthy of sending troops to gather information." He trailed off, wishing the information could have helped things turn out differently.

"Why didn't you tell me about this plan before it was implemented?" Marie bit her lower lip, still trying to calm the emotions surging inside her. "It has been an awful experience, one that I should not wish upon any mother. When can I see him?" she asked.

"I am truly sorry for what you have had to endure," he spoke sincerely, looking between the two and meeting her gaze. "But know that I did what I felt had to be done. I could not trust this information to be handled by any courier, lest Orgle's troops intercept the visage. I know not what will transpire over the coming days, more so after the unholy pact the gnomes have entered with the trolls on the field today. However, I know in my heart that no matter what Orgle, throws at our city walls to bring them down, our son Edward will be my ultimate revenge for the atrocities committed against us." He was excited now, his voice rising until he realized that secrecy was still of the utmost importance.

Stephen was alarmed. "What is this alliance with a troll that you speak of? Should you not have mentioned that when you first entered the castle? And what has prompted you to take up reading old books?"

"The answer to our problems is in one of these leather bound books, or at least I hope it to be. I believe that if we are to defeat this army of gnomes we need to rediscover a tale, or what we thought of as just a fairy tale, from our childhood readings." Samuel gestured to the pile of books that he'd already assembled.

"Within these books is the legend of the Black Knight as it was originally told, not the version parents tell their children in an attempt to make them behave. There were clues in the story, that if one was paying close attention, could be interpreted to solve the problem facing us now. I believe I remember father mentioning it may have actually been a prophecy told to our ancestors by some wizard or seer to help protect the kingdom in some future time and place." He tapped the book below his fingers in thought. "I'm sure of it."

Stephen spread his hands before him in an apologetic gesture. "All that I remember of the story is that a knight wearing black armor came forth wielding an axe that had some certain importance. It was usually at that point that I would fall asleep and dream of my own adventures."

"I'm sorry. I was five and didn't realize that the story would be important twenty years later."

"I realize you were young, but that is not an excuse? Where was that stubborn side of yours? I never thought you one to use resort to excuses when something so important is at stake!" Samuel's mock temper, trying to make light of a trying situation, lasted only a brief moment before finally allowing a grin to sneak onto his face, mirrored by his younger brother's.

"It was always you they compared to the dwarven Prince Rommel for being so stubborn," Stephen responded. "It was you who walked ten miles when Father revoked your riding privileges so that you could visit a certain young lady. Only to turn about straight away and walk home so as not to suffer the punishment for being late to the dinner table." Stephen was beginning to enjoy this lighthearted exchange and realized how much he missed the carefree days spent as a child with his brother.

"Well, can you blame me for making the journey? My investment has paid off many times over with the marriage to the prettiest girl in the kingdom." He looked over at his bride who sat by and listened to the two exchange barbs.

"My dear Marie, you should get some rest. Stephen and I can find this tale. You run along to bed and hopefully the morning sun will find me nestled by your side."

She couldn't argue her need for sleep after the long emotional day she'd endured. She nodded quietly and slipped out the door after pausing to hug her husband tightly and pressing her lips softly against his. It was a long quiet walk to her bedchambers, but for once sleep found her quickly and she drifted off hoping that all would be well when she woke.

The seriousness of the situation settled in after Marie's departure and the two brothers stood and looked about at the many volumes that could possibly contain the ancient story.

"Well, as soon as you are done patting yourself on the back for snaring such an engaging young women, why don't you start handing books down from the top shelf? They are dustier than the others and probably haven't been read since father stopped reading to us." Stephen suggested to his brother.

Samuel rolled a ladder into place and began to climb towards the highest shelves, glancing at various volumes as he passed them by. He recognized some from his studies and discounted those immediately. They weren't filled with anything but

71

numbers and language studies. He could almost picture his father sitting in their room reading from a plain looking leather-bound book, but nothing stood out in his memory to aid in the search. He handed a book or two down that looked as if they had potential, but Stephen seemed to dismiss them without even cracking the bindings.

"Was there something distinctive that you remember about the cover?" Samuel asked, growing irritated. "I could use some insight if you have something in mind that you are looking for. You barely even looked at those last two I handed you."

"If my memory serves me, I'm thinking the cover could have been imprinted with the family crest, but different somehow and it's that detail that I can't remember." Stephen stood scanning the shelves, looking past his brother. It had to be there.

Samuel too searched the shelves, his brother's memory now aiding his own and hopefully bringing him one step closer to remembering. He felt he was very close to remembering the tome that he sought when a guard knocked on the door and announced that he had a message from the main gate. In that instant, the memory scampered away.

"Your Highness," the messenger began after entering the library. "Commander Relysis would like you to know that nothing has happened since your departure and that he is starting to rotate troops to their quarters so they may rest." He bowed and began to back out of the room, asking to be excused.

"Permission granted, and thank you for your service to the crown. Please report back to Commander Relysis that his decision to rest the troops is a wise course of action. Thank you." Samuel tried not to sound perturbed at the interruption, but wasn't sure he had accomplished that. He had been so close to grasping the elusive memory only to have it pushed away by the simple knock at the door.

He turned back to find Stephen scaling the ladder to its highest shelf. Curious about his brother's action, he watched silently as he stood on the top rung of the ladder, reaching up beyond where he could even see. He began to grope about, stirring up dust that had eluded the cleaning staff for many years. His hand slid along the shelf until finally it met some slight resistance. It was a book of some bulk yet curiously light. The tattered leather-bound book, covered in years' worth of dust, seemed to tingle beneath his touch making his heart beat a tick faster.

"Samuel, I think this is it!" he called as he pulled the book down and began to brush the dust aside, looking for the crest that he believed would be there. The Ellingstone crest was indeed emblazoned on the cover, faded with age, handsomely crafted by a true artist. Clambering down the ladder he laid the book upon the table, setting it nearer to Samuel.

Samuel stared intently at the cover of the book, in part to delay the opening of it for fear of what he may not find, but also seeing for the first time that the crest included a special design. The design matched the tattoo he had carried from birth indicating that he was the heir to the throne in addition to being of the royal family. How he had not remembered that seemed foolish now, but he was so used to seeing the tattoo on his forearm, and little Edward's too, that he had become desensitized to its presence. He curbed the urge to beat himself up for the oversight and reached to open the cover, knowing now with great certainty that the answer did indeed lie within this text.

"*The conquerors from the south had never rebuilt the city gates...*" he read aloud. It was how he began the story when he told it to Edward, but then it would always divert into tales about the Black Knight. Here though, in front of him, was the version of the story his father had told them.

Troy A. Skog

Chapter Seven

Kurad sat within the pine grove feeding small twigs into the growing flame, nursing the fire into a small smokeless blaze. Across the clearing from where Kurad tended his fledgling fire, a young boy played with a newly formed stick sword, dancing and parrying with his own shadow. It had been only a day since he'd brought the boy out into the woods, yet the young lad was already completely at ease with him. Kurad had to wonder if a boy so young could remember faces and perhaps recognized him from one of only a few sporadic visits with his father. He had also given the boy a necklace bearing a token from his father, one that Edward recognized immediately as his father's. It was enough to gain Edward's confidence and trust, and he had eagerly slipped it over his head. Kurad could only guess at the boy's actions and freely admitted he wasn't well versed in children's behavior. He figured to learn much over the next few weeks.

That was the plan Samuel had outlined that night in the tent with the front lines of the battle not more than a bowshot distant: keep the boy safe from harm for a month. He had been very confident during the meeting that a siege could last no more than that and at that point in time Kurad was to move closer to the city and determine when it would be safe to return the prince to his home. Beyond those instructions Samuel had left the details to Kurad, trying to remain removed from the knowledge of where his son could be found should he himself fall into enemy hands. Kurad had left the meeting working over in his mind the options for his destination, confident that the actual abduction was going to be the easiest part of his assignment. What direction to go with the boy was more complicated.

He decided that the gnome army would be in pursuit from the south, the fleeing peasants from Pendar would be heading towards the east, and that barren lands to the west didn't offer much for shelter and sustenance. His only option left was to take a northern path, one that would hide him within the forests that bordered the Ellingstone kingdom to the north. They could find refuge there for a short time. Thus far, the plan had gone without a hitch. Now he sat in the forest clearing watching the young prince in his pursuits and with the fire going well enough for cooking his version of a traveler's stew. With the stew now simmering over the fire he took the time to retrace his steps over the past few days, looking for any possibility that he had left a clue behind. He wanted to make sure no one would know to look in this direction to find them.

The trip back to the castle had found him in his own element, traveling alone with no one aware of his passing. He'd made great time, making the most of his horse's long stride and tireless stamina. He crossed the many miles, taking trails known to few but himself, confident in his mount's knowledge of the terrain to carry him safely through the night.

The city walls had held little challenge, for he had scaled them before to meet secretly with Samuel in the castle more than once. Guards atop the wall had been increased, but Kurad found little challenge to eluding men trained to battle armies, not cloaked forms that didn't want to be seen. The route to the castle and the brief time he felt exposed in the wide open hallways made him feel vulnerable, but every job carried its own risks. Everything up until that point had been routine, then the mission had taken a definite turn towards the dangerous.

The room had been dark, forcing him to feel his way to the bed where the boy slept. He had knocked the play sword from its place. Fashioning a gag from the cloth of the bed sheets to stifle any cry for help was necessary but he had felt it somehow wrong to do that to the boy, the child of his friend. He was there to save the boy's life and an alarm would surely have foiled the plan. Bundling the boy in the bed sheets and keeping the noise to a minimum had been the biggest challenge. Infiltrating the castle grounds and even entering the castle itself had been nothing compared to quieting, without hurting, the boy.

Once ready to travel, he'd doused the bed in goat's blood from the wineskin he carried tucked into his belt. It had to appear as if the boy had been slain so that Orgle's search for the heir to the throne would stop there.

He slid out the window and down to the ground, burdened with the additional weight of the child, aided by the climbing rope he carried coiled about his body. With a quick shake upon reaching the ground, he loosed the rope from its anchor point.

The boy was fully awake now, yet offered no resistance as Kurad repacked his rope. He shouldered his charge, cleared the castle grounds and scaled the city walls.

Once he cleared the outlying posts at the perimeter of the city, he slipped into the concealing darkness of the forest. He began making his way to a small supply cache he left behind earlier in the barn on an abandoned farm just a couple of miles into the woods. The farm had been abandoned many years ago and the small fields painstakingly cleared back in days gone by, left untended. The forest was doing its best to reclaim the land with many saplings finding purchase in the once open fields.

The farmhouse hadn't weathered the change as well as the barn and was mostly uninhabitable while the barn still stood. Well, mostly stood. It provided Kurad a dry piece of ground when the weather was bad, although it was drafty when the wind came out of the south. He had approached the barn cautiously, trying to determine if anything had changed since he stabled his mount there en route to the castle.

Kurad was tired now, the extra burden of the boy beginning to take its toll even in his peak physical condition. He stopped to catch his breath. The boy had been sleeping quietly, seemingly tired from the night's journey, and Kurad felt safe in putting him down to do some quick reconnaissance of the barn. Kurad spent a moment camouflaging the boy in the brush and then he had hurried off to make certain that the barn was as he left it.

He circled the homestead in search of sign other than his own then quickly made his way to the side of the barn. He sat with his back to the wall listening to the night sounds that floated through the air. He heard nothing but the wind disturbing the leaves in the trees about the barn. The little critters that lived in the forest had all gone silent at Kurad's approach, for not even he could hide his presence from those whose very lives depended on being ever alert.

After determining that all within the barn was quiet, he slipped in through the hole in the wall, bringing him into the stall his horse occupied. Again he stopped to listen to the sounds of the night to get a sense of those that occupied the building. A soft rustling of hay told him that his mount was aware of his presence, but was otherwise calm which meant he was alone.

He went to his horse and slid his hand along its side in a silent greeting before checking that his supplies were unmolested. It was safe to bring the boy in out of the night.

Kurad quickly retraced his steps and found the boy still asleep, concealed in the brush where he had left him moments ago. The boy had been through a lot tonight and the morning would bring more of the same. They were back inside within a minute or two and he put the boy to bed on a pile of musty hay so that he could continue his slumber while Kurad organized his supplies for the next leg of the journey.

Kurad took a moment to rest his eyes. The lack of sleep was catching up to him and he needed to be sharp. Morning would bring searchers and patrols looking for the heir. The ruse with the blood might buy him some time, but it would be a lynch mob that was on his trail, not just a search party. Without Samuel to explain the situation, people would be hurt. He carried a signed and sealed letter from the king detailing his mission, though he doubted anyone would wait for an explanation. Miles needed to be covered before the rising sun caught them in the open. A few moments spent resting would be just as valuable he decided. Nodding off, he counted on his horse to alert him to any danger.

He had awoken an hour later, feeling far from refreshed, but the nap had taken the edge off and his senses were sharper. He knew he had made the right choice. Kurad checked on the sleeping boy to assure he was fine before he saddled his horse and loaded up their supplies. Edward stirred slightly when Kurad lifted him into the saddle and swung up behind him, but didn't wake as they made their way through the open barn door into the predawn morning. The forest was quiet in the muted light and Kurad sensed nothing unusual as he guided his mount northward.

They traveled for a short time when Edward finally awoke. The quiet boy had regained some pluck from his sleep and began to try and figure out what was taking place.

"What was your name again? What is your horse's name? Where are we going? Why is it still dark out? My mom doesn't let me play outside in the dark, and never in the woods." He finished with a cautious look about him as they pushed their

way through the brush overhanging the game trail that Kurad
followed.

"Well my sleeping prince awakens," Kurad began. "My
name is Kurad, and I'm a friend of your father's. Dancer here is
my fine steed and he's going to be taking us on our little
journey until we meet up with your mom and dad. Let's see,"
Kurad paused, wanting to respond to all of his young charge's
inquiries.

"Oh yes, it's not yet morning, and finally, your mother
would approve of you being out with me. You're definitely safe
with Dancer and myself. We have a little farther to go before
sunrise and we should probably keep quiet so that we don't
attract any wolves."

The boy fell silent and seemed to understand that he was
safe. Nothing had harmed him since coming under the care of
Kurad and he was confident that his dad would be waiting for
him when they were done riding. They had covered many miles
together by the time the sun began to rise above the horizon and
Kurad guided Dancer into a well-concealed clearing where they
now sat cooking dinner and playing with stick swords. He
napped some, and when the boy napped for a while at midday
he slipped out to gather some game for dinner. The forest was
teeming with life and he was back before the child awoke with
several dressed hares.

Kurad found a suitable stick and fashioned a sword for the
boy, knowing it was important to keep the little guy occupied.
Later he was glad he had thought of it as they had spent the
afternoon fencing and resting. Even while resting the boy was
inquisitive and had many questions for his keeper.

Now, as Kurad sat tending the fire, he decided that all had
gone as well as he could have planned. They didn't appear to
have been followed thus far.

Tonight they would set out again and travel northward.
Kurad knew they needed to keep moving to avoid any patrols
that might be out searching for the boy. He rose from his spot
by the fire and went to the bedrolls, beginning the chore of
packing the bundles to ready them for tonight's ride. He staged
them in a neat pile near Dancer, not quite ready to burden the
horse for they were still a couple hours from setting out. Kurad
settled back down in front of his bubbling stew and slowly

stirred the contents. His ever watchful gaze fell on the boy at play with his sword, practicing the few stances that Kurad had taught him.

He stirred the pot in front of him absently, waiting patiently for the stew to finish boiling, wondering about the plight of Edward's family. Was Samuel still holding Orgle at bay in the ravine? Or had Orgle managed, with the aid of his vast army, to push back the Pendarian army? He really hoped for the former, but the latter was more likely to be the truth.

He began to ladle the stew onto two plates, savoring the aroma of his first warm meal in a number of days. Edward was already on his way over to accept his plate when Kurad looked up to call him to eat. He too must have smelled the stew and been reminded by his stomach that they hadn't eaten all day. Kurad handed him his plate and watched as the boy nearly inhaled the plate of food.

"Slow down there, little man. There is more in the kettle."

Edward grinned, his mouth still full. Looking down at his plate, he realized he had already eaten nearly half his plate. The kitchen staff at the palace would not be happy with his behavior. Remembering the palace reminded him of his mom and for a moment he wished he was home with her.

Kurad saw the grin turn to sadness. While he wasn't sure the exact cause, he could imagine it was related to home and moved to interrupt the boy's reverie.

"Edward," he spoke, getting the boy's attention. "Tonight we are going to continue our quest north. I'm going to need your help, so you will be in charge of watching for bad guys. Do you think you're up to that? Or will you sleep all night like you did last night?"

"You mean the Black Knight? He lives in these woods and catches little boys who don't have a sword to defend themselves with. That's what Uncle Stephen told me. Now I have my own sword and you showed me how to use it, so he had better look out." His excitement level was rising and his lack of attention nearly cost him his plate of food. It was barely saved when Kurad reached out and caught the edge.

Well, Kurad thought, that really perked up his mood but now it had swung so far the other way he probably wouldn't be able to settle down to finish his dinner. Kurad motioned with his fork to get Edward back on task and, despite the boy's new level of excitement, he eagerly fell back to eating his stew.

When the last of the supplies were loaded, Kurad lifted the boy up into the saddle. He handed the reins to Edward and went about erasing evidence around the campsite that the boy was traveling with him. He wasn't overly concerned with his own footprints, the tracks would look like any other traveler stopping to camp and take a meal. It would be more suspicious if he attempted to erase his passing too and failed in some fashion. No, he thought, let anyone trailing him find his campsite and maybe the absence of sign from a child would halt further pursuit.

The sun was just disappearing beyond the horizon when he finished his sweep and promptly swung up into the saddle behind Edward. He took one last look about the camp, satisfied with his work, and decided it would be only the best of trackers who could possibly make a connection to him and the missing prince. Knowing that he had taken care of everything he could to throw off any pursuit he nudged Dancer and once again took flight through the night.

Hours ticked by uneventfully as the horse picked his way through the brush and over fallen trees that crossed the game trail that they followed. Kurad guided him in the general direction he wanted to go, but in the darkness that enveloped them he left the specifics to Dancer.

Edward remained alert and very much a part of the game for the first hour or so, but as the sun disappeared so did the boy's resolve to remain awake. Kurad enjoyed the quiet that replaced the boy's questions that, even though whispered, exposed them to any others who may be traveling these same woods. He was used to traveling alone in silence, his senses probing his surroundings, searching out the anomaly, the one thing that wasn't as it should be that would trigger his body into action.

In the wild lands there were always those looking for an easy target, wanting to lighten someone's load of coin or other possessions of value. Many times the victims would be left battered and bruised but alive. However, there were criminals that had little regard for the lives of those they plundered. Kurad had taught many a thief a lesson about preying on the seemingly weak, the lone traveler. He cared not for the lives of those criminals who would seek an easy target and many a corpse warned of his encounters. Now that Kurad had the young prince as his charge, those senses were working overtime.

The woods were still, most creatures falling silent as the pair passed by, not threatened, yet always cautious. Kurad read the forest signs as only someone who spent his life immersed in its ways could. He found little evidence of other travelers and wondered if the conflict to the south was affecting the normal movements of folks in this area. Those who made their homes in these woods, including the criminals, knew enough to steer clear of a major conflict. They knew that eventually the entire area would be plundered to support an army and that meant they would be found out and possibly suffer for it.

The pair continued on through the night, stopping every few hours to rest Dancer and to get a bite of waybread and water to drink. Edward would wake at these stops but Kurad never let on that he knew the boy slept between these rest stops for he knew that would dampen his spirits. Kurad also knew that hurrying through the forest in the dark of night when it wasn't necessary risked injury to his mount, so the miles were logged beneath Dancer's steady gait; not fast but consistent. Even so, they covered fifteen miles before the false dawn began to illuminate their surroundings. Kurad had estimated well the progress to expect and angled off the trail to another secluded clearing he knew where their small traveling party could wait out the day.

Once camp was established and a small breakfast had been eaten Kurad tucked Edward into his bedroll and followed suit himself, hoping to get a few hours of rest before the boy awoke. It was in that moment, as the sun began to rise above the landscape, that he noticed the utter silence that hung over the woods. Kurad's gaze immediately swung to Dancer for confirmation, knowing already that he would see his mount standing as still as a statue. Dancer's head was up and he was looking back down the trail from the direction they'd come. He wasn't agitated as if something dangerous were nearby. No, Kurad thought, it was a more distant threat. A feeling of dread fell upon Kurad as his gaze followed Dancer's to the south. There was nothing he could pinpoint and no way to know yet, but a force foreign and forgotten had come back to this land, and its purpose was to destroy.

Chapter Eight

The silence of the castle was broken by the ancient war horns calling out to all able bodies within the city. Samuel and Stephen, startled by the blast, jumped to their feet sending piles of books cascading from their resting places next to the men. They had both succumbed to sleep sometime during the night, exhausted by their search for the answers given by the prophecies so long ago.

Samuel reached the window and drew aside the curtains, revealing the new day's light creeping over the horizon. The sun looked the same to Samuel as it had for all the days that came before this one, but today it felt somehow different to him. It brought with it a feeling of dread that permeated the air, and it seemed to radiate over the countryside, intimately intertwined with the powerful rays of the sun. The feeling reached out across the landscape with an almost tangible pallor that gripped and pressed down, causing the men to gasp for breath as the sun chased away the shadows of the night. Stephen shook his head in an attempt to clear the effects and looked at his brother.

"What is this that grips our very souls?" Samuel asked in confusion as he dropped the curtains and turned back to his brother.

"It must be connected to Orgle and that stone he carries with him. Some otherworldly power he brought forth with that troll we saw yesterday. Could it be that the stone draws power from the sun, and with the dawn breaking, it's sending out a wave of power to break our very spirits?" Samuel staggered against the weight. He realized the implications of this power at work against those who would be standing ready to fight atop the city walls.

"We must go to the walls," Samuel stated in a defeated tone. "That is where we are needed right now. That's the only place we will be able to get a full understanding of what it is that Orgle intends to use against us. Then we will better know how to stop him and his unholy power." He slammed his fist down on the table, breaking the grip of the spell through sheer will and fueling his confidence; convincing Stephen that not all was lost yet. His determination was contagious, and the two strode from the room, confident with the belief that they would stop

Orgle instilled in their hearts. They left knowing they would have to come back later to finish looking through the tome for a possible answer, an answer that still lay hidden within.

The soldiers they encountered within the courtyard were moving about in anything but an orderly fashion. They were confused and filled with dread until seeing their king striding past, calling out orders to defend the walls. His presence broke their trance and they immediately began to organize into squads and follow him out to take their assigned posts. Samuel could only wonder what he would find when he finally made it to the walls. Would anyone be ready to answer the call to arms? Somewhere someone blew the horn and he held out hope that there were some still prepared to defend the city.

The brothers raced their mounts to the gates of the city, dismounting as they skidded to a halt and running up the stairs to the top of the wall. The men atop the wall were moving about apprehensively, caught in the spell that permeated the air

The dwarves seemed to resist the influence better than their human counterparts and were directing the men, trying to keep them on task. It helped the men shake the feelings of dread to see their king striding confidently to the top of the wall taking charge.

Samuel found Relysis barking orders, trying to get his troops ready for whatever it was that Orgle was preparing to send against them. When he saw his king, Relysis simply pointed across the battlefield, not knowing what to say about the scene before them, and letting Samuel and Stephen decide for themselves what it was they saw.

It looked as if there was a dark cloud of dust rising in the distance, moving steadily closer as they watched. Upon closer inspection, it didn't behave like dust as it moved across the already trampled ground. Rather it had an unearthly quality to it. It didn't billow up as one would expect dust to. Instead it was darker, moving more like a storm of unnatural creation. Whatever it was that created the cloud, it was moving at a swift pace.

Orgle's army had moved to the flanks, creating an opening for this new force to pass through en route to the city. Samuel continued to look ahead, trying to discern what form the next challenge would take. He was out of answers and his confidence was slumping, mirroring his physical state. It had been a draining campaign and his army had continued to retreat before this enemy. Now a new force was materializing on the field before him and he had little hope left of saving his kingdom. Those around him looked to him for strength and now he worried he was letting them down when they needed him most.

"Can anyone see beyond the gnome army and tell me what this demon is going to throw at us next?" Samuel asked, more to break his own mood than expecting a response. Action was needed now; he couldn't let his troops be captured as he was by fear of the unknown and they needed to get their minds off this new menace.

"As soon as someone with an eyepiece can determine what we are facing, I must know. Relysis, send a runner instructing everyone to recheck their weapons." He turned back to the cloud, waiting for something to materialize on the field before him. He also watched the gnome troops. They were off to the flanks and appeared as nervous as his own army, maybe more so because they weren't behind the protective walls of the city. What alliance had Orgle struck? Orgle's own army is afraid of what approaches, wondered Samuel.

"Has anyone got a sighting on what Orgle has conjured to bring against us? Surely this evil cloud can have no other purpose." Frustration was creeping into, and taking a firm hold, on Samuel's emotions. The inactivity, combined with the unknown, was slowly pushing him to the brink of losing control. His thoughts bounced between the soldiers around him and his family, especially Edward, wherever he may be. He wasn't sure if Orgle's stone was sending out the waves of despair or whether the situation had finally caught up to him. He was glad Edward was out of the city. If only his wife had agreed to leave with the rest of the citizens. Then she too would be spared the storm that brewed on the field before him.

Stephen interrupted his thoughts by handing him an eyepiece and pointing towards the cloud that swirled about between the flanks of Orgle's army. Samuel held it to his eye and realized the worst of his fears. From within the cover of the swirling dust, rock trolls began to march out into the daylight and, with extreme discipline, began to assemble into formations on the field before the walls of Pendar. The walls of Pendar had always been believed to be impenetrable against any enemy that should choose to war against the inhabitants, but trolls had disappeared from the world and had never been listed among those enemies. They were called rock trolls because they resembled the rock they tunneled in to make their homes in far off distant mountain ranges. They looked like rocks that had taken a humanoid shape and were as solidly built: skin nearly impenetrable and standing nearly thrice the height of the tallest man in Samuel's army.

"Where did Orgle bring these beings back from? They have been gone from the land for untold years. This is impossible! What can we do against them?" Samuel stopped himself, realizing he'd spoken aloud. He looked about at those gathered around him. They too were seeing now what he had in the looking glass. Disbelief and horror at what faced them this morning on the battlefield was evident on their faces. It was his duty to get the army ready to do what even he believed to be an impossible task. His mind raced, trying frantically to remember a way to defend the city walls against the monsters that continued to issue forth and form up in the growing ranks across the field.

"Prepare the oil cauldrons! Put flame to the wood beneath them! The oil must be boiling hot! Archers prepare coals to light your fletching! Focus your arrows on the oil once it has been spilled down upon the trolls. Fire is the one weapon that will work against this new foe!" Turning to Relysis, he continued his orders, building up his own confidence as well as those around him. The commands exuded strength and a call to arms. The soldiers responded to him immediately, rushing to prepare the defenses that would turn aside the trolls. With everyone moving to take their positions, he spoke quietly.

"Relysis take your dwarves and position them inside the gate. That's where the trolls will attempt to break through. Make sure they are wearing their armor and their axes are sharp. The gates won't hold up against the beasts that take the field against us. The hot oil and fire will slow them, but if they are determined, the gates won't stand against their strength.

"It will be up to you and your warriors to cut the trolls down as they break through. Work as units. Alone, one warrior, even your best, is no match for a rock troll." He dismissed his commander with a salute and a pat on his back.

"I will be there to help as soon as I can. Take care of yourself. I'm going to need you to get us through this one."

Samuel turned his attention back to the field. The trolls had stopped emerging from the dust cloud and were settling into and adjusting their formations. He couldn't count the trolls behind those that stood at the front of the formation, but the fifty that comprised the first row looked like more than enough to rip through the gates that had protected his people for so many years. He knew more lurked behind, but if he had known that they were fully twenty rows deep behind the front line, he would have thrown down his weapons in despair and abandoned the city. He still held out hope, believing his army would rise to the defense of their homes and loved ones.

So much of the coming battle depended on turning back the initial thrust of the trolls. They couldn't be allowed to reach the gates at full strength and not with any momentum. They had to be slowed and they had to feel the bite of his army. It had to be a deep and brutal thrust. The trolls had to pay for this alliance they had created with Orgle. They needed to understand that they would be paying dearly for whatever it was that Orgle had promised in return.

There was a fire in him now, the battles waged over the last couple weeks had nearly smothered the flame, but Orgle had angered him now. It was unconscionable to bring forth a new ally at this point, and one such as this. The rules of conduct precluded bringing in allies who weren't involved in the dispute. The trolls had nothing to gain or lose from the outcome. Samuel knew from history that the trolls had never lost a campaign. There wasn't a weapon that could turn them aside. He didn't have a magical weapon either. However, he did have a skilled army that was making its last stand to defend its homeland. He could only hope that it was enough today.

Samuel watched as the trolls began to march forward, slowly and purposefully, forming a giant wedge at the front of the army. He could see that the point of the wedge was aligned with the main gate, which would be the weakest link in his defenses. It hardly seemed to matter though, considering that the creatures were beginning to gather speed as they closed the gap. Samuel noticed too that the gnomes and their leader did nothing to give the impression that they would be helping the trolls tear through his defenses. What was this pact that brought these mercenaries back after all these years? If he survived this assault he would have to get an answer to that question. Right now he had to stop these creatures. They were beginning to get closer to the wall and it was time to act.

When the trolls had advanced to within a hundred paces Samuel gave the order to spill the oil, effectively coating the field before the walls. Gallons upon gallons of the warmed oil flowed freely, soaking the ground, lying in wait for the trolls to march over. Archers atop the walls prepared their arrows and sighted in on the oil soaked ground. The arrows wouldn't do much against the thick skinned trolls, but once the fletching was put to flame the trolls would be up against a force that even their thick hides couldn't withstand. The trolls marched forward, unconcerned with the oil sloshing underfoot as the gate to the city loomed in front of them.

The signal was given and the arrows rained down on the attackers, a precious few finding a crack in their natural armor; most bouncing off to land in the deadly fluid under their feet. The oil ignited in a firestorm, flames leaping high, and thick black smoke choking the air. The advancing trolls faltered as the lead ranks fell to one of the few tactics known to have success against their kind. Many, though not enough, fell to the heat and flames. As the flames died away the remaining trolls began to push through the dead and dying, once again focused on the gate to the city. A few of the archers tentatively loosed arrows, trying to find a way to bring down these creatures. Samuel signaled to the company of dwarves stationed inside the wall to prepare themselves should the unthinkable happen and the gates fail.

The dwarves, armed with their double-edged battleaxes, began to form up into squads, ready to meet the challenge of any troll that might breach the walls. The squads were comprised of fifty dwarves each and designed to move fast in compact units, inflicting damage then quickly moving away. The trolls were an adversary that would stomp flat an army trying to meet them head on.

The dwarves knew that to stand still against such a beast would invite disaster to every last one of them but still they scurried to get into position inside the gate. Along the flanks of the dwarves the lance-bearing cavalry took up positions, hoping to gain some advantage against the trolls, distracted by the swarming dwarves. They were still gathering in their assigned areas when the first trolls reached the outer wall. With a resounding boom from outside the walls, the trolls made contact with the gate. Those inside stopped their preparations and looked to the gate.

The gate creaked under the massive pressure being applied from without. Again the trolls rammed the gate and again the gate groaned in protest. Never before had it been tested such as this, no other army could bring such a force against these ancient stones. Seconds ticked by as Samuel's entire army held their collective breaths, waiting to see if the gates would hold. Another boom echoed through the courtyard and it was followed immediately by a piercing crack as the massive gates, no longer able to protect its inhabitants, surrendered to the invaders.

Wilgar's arrangement to only breach the walls was forgotten. Lost in the battle lust, they demanded revenge for those lost in the fires. The trolls funneled into the city, swinging log-sized clubs and fists at whoever dared challenge them. They stomped down any dwarves who weren't able to fall back beyond their reach.

The cavalry raced forward, breaking their lances on the armor-like skin protecting the trolls. Few lances found purchase and even fewer wounds were fatal. Once the cavalry closed on the trolls, they became the focus of the trolls' attack and were felled by the hundreds as men and mounts screamed and fought back.

Samuel watched from the walls as the trolls pushed through his defenses, dealing death as they waded through his army. He had seen enough and decided that now was the time to enter the fray. There was nowhere else to fall back to now. The city walls no longer offered safety and the future of his kingdom hung in the balance. Handing Stephen his sword, he reached for his own axe.

"Take this, our father's sword and his father's before since the birth of this kingdom. It will serve you well. Now take a regiment and return to the castle to protect Marie. Tell her that I loved her and did the best that I could for the kingdom. If given the chance, flee the city with whatever army you can gather."

Before Stephen could object, Samuel was leaping down the stairs to join the battle below. The dwarves rallied and charged forward under the leadership of their king. Axes swung with precision strokes, cutting into the legs of the trolls that continued to swarm through the broken gate. The battleaxes powered by the broad shouldered dwarves seemed to work better than any other weapon, though they were still at a disadvantage. Stephen watched for only a moment more, then said his goodbyes silently to himself, putting it out of his mind as he gathered together a regiment to escort him to the castle.

He pulled aside one of the commanders and promptly relayed Samuel's order to protect the queen to the last man. The commander, charged with the honor of protecting the queen, began barking out orders for his troops to fall back to the castle. Stephen began to move out towards the castle but paused to look back at the melee that was anything but an organized battle.

He located his brother momentarily. He was standing between two trolls, swinging his battleaxe with a singular vision of cutting down every last troll that dared stand before him. His passion carried him through and the trolls were beginning to back down from the king and those dwarves that fought by his side.

It was as the trolls began to hesitate against engaging the enraged king that a large troll pushed his way through the stagnated assault holding a large piece of the gate aloft. They all identified the danger, but before Samuel and his supporters could scatter, the slab was hurtled into their midst. It crushed King Samuel where he stood, his battleaxe raised futilely in an attempt to protect himself and those who had fought so valiantly beside him.

Stephen stopped, his knees going weak. On the brink of falling to the ground before him, a hand grabbed his arm to steady him. He turned and looked into the eyes of the commander charged with returning with him to the castle. He too had seen the king fall at the hands of the trolls.

"Your Highness, it is now your army that stands and dies at the hands of these monsters. Nothing more can be done here.

Call for a retreat and have the army fall back to the castle. Maybe a smaller front will be more easily defended."

Stephen saw the truth before him and gave the order to fall back to the castle. The bugler raised the horn to his lips preparing to signal a full retreat. He never played a note, as a spear pierced him through, sending him tumbling to the ground below. Stephen looked on in disbelief. The gnomes had decided to join the fray and were streaming in through the trolls' ranks, loosing their spears with deadly accuracy against the dwarves and men distracted by fighting the large trolls.

With his bugler lying dead down below the wall, Stephen scrambled down the steps and over fallen soldiers to retrieve the horn. Grabbing it up while still kneeling, he brought the horn to his lips and pierced the air with the call to retreat. The fighting units tried to break away from the attackers to fall back to the castle but the gnomes pressed the attack and many of Stephen's soldiers continued to fight where they stood. By doing so they hoped to buy time for the others to make it to safety.

It was a beleaguered force of only a few thousand dwarves and men that reached the castle walls. Walls which were in no way up to the task of holding back the army that was in pursuit. The retreat was a costly maneuver and while it saved the lives of those that made it back, it was at the expense of two or three times that number that now lay dead in the streets of their beloved city. Stephen found the highest ranking soldiers amongst the survivors and put them to the task of organizing squads to evacuate the castle. While they began scrambling to gather the troops, he was off to find the queen.

As soon as Stephen entered the castle, he knew something was amiss. No guards stood at their posts. Where could they be? Who would have dispatched them to other duties? His mind was reeling. Leaving Marie defenseless at this time was unthinkable. However, as he rounded the corner into the main corridor his questions were answered.

Bodies of both the royal guards lay amongst those fallen and the bodies of the gnome invaders littered the hall and stairway leading upwards to the royal chambers. Stephen reached for the ancestral blade now strapped across his shoulders, pulling it free from its sheath as he leaped over the bodies of the fallen, their blood still flowing as he rushed up the grand stairway.

He closed on the doorway to the queen's chambers, fearing what he would find upon opening the door, almost hoping he would be intercepted by gnome soldiers and therefore spared the sight of what had befallen his brother's wife. He dismissed the thought of calling for reinforcements, fearing he would alert those within of his presence. From the number of dead guards, it could only be assumed that it was a large force that had entered the castle, sneaking through the city and getting ahead of the retreating forces now protecting the castle walls. His goal now was to take the lives of as many of the vile creatures as he could before he too was struck down. The desire for revenge burned through him, boiling his blood with the need to dispense justice on those who committed these atrocities in his home.

The door to Marie's chambers was adorned with the last guard that had stood in her defense, pinned to it with a gnome spear. It was a clear statement that the city was no longer in the possession of friendly forces. Stephen stopped his mad charge long enough to lean his sword against the door frame, and with the rage that filled him, he wrenched the spear that held the faithful guard to the door. With that rage burning intensely, he kicked aside the door and, still holding the slain guard's body before, him he bulled his way inside and through the gnomes that were trying to cut him off. It was the scene that he had most feared he would find.

His brother's wife lay on the floor in a crumpled heap, a small blade still clutched in her hand, though it had done her little good. A gnome officer stood leering over her still form, obviously pleased with himself for slaying the woman. His joy was cut short as Stephen, using the guard's body as a shield, rushed forward and drove the spear through the gnome, killing him immediately. Dropping the overburdened spear he reached for his father's sword, but realized quickly that he had left it at the doorway. He grabbed the ugly gnome blade from the newly dispatched officer. Wary because he had a blade, the other gnomes circled about looking for an opening in his defense.

Slowly they circled. Clearly they outnumbered him, all but sealing his fate it seemed. The gnomes were becoming bolder now as they realized that Stephen couldn't fend them all off at the same time. A few fell to his blade, and though he took some joy in their deaths, it was his knowledge that someday King

Edward could come forth from hiding and finish that which he today wouldn't be able to that sustained him as he fought on through wounds that should have felled him time and again. In the end their numbers, though greatly reduced, finally took him down. The gnomes celebrated his death, believing they had finished the job of wiping the entire Ellingstone family from existence.

Orgle listened to the reports later that night as he sat upon his newly acquired throne. He sat idly holding the stone that Wilgar had given to him in exchange for the mighty Starrock when they had departed. It had crossed his mind to back out of his part of the agreement, but he had thought better of it after surveying the damage caused by the trolls. They were certainly not a force one would want to face. Not even the legendary walls of Pendar had slowed them down.

Orgle had dispatched teams to remove the fallen from the castle and clean the signs of battle from his new home. The city had been swept clean of its former occupants after the fall of the castle. Some had escaped the carnage and fled the city, but Orgle had instructed his soldiers to round them up with the other refugees who thought they could hide from their new king. In the process weapons were collected from the fallen, including the Ellingstone's ancestral blade found leaning against the doorframe of the queen's chambers. It was piled with the rest and stacked in a cellar to be forgotten about by history, as were those who had borne it.

Orgle assembled witnesses who could verify the deaths of the royal family, accounting for both the king and his brother and also the king's wife, should she possibly have been with child. It was a rarely-seen happy Orgle that now strode through the hallways of his new castle, peering into rooms, looking for treasure which others not as smart as himself might overlook. It was in one of these rooms, in the hallway of the royal family's quarters, that he came across something completely unexpected; the obvious furnishings and toys of a child. He was in the middle of tearing apart the room in a fit of rage when one of his commanders finally responded to his shouts.

Orgle questioned the commander about the whereabouts of the child's body. He had been assured that no royal family members had been left unaccounted for. The commander didn't have the answers Orgle was looking for and thus died on his own blade. Orgle strode from the room wiping blood from his hands and dropping a small wooden sword atop the body of his slain commander. He went looking for someone more capable of answering his questions. Commanders immediately dispatched squads in an attempt to locate the boy or determine where he could possibly have been taken, trying to avoid the same fate as their predecessor.

Three days passed while the gnomes searched the entire city. Guards were posted along the walls and those in the streets were on high alert. The gnome soldiers searching for the boy knew their commander would only be happy when they found the lost boy and that whoever found him would be mightily rewarded. Those in charge of the search who failed to find him were growing fewer in number, paying with their lives to make up for their ineffectiveness. It was not safe to bring word of the failed search to Orgle, his mood worsened as the days passed.

Orgle's supreme plan to end the pain caused by the Ellingstone family was falling apart because of a simple little child who could not possibly know the power he held and what he symbolized. Orgle was unaware that at that moment the prince was in a small clearing just a few days' ride to the north of the city. Under the watchful eye of his protector, Edward played his games oblivious of the creature that vowed to find and destroy him for reasons that the child couldn't begin to comprehend at his young age.

Chapter Nine

The weeks passed as Kurad and his young charge traveled the woodlands north of the city that Edward called home. They never moved more than a distance of even twenty miles from the city, expecting to return shortly. Too, Kurad didn't want to tax the boy's endurance. They traveled, moving camp every couple of days, maintaining what Kurad thought would be a safe distance from any gnome troops that might be outside the city walls as they lay siege to the army trapped within.

Kurad knew Samuel to be a knowledgeable leader on the battlefield, guessing he had most likely been pushed back to the safety of Pendar. Based on that scenario, he believed it would only be a matter of time before Orgle would tire of losing troops and give up this campaign. In Kurad's mind, the walls that protected the city had withstood greater assaults than Orgle could assemble. So his job was to lay low until the gnomes had cleared out and then he would bring Edward back home. It was only a matter of time.

Kurad used the forest activity as his gauge as to what was happening outside the confines of the woods. Of particular note was that the usual riff raff that lived in the woods had moved out and into the deeper, more remote regions that lacked even the accessibility that this area presented. The ruffians and cutthroats had a highly developed communications network. Obviously word had spread that a new force was in the area. In a situation like this, avoidance was the best tactic.

Kurad lacked his own network of informants so he was relying on his own powers of observation to bring him through safely. The absence of these usually undesirable individuals was more than a little unnerving and left him wondering what was transpiring back at Pendar.

Kurad didn't know, but Orgle did have patrols out searching for the boy, though mostly to the east; the direction the residents of Pendar had fled in advance of his arrival. He assumed the boy must have left with the commoners or had been spirited away when small units of the defeated army had given up the fight and deserted. The patrols were bringing in stragglers and small pockets of captured soldiers to work in the newly created labor camps. No sign of the boy was found, and none in the ranks of prisoners admitted to knowledge of his whereabouts even under extreme torture. One member of the castle guard spoke of a tragedy befalling the young prince prior to the city falling before he died, but no others spoke of this incident. Someone had to know where the boy was; the uncertainty was spoiling Orgle's triumph.

The only other problem plaguing Orgle were reports from his scouts indicating the former inhabitants of the city had made it safely to the ancient mountain stronghold and were setting up to defend its walls. He called his commanders together and put them to the task of routing the escapees and bringing them into line with the new rules of the land. Once they were brought under control, he would bring forth his subjects from the south so they could resettle this new kingdom.

The gnome army had had the mountain city under siege now for two weeks, waiting for time to do the fighting for them. There were a limited amount of supplies in the city, and the longer they sat trapped behind the tall granite walls the more desperate they would become. The city of Zoisite had been left to ruin many generations before, and while the walls had been built tall and strong, years of neglect had compromised the defenses. The remainder of the army, nearly two thousand strong, was comprised of men and dwarves resolved to fight Orgle's horde one more time if they had to, though most were nicked up and feeling the effects of the long battles they had fought the weeks before.

Samuel had given his life along with thousands of others at the gate that day so that those that survived could fight another day in the name of freedom. The survivors were determined not to let their king's death be without meaning. They were a proud nation and they weren't going to surrender without a fight. That wasn't an option.

Escaping, however, while Orgle thought he had them trapped was an option. The surviving members of the army had gone to work immediately on reopening the tunnels carved though the mountains by the dwarves that had inhabited this once great city. The tunnels issued forth into a valley on the opposite side of the mountain. They had gone unused for so many years that knowledge of their existence outside the dwarf community had virtually vanished, and it was this misstep by

Orgle that gave them hope. The army, weary from battle and flight, continued the fight for the freedom of their families, albeit with shovels and picks now. The tunnels were in disrepair and needed to be cleared before the exodus could begin. The dwarves were tasked to work removing the stone while the men took up the watch atop the cracked and broken ramparts. The men were hoping to create the illusion that they now intended to defend these ancient walls against the gnome aggressors.

Orgle's army was growing bored waiting for the occupants of the city to surrender, instead of facing death by starvation. He knew that waiting much longer would result in his troops wandering off to pursue more pleasurable pastimes. They had been camped outside the city resting and recovering from the chase, but now they just wanted to be done with this campaign so they could enjoy the spoils of war. Without the Starrock to control their minds, Orgle was forced to use conventional means to persuade them to cooperate. He knew they thrived on action, so he decided that tomorrow morning at dawn he would give them their wish.

His decision came one night too late though, for the remaining debris from the escape tunnel had at long last been removed. The race to escape into the tunnels began in earnest as the guards reported renewed activity within the siege army, indicating they were preparing for an attack. The few personal effects they'd carried from their homes to Zoisite were now going to be taken from them just as most of their belongings had been left behind in Pendar. Tonight the occupants laid aside anything that wasn't immediately necessary for survival in preparation for the march through the bowels of the mountain. Orgle had effectively stripped away everything they had ever owned. In the end, all they took with them through the mountain was their memories of better days and whatever pride they could muster.

The flight from the city began the very night that the tunnel was cleared. The evacuation took the better part of the night just to get everyone through the portal leading into the mountain. The men standing watch were the last to surrender their posts, slipping away at points along the wall, where the gnomes camped out in front of the city couldn't see them depart. Once they joined the trail of evacuees and the city was entirely deserted, dwarves set about knocking free the keystone that sat atop the tunnel opening. It took several attempts to dislodge the giant stone but as soon as it slipped from its perch, the entire entrance to the cavity came tumbling down. The dwarves scrambled back from the collapsing opening. Inside the dust was thick, choking those within until it settled. Outside, the opening was covered by what they hoped appeared to be a natural rockslide hiding their escape.

The next morning Orgle emerged from his field command post ready to give the order to attack this last bastion of King Ellingstone's reign. Today would be the final stroke against the old regime and then he would be able to begin shaping his new world. According to his plan, his army would round up those remaining in this old city, kill any that resisted, and most importantly, get their hands on the boy prince, who until now, had eluded his grasp.

In his right hand he grasped his newly crafted scepter, complete with the new black stone in place of the Starrock. Orgle was annoyed that he hadn't been able to make the stone respond to any of his demands yet, though at times he thought he could see Wilgar within. Someday, he knew he would learn to call him forth. For now he was satisfied with looking at this new instrument with its black stone mounted atop the silver handle that was half as tall as Orgle himself. It was truly impressive.

His only regret was that he wished that his own craftsman had made the scepter. Instead, he had found it in Samuel's personal war treasury. Orgle's main concern was how his subjects would perceive his new instrument of power. They had respected, even feared the Starrock, but what of this new talisman? The scepter displayed the stone wonderfully allowing it to shine brightly in the sunlight. Judging by the reception they were giving him, it would be enough for now to intimidate them.

His troops cheered as he walked to the front of the assembled army. They were excited to be getting back into action and more than just a little fearful of their scepter wielding leader. They had all witnessed the atrocities committed against those that opposed Orgle when he possessed the Starrock, and this new stone looked equally intimidating to those in the ranks of the army. Too, they wondered if he would once again call forth the trolls to tear down the walls of this city as they had done just weeks ago. For good reason they feared the trolls.

Rumors circulated that the trolls hadn't limited their energies to tearing down the walls, but had also crushed many gnomes with the swings of their massive clubs.

Orgle waved the scepter overhead a few times, finally calling out to the city to surrender or face retribution at the hands of his army. He waited for a moment or two and, when no response came from within the walls, he signaled for his troops to attack. They charged, calling out their battle cry as they closed the gap to the stone walls.

There was no response from within the city. The inhabitants had been gone for several hours and were miles away, snaking through the depths of the mountain. They estimated it would take them the better part of three days to get the column of refugees through the tunnels and into the valley on the other side of the mountain. Even then, it wasn't going to be an easy march. They had to traverse the underground pathway and slip out of the adjoining valley and disappear beyond Orgle's reach. If he located the escape tunnel, he could move his army to the far side of the mountain to block their escape. Then they would be trapped within the mountain with no way out.

Troy A. Skog

Chapter Ten

Nearly a month had passed since Kurad had spirited Edward away from his home and still he'd heard nothing of the battle for the city. Night was closing in and the woodlands were quiet and the two traveling companions sat around a small smokeless fire eating roast rabbit provided by one of Kurad's snares. There hadn't been any news from the south. The less desirable inhabitants of the woods were still absent. Kurad knew at some point he would have to get an accurate assessment of what was happening back at the city. The thought that things may have gone terribly wrong and that Samuel defeated replayed in his mind just as it had more than once in recent days. The feelings were so strong they decided it for him. He depended heavily on his sixth sense. He attributed it to helping him survive alone in the wilds for so many years and he wasn't going to start ignoring it now.

It was time to have a firsthand look into what was transpiring, so he decided they would set off first thing in the morning. The sooner he found out what was happening, the better off he and the boy would be. Besides, all the sitting around being inactive was beginning to wear on him. Kurad knew lack of knowledge about the progress of the battle and the lull of inactivity, which dulled the senses, made for a potentially deadly combination for a pair of fugitives in hostile territory.

The next morning greeted the pair with overcast skies and a mist that on most days would have brought their spirits down. However, today Kurad would be able to use it to his advantage as he moved back towards the city. He needed to find out who controlled the city and the outlying areas, how the battle was progressing, and if they were still under siege. As he packed up camp, he pondered the question of what he was to do with the little prince when they drew closer to Pendar.

The two had become quite close during their time together traveling through the woods. The boy was obviously clinging to the only constant in his disrupted life, Kurad. It was a testament to the boy's resilience, even at his young age, that he still kept his spirits up. Kurad had been fortunate that he had been able to establish with the boy that he was a friend of his father's. Without that, things might have been different.

As soon as they'd collected their gear and loaded up Dancer, they climbed aboard and headed south. Edward was accustomed to the process of moving camp and didn't question Kurad about this morning's activities. It had become routine to move camp every couple of days so they didn't become a stationary target should someone be actively searching for them. If Kurad wanted contact, he would initiate it.

Though it seemed unlikely that they would be tracked too far from the city, Kurad had begun to emphasize the importance of moving silently, training Edward to move with stealth through the woods. To Kurad's amazement the boy was a quick study, maintaining his silence as Kurad instructed. The boy was naturally inquisitive and had initially struggled with not being able to blurt out whatever crossed his mind at any given moment. To combat this urge, the pair had established a hand signal system whereas when Edward felt it important to tell Kurad something or to ask a question he could ask permission to speak without making a sound. Now, as they headed closer to the city, the training was paying great dividends by allowing Kurad to focus on other details while Edward joined in the game and added another pair of eyes.

As they headed out, Kurad was still struggling with the question of determining what he was going to do with Edward when it came time for him to do some close observation of the city. His initial thought was to return to the barn in the woods and leave the boy during the night when he was fast asleep. The barn would provide some shelter from the elements and he could leave Dancer stabled to watch over Edward. He felt the barn was probably the natural choice to base his operation, though it depended where the gnomes were positioned outside the city. If their camp was set up on the north side of the city he would have to work around them, and no matter where they were, they could have patrols hunting in the forest looking for game to feed the army. He realized that worrying about such scenarios until he encountered them did little good. Stay sharp and read the signs, he told himself, and the gnomes would reveal themselves long before they were aware of him.

The day progressed as most did when they were moving their camp. They stopped, stretched their legs, and took a light meal at midday. Kurad picked a spot with fresh water to refill their canteens and it provided easy access for Dancer to quench his thirst too. The mist from the morning had developed into a light rain that dampened the boy's spirits, not that Kurad blamed him. Riding through the forest where leaves continually emptied their collected raindrops had a way of bringing down the spirits of even the most optimistic of travelers. Kurad empathized with the boy, but used the precipitation to his advantage as it helped to silence the trio's movements.

They were nearing the old barn by the middle of the afternoon and Kurad subconsciously increased his awareness. The difference between now and his past travels was his young charge. Edward was normally very obedient and took instruction well, but a child's exuberance can distract most when they see something out of the ordinary. A gnome soldier would definitely get the boy's curiosity up, and at that point an outburst would prove disastrous. Kurad had been playing a game with Edward over the past couple weeks that focused on being completely still. The game exceeded the normal hand signals that they had established, and called for him becoming as still as a statue.

"Edward, I wonder if you can become a statue today?" he asked in a voice barely audible, hoping the boy would follow his lead and keep his voice at a mere whisper.

"Of course I can," he replied in the same quiet tone. "The Black Knight himself could walk past me and think I was made of stone. You just watch me." Excited at the prospect of playing, his voice rose slightly as he rushed his sentence. Playtime was limited to different games now that he was traveling with Kurad but, like all little boys, he jumped at any chance to play games.

"Well little man, today it will be even more important that neither of us gets caught moving. The game is a little more realistic today than at other times that we've played. You should probably know that there may be those in the forest who would like to take you away from me and not let you camp out anymore. Some people out in the forest who aren't friends with your father like I am." Kurad didn't want to completely frighten the boy, although he needed some additional incentive to keep the boy focused on the task of remaining still.

"Camping is lots of fun and you still need to help me catch the Black Knight," Edward's words rushed out, hoping to get everything out before the game started. Once the game started he knew he would have to keep his mouth closed and quiet until Kurad let him know the game was over. Even at his young age he could figure out that sometimes adults had other motives behind their behavior than they shared with him. He had come to the conclusion that this game was probably more than a game. What it was he didn't know, but the longer they remained camping the more he started to pay attention to what his protector taught him.

"If you are ready let the game begin, and remember that today the consequences of losing may be even greater than having to clean the dishes." Kurad looked down at the boy sitting in front of him in the saddle, wondering if he wasn't giving the boy enough credit. He seemed to be brighter than he expected a child to be, but then again he hadn't spent much time around them in the past.

They came upon the old barn just as the sun was setting in the western sky. Kurad began a long slow circle clockwise, scanning both towards the barn and beyond the arc that they now traveled. Noting that the animals of the forest were going about their activities as was normal for this time of day reassured him that he was right in his assessment that nothing felt out of place in the abandoned farm site. It was mostly small birds and squirrels flittering and scampering about amongst the treetops, melting away at the approach of the riders. As he passed by the setting sun's fading light, he took care not to silhouette the trio from any who might be watching from the safety of the barn should any have eluded detection.

After considerable scrutiny of the surroundings, he finally decided it was time to dismount and approach on foot. Edward was left perched atop the saddle. If he had missed some clue and indeed someone lurked within, the horse was trained to either flee or fight at his command. Kurad stalked forward, all senses focused on the small barn ahead of him through the trees.

It was completely dark by the time he'd dismounted and nothing but the nighttime noises of the forest reached his ears.

The last short distance to the barn he covered in a quick rush, remaining quiet yet making sure he didn't expose himself in the open for more than a brief instant. With his back to the side of the building, he circled the barn until he came across the lone window opposite the door. Hoisting himself up and through the window, he landed softly inside and immediately slid several paces away from his initial point of entry. He paused, knowing that any persons hiding in the barn would have their weapons aimed towards the window.

Several long moments passed and Kurad continued probing the darkness, casting forth his sixth sense, searching the darkness with this highly attuned ability to detect that which was out of place. Already his posture had relaxed a degree from that of a tightly wound weapon ready to strike. Anyone in the building would know that he was there by now and there hadn't been even so much as a rustle of the hay. He struck his flint to a torch to let the meager light search out the corners for someone lying in wait that would cause him or his charge harm. When his interior search confirmed that no one had been in the barn since his last visit, he slipped out the door and retrieved Edward and Dancer.

He waited with the boy until Edward seemed comfortable with his new surroundings. Then he tucked him into bed, telling him that he needed to get to sleep right away while Kurad did some more scouting and maybe would find some fresh berries for breakfast. It had been a long day in the saddle and Edward couldn't have put up much resistance even had he wanted to. Saying goodnight, Edward snuggled into the warmth of his dry bedroll.

Kurad left Dancer with Edward, knowing that he would protect the young boy should someone stumble upon him while Kurad was away scouting. Kurad was certain that whoever came into the barn in his absence would be sorely pressed to reach the boy unscathed. Kurad knew he had only a short distance to cover and he hoped that being on the ground would reveal more traces of the traffic through the woods than if he was mounted. He was rewarded for his decision in short order by finding gnome tracks within a mile of the barn. It was a miracle that they hadn't discovered Kurad's way station during their traverses of the area, but he was certain they had not been within the building and, had they known of it, they surely would have left sign. Kurad could tell, based on the pattern of the tracks and the utter disregard for covering their trail, that they weren't overly concerned with hiding their presence in the area. Kurad fought the urge to jump to conclusions concerning the fate of the city but he was too near now not to wait and find out first hand, but this wasn't a behavior that an invading scout squad would employ. Rather it was more like a scouting party that felt secure and comfortable in the area.

He covered the distance in a very short time, traveling quickly and quietly. As he neared the edge of the wood that surrounded Pendar, he slowed his pace to a near crawl. He carefully checked his foot placement amongst the branches on the forest floor so that no dry branch could betray his presence to a perimeter patrol of Orgle's siege army that could be stationed in the vicinity.

At the edge of the tree line he scanned the open grassland between him and the city walls. He found no siege army camped there but that was of little comfort. The next discovery by Kurad confirmed his worst fear. The guards atop the city walls, even from this distance, were clearly not of King Samuel's army. These troops were highly undisciplined and Kurad could tell they were simply going through the motions. Their behavior played perfectly into his hand, however, for now Kurad would be infiltrating an enemy's hold.

He counted the number of sentries atop the wall and quickly discerned their pattern. The predictability of their circuits combined with the fact that they paid no attention to the field outside the walls made Kurad's crossing of the open field almost too easy. They jabbered with the gnome guard in front of them as they walked back and forth along the wall.

Crossing the field without raising an alarm he waited with his back resting easily against the stone, calculating where the sentry on the wall would be positioned at that moment. He counted off the steps in his head, waiting for the guard atop the wall to reach the point in his patrol that would find him farthest from Kurad's position. When the paces were counted, he gave a quick flick of his wrist and his climbing rope was firmly hooked atop the wall. Kurad scampered up the rope to hang just below the edge of the wall while another circuit of the sentry passed.

Then Kurad quickly crossed the parapet and dropped down to the street below, his presence within the city completely unknown. It was eerily similar to his last visit, with the exception of the guards atop the wall last time being more adept at their assignments; ultimately it had the same result. This time though it was a different mission that brought him into the city. No, he thought, actually it was a continuation of the mission, a mission that had apparently been altered by the fates of the army that had come against the city of Pendar

Kurad was on a different path now. It was a contingency that he hadn't planned for, at least not entirely. The possibility had been discussed briefly with Samuel that night in the tent, yet it hadn't seemed realistic at the time. Nevertheless, the city had fallen to the gnome horde and Kurad's goal now was to find out if there were any surviving members of the royal family and get them out of the city. One of them, whether it was Samuel, Stephen, or maybe even Marie, had to be alive and it was up to him to find them. He gritted his teeth against the emotions that pushed against his resolve when he thought of their possible fates should they have fallen into the hands of Orgle.

The city was quiet and Kurad made good time working his way through the deserted streets, maybe too deserted for what he thought of as an occupied city. Perhaps Orgle still followed and harassed an enemy on the move and there was still some fight left in Samuel's army. Orgle may have left the city with only a small force of gnomes to hold it against a counterattack.

It was a nice thought, but until confirmed, it did nothing to improve his present situation. Information gathering was the mission and he wouldn't make any decisions on future actions until he had gathered all that he could. He closed to within a city block of the castle before he had to duck into a shadowed doorway to avoid a patrol. They were headed towards the main gate and were probably sent to relieve those that walked atop the city walls. He moved quickly, knowing that those relieved from sentry duty would be back this way shortly.

The castle's walls were not even patrolled so confident was the new ruler of the city, again making Kurad's task easier. What greeted his eyes as he crouched atop the stones, however, erased any feelings of triumph. He looked upon an enclosure constructed to imprison what Kurad surmised could only be what was left of Samuel's great army of men and dwarves. A detachment of gnome soldiers stood watch over the dejected and beaten soldiers. Some sat huddled around campfires while others, most likely wounded, lay nearby. Kurad knew immediately that he could do nothing for them. They were a defeated force imprisoned with superior numbers standing watch. Hopefully, though, they could help him with the information he needed.

The guards posed a bigger problem now. The area was well lit both from within and without the fenced area from small fires holding off the wet chill of the night. The gnomes were more attentive and would likely take note of any movement towards the prisoners. If he didn't have the boy under his care to worry about he could have risked capture, confident in his own abilities to escape once he attained the information that he needed. Knowing that wasn't a viable option, he scrubbed it immediately. He would need just a moment or two with the prisoners to gather the information and felt a diversion should give him just that. Moving back into the city he quickly began preparing to implement his plan, and getting to work on his diversion.

Back in position atop the castle wall within half a candle mark and now sat waiting for his primitive yet effective diversion to catch the attention of the guards. The flames from the fire Kurad lit in the nearby building soon leaped into view from within the castle. As he'd expected, the alarm was sounded and the soldiers on prisoner detail were dispatched to extinguish the flames before they could spread throughout the city. As anticipated, soon the immediate area was largely cleared of gnomes. Kurad made short work of crossing the space separating him from the prisoners. It took but a moment to attract the attention of one of the imprisoned dwarves kept within the enclosure.

"Quiet, dwarf," Kurad hissed, not wanting the dwarf to blurt out a word that would give him away. "I need to know what happened to our King Samuel. Does he yet still draw breath or is his brother Stephen now the High Ruler?"

"It is neither of the two that sits on the throne." The soldier answered in an angry controlled whisper. "Orgle rules Pendar now," the dwarf snarled, nearly spitting in his rage as it boiled up within him. "Samuel and his brother have both been slain along with the queen. Even the crown prince has been slain while asleep in his own bedchambers in some foul plot before the trolls breached our walls."

Kurad cut him off, realizing the dwarf's mounting anger would soon cause him to explode into a violent fit of rage.

"Listen to me very carefully. I have very little time remaining before the gnomes return. You must find the highest ranking officer among the captured and tell him to have his army ready to rise in twelve years and seventy-three days. That will be the day that the city of Pendar will be returned to its rightful heir. Know what I am about to tell you with all certainty and guard this next piece of information I am about to tell you as if your life, nay your king's life, depends on its secrecy. The crown prince Edward still lives and will return on the appointed day. Remember, twelve years and seventy-three days, his eighteenth birthday. The flames of my diversion are surely dying down by now and I must be away." With that he turned from the stunned dwarf and disappeared into the dark night and over the wall of the castle.

Relysis sat and watched the mysterious man disappear and promised to himself that, as the highest ranking soldier remaining in his defeated army, he would personally see to the preparedness of the men who would once again rise against the evil usurper that wrongfully sat on the throne of Pendar. He went over the mandate again in his head, twelve years and seventy-three days. It was a long time to wait in captivity but he was going to need it, he thought, as he looked at the soldiers around him.

The trip back through the city was a blur as Kurad moved with all the stealth he could muster. The king was dead and the only living heir to the throne of Pendar lay asleep, virtually unprotected, in a small barn not more than a couple of miles from his occupied ancestral home. His home and everything he had known including his mother, father, and uncle had been taken from him in one fell swoop. Kurad's mission had just been officially altered and it was time to put distance between this city and his charge. It would be many years before he could bring the king back to reclaim Pendar. Hopefully the army he requested, and desperately needed, would be at his disposal on what would be his eighteenth birthday, the day of ascension based on the laws governing the land. Had Kurad known the dwarf he'd charged with the monumental task of raising an army was Relysis, he would have rested much easier in the years to come.

The city wall loomed ahead of him. He made quick work of going up and over and was quickly gone across the field and into the forest without even a stirring of the brush along the tree line. Kurad continued moving fast and slowed his pace when he had the barn in sight. Nothing stirred as he closed rapidly on the building. Kurad slipped through the door and was greeted by the soft nuzzle of his horse. That was the final assurance he needed that all was well with the boy. After checking on the sleeping child, he quickly went about packing the gear and loading the horse. At long last, he roused the young prince and hefted him up atop the saddle before he moved out through the door and into the night.

As he stopped to shut the door behind them, it was the barely audible snap of a twig cracking in the quiet night that caught his attention. He couldn't be certain of its source and continued to shut the door as if he'd heard nothing. Stretching the limits of his senses, searching for any clue as to the identity of who waited in the darkness. He had been hasty, skipping even a cursory sweep of the perimeter as he neared the barn. Now he was unprepared for whatever lurked in the darkness. His carelessness left Edward exposed and in considerable danger. His pulse quickened, muscles prepared for flight or fight.

Chapter Eleven

Dancer was his barometer, the horse's uneasiness alerting him that something was wrong with the unusual quiet hanging over the forest. Kurad continued the slow swing of the door, attempting to disguise his awareness that someone lay concealed in the brush nearby. Kurad had nearly shut the door completely without getting any more clues about his attackers, when finally the faint scrape of a weapon against a tree trunk alerted him to the ambusher's position to Kurad's right. He continued his ruse that he was completely unaware of the impending attack, all the while plotting his escape route based on the little evidence he was able to gather in those brief seconds.

He gripped the reins of Dancer tightly as the door came to a stop against the frame. Then he exploded into action, planting his foot against the door, pushing off with all his strength, leaping high, and spinning about to land behind the boy atop his horse. Dancer was on full alert to the danger that surrounded them and responded with a burst of speed even as Kurad was finding his seat. Kurad let him have his head and merely spurred him on, trusting that Dancer would find a hole in the net that threatened to ensnare them. He held on with his knees as he drew forth his sword, hoping not to have to use it to, but rather to make a clean pass through the circle of would be captors.

The edge of the tree line was fast approaching when the rush came. As he had feared it was a gnome patrol that faced him, hoping to intercept the charging steed and its precious cargo. Dancer had accurately sensed the strength of the patrol and unerringly veered for the weakest link in the circle of attackers. Kurad's sword swung low, catching the closest gnome as he tried to close in from the side. Dancer's hooves reached out and clipped the lone gnome standing between them and freedom. They only felled the two, yet it was enough to stop the pursuit as none had mounts to give chase.

Kurad had to assume the child had been noticed even though Edward rode crouched down low in the saddle in front of him. Kurad knew that eventually the patrol would regroup. After reporting to Orgle, it would be a much stronger and better

111

equipped force that took up the trail if any determined that the child was indeed the young prince. Now Kurad had to shift his actions from hiding nearby and awaiting the victory of Samuel, to that of putting distance between Orgle and his relentless pursuit.

These thoughts and others raced through his head at a pace matching his charging mount as they flashed through the trees putting distance between them and the gnomes. One question rose to the surface amidst his churning thoughts. How had the patrol found the barn? He feared he had made a mistake and was seen leaving the city. If they followed him it could mean only one thing: Orgle already knew the boy was alive. He would have time later to ponder all of these possibilities but now he needed to focus on their flight through the night. Right now he wanted to put distance between him and the patrol before dawn provided the light needed by his pursuers to take up their trail.

That same dawn found Orgle in a rage when it was reported to him that the ones he valued so much had eluded him. The refugees of Pendar had slipped from his grasp, apparently vanishing into thin air, leaving the old dwarven mountain stronghold completely deserted before Orgle's army arrived. The captain of scouts assured him his army would have no problem overwhelming any resistance that the refugees, mainly old men, women and children, could muster from behind the ancient walls. He also reported that the walls were still formidable after years of neglect and exposure to the elements but without an army of consequence, the walls could be breached. Even though the plan had been executed perfectly and the dwarven stronghold taken, it was a hollow victory without the capture of the refugees. Somehow they had simply disappeared without a trace, even though the scouts had reported they were securely sequestered behind the ancient walls when the raid began.

Orgle, in his fit over the loss of the Pendar refugees, tallied the only two casualties of the campaign to take the city. The first was the messenger that brought the news, the second the scout captain. With his rage appeased, Orgle appointed a new captain of the scout squad and sent him out to investigate possible routes the people could have taken to flee the city without being seen by his troops. It was at that moment he decided he might have been a bit hasty in executing the scout captain. He may actually have been able to give some valuable input on the lay of the land; what was done was done. There were always more to take the place of the incompetent, whether they desired the post or not.

It took the better part of the day searching the city in the mountain for escape routes before searchers found the rubble from the recently collapsed tunnel opening and determined that this was the route they had taken out of the city. The escape tunnel they used burrowed deep under the mountain that for centuries had protected the rear approach from any who would come to wage war on Zoisite. Beyond the height of the mountain, one that would not be easily crossed by a lone tracker much less an entire gnome army, there was a valley that surely now held the refugees. The peaks were jagged and covered with snow most of the year and the passes were treacherous even then. For now, the remnants of Pendar had bought themselves some time, although Orgle would surely give chase, with the prize of capturing and enslaving the last of the once proud and previously unconquered nation.

After much persuasion by his commanders, it was decided that a small exploratory force would give chase over the mountain to try and find a pass where Orgle could send an army to finish what he had started with the taking of Pendar. There were other tasks that needed his attention now. Once his newly acquired kingdom was running smoothly, he would return and round up the remaining refugees and drag them all back in chains.

One of the tasks before him was listening to reports on incidents within the city to determine if any holdouts were striking back at him. Orgle suspected they would use guerilla tactics, and his mind wandered as the captain droned on about a fire his squad had responded to. He knew the holdouts would be gathered up in short order and his lack of concern found him staring out the window until a clamor arose in the hall outside his throne room.

"What is that racket? You know I don't like distractions while I'm holding my briefings. Come and state your concerns, you've already disrupted me." He waved in the sergeant who was being detained in the hallway, secretly thankful for the distraction.

"Your Excellence," began the sergeant, hesitating before his king. He knew Orgle's reputation for dealing with those that angered him and he was fearful. Realizing though, that Orgle was waiting for him to speak, he hurriedly began his tale so as not to further annoy his king.

He'd led the patrol that had come across Kurad and Prince Edward at the barn in the woods. Although they hadn't identified the pair from the brief encounter, it definitely got Orgle's attention. The sergeant began the tale at the point where the patrol spotted the barn through the trees and began to investigate. He left out the part of the story that they were just looking for a place to kick back and rest their legs, but rather explained it as they were approaching to look for more holdouts they could bring to justice. As he progressed in the telling, he got to the point where Kurad came out of the surrounding night and quickly bundled a young human onto the back of a horse that he brought out of the barn. At that point Orgle sat up and became much more interested. The fight for freedom by Kurad was exaggerated to the point that the pair of fugitives were nearly captured except for an unlikely chain of events that left them scrambling away into the dark night. The patrol pursued the pair through the dark of the night for a brief time, but was forced to give up pursuit in order to report their findings to their commanders.

Orgle listened intently, wondering to himself who would be this close to his city without fear of being captured and brought before him to explain themselves. And who would bring a child this close to a city ravaged by war when the dust hadn't even settled yet? Orgle sat and pondered while the sergeant stood by nervously. Could there be any connection to the events that occurred within the city that night?

The man had come from somewhere close by because he had been on foot until he reached the barn. It only made sense that he had come from the city but could he have infiltrated the city and then escaped? There hadn't been any reports of dissidents captured after the mysterious fire was under control. And there hadn't been any other sightings of fugitives reported since the very thorough sweep of the city after he had conquered Pendar.

The timeline was too coincidental for Orgle to ignore, and he knew that with just a little more information the whole story would reveal itself.

The flight through the woods that night for Kurad and Edward was wild and chaotic for as long as it took to clear themselves of the net of soldiers that threatened to snare them. Kurad had given Dancer his head only as long as was needed to break through the would-be captors, allowing the horse to search out the best avenue of escape as he sensed the openings in the circle. Kurad made sure the initial pursuit had faded behind them and when he was confident the threat was sufficiently behind them, he took control of the reins and asked Dancer for stealth and cunning. Kurad put more distance between them and the barn before he stopped to dismount. He checked over both his charge and his mount for any injuries, no matter how minor, they may have received during their chaotic flight. Both seemed to be unscathed. He hadn't expected to find a wound on Dancer, for he had never missed a stride during the escape. The boy though, hadn't spoken a word even after they had stopped.

"Edward, are you okay?" Kurad asked the boy, trying to remain calm but the concern for his welfare still came through. "Did you get hurt at all during our ride through the trees? I do not see any wounds, but the lighting is poor."

"Why were those men trying to get us? We did not do anything to them. Was it their barn that I slept in that made them so angry?" The boy's little voice quivered slightly even though he tried valiantly to conceal his fear.

"We did nothing to offend those creatures tonight. Do not worry about being guilty of doing anything wrong. They were not men though, and you need to learn the difference. The group that attacked us tonight and tried to capture us were members of the gnome army. They are enemies of your father and are not friends to either man or dwarf. Some day you will better understand why they were after us, but tonight know only that we need to travel a few more miles away from here so there is no chance they will catch up to us. As soon as you're ready to ride again, we'll be on our way."

It was going to be hard to explain to the boy what tonight's raid had meant to accomplish, but that was for another day, he thought as he patted Edward on his leg before swinging up behind him.

Kurad had to assume that the patrol knew the identity of the heir to Pendar and that was why they had made the attempt to capture the pair. Any other assumption by Kurad could prove deadly. He had to act as if their identities were known, and when one of them was the only living heir to the throne, the stakes were compounded many times over.

They traveled until first light then stopped to take a small meal of way bread and wild berries. Kurad had developed a plan as they passed silently through the forest and dawn found them many miles from the abandoned barn. They were headed north to lands that would be friendlier to a pair of travelers than the forests that they currently traversed. He had a few contacts up that way and someone would surely know a place he could hide Edward until the time was right for his return.

When they remounted after a quick breakfast and started off once again, they soon left behind the forests that had been under the rule of Samuel Ellingstone and his forefathers. Someday Samuel's young son might be in the position to retake what was his by birthright, but that day seemed quite distant to Kurad right now and not yet a concern to the little boy sitting in front of him.

The days passed, one after another, and still the pair trended northward, winding through the mountain passes. They began to encounter others on the roadways, getting no more than curious glances from those that lived in the lands they crossed and even less acknowledgement from those like themselves who were just passing through. The lands they crossed became less mountainous as they left behind the range that had protected Pendar for so many years.

The nations to the north hadn't always been friendly to Pendar, but in recent years Samuel had worked hard to secure truces and even open some trade between them. However, they hadn't felt so closely allied that they were compelled to respond to King Samuel's request for aide in turning back the gnome threat from the south. The northern nations felt the gnomes would be hard pressed to defeat Samuel's army, and even if they did, the same mountains Pendar had used for generations to hold back any threats from the north would also keep the gnome hoards from advancing any further.

Even though the northern nations had not come to the aide of Samuel while he lived, Kurad thought, they would unknowingly help in protecting the young heir Kurad now brought into their lands. They wouldn't know who he was, yet they could offer them a place to hide and the protection while their forces kept the gnomes at a distance. That would leave Kurad to make sure Edward grew up strong in mind and body. The time needed to accomplish the tasks ahead would be short and there were many things that the young prince, sitting quietly in the saddle before him, would need to know before he was returned to his home and took his place on his father's throne.

Kurad had to work hard those first days on the road to keep his thoughts as positive as possible, for he knew countless challenges would present themselves before that day could arrive. Foremost on his mind was finding an army for Edward to lead in his attempt to retake the throne someday as his father had envisioned. He shook his head in resignation. Without an army, all the training Kurad planned as well as the preparations would be for naught. He reminded himself that their flight from Edward's homeland had just begun and they had many miles to travel. Years would pass before he could start thinking about Edward's triumphant return. No, those were thoughts for another day, he decided, as he nudged Dancer into a trot. They needed a place to disappear, so that would be his first priority. Neither one looked back as they descended into the foothills on the north side of the mountain range and crossed the border into Mycilia.

Chapter Twelve

The night air was cool against Edward's sweat covered back. They trained at night at Kurad's insistence, though Edward thought they could accomplish more if they could find one another more easily. Then they would get to do more sparring, which he preferred. How was it, Edward wondered, that he could never elude his uncle whether it be by climbing a tree or hiding in a cave, to name just a couple of his past attempts? Kurad could track him across water, even if he were able to cross a lake without leaving a ripple to mark his passage. Maybe it was that he was only sixteen and lacked Kurad's experience when it came to his hiding places. With that in mind, he thought, what could he do tonight that would be different? He didn't have much time to ponder his choices Kurad was probably just moments behind him on the trail.

Okay, Edward thought to himself, let's try something simple. Step off the side of the trail and when Kurad passes by, I'll double back the way we came and he'll never be the wiser. He had tried a variation of this tactic in the past, but he always remained in his initial hiding spot while Kurad invariably doubled back in short order to find him. Tonight he would not be in there when Kurad found his hiding place. He slowed his pace to a walk, hoping to minimize his tracks before he got to a suitable bush to hide behind. Stepping onto a large rock lying on the trail, he pivoted as he stepped off the trail leaving no discernible track on the path. Then he sat, crouched in the shadows, waiting for Kurad's dark form to come along.

As he had expected, he didn't have to wait long as Kurad moved swiftly on his long legs, scanning the ground before him and scouring the branches that hung along the trail looking for sign of his quarry. Edward sat silently, barely daring to breathe as Kurad made his way past, moving beyond the bend in the trail ahead. Quickly, and hopefully without a noise, Edward stepped back onto the trail and began to move cautiously back in the direction he had come. He had gone some twenty paces and was feeling pretty good about himself when suddenly he was knocked from his feet in mid-stride.

"That was very clever young man," Kurad began, "but you'll need to be a little quicker on your feet if your plan was to outdistance me." There was a bit of jab there from Kurad, but also a hint for future success and Edward would definitely remember both. He helped Edward back up from the ground and steadied him until he recovered his feet. "Come along now, Edward, we need to make haste back to the cottage so that we are back in bed long enough to catch a few winks before the cock crows."

"I was wondering if we could travel to Stonebrook this summer." Edward's question pulled Kurad's attention away from the moonlit trail and Edward, seeing his opportunity, hurried on with his inquiry, not wanting to give Kurad a chance to answer before he had chance to plead his case.

"You know its Jessica's birthday this next month and I wanted to get her a present from the city instead of one from our own village." He paused now, looking up at Kurad, hoping to read the man's mind through the stone-faced expression that he often wore during training. Hoping he could influence him, assuming that Kurad still needed some convincing, he plowed ahead with the speech he had rehearsed earlier in the day.

"She is always talking to Helen about that little porcelain figurine that we saw two years ago when we all made the trip together. It wouldn't fit in at the farm, but maybe someday..." Edward stopped himself, realizing that he had gotten off topic and was beginning to divulge things that only Jessica and he had spoken of in their brief moments together. The manor they hoped to share together when they were grown and Edward had become a lord of some sort with landholdings and their own stable of the finest horses around. He looked up quickly at Kurad hoping the man hadn't heard the daydreams sneaking through his consciousness and into his conversation.

"It might be a nice break from the chores and the farm. It would be fun for all of us don't you think?" He hoped he had recovered well enough, but how could you know by looking at Kurad's stone-like visage? The man was impossible to read.

"I'll think about it today. Right now, you get your feet moving instead of your mouth and when you get your chores done tonight I'll have an answer for you." With that said, he started out at a brisk pace through the trees in the direction of the farmhouse. He could hear Edward falling in behind him, trying to match his shorter stride to Kurad's considerably longer one. It was no more than three miles back to the farm but the run would help Edward with his endurance.

The young man would never be able to sustain a full-out run for a long period like him, for Edward was an exact duplicate of his father. He was more compact and broader of shoulder than most boys his age, lending credence to the myth that dwarf blood flowed through the Ellingstone family. Edward was built low to the ground and more suited to short bursts of speed. Even Kurad himself could not match him from a standstill.

Kurad wasn't sure if now was the time to travel to the city. Rumors of gnomes in the area were particularly disturbing considering the identity of his charge. Kurad had been told, when he inquired of those that had seen the gnomes, they were simply traveling through the area looking for new trading opportunities. They had not appeared hostile in any way. Outwardly, it appeared as if they were concerned with improving their image with their new neighbors since they had defeated Samuel eleven years past.

It seemed to Kurad, in retrospect, that Samuel hadn't been completely trusted amongst his peers in the neighboring kingdoms. Kurad couldn't understand their position based on what he knew of Samuel. He has always been fair in his dealings, no matter one's position in life, and his interactions with surrounding royalty were consistent with that practice. It must be assumed that it was his allegiance to the dwarves who shared his lands that those outside the kingdom didn't trust. For whatever reason, it was widely believed that dwarves weren't to be trusted. Kurad could only believe that people were afraid of what wasn't familiar to them. Even he had to acknowledge that dwarves were certainly different then humans, a point any dwarf would proudly point out.

The distrust of the dwarves aside, any king should be fearful of how easily their new neighbor conquered such a powerful kingdom, and should have some concern over how safe their own borders were. Those same borders had been protected by Pendar from the gnome hordes to the south. Now those same gnomes traveled with apparent freedom throughout the lands. Orgle had either intimidated his new neighbors or it could just have been the lack of hostility he displayed once he had established himself. It was another riddle for Kurad to unwind should he ever have the time to investigate the happenings over the past decade.

The last ten plus years hadn't left much time for investigating what went on so far from his temporary home. Upon fleeing Edward's homeland, they had traveled north for several months, crossing several more borders until he reached Stonebrook, the capital city of Chalcedony. There he had turned west and continued on for another few weeks. He had remembered a woman, Helen, whom he knew to be trustworthy from previous travels and also knew that she could use a hand running the family farm. Edward would benefit from growing up in a more traditional family setting. In the long term, they would have time to blend into the community and establish themselves as locals while Edward was still young.

Becoming one of the locals had been critical if someday anyone came looking for someone who fit either of their descriptions. It was important that they blended in and grew roots. Helen had readily agreed to the arrangement without asking many questions about Edward's origin. She only knew that he was an orphan Kurad had taken in to see that he grew up strong and healthy.

Helen had been widowed many years ago and left with a young daughter herself who would enjoy a playmate. And Helen would appreciate having a strong back around to help with chores. The pair had moved into a cottage tucked into the woods not far from Helen's and began the process of becoming a part of the community.

A small village was located a couple miles just down the lane where Edward and Helen's daughter Jessica attended school. Edward's education was not overlooked. Kurad had known that Edward would require the right upbringing, one that a village could provide, rather than growing up amongst the creatures of the forest or in the dark mountain passes Kurad typically called home. It was a sacrifice he was more than willing to make for his friend Samuel.

In the early years, Kurad would leave Edward under the watchful eye of Helen and make excursions south, spending months at a time scouting the developments of Orgle's new empire. He continually probed the region, learning all he could concerning the fate of those chased from their homes. Over time he'd learned that a host of refugees had escaped from the old dwarven stronghold and disappeared into the mountains, but he had always been thwarted in his further investigations to find them. He could only assume they had disappeared to the north in an attempt to hide from Orgle, but his time away from the farm was limited and all Kurad ever found were dead ends.

As Edward grew older, Kurad's solo excursions were scaled back. Edward needed more attention and the training only Kurad could provide. After a time his trips began to include Edward as they were a natural extension of all Kurad had taught him. Edward was unaware of the underlying reason for the trips and assumed that he and his uncle, as he had taken to calling Kurad, were just taking vacations away from the farm and enjoying living off the land. The trips usually coincided with school breaks and never during the planting and harvesting seasons. Helen had come to rely heavily on their help and could ill afford to have them traipsing through the woods when there was work at the farm. She had accused Kurad on more than one occasion of doing just that.

The trips had reinforced his woodcraft training and had hardened his young body through the rigors of living off the land and logging many leagues on the backwoods trails. Both of these attributes would be important once the time was right to return the prince to his home. These skills would not be required to govern his father's kingdom. No, it was the journey that would begin when they set out from Helen's little farm and would go on until they wrested the throne back from Orgle that would tax them both. That was the reason behind all the arduous physical training. It was the hand-to-hand combat drills and weapons training that Kurad placed great emphasis on, knowing that these skills would be necessary someday.

Once Edward had regained his rightful place on the throne he could draw on his schooling and book learning, for they would be his greatest asset. So with that vision of the future in mind, he had divided Edward's training between that which would not only serve him well once he wore his crown, but also that which would enable him to survive until that day arrived.

While most boys reveled in physical contests of wrestling and mock battles few, if any, would ever draw on these lessons as Edward most assuredly would. Kurad knew that Edward's destiny was to be a king and a warrior. With that picture in mind, Kurad taught him the use of the sword in close combat situations. Another skill Kurad also concentrated on was the art of using a bow in stealth to eliminate an enemy from a distance before they were able to get close. The bow felt natural in Edward's hands and his skills had progressed faster than most when learning its use.

The sword, though, was a different story. He couldn't shake the awkward feel which left him vulnerable in an attack. It wasn't as if he was inept, for he grasped the concept of thrusting, blocking, and even how to use the hilt to pummel an opponent, yet it didn't flow for him as well as Kurad knew it must.

It wasn't until one day when Kurad watched Edward plying an axe against a tree that he realized what weapon Edward's broad shoulders were best suited to. At that moment, Kurad decided that a dwarven battleaxe would be Edward's weapon of choice. Most men found the weapon cumbersome and not as effective as a sword in battle, but then most men didn't have the strength of a dwarf to properly wield it.

Finding one was going to be most difficult for they were not readily available in Chalcedony and the craft of making one had almost exclusively been kept within the dwarven nation. Now, with the metal workers of Pendar scattered to the winds, the prospect of finding a well-crafted weapon seemed unlikely. He did know of one man who lived a month's travel to the east of Tourmaline, the capital of Mycilia, in the wilds outside the city. The craftsman had lived with and apprenticed under a dwarf smithy as a young man. He had gained the respect of his master and been taught the art of forging the dwarven battleaxe. It was an art for even a skilled metal worker to create a well-balanced, perfectly weighted axe.

The desire to acquire an axe for Edward swayed Kurad in his decision to take an extended trip into and through Mycilia precisely as Edward had asked him to consider. School was on hiatus to allow children to help on their farms with planting. Kurad and Edward had the planting done for the year already which was good, time was becoming a factor. With only a couple years until the age of ascension, now seemed like as good as any to take leave of the farm and take Edward on a longer excursion. With the decision made. he went about his daily chores and began to make a mental list of the items he would need to acquire before they struck out on their journey.

At dinner that evening Kurad announced that he and Edward needed to make a trip to Mycilia. They would be gone for a good share of the summer and most likely later into fall. He emphasized, upon noting Helen's frown, that they most assuredly would be back well before the harvest. Her features softened, yet left him realizing more assurances in the next few days would be required. Their summer excursions were common so it didn't take Helen completely by surprise although, Edward noted, Jessica was rather shaken up. The rest of the meal was quiet and nothing else was said of the upcoming trip except by Kurad to establish that they would be leaving at week's end.

That night, as Edward finished feeding the livestock, he heard soft footfalls coming up behind him. Instinctively taking a quick look over his shoulder, he was pleasantly surprised to find Jessica approaching him on the worn dirt path alongside the barn. She reached him just as he was putting down his feed bucket. He suddenly turned, catching her by surprise, and hugged her about the waist. He lifted and twirled her around a couple of times before setting her back to her feet.

"Edward," she giggled as she tried to catch her breath and straightened her long auburn hair. "Don't you be doing that. If my mother caught you behaving like that she would likely tell you never to return from your stupid trip." The giggle hadn't given away her true feelings about the trip, but her comment regarding it as stupid certainly did.

"Jessica, you know these trips are important to Kurad. That's the only reason I agreed to go along with him. He needs my help. We'll probably be gathering supplies for the farm and you know what a burden some of those things can be." He decided not to mention that it was, at least in part, his idea to go. Except Kurad had extended the trip considerably from Edward's proposed few days. He wondered why Kurad had decided on the extension, then justified the trip by telling himself that the gift he picked up for Jessica would more than make up for his absence.

"Maybe I can find some trinket or piece of jewelry when I'm there so that you'll know that I was thinking of you while I was gone."

"I know that you'll be back by the harvest. Kurad promised my mother as much, but I had hoped to spend the school break doing things together." Jessica ignored his hint of a gift, instead revealing her true feelings.

"You know better than to think your mother and Kurad would let us spend our days taking walks and going on picnics." He almost laughed at the image of Helen packing them a lunch so they could stroll down the lane hand in hand. "Besides, this way at the end of the summer we'll have plenty to talk about. You can tell me how you collected eggs every morning and I can tell you about the exotic creatures we discovered as we trekked through the mountains." Laughing, he jumped back in time to avoid a good natured jab from a vexed Jessica.

The next two days passed rapidly for everyone. Helen was baking way bread for the trip and Jessica helped pack travel bags. Kurad, along with Edward, made sure the horses were properly shod and fit for the journey ahead and the bows they would use for hunting were in fine shape along with a good supply of arrows. At week's end it was a quiet group that bid farewell in the pre-dawn hour as the men climbed aboard their horses and waved good-bye to Helen and Jessica. Jessica watched them disappear down the lane, continuing to wave until they rounded a bend in the road in case they turned back one more time. Then she turned towards the house, discreetly dabbing away a small tear sneaking from the corner of her eye.

Chapter Thirteen

It had been a late night followed by an early morning and now Edward was feeling the effects of a full stomach from breakfast. Helen and Jessica made sure the two men had gotten off to a good start. Rising early, they collected fresh eggs from the hen house, milk from the barn, and smoked bacon and flour from the cellar. Edward and Kurad devoured the meal with a passion knowing that, at least for a while, they wouldn't be getting any more home cooking.

Edward dozed in the saddle as he and Kurad crossed an open area along the wooded path they followed on their way towards Stonebrook. Edward was somewhat of a romantic and enjoyed the adventures that played out in his mind, always concluding with fairy-tale endings he dreamed up. In his reverie, he dreamed of coming back from their summer travels to the farm and giving Jessica her gift and thinking how much she was going to enjoy it. Then she would understand why this trip had been a good idea and that would make everything okay.

The morning passed on into the afternoon, both men lost in their personal thoughts, so much so that they hadn't spoken for many hours. Suddenly Kurad pulled up hard, motioning for Edward to do the same. Even as Kurad was bringing his horse to a halt, guiding it towards the side of the road, Edward and his mount were doing the same. Having spent so much time training in the woods with one another, moving together was instinctive for them.

Kurad slipped from his saddle and began going through his packs as if he were getting ready for lunch. Edward mimicked the actions of his traveling companion, emulating Kurad's actions, wondering what had caused this sudden stop.

"I thought it was about time to get some grub in our stomachs." Kurad stated, scanning their surroundings. He never really looked at Edward, but made it appear that he was merely talking to him.

"I guess I could eat. I'm still remembering breakfast, but that's never stopped me before." Still unsure of Kurad's actions he felt it best not to question him on his motives.

"Don't unpack much," Kurad began speaking quickly in more hushed tones. "Get just enough bread out so that it looks like we're stopping to eat lunch. Move the horses over to the brush and tie them up there, loosely," he added. "I'm going into the brush as if to take care of some personal needs. Be at the ready to take flight at a moment's notice." With that, he stepped off the roadway into the woods, instantly disappearing from sight.

Edward stared after him, trying to discern where he had gone. After a quick look he turned back to the horses and went about getting a little lunch put together. He had to wonder, though, what had Kurad seen that caused this unexpected stop? True, Edward admitted, he had been dozing in the saddle so he probably hadn't noticed what had been going on ahead on the road. This behavior wasn't totally out of character for Kurad. He always seemed what would he call it, edgy? Kind of like Kurad wasn't really in his own element. Make that, he wasn't in his element on the farm, Edward amended. This string of thoughts caught Edward off balance. Was Kurad changing or why hadn't he noticed this before? Edward decided it was he himself who was growing and changing, noticing more about those around him. Maybe when Kurad got back out of the woods and they got going again he would find out a little more of the history about his traveling companion. His own memories didn't extend beyond living in the cottage down the lane from the farm and Kurad wasn't typically talkative about his history.

Pulling his loaf of bread from his pack, he tore off a small piece and quickly put it into his mouth. He looked around, trying again to piece together just what it was Kurad had found so unsettling. The roadway was nothing more than a couple of worn wagon wheel dirt paths, encroached upon by the overhanging branches of the forest that it passed through at this point. They had been in and out of the forest all morning long, making brief but welcome respites from the increasing heat of the day. But in other less developed tracts, such as the one they found themselves in now, the forest stretched into the distance beyond Edward's view. Maybe this seclusion was what Kurad had gotten nervous about. Now that Edward thought about it, it probably would be a good spot for someone plotting a robbery to ambush them, and with that thought came a sense of urgency about Kurad's whereabouts and safety.

That was all the further Edward got. He was interrupted as Kurad came bursting from the brush, grabbing the reins of his horse from Edward and vaulting into the saddle and calling for Edward to follow. Edward dropped the bread loaf he was holding as he scrambled into his saddle, worried only about what it was that Kurad was fleeing from.

His question was answered almost immediately. Even before he was completely in his saddle, a mob of howling creatures burst through the same brush that had just seconds before given way to Kurad. Thanks purely to Edward's reflexes and the training of his horse, they bolted away together just as the gnome soldiers reached the fallen bread loaf.

It was a terrified duo, young man and horse, that overtook Kurad who, while waving them onward, had paused to make certain his charge had gotten away clean. Immediately wheeling his horse he followed the flying pair back down the roadway in the direction they had traveled that morning. Before easing up, they kept up their gallop for a mile and realized then that their pursuers must not have mounts available to give chase.

"Kurad, what were those things chasing us?" Edward got out through his ragged breathing, still feeling the rush of the recent escape.

"The short answer is that they are gnome scouts. The long answer will have to wait until we have more time. My question is what are gnome soldiers doing this far North? They shouldn't be anywhere near here."

Edward looked back down the path, following Kurad's eyes, and trying to see something that his uncle was missing. Neither saw anything that suggested they needed to continue their flight in haste, so they turned their mounts off the trail with Kurad in the lead and began moving through the woods towards the north.

They pushed to the north for the rest of the day, eating in the saddle and stopping only when the horses needed to be fed and watered. It was during one of those stops that Edward decided to inquire about their recent encounter.

"Exactly what were those gnome soldiers after? And you mentioned that they shouldn't have been this far north so where do they live? Is there something...?" Edward stopped his questions abruptly when Kurad raised a hand.

"The only answers I can give you," Kurad began, "will only cause you to ask more questions. I will give you the information that I think will help you right now, but anything further will have to wait. Agreed?"

Kurad always seemed to know more than what he divulged, and he always justified it by saying that there wasn't enough time right now or it only would confuse him. So knowing this, Edward shook his head in agreement with more than an air of resignation.

"Well, for starters," Kurad began anew, pausing momentarily to collect his thoughts about what to include and what to hold back, "I happen to have dealt with these characters on an occasion or two." Pausing again, he realized he probably didn't remember seeing these creatures before. "Edward, what do you know about gnomes?" he asked.

"Well the boys in school used to tell stories about gnomes and those kind of creatures, but they always said they were nearly twice as big as what we just encountered and even fiercer. But besides the exaggeration about the size, they were pretty accurate about how they walk all stooped over and have thick hair on their long thin arms." Edward responded, showing that he knew at least a little about their pursuers, feeling there was much more to learn.

"Good, at least we have some sort of base to start with," Kurad paused wondering how to continue. "I told you that I have had dealings with these creatures before. Well, that was some time ago, perhaps ten years or more. Right before you and I traveled north to Helen's farm. It was a brief encounter, a run-in of sorts that I wasn't even sure if you would remember. You were young." Kurad knew at some point the story would come out and Edward was shaking his head indicating that he didn't remember.

"Right now though we should concentrate on covering some ground, and if we are being tracked, lead them away from the farm."

"Do you still think they are following us?" Edward stopped, captured by a series of memories floating in his mind. He was trying hard to recall the incident that Kurad had mentioned but struggling as the pieces refused to come together. He was afraid that he would lose hold of them before they resembled something cohesive, when he was suddenly struck with a terrifying thought.

"Wait a minute! Why would they care about where we lived on the farm? Are Jessica and Helen in danger? I thought they were just highway robbers."

"Hold on young man," Kurad interrupted, his voice taking on an authoritative tone.

Edward shot him a hard look, not appreciating the edge that crept into Kurad's tone.

"There are plenty of things about this that you don't know," Kurad began, softening his tone, "Right now I think it best if I tell you only that which will help us right now, in the present. For starters the answer is yes, they know who we are or at least I have good reason to suspect they have figured out the truth. Second," Kurad stopped and held up a hand, asking Edward for silence as he tried to put the final pieces of the puzzle that had until this moment eluded even himself. How did these scouts know who they were? The boy was grown now and the years of farming had changed him. They had to have known our identities based on something, but what?

"We need to get back to the farm. I'm not sure if they've been there yet." He exchanged looks with Edward knowing that he was right in amending that the both of them needed to know about the welfare of Jessica and Helen.

"Even if we leave now it will be dark before we reach them." Edward spit out between clenched teeth as he wheeled his horse. He wasn't sure who he was angry at; Kurad who had left out key details about the past, or the gnome scouts that might be in a position to harm Jessica. Maybe both but the important thing was getting back to the farm so he could protect Jessica. At that moment her wellbeing was at the forefront of his thoughts. Kurad would have to fill in the details about the past later. Both men put their heels to their horses' flanks.

Troy A. Skog

Chapter Fourteen

The pair traveled quickly back towards the farmhouse. Kurad had caught up to Edward as they rode and assumed the lead. All of their time spent together made it instinctive to let Kurad lead. As they fell into a steady pace, Kurad was already working through the possible scenarios that would be facing the pair shortly. He had to figure out how the gnome scouts could have known about the homestead where Edward was living. It was the only way that they could have known who they were when they attempted to ambush them along the roadway, he was certain he had heard them shout out the gnomish word for king. There could be no other explanation. They had to have been followed. Even gnome soldiers wouldn't dare to openly attack peasants in a foreign land this far from the protection of their throne. No, Kurad was convinced that they had been found out. It was a mystery to be certain, but one that would likely go unsolved in the immediate future or maybe ever.

Kurad decided early on during the return trip that Edward needed to be told of his past as soon as time allowed so that the boy would be ready when the time came for action. For now though, he would have to trust in his training of Edward and that he would follow his lead. His actions and reactions depended on the two of them working as a cohesive unit, just as Kurad had trained them to do. The young man was definitely growing up, but Kurad wasn't sure how he would react to fighting gnomes. He was confident that he would know the answer soon.

The rush back to the farmhouse had gone quickly still it was dark when they arrived. Kurad wasn't sure who was waiting for them at the farmhouse, so he slowed their approach to a crawl. They dismounted and led the horses, hoping to get as close as possible before they had to leave their best means of escape behind. When they were within a half mile of the fields that surrounded the house and outbuildings, they tethered their horses in some dense brush and hoped that they would still be there when they needed them most.

They followed one another through the trees taking turns at point. First Kurad would move ahead, scouting as he went, going only as far as he knew Edward could keep him in sight. Then Edward would move forward, using the same stealth that Kurad used, drawing even with him and then moving out ahead of his teacher. They scanned the trees for soldiers. It was completely dark that night and the little bit of moon shine that would have shed light on the land below was obscured by a thick bank of clouds that were making their way across the night sky. The conditions worked both in favor of and against the duo making their way back to Helen's farm.

It was Edward that met with the first gnome as he was crawling ahead through the brush. Both young man and gnome were frozen into place by the shock of suddenly coming into contact with one another, even though both were looking for the other. Edward was down on all fours and winding his way through a particularly dense section of brush and was at a distinct disadvantage upon meeting the soldier. He knew instantly that he had made a mistake by entering that thicket. It was obviously a perfect place to hide to ambush a target, and that is exactly what the gnome soldier had done. Now, staring at the legs of the soldier in front of him, Edward's training and reflexes took over and pushed him into action, automatically taking him from his crouched position and making the decisions for him.

Edward powered up to his feet, reaching for his knife tucked into his belt, expecting to feel the sting of the gnome's weapon in his back before he was able to reach his full height. Trying to compensate for his awkward position, he struck out wildly with his knife, reaching for his opponent's midsection, hoping to distract him and lessen the blow that was undoubtedly coming at him at that very moment. His thrust struck the gnome soldier solidly. It apparently had been enough to make the gnome hesitate, because the attack he expected never came. The gnome kicked weakly at him, struggling to grasp his own weapon.

Taking a moment to regroup, he realized that the soldier hadn't resisted at all. Even now, with a very painful, but not fatal wound, it stood unmoving. Seeing his chance to put some fighting space between them so that he could get on even footing, he pushed backwards and planted his feet beneath him, crouching low. Looking up, he stopped and stared at the silent form leaning back against the tree he had been hiding by as if suspended. It was then that he spotted an arrow buried in his neck, pinning his victim to the tree.

Kurad had seen the outline of the gnome even as Edward started to enter the thicket. Kurad came forward and checked to make sure he had dispatched the soldier. He slowly retrieved his arrow and helped the lifeless body slide down the tree as quietly as possible, trying not to attract any more attention as the two men both crouched down in the darkness.

Kurad leaned over and put his hand out to steady Edward, not sure how the young man would be handling his first real hand-to-hand combat. Edward seemed fine and Kurad decided that focusing on the mission would serve them best right now.

"Edward," he whispered into the young man's ear, "we must make haste for chances are that another set of eyes or ears took notice of our encounter. We still need to practice stealth, but with the very good possibility of scouts descending on our position, we need to put distance between this spot and ourselves. They may not be sure that anything has happened until they find their comrade. When they do, you can be positive they will sound the alarm and pursue in earnest. Hopefully, we can get this to work in our favor. If we can get close to the farmhouse before the alarm sounds, the ensuing commotion may afford us the opportunity to slip in undetected."

Edward nodded solemnly, still unsure of what he had just done. He was trying to figure out why it had been so easy and instinctual to thrust his knife into a soldier that he knew nothing about. He hadn't even looked at the gnome's face much less into his eyes. Why were these soldiers after him and his friends? They had done nothing to offend them. He must learn from Kurad what he knew. He broke off his thought as Kurad moved ahead of him expecting him to follow close behind. Edward, not wanting to risk being separated, quickly caught up.

They reached the edge of the fields where the milk cows grazed surrounding Helen's farmhouse. Over the years, cow paths had been worn into the pasture. Having herded the cattle morning and night to milk for the past ten years, Kurad and Edward knew these pathways like the backs of their hands. Keeping to the pathways where they knew there would be no unexpected holes or tufts of grass to trip them up, they began crossing the space between the woods and the barnyard.

They had closed to within one hundred paces of the barn when behind them in the forest the alarm was sounded. Kurad pushed ahead faster now, his legs stretching out underneath him in his ground-eating stride. He looked from side to side, searching for an enemy that might or might not be there. Edward followed closely behind his legs pumping feverishly, trying to maintain the pace the much taller man in front of him set. He waited to draw his weapon, waited for his teacher to do likewise, realizing after the encounter moments ago just how dangerous this man was. Kurad had been places and experienced things he had only imagined and this new insight piqued his curiosity more than just a little.

It wasn't until they stood with their backs to the wall of the barn that they reached for their knife belts. Kurad drew first and was quickly mimicked by his understudy. Edward also copied his surveillance technique, looking everywhere, never focusing on any one object. Kurad had taught him that if he stared long enough, he would see movement that was not there. It was a simple trick of the eyes. These were things that Kurad had spent years training Edward for and now they surfaced with little conscious effort.

They continued to hear shouts and curses from across the field, yet nothing stirred on this side of the field and they began to work their way through the out building towards the house. They tried to find the perfect mix of stealth and speed, needing to reach the house before their pursuers, not wanting to walk into any traps. Kurad continued to set the pace with Edward following on his heels. The two were once again at an advantage over the gnomes and were partially relying on that advantage to help them reach their current objective.

Edward bumped Kurad from behind as Kurad had stopped suddenly and caught him unaware. Edward steadied himself. Kurad reached back to help him recover although he never he never took his eyes off the front porch. That was enough for Edward to know that Kurad had seen something wrong ahead of them and that he should be prepared for whatever Kurad needed. Kurad simply nodded in the direction he was looking and, after focusing, Edward saw the dark form standing off to the right of the porch, nearly hidden in the shadows of the house. Nearly, but not entirely hidden, especially from someone who was specifically looking for an ambush.

From there they scanned both to the left and right, looking for others. Nobody else was discernible in the shadows so Kurad began moving around the yard, circling back so they would avoid the lone watchman. They moved back along the way they had come, aware that the forest on the other side of the pasture had become quiet and they had no way of knowing where their pursuers were. Had the soldiers started to cross the field or were they searching the woods for sign of their flight? They could only assume the former and hope for the latter. Either way, it wasn't a gamble they could afford to lose and every second it took to avoid the gnome guarding the house made it more likely they would be caught from behind.

With weapons still drawn, they circled behind the barn and began to make their way to the house. They reached the back of the house after what seemed all night to the pair, when it was actually only minutes. Kurad and Edward encountered no one en route, which almost made it worse for the two. Kurad knew there had to be more than the one soldier standing guard by the front porch. Wherever they were, they were succeeding in avoiding Kurad's detection.

At the back of the house, they located the cellar door that would lead them inside. Kurad leaned down and firmly grasped the handles and began to ease the doors open. They groaned almost inaudibly, opening against their will, but Kurad continued to apply a steady pull knowing that the noise from the hinges wasn't as loud as his senses indicated. When the door was open enough for Edward to slip through, he nodded to him, taking over as the watchman as Edward ducked down and clambered over the threshold. With Edward safely inside, Kurad took one last look behind him before following Edward into the darkness below.

Kurad eased the door back down into place. Turning, he located Edward waiting at the bottom of the stairway leading up into the house. Kurad didn't hesitate to take point as he passed the boy, creeping up the stairway leading to the kitchen. He had gone up just over half the staircase when suddenly he was pulled to a halt from behind. Expecting trouble Kurad spun to see what had caused Edward to grab him. Seeing nothing in the dark cellar but Edward's shadow, he stopped moving, waiting for Edward to explain his need to stop.

Edward leaned past Kurad and pointed to the step just ahead of where Kurad was standing and shook his head. He paused for a moment contemplating the gesture, wondering what Edward was concerned about, when suddenly it clicked. That was the step that was chronically loose and Edward had always compared the noise to having stepped on the cat's tail. Kurad, though, rarely went into the cellar as he was usually working the fields or other such chores around the farm. He nodded to Edward, silently thanking him for his caution. The noise would have been heard by anyone near the perimeter of the house. Stepping lightly over the tell tale board, Kurad made his way to the top of the stairway with Edward following close behind.

Pushing the door at the top of the stairs open slightly, Kurad took an inventory of where everything was ahead in the darkened room. His eyes were adjusted fairly well to the limited amount of light and he also knew that Helen always kept a meticulous house. She would never think of leaving chairs pulled out away from the table and other items lying about where they would trip someone who wasn't watching where they were walking. With that knowledge, he moved into the kitchen, confident that his path would be clear to the bedrooms up on the second level.

Upon reaching the landing on the second level, they made quiet, hurried plans to meet back in the cellar with their appointed charges and not to leave without anyone unless their situation demanded it. With plans made, they separated and went to collect the women, allowing minimal time to put together a light travel pack for them, not knowing where their flight would take them. They could be in hiding or on the road for an extended period of time and some time would have to be expended now in making provisions in case nothing improved in the near future.

Edward crept away to Jessica's room. He had traveled this hallway often while growing up, helping with household chores; only now everything was different. He wasn't coming in from chores late after school. Now their survival depended on him. He felt the weight pressing down on him as if it had a physical presence. From the other end of the hall he heard Helen's door creak ever so softly. He wasn't even to Jessica's door yet, 'hurry or you'll be left behind' his mind called out. Kurad had already demonstrated tonight that he was their best chance to get out safely and he wanted to make sure to stay close.

His hand fumbled for the door latch, misjudging the height in the dark and rattling the door slightly before getting a firm handle on the release. From within the room he could hear Jessica adjusting her position in her sleep, disturbed from her slumber by Edward's fumbling. He lifted the latch fully and slipped inside the room, trying to let Kurad's training take over and pushing his fear back. Everything depended on him getting Jessica out and away from danger. Within a heartbeat he'd crossed the floor to the side of her bed.

Jessica had settled back into her slumber, breathing easily as she rested peacefully. Edward hesitated, trying to wake Jessica quietly. He had to make sure he didn't scare her to cause her to call out upon waking. Gently nudging her, trying to coax her awake slowly. He didn't have a lot of time, Kurad was down the hall in Helen's room going through the same process, though probably more smoothly. This all came so natural to Kurad. Throughout the years Edward had always watched him during training with respect, but it seemed that now, with their lives on the line, Kurad took his intensity to another level. How could Edward ever live up to Kurad's expectations?

He reached up to gently touch Jessica's arm. Touching her lightly, trying to imitate an insect landing on her arm, hoping that would get her to wake up naturally. She mumbled something incoherent and brushed at Edward's hand.

"Jess, it's me, Edward," he whispered as he took hold of the hand that was trying to brush away whatever it was that was disturbing her slumber. "Jessica I need you to wake up." Now with more force behind his words, yet he was still trying to remain calm.

Her eyes blinked a couple of times as she tried to figure out if she was dreaming.

"Edward?" it came out as a question, still not believing what she was hearing.

"You're not dreaming. You need to keep your voice down. We're in terrible danger. Don't make any unnecessary noise." Maybe that wasn't the best way to alert her of the danger for she sat straight up and began trying to talk. Her voice turned to a mere squeak as Edward's hand shot out to cover her mouth and silence her before more than a single peep had escaped.

"Now that was exactly what I didn't want you to do," he admonished her. "Listen carefully and do exactly as I say. I don't have time to explain twice." She relaxed and he released her mouth as he talked in a hushed whisper. He continued his instructions.

"Kurad is down the hall at this very moment gathering your mother and some traveling necessities. You need to do the same. We need to get you away from here and leave the farm for a while. There are armed soldiers of a race called gnomes. I am not sure exactly why they are after us, but they certainly mean to do us harm. We need to pack a light bag and meet up with Kurad and Helen; they are waiting. Change out of your nightclothes and dress in something you can run in. I'll be out in the hall outside the door waiting, and remember, no noise." With his instructions laid out, he squeezed her hand and turned back to the door, crossing on hands and knees until he slid out the door.

It was only moments later that Edward and Jessica met up with Kurad and a very anxious Helen. They descended the stairs making for the cellar where they hoped to launch their escape.

Nothing had changed by the time they reached the kitchen and passed through. They crept down the stairway into the cellar, careful to avoid the step that would alert the gnomes outside. Kurad led the foursome with Edward bringing up the rear. Edward hoped nothing threatened from his position and exposed his inability to defend the party. He wasn't ready to find out how well he had been trained when he was up against a real enemy. What if he couldn't perform to Kurad's high standards? Couldn't match his teacher's deadly efficiency he had witnessed in the woods?

The group stopped, collecting their thoughts and catching their breaths, preparing to make their break for the cover of the trees just across the field. Kurad was instructing them on how much ground needed to be covered before they reached the trees and that the first steps would be the most dangerous. They had no way of knowing what might be awaiting them just outside the cellar door.

Kurad led the way, pushing tentatively at the door. He knew instantly that something was wrong. There was more than just the weight of the door against his hands. Somehow they had been found out. There must have been another scout watching the cellar door from concealment, waiting for the duo to come back to rescue the women. The question that Kurad wrestled with now: Was it a lone gnome? Or had the whole detachment been alerted? Were they awaiting their final orders before rushing into the cellar from this door as they simultaneously flooded down the stairs that Edward continued to guard?

Urgency required Kurad to push ahead, so after a quick exchange of glances with Edward, he turned back to the door in front of him and began to push. He could sense the movement of bodies outside now, and with a lunge he threw the door upwards, rushing forward with sword and long knife drawn, meeting cries of alarm and confusion.

Chapter Fifteen

Kurad led the charge from the cellar, catching the gnome soldiers still setting their defenses that they had figured would contain those trapped within. The gnome squad leader had his back to the door as it burst open and was cut down without ever seeing the man whose sword thrust burst through his chest. Kurad pushed the squad leader away leaving him to fall forward into the path of the onrushing soldiers and helping to clear his way to the next opponent. Edward came out right behind him, blocking the path to Jessica and Helen. They needed to break through the ever tightening circle of soldiers before the sheer numbers overwhelmed them and forced them back into the cellar where another group was sure to be coming at them from inside the house. The trap had been sprung and the fugitives could hear them banging at the door leading down from the kitchen to the cellar, and they all knew it wouldn't hold them off long.

Kurad was thrusting and dodging, trying to set the gnome soldiers back on their heels and push a way through the circle of swords that held them at bay. Edward was trying to help Kurad as much as he could, but he was also concentrating on protecting the two women hiding on the cellar steps. The numbers were stacked against the two men, but that helped the pair fighting for freedom because the attackers couldn't use their numbers to their advantage for fear of striking their own. The gnome soldiers were giving ground grudgingly as a few of their comrades learned what could happen against a foe such as Kurad. The confusion of the battle began to create an opening to break through for the trapped humans.

"Gather the women, we must go now!" Kurad shouted to Edward.

Edward turned to the women behind him and reached his hand down to help them up and out, to make their break through the gnome soldiers ahead of them. Already trying to divide his attention between the women and the soldiers battling Kurad, Edward was unprepared when those who finally gained entrance to the cellar from inside the house appeared at the bottom of the cellar steps. It was enough of a distraction to allow the soldier in front of him to connect an effective blow with his staff into Edward's midsection. It required him to concentrate on defending himself and brought his focus back to the battle outside. Kurad was fighting with two others and wasn't able to give Edward a hand, nor was he able to help the women now trapped in the stairwell. It took Edward a moment to fend off his attacker with a fatal thrust of his sword, it was all the time the gnomes in the cellar needed to tackle the fleeing women and drag them back into the house. The last sight Edward had of Jessica was of her being dragged back down the steps, fighting her attackers every step of the way.

"Jessica!" he yelled after her disappearing form. Leaping away from the battle in front of him to help the women brought him straight into the middle of another one. Gnomes brandishing swords were coming out of the dark cellar opening causing Edward to retreat back up the stairs and away from Helen and Jessica's abductors.

The two men were surrounded completely and the women had been taken from sight. Kurad made the decision that their best hope was to get clear of the gnomes immediately. Fending off the blows aimed at him he grabbed Edward, who was being pressed on both sides, and began pulling him through the throng that now closed in on the pair. Edward tried to pull away at first, to follow the women into the cellar. Confused, Edward wanted to question Kurad's decision to leave, but the battle didn't allow it. He finally had to give into Kurad's iron grip and help him fight their way free of the enemy.

Combining efforts, the two of them quickly broke the ring of would-be captors striking down any that would oppose them. Once outside the throng they spun about to counterattack from outside the circle catching the soldiers by surprise. The hesitation cost at least one gnome soldier his life and wounded another that would be litter borne on the return trip if he survived the night.

Edward and Kurad took advantage of the momentary break in the attack spinning on their heels taking flight across the field they had so cautiously crossed earlier in the night. They needed speed instead of stealth for this crossing, relying upon pure reflexes honed by years of training to deal with any surprises they might come upon.

Fear pushing him faster, Edward had no problem keeping up with Kurad's longer stride. As they reached the brush along the tree line and began to clamber through the undergrowth, Edward risked a look behind to measure the lead they had built. The lead was greater than expected, but not enough to stop running. Turning back he continued to race on after Kurad.

The gnomes gave chase as far as the woods before realizing the two ahead of them were fleet of foot and were not willing to be caught this night. With the fleeing pair ducking into the underbrush a good distance ahead of them, the squad leader also realized that the women of their party had indeed been caught. He called a halt to his troops who immediately stumbled to a halt trying to catch their breath. Some amongst them mumbled that, given a little more distance, they would have overtaken their quarry though they made no effort to dissuade their leader from stopping. They turned away and marched back to the farmhouse wiping beads of sweat that formed on their brows despite the chill in the night air. They would pay for the loss of the pair when they reached the farmhouse, but maybe their commander would be gladdened by the capture of the pair of females.

As they expected, their leader wasn't happy when the squad showed up without the pair they had chased after into the night, but he did see the advantage of holding hostages. This situation could still be salvaged, he decided. Now they wouldn't have to spend time tracking the young prince, he would come looking for them without fail.

The gnome soldiers moved into the barn for the remainder of the night, posting a perimeter watch in the event the attempt at rescue came before dawn. With their prisoners secured to separate support posts in the barn, the gnomes not charged with the first watch sought out the relative comfort of the hay in the loft above. The two prisoners tied to the posts were not given such consideration and thus slept little, standing throughout the night.

Just before dawn the gnome soldiers were awake, gathering up gear and re-supplying their stores at the expense of Helen's stock. They began marching as the sun rose above the horizon. Advance scouts led the way across the fields surrounding the farm, keeping their eyes peeled for the two that got away, although it was merely an exercise in futility; Edward and Kurad had put many miles between them in their flight through the night.

After losing their pursuers, Kurad had pushed on, not believing that they had left the gnomes behind that easily. Experience taught him to go on until he thought no one was left, and then keep pushing on. He would slow his pace only to disguise his trail, never thinking that his pursuers would give up any sooner than he himself would stop the chase.

They reached the tethered horses without any resistance. The men noted their animals' calm dispositions as a sign that they had spent the night undisturbed, unaware of the crisis that had unfolded across the field. Taking up the reins, they climbed into their saddles and urged their mounts to move out silently. They traveled as safely as possible, implementing numerous tricks to hide their passing. Tricks Edward had spent many days learning.

Morning found them tired, their horses nearly spent. As the sun broke the far horizon Kurad pulled up his mount, signaling for Edward to do likewise. Edward was only too willing to get out of the saddle. It had been a long, grueling, and disappointing night. They had gone back to rescue the two most important people in their lives and had barely saved their own. Two questions plagued him through the long night. What had become of the women, and were they even still alive?

"What will those soldiers do to Helen and Jessica? They won't kill them will they?" Edward's words were hesitant, fearful of Kurad's answer.

"No." It was Kurad's only response. Tired from the ride, he was not sure how to explain to Edward that this was all about him and the threat he represented to Orgle.

Kurad's answer was clearly not enough of an explanation for Edward so he rushed up to Kurad, dropping his reins as he came to the end of their length.

"How can you be so sure? We bolted out of there and left them with those creatures. Who knows what they did with them after we left. Probably tortured them all night and then left them for dead, maybe even burned them up in the farmhouse." His eyes held more than a hint of accusation, boring into Kurad. He was looking for answers that would explain what had happened last night. He also needed to hear that they were okay to help with his feelings of guilt for leaving them behind as he ran off into the night.

"It's a long story," Kurad began, holding up his hand to defer any further questions from the young man standing in front of him. He really had grown up since that night he spirited him away from a city under siege. It wasn't how he wanted to explain it. He had envisioned it differently; not sure how, but certainly not while running for their lives. That had never been the plan.

"You are what, or rather who," Kurad corrected himself, "they are after. That is why they captured the women. They never really wanted them and we spoiled their plans by leaving the farm too soon. The soldiers will take care of the women as long as you are free. Not that the women will be treated like royalty to be sure, but they must keep the bait alive so that you will be tempted to rescue them. They are the cheese in this mousetrap and you are the mouse."

"Why me? What did I ever do to them?" Edward looked around at the trees they were hidden in as if searching for clues.

"Let's make camp and we can tend to our mounts. It's important now that we always have as fresh a horse as possible. After that we will have time to talk, I promise you that. Then you will have your answers. However, there are also some decisions that have to be made and I will need your full attention, for they will not be easily made." He turned back to his horse leaving Edward to stare after him.

..

Chapter Sixteen

Kurad sat across from Edward, both resting weary bodies on the bare ground while the horses grazed on the short grasses struggling to grow on the shadowed forest floor. Only the basics were unpacked. Bedrolls would be a comfort lost if they had to make a hasty departure. Even if the gnome soldiers didn't find them, they would be moving on by midday as it was. Kurad needed Edward to come to this decision with him. It must be a mutual choice, but they needed to put distance between them and the soldiers if that's what they decided to do. How was he going to convince his young student to follow the path that would take the most time, even if it was the path that would give them the best chance of success? How would rescuing the women now fit into what Kurad knew must happen? It was a horrible thought but they, like others, might become victims in a war that started so long years ago, few even knew it yet continued.

"Okay I'm ready for your revelation," Edward looked across at Kurad as he spoke. "Why would a bunch of soldiers from a foreign land come all the way up north to find me? I'm a farm boy. They must have me mixed up with someone else. What is the excitement...?" He stopped himself short, not finishing his last question and looking across at Kurad. He knew the look his mentor wore; this was much more serious than a case of mistaken identity.

"A little history lesson might be good right now. The gnomes come from the land of Pendar, but before that they originally ruled the gnome empire in the wild lands to the south." He held up a hand to deter Edward, knowing the young man and that an interruption was inevitable.

"Orgle, the leader of the gnomes, defeated his neighbor King Ellingstone in what was a horrible war that had a dire outcome for the ruling family. They were all killed when the walls fell. Orgle was convinced that killing the royal family would eliminate anyone challenging his rule. And until today, everyone went along with him." He paused to make sure Edward was keeping up and that the links were connecting.

"Today is the day Orgle acknowledged that he did not succeed in his original attack; one threat to his throne remains. You, Edward, as far as they are concerned, are a wanted criminal because as the rightful heir, you are to be the next King of Pendar." He had decided not to buffer the truth from his young charge. Now he sat across from a young man who had just learned that everything he had thought of himself, had been overturned. Waiting for the normally talkative boy to say something, it seemed longer than the few minutes that actually ticked by.

"Kurad," Edward began then paused, still turning around in his mind that which had been just revealed. "I'm to believe that I am not just a farm boy, but rather some kind of a prince of some country, I mean Pendar." His words were laced with nervousness and he spoke haltingly, trying to fit this new information into his logic.

"I know this is a shock to you. I always meant to tell you, although a little less abruptly." Kurad stopped, visibly searching for the words to say. "You know, to soften the blow, but with Orgle's troops chasing us and kidnapping the girls, that luxury has been stripped from us, along with a few other things I had hoped to take care of before your eighteenth birthday."

"What does my birthday have to do with anything?" Edward was still trying to digest the implications of what his mentor was telling him. Who was Kurad then? How did he come to be with this man?

"I guess I'm a little shaken by this. Can we wait a moment before we talk about my birthday? I think we should start at the beginning of the story, rather that the end. Or, not the end, but where we find ourselves right now, hiding in the woods." Edward stopped talking, continuing to mull over questions in his mind.

Kurad waited until the young prince looked ready to take in more information. He began his tale at what he considered to be the beginning.

He started with the time he met with King Samuel, a man the boy could barely remember, when it was decided that a drastic plan to save Edward was needed. That plan would allow the family, and ultimately the nation he represented, to be reborn when the time presented itself. The first part of that plan was carried out effectively, or so it was thought until now. Abducting Edward and staging his death had certainly fooled his enemies and ultimately delayed their pursuit of the boy. It was at this point in the narrative that Kurad stopped.

What had changed for Orgle? He must have come across some evidence that made him doubt the apparent death of the heir to the throne. It was something that must be determined before they returned to the Ellingstone nation. The implications of the only possibility worried, even scared, Kurad. There was still so much to be done and now they had little, if any, time to really prepare.

"And that brings us to today," he tried to hide the concern in his eyes, "and your question about your birthday. Your eighteenth birthday," he then stated with as royal a tone as he could muster, "is the day you will become the official king of Pendar," he pointed at the tattoo on Edward's forearm. Watching Edward, he could see he was completely overwhelmed. It was understandable. He had just revealed an identity to Edward that had been hidden for so many long years; it was almost a relief for Kurad to no longer have to hide that anymore. Now he could begin planning with Edward, both of them aware of the final goal and with no more secrets.

Edward looked at his forearm. "I thought you said all the boys back home had a family tattoo." Clearly he was struggling to assimilate this previously hidden identity into his perception of himself. He fixed on the image inked into his skin as the only tangible link to a part of his life for which he had no memory. A family he didn't remember was revealed and then taken away once more. Helen and Jessica had been there with him all these years and now they too had been taken from him. He needed to get them back before he lost them forever.

"Okay, so now that you've turned my world upside down, how do we get the girls back from that squad of gnomes before anything bad happens to them? We can't let them get too far ahead of us or we'll lose the trail." He looked over to Kurad waiting for an answer.

"That's a decision we need to make." He paused, trying to size up the young man. "We need to sit awhile and figure out the best course of action. Now that you know what is at stake; your father's country, your country." He corrected himself trying to make sure that Edward understood the weight of the decision.

"We must think of the welfare of thousands, the people of your country that have been made slaves or homeless refugees. We must honor those who gave their very lives in the attempt to stop what is currently happening to their loved ones left behind. I know it is your first inclination to rush to the aide of Helen and Jessica. They are the only family that you know. But you must trust me in that I know where the soldiers will take them, and that they will not be in mortal danger while you are yet alive.

"As I said before, Orgle needs them as bait. He knows that we are on the run and will be very difficult to locate. He also knows that you will come to rescue them if they are still alive. What we need to do is plan the best way to accomplish this task along with putting you, the rightful heir to Pendar's throne, where you belong. These things can be accomplished simultaneously if we agree on what must happen between now and our attempt at a rescue." Kurad felt he filled him in enough and begun to lead him down the right path.

"Do you see my logic if we go after the girls?" Edward started again where he had left off. "They can't be far from the farm house. There are too many soldiers for rapid travel. Plus they are burdened with hostages. We can travel much faster than they can, overtake them, ambush them, and then free Jessica and Helen. The soldiers would never be able to track our small party." He stopped and waited expectantly for Kurad to agree with him. He continued to watch his teacher, but the look on Kurad's face didn't look like he was going to agree. Without even waiting for Kurad to respond, he went on the offensive.

"Why aren't we going after them? They need us! We can't just abandon them! I can tell you right now there is no way I'm not going after them, no matter what you say or do. I'll go alone if I have to." He was up on his feet, gesturing towards the way they had just come from.

"Please seat yourself," Kurad calmly replied, gesturing to match his directions.

"We have a lot of things to discuss before any choices are made. You are barely more than a year away from your eighteenth birthday and if what I just told you wasn't clear, allow me to repeat myself. You will be the king of Pendar, a nation ruled by your father and his before him, a father that died in the defense of that city along with his entire family except for you. Only the foresight of that man saved your life.

"Now I want to discuss your options with you." Kurad's voice had become much sterner as he continued to talk. He hated bullying the young man but there seemed to be few options other than becoming teacher and pupil for the moment.

"However, for now, I think we need to both get a bite to eat." Kurad stopped the lecture before he got angry with the young man. "Some quiet rest would do us both some good. Take some time to think about everything I have told you just now. And I mean everything. We'll be leaving this area, no matter what course we decide to pursue, shortly. Let's talk about it then. Agreed?"

Edward nodded his agreement. Kurad always knew when it was best to rest and regroup. So long had they trained and traveled together that Edward had learned that much from his teacher.

Later that afternoon, rested and with something in their stomachs, they remounted their horses and set out in the direction they had decided, though somewhat heatedly and with reservations would best serve their mission. They departed the small glade that had welcomed them in to rest and talk. It had paid no heed to raised voices and emphatic gestures, oblivious to the decisions that would hopefully bring about the rebirth of a once honorable and proud nation. The forest glade simply waved its slender branches in response to the horses pushing through the tangle that had protected the pair, never knowing if the men achieved the goals set in motion so many years ago.

Chapter Seventeen

Jessica and Helen were battered and bruised from their months on the trail. Their captors kept them alive and healthy enough to keep walking but just barely. The first days had been a battle of wills between the captives and the captors. The former firmly believing that help would arrive soon and this nightmare they were living would come to a swift end. The latter hoped too that that same help would arrive so they could capture Edward and thus be able to dump these women who were nothing more than extra cargo. The days and weeks passed and while much time and effort were spent looking for Edward and Kurad, there never was a sign to bring encouragement to anyone.

They continued their forced march, the gnome soldiers harassing and herding the captives towards their destination. Jessica and Helen helped one another the best they could physically and emotionally whenever they were allowed to interact on the trail. The long lonely nights were spent separated from one another so if an attempt was made to rescue the pair they would not be easily taken. They would be reunited each day and allowed to walk together, yet discouraged with the blunt end of a spear or the flat of a blade from excessive talking.

The women tried their best to keep their spirits up though it began to look as if something had happened to the pair they hoped would come to their rescue. As the days passed they began to doubt that Edward and Kurad had survived the encounter with the same creatures that held them prisoner. If the women had realized the purpose of the soldiers' constant coming and goings as they scouted the surrounding area and the reason they were being kept alive, their spirits would have been buoyed. Their friends were alive.

Now, months later, they stood in the throne room of an ancient castle, bound and dirty from the long and arduous journey. Surrounding them was an assembly of what appeared, based on decorations on their uniforms, to be high-ranking members of the military. Jessica looked around the room at all the officers of the gnome army. Many of them were looking over the dirty pair with equal curiosity.

Looking beyond the gnomes in attendance, she began to take notice of the castle where they had been brought immediately upon their arrival in the city. The throne room looked out of character for the residents. It was cluttered and quite full of filth, but the decay wasn't what held her attention. It was the furnishings and wall coverings under the grime that hinted to her that things had not always been this way. It was apparent that something had happened and changed the way the castle was kept. What could possibly happen that would make a ruler let his castle fall into such disrepair? There was a great commotion to the rear of the throne that forced her to tuck that thought away for later.

A door hidden in the prevailing shadows, not apparent at first, opened to reveal a contingent of gnome officials arguing amongst themselves. They were not worried about the presence of the others already gathered in the room. Their only concern was that several of the members were in disagreement with the others. They continued their discussion while they moved into what appeared to be their assigned positions. Although Jessica could not understand what they were saying in their guttural language, she was getting the feeling that they, Helen and herself, were the topic of discussion. Had she been able to understand their speech, she would have been upset to learn that they were deciding the women's fate and few of them felt any need to keep the women alive.

A trumpet blasted and, with the exception of the two prisoners, everyone else knelt down on one knee as once more someone entered from the rear of the throne room. Jessica squinted, trying to pierce the shadows to see who garnered this much respect. As Orgle came into view, the room took on a different feel, more fear than respect.

"Who are these two?" Orgle screamed in the common tongue of man when he saw the two women standing in the middle of the throne room. "I wanted the prince dead! I do not want women and children brought to me! Where is the commander that led this hunt?"

There was some movement in the group directly behind Jessica. Turning around, she saw the troop leader who had dragged her so arrogantly from her home and life. Only now he had a whole different demeanor; hesitant and unsure as he shuffled his way to the front of the throne where his king sat. He was visibly trembling as he walked the last few steps, bowing as he reached the foot of the stairs leading to the throne.

"Your Highness, Captain Tolys reporting. I have retrieved two very important hostages; people the young Prince risked his life in an attempt to rescue. I brought them because I believe that he will do so again." The captain spoke quickly, but clumsily in the common tongue of men that Orgle insisted on when the gnomes were speaking in his presence. Speaking the language of men made Orgle believe he was more than just an outsider, instead the rightful ruler of this kingdom.

"Where is the Prince? Is he here, in the midst of this rescue attempt? I do not see him anywhere! Has he died avoiding capture and you are not telling me? Why have you come before me without proof of his death?" Orgle had worked himself into a rage and had passed the point of reason. "Did I not give you highly trained soldiers to expend as necessary?" He paused as if he had just come to a decision and rose from his stolen throne, pointing at the trembling officer in front of him.

"You, Captain Tolys, have failed me. When I give orders they are to be followed. Let this be a lesson to all the others in this room who would consider disobeying High King Orgle." As he finished his threat intended for all, he motioned to a pair of guards standing to either side of the platform. They immediately stepped forward towards Captain Tolys with spears at the ready. "Remove this traitor from my presence and carry out his sentence at once." Orgle turned and sat back upon his throne, not watching the scene unfold in front of him.

Tolys, upon hearing Orgle's proclamation of treason, spun about and began a desperate charge through the assembled crowd, bowling over the two prisoners in a futile attempt to escape. The two guards, knowing they would be held accountable for the escape of a prisoner, didn't hesitate more than a breath. They took aim and simultaneously loosed their spears towards the back of the fleeing captain. The first caught him in the back as he fought clear of the now prostrate women and the second sailed past where the women had just been standing to catch an unsuspecting bystander in his midsection.

Jessica clutched Helen tightly as they tried to come to grips with the brutality of their captors and the realization that, had they not been knocked out of the way, either of them could be lying wounded and dying as were the two gnomes. Jessica looked from the two victims to Orgle sitting upon the throne again. She watched him give a dismissive wave towards the dying gnomes, indicating to the others that they should remove them from his sight. Those nearest the victims hastily grabbed them and began to drag them towards an exit. Both were treated equally and without compassion as their bodies were dragged from the room, stopping only momentarily for the guards to retrieve their weapons.

Much to Jessica's dismay, Orgle now turned his attention to her mother and her. She stared up at him with a fear she had not known before. This creature had just ordered the death of his own kind, an officer in his army that had seemingly made the best out of a failed attempt.

Her thoughts were confused. What had been said right before the killing of the gnome? Who could they have been after? Someone of royalty, but Jessica knew of no one that was a prince, and the only rescue attempt had been by Kurad and … Edward. His name shouted itself in her mind as the final piece of the puzzle slipped into place. She needed to let her mother know what she had just figured out but how could she communicate this? She could only hope her mother now knew too. Helen was trying to shield Jessica by stepping to the front but Jessica knew by her body language that she was as frightened as she was.

"Who are you?" Orgle asked them directly, still speaking in the common tongue, a curious expression on his face.

"I apparently have a couple of prisoners on my hands, valuable according to what our good captain said before his untimely demise. A little bait to entice our young prince," he paused as he stared off into the darkness of the upper reaches of the room. Thinking briefly on the situation before he began again. "Is it possible the prince doesn't know you two have been brought to my doorstep? Maybe he does know and he has been watching your entire journey. I don't see that it matters much either way. He will not know that you have been killed until he shows up looking for you." He motioned once again to the guards flanking his throne.

Jessica looked to her mother who stood motionless. She was unable to respond to Orgle's proclamation for the events of the last months had drained any reserves she had. Jessica stepped past her mother, positioning herself directly in front of Orgle. She didn't know exactly what she thought she could do to prevent their deaths, but she was buoyed by her newfound knowledge of Edward's lineage. She knew that if they could stay alive he would come for them.

"Sir," she began, not knowing how to address this creature. "I would not be so hasty in deciding that we are of no value." She took a quick look at the advancing guards to gauge how much time she had to state their case. She held up her hands to motion them to wait, which to her surprise, they did. Seeing this as her last chance, she took up her cause with Orgle.

"Prince Edward will come for us, in that regard you are correct. Something that you are not considering is that he would trade his kingdom for us." She motioned to her still silent mother to remain so then looked quickly back to Orgle.

"Young lady, who do you think you are to be bargaining for something I already posses? This kingdom is mine by right." He spread his arms wide indicating everything in the room and beyond was his.

"And by might!" He finished by smashing his fist onto the arm of the throne for emphasis, his voice rising to a roar.

"This puny little boy hasn't the army to take these lands from me. So to think that he can trade nothing for something makes me laugh out loud." And he did just that. His was not the laugh of someone amused, more like someone who wasn't entirely in control of his mind.

The guards resumed their march towards the women, spears at the ready, should these two decide to take the same path as the captain.

"Wait!" Orgle spoke to his guards, having regained some sense of control. "These two amuse me. I think we shall keep them around for at least a day or two. Take our guests to the dungeons and make sure they are kept alive until I decide otherwise." With that he waved them away dismissively.

It appeared to Jessica that she had saved them for now, but for how long? Orgle had stated that at most they had two days and only then if he didn't change his mind. As the guards grasped the women's arms and began to haul them from the room, she looked around at those in attendance and wondered if she would be seen again by anyone in this room. The women were escorted out from the room and down into the bowels of the castle, through countless hallways and stairways, until at last they arrived at the castle prison. The guards quickly dumped them in a cell together and slammed the door behind them.

They huddled quietly together trying to get accustomed to the darkness that surrounded them, waiting for their eyes to adjust. The light from a burning torch in the hallway peeked in through the tiny window in their door giving them a small amount of illumination. Looking around the small cell they began taking note of their lack of amenities. There was a small pallet covered in dirty straw to sleep on and an equally dirty little bucket for personal needs. It sat next to a small opening along the wall, probably to empty their bucket. It had cold, damp stone walls, ceilings, and floors and was no more than a couple of paces in either direction. Maybe Orgle was doing them a favor, Jessica thought, by only giving them two more days if this was to be their existence.

When they finished assessing their new surroundings, they relaxed their hold on one another and tried to find a way for both of them to at least sit on the pallet of straw. They had spent enough time on the dusty trail to no longer worry about the grimy straw bedding.

"Jess, I can't believe how you stood up to that creature." Helen said in a whisper, not knowing if they were being monitored or if there were other prisoners that would hear them. "I thought that we would be killed like the captain. I still don't understand all this talk about Edward being a prince. Kurad never once mentioned any of this."

"He probably knew it would put us in danger," Jessica said, understanding now at least part of what had happened. "He wanted to avoid this very situation. I would question whether Edward even knew of his heritage." Edward couldn't have known and kept it from her. He was too innocent to deceive her. Just then her thoughts were interrupted by a voice, coming to them from the other side of the wall, through a crack hidden in the darkness. It was a gruff whisper and barely audible to the two women.

"If what you say is true, our king yet lives, and with him our hopes too."

Troy A. Skog

Chapter Eighteen

Kurad pushed hard that first day, determined to keep Edward's mind from dwelling on the decision that they'd made. It was tough on Edward, and him too, not to follow the gnome troops, but Edwards's path pointed east first. It had taken a lot of convincing to get Edward to agree to catch up to the women later. How much later Kurad wasn't sure, but once they started down this path it would be difficult to backtrack with little to gain if they did.

If he knew the gnomes, they would be beating a trail back to Pendar to present Orgle with their hostages. The gnomes would be on alert for any escape attempt so it would be impossible to free the two women and make an escape without horses for them all. If it was just him scouting it would not be an issue, but rescuing the women would be impossible without a fight. The odds on the outcome of that fight would be stacked against the two men.

They were travelling a different path now, a path he promised a very close friend many years ago to travel. Samuel had ruled his nation fairly and justly, searching for the truth before passing judgment. For this, Kurad felt, even if he fulfilled his promise and brought Edward back to Pendar, he would still be in his debt for what Samuel had done for him so many years ago.

There was little communication between the two men throughout much of the afternoon and stretching into the evening hours. They were both too busy reading the woods around them, always ready to react to any threat that should present itself. With several hours behind them and the sun slipping from the sky, they stopped in a forest clearing to take another meal and get some rest for themselves and their mounts.

"Do you think Jess and Helen are alright?" The sound of Edwards voice seemed louder in the stillness. The night was quiet and they had yet to speak since entering the clearing.

Kurad looked at Edward who would not look at him even when he spoke to him. "They will be treated as prisoners." He knew the truth would be tough, yet he felt he owed Edward that much. "However, I don't think they will abuse them. It is foolish to burden oneself with those unable to continue under

163

their own strength. It would only slow the march down. Orgle will be waiting for them, or rather you." He said looking directly at the young man, waiting for some response.

"I just need to know that they will be alive when we get back to them. I don't think I could live with myself if I thought I abandoned them to their deaths." He shook his head and finally looked up at Kurad with a certain hardness in his eyes. "We would both be at fault if they are harmed because of our decision."

"We should keep moving tonight," Kurad's voice broke through Edward's thoughts. "There is a pathway ahead where we can make better time. Orgle's troops won't know of it so we can pass quietly out of their reach."

"How long will it take to reach this man you know and what does he have to do with the girls?" Edward pushed again to go after the women. "Why don't we just postpone this trip east? What can be so important?"

"It's still the same reason for going that we discussed before. Have you ever retaken a city or castle?" Kurad knew he needed to squash this thought before the boy drove him to anger. "We are in search of an army. They come in very handy when overthrowing a castle. I'm not sure where they are now, although I think I know the general direction your people went to avoid Orgle. From there we will pick up the trail." Kurad looked sternly at the young man, taking on the role of the teacher he had used many times over the years.

"Do they know I'm here? How come they haven't come looking for me instead of Orgle's troops?" Edward asked.

"No, they don't know where you are or quite possibly if you are even alive. I had left a message of your existence with a lone dwarf after the city fell. I don't know what became of him; he was a prisoner in the city. He was to pass the word, secretly, of your existence to organize resistance." Kurad paused. What if something had happened to that dwarf before he could spread the word?

"Does this man know where the army is waiting?" Edward jumped in during Kurad's pause.

"Maybe, maybe not." Kurad regained his thoughts and continued. "But, if anyone would know, it would be him. That's just one reason that we are traveling to find him. The other is the weapon I envision you carrying when you lead your army back into the city of your childhood." He had piqued Edwards's interest now and, seeing it, continued on without pause.

"It's a weapon familiar to your dwarven heritage, if the legend is true. It is their weapon of choice, the battleaxe. Most men prefer the sword because it is lighter and more agile. The battleaxe takes a stronger individual to use it well and dwarves with their broad shoulders are naturally suited to the battleaxe. You would be a rare man to have their blood flowing in your veins, but your stature is a reflection of that mix. You are taller than your dwarf ancestors, but broader of shoulders than your average man." Kurad stopped to look the boy over. He was becoming a powerfully built young man. He would be a force to be reckoned with if he could contain his emotions in the heat of the battle and remain disciplined.

"If we can find this man, who at one time studied under the dwarven weapons masters, he may be able to give us what we are looking for. The crafting of the weapon may take some time. Most axe bearers are shorter and can't make use of the longer handle I envision you having." Kurad stopped, waiting for the obligatory objection from Edward. He was young and in a hurry, of course.

"Does this man have a name?" Edward asked. "And where will we find him? He could have moved since last you visited."

"He goes by the name Tyvig. It's a name his teacher stuck on him so he would carry the name of a dwarf. I suppose that's something you should know concerning your brothers of dwarven ancestry. They don't take to outsiders, and that is anyone who is not a dwarf. It's a certain pride they carry, almost a birthright to them. Your nation was always a curiosity in regard to how the two races blended together after the marriage of your ancestors. Politically and socially they integrated, though with some reservations." He shifted to get back on track explaining Tyvig.

"Anyway, we will have many days on the trail when I can fill you in on the intricacies of your kingdom, for now I must tell you what I know of Tyvig.

"He keeps very much to himself, never seeking out the company of others, rather letting those with need of his services come to him. That's why he will be the one to know what

165

happened to your people. Eventually they may find him for reasons similar to our own for his weapons rival those made by his teachers. That is the goal of every teacher though," he paused realizing how it pertained to his student and himself, "for your pupil to go farther than you were able." He stopped and looked over at his student sitting in front of him.

Had he done enough training with Edward? They were different men with different paths ahead of them so maybe it wasn't always an easy task to judge such results. By comparison, it was easy to hold and feel a weapon but much harder to compare the skills of two different crafters. When the student's job would be to lead a nation back from exile, how does one know what they need for training?

What did Kurad have to compare? He had never been a leader of men. He had usually worked alone to accomplish what others were unable. It would boil down to the skills at arms he had been taught, his ability to weather hardships, and hopefully his inherited traits as a leader of men from his father. It would have to be enough, Kurad thought. He had done all that he could.

"We need to get some rest for ourselves and our mounts. Let's make a quick camp and get some sleep. We have a long journey ahead and plenty of time to continue this discussion." Kurad was tired and knew that Edward must be as well. "I'll take the first watch and wake you later. Get some sleep whenever you can. You never know when your next chance will come."

For once Edward didn't protest about wanting to take the first watch or even that he wanted to continue talking. He was obviously as tired as Kurad felt and within a few moments of climbing into his bedroll, had fallen into the rhythmic breathing of someone sound asleep.

Kurad waited a few moments, listening to the sounds of the forest, and getting a feel for the natural rhythms. Then, taking advantage of the little remaining light of the day, he slipped off into the woods. He circled the camp several times in ever-growing rings, looking for any signs of activity. Convinced now that they weren't being tracked, he returned to the camp. He stopped short of the clearing but within sight of it and settled in for his share of the night watch.

Chapter Nineteen

Edward and Kurad traveled east for the next several months without encountering any gnomes along the way, nor did they hear of any pursuit from those they met along the road. Kurad never relaxed his guard. Too many years of living on the road had taught him that those who got complacent often found themselves on the wrong end of a sharp sword. Communication with other travelers occurred only when Kurad felt that contact would be safe. The easy manner in which he brought up subjects with those he talked to raised no suspicions that he was on the run. Those he spoke with went on their way without realizing they had been questioned about the pursuit he had expected. Always it was just him they saw, for when they met others Edward kept well away from the road so no one would report seeing the pair traveling together.

At night they would come out onto the road and move along at a good pace, allowing the horses to stretch out their legs and cover ground faster. As the sun began to break the horizon they would slip back off the roadway and disappear into the undergrowth. They rested during the day, hidden in small clearings out of sight of the common traveler. They foraged for supplies, sometimes buying them from merchants traveling the roadways, but sometimes finding them on homesteads when no one was watching. They never took more than what could be easily missed for they did not want to cause anyone a hardship.

The miles ticked by as they moved steadily south out of Chalcedony and closer to Tyvig. Kurad felt the guilt weighing on his shoulders, worried about the fate of the women that had been taken into custody by Orgle's soldiers. Helen and Jessica would be to the castle soon and their lives depended on Orgle realizing the value of holding them as hostages to lure Edward home. He had to be willing to hold them for an extended time. It would take months for the men to travel and find Tyvig. Once there, they needed to get Edward's battleaxe crafted and hopefully get a lead on where the people of Samuel's kingdom disappeared to a handful of years ago.

The trail was cold and likely dead. The dwarves could go to ground and live quite well without any of their neighbors knowing that an entire city existed beneath the nearby mountains. Unless they were lucky and came into contact with someone who had just the right scrap of information, this task could well prove impossible. Kurad was counting on the fact that Tyvig was that someone and was trading with them for basic goods that couldn't be found in the seclusion of the mountain hideaway. He figured Tyvig would agree to fashion a battleaxe for the heir to the Ellingstone family. Beyond that, it was a leap of faith that he might provide some insight. No, he amended, not just insight, but actual contact. Was he putting too much faith in Tyvig? It was a gamble that he felt he had to make. It was a long shot but Kurad was running out of time. Edward was coming of age and the women were being held captive, or at least he hoped they were captives because the alternative was unspeakable. Too much of this whole mission was based on thin strands of a frayed rope, but how long could he keep it all from unraveling? Only time would tell and all they could do was hold on and pray that it all fell into place, and so they pushed on to find Tyvig.

A few days short of six months on the road, they arrived at Tyvig's place in the woods. The locals had been willing to give Kurad and Edward directions to his place when they asked around in town. The trip had gone well. They had successfully avoided any pursuit by Orgle's soldiers and Kurad had been able to speak of Edward's parents and the nation they had faithfully built for the people of their country. Now that they had finally made it to Tyvig's, they needed to convince him to begin working on Edward's battleaxe.

"Let's go up to the cabin and see if we can rouse Tyvig and get him to work on his forge." Kurad said as they dismounted and led the horses the last few paces to the porch and tied them off to the railing. They had climbed barely a third of the steps when a burly, bearded man came out from the barn with a goodly sized mutt padding alongside.

"What brings you my way Kurad? I haven't seen you in a couple handfuls of years. Nay, maybe more if my reckoning is correct," he said as he closed the gap between them. "And who is your protégé? I can't think that anyone would get into your line of work willingly so there must be a story." He stopped and extended his hand to Kurad.

"Well met Tyvig," Kurad began, feeling the strength of the other's grip. Here was a man that worked the raw metals of the earth to create dwarven tools and weapons.

"It's been a long time and I apologize. I've been busy, out of circulation you could say. I have someone you should meet. This young man is Edward Ellingstone." There was no sense in hiding anything from Tyvig. It was the best course to take if he meant to enlist his help. Kurad watched Tyvig carefully for any reaction that might be a clue as what he knew about the situation.

"So it is true what they say about an heir to Pendar." Tyvig replied, his face remaining unchanged except for a slight widening of his eyes as he looked Edward up and down and extended his hand in greeting.

"I thought you would be by someday, just not in the company of this rogue." He broke into a grin and thumbed towards Kurad, obviously happy to give Kurad a verbal jab.

"You're a bit taller than I thought, but I think we'll be alright. Let's go knock some of that dust from your clothes and get some grub. You can tell me your tale while we eat.

Oh, and this guy here is Blue." He pointed at the dog. "He's as big as a pony and weighs near as much as meself but he won't hurt a fly, unless it's for biting 'em," he chuckled before muttering, "Stupid little gnomes." The last statement caught both visitors attention and, looking at each other, they knew there was a story awaiting them. He continued to chuckle and shake his head as he tromped up the steps of the porch with the two very interested men in his wake.

It was a simple home fashioned from the logs of the surrounding forest with few creature comforts save the tools that he created with his forge and those strong hands. There was an artist hidden behind that gruff visage and it showed clearly in even the simplest of kitchen utensils he used as he prepared their evening meal. They had been able to do more than brush the dust off in the tub in the back room and even if the water hadn't been much more than warm, it was still refreshing. When they had scrubbed themselves clean, a first in a month's time, they did the same to their clothes. Tyvig supplied them with wraps to, as he said, 'keep out the drafts' while their clothes hung by the fire to dry.

As he sat at the table and looked down at his now empty plate, Edward couldn't remember how long it had been since they had been afforded the opportunity to sit and eat a meal without the fear of discovery. Many nights they had to do with dried meats and trail bread that Kurad had bartered from other travelers. When he did stop to think back he came, of course, to the dinner that Helen had prepared the night before they headed out for their trip. It seemed like a whole other life he'd led in the distant past. How could he have left Jessica in the clutches of the gnome soldiers? Was she even still alive? It was a question he'd tortured himself with so many times he lost count. Kurad was convinced that this was the best plan. The best plan? He questioned that choice again, but got no further when Kurad's voice interrupted his thoughts.

"We've been on the road for what must be better than half a year now and haven't seen nor heard of any pursuit." Kurad responded to Tyvig's question Edward had missed during his reverie.

"When do we get to hear this tale of Blue taking a bite out of a flea?" Kurad asked, grinning wide at Edward, knowing that Tyvig most certainly was waiting impatiently to tell his story.

"Let's see," Tyvig began, "it was a group of weeks back, could have been more." He stopped and scratched his beard as he searched his memory, then he shrugged and continued on. "This little band of gnomes comes wandering in, looking for a tribe of dwarves. Apparently they had talked to some of me neighbors and thought I might have knowledge based on my wares. I took that as a compliment, not so much to make it enough to make me talk." He paused and smiled.

"Dumb little critters, they started getting excited when I wouldn't spill the beans and give up what I knew. Well Blue here doesn't take to folks gettin' excited toward me." Tyvig stopped to rub Blue's head as the big dog sat quietly unaware that he was the main character in the story.

"Well there was some bad feelings by the time they left. I'm pretty quick yet with me axe if given a chance to get me hands on it. Blue here gave me the time I needed when the mob started getting grabby and brandishing some steel. Yeah, he saved me hide for sure," he said reverently.

"The little buggers run off a little bloody and bit up but I'm sure they're all still breathing, unless they crossed your path, I'm thinking." He eyed Kurad up without getting a response and then looked over to Edward to get a read of his young features.

"I thought as much. I don't need a body count, but you two look like you're a long way from home. How about you get me familiar with your story concerning these gnomes and then we'll figure out what we're doing next? This isn't close to being over, is it." It wasn't a question, but more of a statement that told the two visitors Tyvig was going to be a big part of whatever happened next on this journey.

Kurad retold the story of the attack at the farmhouse and the abduction of the women and how they had traveled all that way to find Tyvig and then about the plan to find the missing dwarves.

"We're pretty tired from being on the road all these months, but we need to keep on task here. We need to find Edward an army so that he can retake his rightful spot on the throne his father envisioned for him." Kurad looked at Edward dozing in the chair by the fire and then back to Tyvig who was still digesting the story.

A few minutes passed and Tyvig stood up and patted Kurad on the back, then turned and tromped off towards his bed speaking over his shoulder as he went. "Get some sleep, both of you, and tomorrow will find you rested. You're a lot closer to your goal than you realize."

Troy A. Skog

Chapter Twenty

Tyvig was getting bacon going in the frying pan and Kurad was sitting at the kitchen table when Edward roused himself from the floor in front of the fireplace.

"The young prince answers the call to breakfast, I see," Tyvig snickered when the lad climbed up off the floor. "Did the chair buck you off during the night? When I wandered off to bed last night you were looking pretty comfortable in the rocker over there."

Edward grinned at the fun Tyvig was having at his expense while he made an attempt to smooth his tousled hair. "The bacon smells wonderful, Tyvig. Sorry about sleeping so long, it's been awhile since I've slept so soundly." He yawned as he found a seat next to Kurad at the table.

"Good morning, Edward," Kurad looked expectantly at Tyvig and continued. "Tyvig was just getting ready to explain his comment from last night before he turned in. I don't know that I would have been able to sleep if I hadn't been warm, dry and clean for the first time in months."

"What was it that he said? I must have not been paying attention, probably distracted by my full stomach." He laughed out loud at himself. "I'm sorry Kurad, but your charred rabbit doesn't compare favorably to Tyvig's cooking." He smiled at Kurad, knowing he wouldn't be angry at Edward's blunt assessment of his cooking skills over an open fire.

"I would dare say we never went hungry for more than a day or so at a time and I don't remember you complaining when we did eat." Kurad's mood was light and self-effacing. "But, young man, you are more than correct that Tyvig is clearly my superior. Now that the bacon has started frying, I'm not sure if I don't want to wait until after breakfast for Tyvig to finish his story."

Tyvig kept working away over the griddle, though he smiled at the compliments from his visitors. He flipped the flapjacks and rearranged the bacon off the hot spots on the griddle so the bacon wouldn't get too crispy. He didn't seem inclined to begin the explanation of his bedtime teaser and the other two men seemed to sense as much and didn't push. Rather, they sat back and took in the smells that they had been missing these past months on the trail. Edward couldn't help but remember back to the days sitting in Helen's kitchen watching Jessica and her mother preparing breakfast after chores had been finished. It was something he took for granted back then and thought that if this whole adventure worked out, he would never take for granted again. How were they ever going to get Jessica and Helen away from Orgle? He didn't dare think about the very real possibility that the two women were no longer being held as hostages and what that meant. They had to be alive. They just had to be! He snapped out of his feelings of dread when Tyvig set an overflowing plate of grub in front of him.

"Eat up, young prince! You're going to need your energy before this day is over." He chuckled and muttered to himself, as was his custom, about sore muscles and lots of sweating as he turned back to load a plate up for Kurad. Edward looked up from his plate inquiringly to Kurad, but Kurad shrugged his shoulders and began eating as soon as Tyvig handed him his plate.

"Like I says boy, eat up. We've got a long day ahead and it starts whether you're done eatin' or not. Unless you're thinkin' this isn't to yer likin'," he added with a wink as he settled himself in across the table with his own plate.

"I would never want to insult your cooking, Tyvig. No more talking until we're finished then," was Edward's polite response.

Edward kept his word and polished off every last morsel on his plate, as did Kurad. After they finished, they helped clear the table and clean up the kitchen. Their conversation centered on the weather and how the cold winter weather was just around the corner. Kurad had known it was closing in on them and had hoped to be farther along the road before it caught up with them. Some things couldn't be rushed though and he knew it would take Tyvig some time, if he agreed to it, to make Edward's battleaxe.

"Let's head out to the barn then," Tyvig said, as he reached down and scratched Blue's ears. The dog rose from his place in front of the fire and headed for the door as soon as Tyvig grabbed his cloak.

"I think this will answer some of your questions. Of course, it may create new ones too." He chuckled to himself, clearly enjoying the game he was playing with his old friend, Kurad. The two men moved quickly to keep up with Tyvig as he headed out the door and across the yard.

The morning air was cool, another hint that winter's reach was getting closer, making Kurad more apprehensive about the time slipping away. Tyvig swung the barn door open, letting the sunlight chase away the shadows from around his smithy. In short order he had the charcoal fire going in the forge and the cold air was receding to the far corners of the barn.

"This is where I spend my days trying to eke out a living making utensils, pans, and tools for the locals." He waved his hand around, drawing attention to a few of his pieces sitting close at hand waiting to have the finishing touches applied.

"They bring a few things by to have repairs done too. It's steady work and it puts food on the table and in the dog dish." He chuckled at himself for worrying about including Blue, but he was good company for a man living alone in the woods.

"Tyvig," Kurad began, "I'm guessing by the quality of your wares that you get top pay for your efforts, but are there really enough locals to keep you busy making utensils, and the occasional tool? Do you ever take your goods on the road to trade?"

"You've got a sharp mind on yourself, you do. I knew you were suspicious of my dealings last night when we turned in, but I had to let it simmer for a bit and figure out our next step. It's not an easy path that's laid before us by my reckonin' but if we plan it out we'll be fine." He continued on, having the plan formulated in his mind and assuming that the other two would have no quarrel with it. "The weather is the biggest concern that we'll have to contend with until we get up and over the Silverback Mountains. I usually leave earlier in the season," he said the last almost to himself, continuing on without realizing his audience was confused. "We'll pack light. I think that's our best chance..." Tyvig trailed off, deep in thought. Kurad saw his chance to break in and quickly did so.

"Tyvig, it seems you've forgotten to tell the two of us some key information concerning this plan of yours, or ours, rather. We're a little in the dark here." He looked over to Edward who simply nodded and shrugged his shoulders, letting Kurad know that he wasn't following where Tyvig was going either.

"Follow me, boys. I think that what I have to show you down in the cellar will shed some light." He led them off towards the back of the barn where the only light coming in was from windows tinted from the soot of the forge. It appeared to Kurad that Tyvig purposefully ignored cleaning these, for everything else seemed to be in good repair and not neglected, though he said nothing as Tyvig began moving straw bundles away from the back corner.

"I keep it dark back here and try to conceal the trap door as best as I can. Nobody has stumbled onto it yet, but I keep my visitors to a minimum." He explained as the men watched him set the bundles aside, clearly a routine process. When he had the door cleared off, he bent to grab the ring set in the face. Edward made a motion to step forward and help only to be waved off by Tyvig as he hefted the door up easily, muscles straining but clearly conditioned to heavy lifting.

"Watch your step. It's a bit of an incline but the steps are solid," he said as he disappeared down the stairway. "I'll get a torch going lickity split once I get down," he said as he descended into the darkness.

Edward and Kurad waited above in the barn with Blue until they saw a faint glow from the doorway and then carefully made their way down the steps, not knowing what to expect when they got to the bottom.

The room was larger than they imagined. In fact, they didn't see Tyvig at first, instead hearing him rummaging about from what must have been a few rows down. Shelves ran the length of the room and the two men, still adjusting to the limited light, couldn't make out what it was that occupied the shelves. They stopped at the bottom of the stairs and waited, not sure if they should follow the dim glow to the back of the room. The mumblings from Tyvig continued as they heard him moving about steel objects, presumably looking for something particular.

"Ah, here it is. It's been longer than I thought since I tucked this away." He talked as he made his way back to the two men standing in the darkness at the bottom of the stairs.

"You didn't have to wait there, boys. You're welcome to poke around if you want. Nothing to hide from friends down here." He stopped on the far side of the nearest shelf and looked up at his torch, realizing he was the only one with a light source before letting out a low chuckle.

"'Course if you don't mind stubbing a toe or two, that is. Sorry about taking the light with me. I knew the general area of this critter but it's been awhile." He explained as he rounded the corner and brought the influence of light back to the two waiting men. It wasn't the torch the men both stared at; it was the object that Tyvig held in his muscular grasp that captured their gaze.

The two men were speechless, as Tyvig, noting the object of their attention, held the dwarven battleaxe up to show them better.

"It's a bit dusty and the edge may need some truing, but I think the length, weight and balance will be what you're looking fer. I can have it ready in no time."

Kurad spoke first, digesting the implications of Tyvig holding the very weapon that Edward needed before they could continue on their path.

"We need an explanation concerning that axe. It seems you did know we were coming. That axe was never meant for a foot soldier. It's got "King" written all over it with the detail and design that has gone into it. Let's get it out into the sunlight and get a good look." He turned and headed for the stairs, giving the other two men no option but to follow in his wake.

The three men made their way out of the barn and into the yard, Tyvig grabbing a rag to wipe the axe off as he passed the forge. After they assembled and gave Tyvig a moment to finish wiping it down, they were finally able to fully appreciate the detail that Kurad had glimpsed in the cellar.

It truly was a weapon meant for the King of Pendar, Edward realized, comparing the tattoo of his family's crest on his forearm to the curves and scrollwork detail on the blades that mirrored it perfectly. It was a weapon that only a master craftsman would be able to create. Tyvig handed it off to Edward, a simple gesture, but one that signified so much more than merely handing over a finely wrought battleaxe. They all recognized the significance on some level and respected the moment.

Edward looked closely at the axe he held in his young hands. This was the new symbol for his fallen nation, the weapon he planned to hold in his hands as he deposed the creature that had taken nearly everything from him. It was in this moment that it all came together in his mind. This wasn't just a rescue mission for Jessica and Helen; he was about to embark on the biggest challenge of his young life. Holding the dwarven battleaxe out before him, he felt the smooth handle meld into his grip and feel as if it became one with him. Though it wasn't a sentient weapon, he had the overwhelming feeling that it had been waiting for him to take it up. The axe had truly been made for him.

"How did you know? It feels like it was custom fit to my hands. I've never felt such a connection to a weapon before. I mean, I've never held a battleaxe, but never has a sword fit me like this does." Edward was overcome by the emotion of holding the axe and took a moment to gather himself before continuing on.

"This is truly of my heritage, a heritage that only a short time ago, I had no idea was a part of me. Even when Kurad told me about my past, it didn't register. I don't know what to say, Tyvig. Thank you doesn't seem to be strong enough. You've given me a wonderfully crafted axe, but you've also given me back who I really am, my identity." The tears flowed down his cheeks freely. He was no longer able to contain them and did not care.

Tyvig stepped forward and reached for the axe. "Let me go get a proper oil to rub this old thing down with. Can't have me king wandering around with a dull axe. You two take a moment and digest all this," he looked over to Kurad and gave a knowing nod. "Then we'll get to planning our trip and showing the boy how to use this thing without lopping off his own nose or some toes, and hopefully not mine either." He cradled the weapon in his arms as he turned and headed back into the barn.

"It's all so real now," Edward began, "Tyvig called me his king. What's that about? Is he a survivor of my father's kingdom? 'My father's kingdom'. It's weird to even say that, and really believe it. I feel like I owe you an apology, Kurad."

"Don't worry, Edward. You had a lot thrust on you after we hit the road and I'm impressed with how you've handled this whole trip. We won't abandon Jessica and Helen, but I think you now know that there is a bigger task before us. Your father saw the possibility of the end of his reign coming and had the vision necessary to get you out of harm's way so that someday you could return to take your rightful seat on his throne. Up until now, it's all been teaching, practicing, and preparation. I know that your father and mother would be very proud of how far you've come already. The truth of it, though, is that we have just entered a new phase, and more is going to be expected of you now." He walked over to Edward and patted him on the back. "Don't doubt that you're ready though, you've had an incredible teacher." He burst out laughing at his own immodesty and Edward quickly joined in, both enjoying the levity of the moment after such an emotionally charged morning.

"Are you two done with your jokes?" Tyvig yelled from the interior of the barn. "We have lots of packing to do if we're going to get that cellar full of goods bundled up and loaded onto me wagon. Snow's going to be nippin' at our heels as it is."

"It seems, Tyvig, that you still have a little more information than you've told us," Kurad said as he walked into the barn with Edward in tow. "When are we going to get the whole story out of you?"

"Well, me boys, there's some truth to that. I figured I should show you the axe first so that you weren't thinkin' that I was making up stories as I go." He stopped his work on Edward's axe and looked up at the two men standing before him. "Now seems just as good of a time as any, I suppose. Of course, storytelling over lunch might be a tad more enjoyable." He smirked, clearly enjoying the act of keeping the other two in suspense.

"You've had enough fun, I think," Edward said with a smile. He enjoyed Tyvig's sense of mischief, but clearly there was more to the story that needed to be told.

"You're the one that called me your king. I mean, I'm new to the idea of being royalty, but I think now would be a good time to fess up what you know or I'll have my loyal companion here," as he pointed his thumb at Kurad, "make you talk. I've lived with him all my days it seems and trust me when I say he's capable of extreme measures of torture."

Kurad came to his own defense. "Oh, that's not even fair. I taught you well the ways of stealth and avoidance, not to mention basic physical conditioning. Which, if I might add, you're going to appreciate once Tyvig teaches you how to swing that axe of yours." Tyvig chuckled and nodded in agreement on that point, leaving Edward a little nervous as to what new forms of torture this was going to entail.

"Grab yourselves a spot to sit. I'm going to keep rubbing this bit of iron while I tell you what I know." He paused and seemed to be trying to pull the details together from the depths of his memory as they settled in to finally hear the story.

"It was some years ago, maybe two hands full, that a dwarf shows up on the porch, looking a bit worse for the wear, and definitely well traveled for sure. I step out to see what Bonnie is growling at. She was Blue's momma," he explained, "not quite as big as her boy, but just as loyal. Well, I see's he's a dwarf and I ain't never met a bad one, so's I call her off and invite him in to rest his weary legs. He sat for a spell at the table and gives me the whole story about the gnomes taking over the castle at Pendar and running a band of survivors off to the mountains. Says there's nothing to be found of the royal family and that the line is believed to be gone." He paused and then went on, "but there was a prisoner that was taken the night the castle fell who swore a man came in the dead of night and told him otherwise." Tyvig looked over to a nodding Kurad for confirmation.

"I thought as much." He looked over to Edward and nodded. "You've done well with him, at least it looks like it." He chuckled to himself again. "Anyway, he tells me he's been searching for me because I had the knowledge and the tools to help design and craft this axe of yours. Well we went to work straightaway on this thing, making some assumptions about your size based on what he knew of your father. He brought the pattern of the crest with him and it was a good thing because I don't usually incorporate crests into my work. It's a nice style, just not my usual stuff, but it worked out well, I think." He stopped his rubbing and held the axe up again clearly proud of the weapon he had helped create.

"Well, after we finished it, he asked me to hang onto it. He said that should the prince ever find the dwarf haven then they would come looking for it. He was a bit nervous about the gnomes coming along and finding them in their weakened state, cleaning up the place, and taking the axe into their possession. It's clearly the talisman that they wanted you to carry when you lead them back home."

"Wait a minute," Kurad interrupted, having kept his silence throughout Tyvig's telling. "Do you know where this dwarf haven is located? We need to get there as soon as possible."

"Of course I do, or at least I can get you close." He gave his customary chuckle. "Like I said earlier, we need to get the weapons and armor out of the cellar so we can bring them along to help outfit your army. They're a bit secretive about it, but I'm thinkin' if I shows up with the crown prince, I'll surely get past the outpost this time.

"It's not an easy road that we'll be travelin', and not to be repeatin' meself all day, but the snows a comin' and we've got some distance to cover. So what do you say let's get ready to roll?" Then he paused and thought for a second. "How about after lunch?" Which brought a fresh round of chuckles from him as he tossed the axe to Edward and headed for the cabin and lunch.

Troy A. Skog

Chapter Twenty One

They didn't get going after lunch that first day as Tyvig had joked. There was much to do, and even with all three of them working together it was the better part of two weeks before they had packed the wagons with everything they would need. Tyvig had an old wagon that he'd used before on similar trips, but it wasn't going to hold all four of them. Blue could pad alongside just fine, according to Tyvig, but he knew that occasionally a rest would be welcome too. Then there were all the weapons from the cellar that he was bringing. After a short discussion the next day amongst the three men, Tyvig went into town and bought a wagon and a pulling team of sturdy workhorses at the livery to compliment the team that he kept. They initially planned on driving only the two teams, but after loading those two and assessing what else they deemed necessary to bring, decided that it would make for faster travel to lighten the loads. Lighter wagons would also help them get up through the mountain passes that they would be traveling. Tyvig went back a week later to acquire another wagon and team.

In addition to the armor and weapons he'd made for the dwarves, Tyvig intended to bring his forge tools, hammers and tongs, along with some of his personal effects. He knew there was a battle to be fought and that meant broken spears, axes, and armor to mend. He loved his home in the woods, but the dwarves were going to war and he meant to be right there with them when they did.

Once they had the house and barn buttoned down, they mounted up the wagons. After some initial jockeying amongst the wagon drivers, they fell into line with Tyvig in the lead wagon, followed by Edward with his team in the middle, and Kurad riding drag with his wagon. Blue padded alongside Tyvig's wagon, scanning the scents along the road. Curious or on patrol, Edward couldn't tell. Edward had his and Kurad's mounts tethered to the buckboard of his wagon. Kurad wanted them close at hand and protected in the center of the caravan. It was the same reason he had Edward positioned in the middle. Edward hadn't questioned the placement, although if he had,

Kurad would have told him bluntly he was there for a reason too.

The plan was to be on the road for at least a month, longer if they didn't get over the high trail before the first snows of the season fell at the highest elevations. It was going to be close and the men pushed the teams harder than they normally would for the first week in an effort to get ahead of the snows. It helped that the road was smooth and well traveled so it was in good repair. The men quickly found their rhythm on the road; setting up camp, tending the horses, and making a traveler's meal over the campfire before turning in for the night. Blue was put in charge of the night watch and nothing was going to come into camp without him taking notice and alerting Tyvig. The two relied on each other exclusively, living alone in the forest. They each had a pretty good read on the others body language and could communicate quite well without making a lot of noise.

The first week sailed by with the men pushing the teams as much as they thought they could while keeping them fresh for the pull over the high pass. The land remained flat as they moved out of the forested lands Tyvig called home and into the rolling foothills that led the way up into the mountains. The trees thinned and meadows began to dominate the landscape as the journey passed into the second week. Even though the cover dwindled, Kurad was still able to hunt for small game with his bow while he scouted ahead in the evening after camp was struck for the day. It was enough to keep the men from using too much of their supplies early on and fresh meat was always preferable over dried.

They met fewer and fewer travelers as they got closer to the mountains. Nobody else seemed to be heading in the same direction they were. It made Kurad's scouting easier as there were fewer individuals to make tracks on the dirt road. Kurad could only assume that there were more gnomes that would be out searching for the two men. Any other assumption could prove costly, so he kept vigilant for sign of their passing and also listened intently as he talked to others on the road. He kept to his usual method of talking with others only when Edward was not around; he didn't want the two linked together should one of the travelers also cross paths with a gnome search party. With their convoy, they were now numbered three traveling together, so hopefully that would aid them to hide in plain sight if the gnomes were focused on finding only two men.

The trail started to trend upwards as the foothills closed up to the leading edge of the range. The road was quiet and it gave the men pause that most folks were already avoiding the mountain passes that they needed to traverse. It was getting cold in the evenings and it seemed like winter got closer with every mile they traveled. Kurad wouldn't allow the other two to build a roaring fire for fear of attracting attention so they built small fires to cook any game that they collected during the day. They heated rocks to put at the feet of their bedrolls to ward off the cold that settled around them.

In the second week, they were forced to slow the teams as they began to climb the roads that would see them over the mountains. The air remained chilly into the mid-morning and was only chased off by the sun overhead on clear days. Edward knew not to complain about the cold to the two men helping him on his quest, but on a particularly overcast day he couldn't help himself.

"Tyvig, how long are we going to be on this road before we get back down where it's at least somewhat warm? I'm beginning to wear out the seat on my wagon from shivering."

"Ah, my young king, you are more patient than others your age. You have been taught well." His pause hanging in the air left Edward with an uneasy feeling in his stomach.

"However, it will be a goodly week before we crest this mountain top and begin our descent. By my reckoning it won't be more than two weeks before we're down to lowlands, though they won't be nearly as low as me own place. Of course, that be only if the snow holds off and doesn't slow us." He finished with a grumble, for it was as if the mountain gods had heard him and let loose the first flakes of what had the makings of a good blow.

And blow it did. The men stopped short of their goal for the day and found shelter off the trail in a small grove of pine trees, bedding down the horses out of the elements as much as possible. Kurad allowed a bigger fire this night as no smoke would be visible through the blowing snow, even the flames would be hidden to most eyes. It wouldn't do for them to freeze to death in a blizzard along the trail and that seemed a much greater danger on this night.

They took turns on watch, though most of the time was spent tending the fire and making sure the horses didn't wander off and get lost. The storm abated some time during the night, but true to form for mountain snowfalls, they were knee deep in powdery white snow by morning.

Kurad headed out at first light to scout the road and see what else might be out moving around in the mountains. Trails were going to be easy to spot for anyone looking for other travelers today and that went for the three of them as well. He came back to camp as the other two were finishing hitching up the horses, packing the wagons and cleaning up the campsite.

"It was an unfortunate snowfall for us. The road, while passable, is covered as deeply as our immediate campsite. It's going to slow us down and tire the horses. I came across several goodly drifts we will need to help the horses bust through too." Kurad paused to consider the strategy.

"I think we should rotate the teams at the front, they will be working harder to break the trail. Slow them down and watch for fatigue. We need the payload we're carrying and we're prepared to spend some extra time on the road." He stopped short of voicing his fear of another storm catching them on the mountain. With two more weeks, if not three, it was a good likelihood that it would snow again before they reached the far side of the mountain.

"I'll take the lead," Tyvig announced as he interrupted Kurad's musing. "I know the route nearly as well as a good dwarf would once they've walked the trail. I'm sure we're going to be guessing at where the road is under this blanket of fresh snow. I've ridden the road more than a time or two without snow so I'm hopin' that will carry us through now."

Kurad nodded while Edward silently hoped they would make good time despite the snowfall. Helen and Jessica were still being held prisoner, that was his hope anyway, and time was slipping away.

They pulled out of camp, the horses' fresh from the early stop the day before. They stomped through the fresh powder, creating their own miniature swirling clouds of snow as they churned the flakes under their feet. It seemed to the men that the horses enjoyed the newness of the scenery as they headed up the trail.

The drivers kept the pace even as they slogged through the varying drifts. At times, when the trail was blown clear, the horses could conserve their energy for those inevitable times where the trail would be nearly belly deep for the first team in line. At those times when the drifts were piled high, Kurad and Edward would stop their wagons and make their way to the front to help the team break through. Once moving again, the teams following had an easier time of it and the two men would catch their breath waiting for the next drift. Following Kurad's plan from that morning they rotated the teams, trying to give them equal time on point.

The day went well and the group covered more distance than they had figured. In an effort to keep the horses fresh, they stopped early and made camp for the night. They built a low fire and dug into their stores to make a meal as there hadn't been an opportunity to hunt game on the trail. The road had been empty of any other travelers and the men felt isolated from the rest of the world on the top of the mountain.

The next week was uneventful as they crested the mountain and began making their way down the far side. They lost a little time due to the slower pace, but overall the trip hadn't been delayed too much.

"We can't be more than a week from my rendezvous point with the dwarves," Tyvig told Edward as the two of them began preparing dinner.

"As soon as Kurad gets back from his scouting trip, we need to start planning how we are going to introduce you to the dwarves. I think they'll acknowledge your right to the throne. You convinced me, but I'm not a dwarf. Their reputation for stubbornness has been earned. That's something that should be considered is all I'm saying." He left that thought hanging as Blue lifted his head from his nap beside the fire, signaling that Kurad was approaching the camp through the trees.

"We're being tailed," Kurad said as he came into camp. "It's a small band of gnomes, maybe as many as twenty, but I can't tell if they know who we are or they're just using our trail through the snow. Either way, I'm not one for waiting to find out. Tyvig," he stopped and directed his full attention on the man. "How far out from your usual meeting point are we?"

"I was just telling the boy that we can't be but six days at this pace. If we push a bit we can lop off a day, maybe a day and a bit more." He seemed to be calculating the distance as he looked down the road.

"Do you think they, the gnomes I mean, will be content to hang back and not make contact to find out who we are?" Edward looked between the two men for an answer that wasn't likely to get them killed.

"My thought is that they won't pursue us like they did back at the farmhouse. If they thought they were this close to the prize they would be traveling faster to catch up to us. However, they aren't encumbered by wagons full of armor like we are. Figuring at the natural pace of their travel, they'll be sitting around our campfire not more than two nights hence." Kurad's estimate wasn't what the other two wanted to hear.

"Is there a chance they won't recognize the two of you as enemies of the state? We could keep plugging away and not act spooked when they turn up." Tyvig began, pausing as he reconsidered. "I'm guessing three wagonloads of dwarven armor might raise suspicions and get us acquainted with the pointy end of sword just as well," he mumbled under his breath. Edward wasn't able to make out what he said though he knew it was less than encouraging.

"I think we need to break camp as soon as we finish dinner and push on down the trail." Kurad began laying out his plan. "It's going to be a snail's pace through the dark, but any time we can gain on them will help. I would like to dump one of the wagons, except then they would realize we were on the run and they would quickly give chase." He paused to try to settle his mind on the developing plan. "We need to gather materials for torches. Driving the wagons when the road is snow-covered is tough. At night, it's going to be even more so without some light." Sensing hesitation from Tyvig, he answered the question before he could be interrupted.

"We'll have to risk that our torches are seen. The enemy at our backs is the biggest threat at this point." He knew they weren't prepared to deal with a band of gnomes. He also didn't like the plan, but their options were limited. The situation could only get worse until they were off the mountain.

The men ate a quick meal and stowed the gear with nothing but a quick rinse of the pots in the snow. No one said as much, but the likelihood of using them again was slim. Materials were scrounged to make some crude torches and the horses, with minor protest, were hitched back into their harnesses.

The horses had already had a long day breaking through the snow and were nonplussed about the proposition of continuing through the night. The men had no choice but to push on. They were now in a race to the dwarven stronghold that Tyvig promised. Either they would reach the safety of the dwarves or they would be overtaken on the snow covered road leading down from the mountain tops. All three hoped they could make great speed and that the roads would be clear of snow. The other option didn't bode well for the three of them or the women being held in Orgle's dungeon.

The wagons moved out into the night unseen by all, with the exception of a single pair of eyes looking out through a hood drawn tight to ward off the cold.

Troy A. Skog

Chapter Twenty Two

Jessica awoke from her fitful slumber when the jailer rattled the keys to get the attention of those within the cell.

"I'm coming," she whispered, trying not to make too much noise so that her mother could continue sleeping. She stood and moved to the door so the guard could see her, then waited as he inserted the key and unlocked the door. It swung open and she stepped out, presenting her wrists so that she could be properly restrained on the walk to the upper floors of the castle. Her mother never stirred as the door shut behind her and they began their walk.

"What is my task today?" She asked, knowing full well that there would be no answer forthcoming. It was always the same; never any communication as she was led up to the surface to work in the kitchen, the laundry, or sometimes even the stable if they were shorthanded. She rotated days with her mother.

Apparently the thought was that neither one would try to escape if they knew the other was locked in the dungeon below. It was actually quite effective Jessica had to admit, for neither one would think of leaving the other to their cruel fate alone.

They had been on this rotation now since nearly the beginning of their stay. Orgle wanted to keep an eye on them and he was always happy to have them working in the kitchen. He craved dishes from the humans and the two didn't complain about the chance to get out and see the sun and breath fresh air. Even the stable was better than the air they breathed down in the dungeon.

The pair walked the halls in silence now that they had cleared the tunnels below the castle. Jessica made certain not to make eye contact or gesture to any of the dwarf slaves they came across en route. That lesson had been driven home on one of the first outings. She hoped the dwarf had survived. The guilt remained with her and the image was painted vividly in her mind. The rule was that no one should talk to the ladies, lest they conspire to plot their escape or enable the return of the prince. It was a rule that they had learned to circumvent.

Today she was off to the garden. Winter was approaching and all the weeding and pruning had paid dividends, the vegetables were ripe for picking. Jessica reveled in the sunlight as she stepped out of the castle and was prodded down the path leading to the gardens. It had been several rotations since she had been allowed outdoors. The garden was bustling with activity as her escort undid her restraints and led her through the gate. There were too many dwarves working in the enclosure to keep her completely isolated and the nature of the work required at least some interaction. The guards frowned on excessive communication, but they spent more time watching for their superiors, afraid to get caught relaxing the rules.

Word of the women's connection to Prince Edward had spread quickly throughout the prisoners. A rumor started by a dwarf had been floating around the prison in the years since the occupation of the city that the prince had been rescued and one day would return. That dwarf was Relysis, and he swore upon his good friend King Samuel's grave that a man had sought him out and told him as much in the days following their capture. Relysis had been the commander of the dwarves and no one would dispute that what he said wasn't the truth, so they had toiled these long years gathering equipment and weapons of any sort in anticipation. If nothing else, it had given them hope and the will to resist. Now, with the revelation that Edward was alive and coming back, there was a new urgency in their preparations. There was an undercurrent of anticipation amongst those enslaved and disguising their new resolve wasn't easy, even if they were dwarves.

Jessica was aware of the effect she had on the dwarves. Without her arrival, they would still be toiling away without hope. Now she was the focal point, their source of energy. She wished she knew more so she could answer the many questions that were directed toward her. When would he arrive? Did he have an army? Initially she tried to tell them his identity had been a mystery to her too, but they wouldn't have any of that. It was thrust upon her that she was the link to their king. Some of the communications she had with the dwarves, quick and sketchy though they were, had her already established as the queen.

That was an intimidating thought, the queen of an entire country. Unfortunately, there wasn't much else to distract her thoughts and she often found herself returning to that idea time after time. Edward and she had discussed a future together, but they were young and at no time were they planning on ruling a country. That was a big shift, something to consider. She almost had to chuckle at herself. Why spend her time worrying about being the queen of a country when she was currently being held in the dungeons of that very castle she would call home? Her life was only now being spared on one of Orgle's whims. She was pretty sure she was a bargaining chip at best, and probably more likely to be a sacrifice in some spectacular fashion meant to demoralize Edward upon his arrival. When she thought of it that way, escape seemed like a better option and she decided it was time to focus on that immediate problem. She spent the remainder of the day getting the latest information from the other prisoners.

The day in the sun passed by entirely too quickly and before she knew it, she was being ushered back to the cell she occupied with her mother. She was encouraged by what she'd learned and was anxious to tell her mother when she got back.

Chapter Twenty Three

The trail was mostly clear of snow as they dropped down the backside of the mountain, with the exception of the deep drifts where the road opened up between the thick trees. It didn't mean they made good time though. The dark of night was just as effective as the drifts in slowing the wagons. They plodded along with Kurad ranging out ahead to scout the trail whenever they stopped to rest the horses. The horses needed breaks because it was unrealistic to expect the animals to continue throughout the night without some respite. Pace was on the forefront of their minds. Too quick a pace and they would run the horses into the ground, too slow and they would be overtaken by the band of gnomes following in their wake.

Kurad called a halt after several hours. The horses were beginning to stumble and would need time to gather energy for the next day's march. The men were beginning to tire too. On the mountain road, Kurad began to fear for the safety of the teams and drivers. Everyone was tired and mistakes became more likely. They found a small clearing off to the side of the road where they hastily bedded the exhausted horses, built a fire, and laid out their bedrolls nearby. Edward was out nearly as soon as he settled in and Tyvig soon after. Kurad gave the area a quick once over and settled in too. It was against his nature, but he was going to have to rely on Blue to keep vigilant.

Edward awoke to Tyvig and Kurad discussing the plan for the day. They were in the middle of trying to decide how best to balance the need to move quickly and also make an effort to save the horses.

"I think if we rest the horses while one of us scouts the road ahead we should be able to rest them adequately." Kurad put forth. Tyvig agreed with Kurad, but still didn't know if they could outrun the gnomes.

"Now that we are not pulling uphill, the horses should stay fresh but the breaks for scouting ahead will help too. At least the road is mostly free of snow. Breaking a trail is going to stall us out and leave us vulnerable. We still have several days ahead of us, even if we can keep up this pace. Obviously if we had to dump the wagons and run we would get there well ahead of the gnomes, but we're going to need the armor and weapons if we're going to be attacking a castle."

Kurad looked over to Edward, "Good that you're up, I was just about to rouse you and get you to help Tyvig break camp. I'm going to run ahead and scout the road, see what obstacles we have facing us as the sun comes up." He barely finished his statement before he was off down the road at a lope.

"The horses are going to be less than pleased that they are already back on the job. Watch yourself, they could get ornery," Tyvig started then paused.

"Actually that might be meself I'm talking about, but at least I don't bite or kick." He chuckled at himself, only half kidding. It had been a long day and short night and from what he could tell, it wasn't going to get much better in the near future. He looked absently back at the road they had traveled during the night.

"Those gnomes better not pester me or I just may kick and bite." There wasn't any humor in his tone.

Edward stowed his gear and then started helping Tyvig harness the horses, taking Tyvig's statement to heart and using gentle persuasion to get them into place. They had the teams all in place and their gear packed away by the time Kurad arrived back at camp with his report.

"We should make good time this morning. There's some snow on the road but not too many drifts that we will have to dig our way through. Looks like you two have been busy. Breakfast will be served on board I would assume." He was ready to roll and didn't waste any time climbing aboard his wagon. The other two men followed his lead as they all took up the reins and coaxed the horses forward. Kurad took point and Tyvig waited silently as Edward assumed his customary position in the middle of the train before Tyvig moved into position at the tail end.

The morning went as Kurad had predicted with few stoppages as the horses navigated the road. As promised, they stopped periodically to rest and do some additional scouting. Midday arrived and Kurad, now riding drag, called out that it was time for lunch and to give the horses a rest out of their harnesses. He wanted to backtrack a bit and see where the gnomes were and if they were gaining on them. The pace had been pretty good for the wagons, but a troop of gnomes on the chase could quickly overtake them. That was information Kurad needed to know.

Kurad headed back up the road moving at a good pace, scanning the trail and the surrounding area for any sign of pursuit. He calculated in his mind as he clicked off the miles. His estimate of the gnomes' speed put them still quite a ways behind the little caravan, so he moved with speed down the trail, sticking to the wagon ruts where the snow deepened. Kurad had run several miles when he skidded to a halt, his breathing heavy from the effort. Looking down at the snow he saw tracks that split off from the road. It didn't take more than a moment to realize whose tracks they were as he spun and raced back towards the wagons.

Tyvig and Edward watched Kurad heading back up the road as they began the process of releasing the horses from the confines of the harnesses.

"It's a good thing we're stopping, these horses need a break. We push them too hard and we're just going to end up pulling these wagons ourselves." Tyvig spoke as he worked around the teams.

"Answer me this lad, does that man ever tire or slow down? Seems he can go all day and night with nary a rest. Right now he's galloping off up the road looking for some gnomes who could probably care less about us except that we're blazing their trail for them."

"He used to drive me crazy with all the training and preparing and I never quite understood what all the fuss was about, but since that day on the farm when the gnomes found us, I haven't had too many reservations about his tactics." Edward understood Tyvig's complaint. They were pushing hard and they were all tired. He had a good point though, the horses weren't going to care about pulling if they were exhausted. If that happened, then the whole plan was derailed and the gnomes would surely catch them before they reached the dwarves.

"I'm sorry for complaining Edward. I've slept too many nights in a row in snowbanks and these old bones are begging for a warm feather bed. We'll get through it though, don't ya fret. Let's feed these beasts and then get some grub for own selves." Tyvig was durable, but the pace was hard. He felt bad for complaining and hoped Edward didn't take him wrong. He knew a little lunch and a chance to nap a tad would get them both back on their feet. They did just as they planned and before long they were sitting down to a bite to eat. Right then, Blue began growling, his hackles standing tall.

Tyvig knew the tone, and knowing Blue was serious, grabbed for his staff. Edward's reaction was a step slower, though he grabbed his axe and was on his feet by the time Tyvig squared up to challenge whatever had roused Blue. Tyvig scanned the trees for a moment seeing nothing, never doubting his four-legged companion's senses. An arrow came slicing in from behind and caught Tyvig in between his shoulders. Pain exploded, bringing him to the ground. Blue wheeled and charged toward the unseen assailant, arrows sailing about his fur as the attackers tried to fend off the raging creature.

Edward spun around to see Tyvig's body crumple to the snow, blood turning the snow red as his life leaked from his wound. The scene was unfolding and events happening so fast that his mind was spinning. He knew instinctively that he and Tyvig didn't have time for him to flounder, and at that moment he let his mind go and relied on his training. Diving towards the protective cover of one of the wagons, he hoped to get out of sight of the individuals loosing the arrows in his direction. He crouched and pulled himself behind the wagon, stopping to assess where the nearest threat was. The arrows had come from across the camp in the direction Blue gave chase and, despite the situation, Edward had to crack a slight grin as he could hear Blue still giving chase. Apparently no arrows had found purchase in his hide yet.

He stooped and took a look out from under the wagon, noticing the arrows had stopped landing about the campsite. He took that as a sign that they no longer had a visual on him. That was until he played back the scene in his mind and realized the arrows had stopped after Tyvig had gone down. Blue? Did he distract them enough that they forgot about Edward? No, that didn't add up. There were obviously more than a couple of individuals surrounding the camp. Blue had reacted to the other side of camp before the first shot was fired. The alarm went off in his head a split second before he felt the pain in the back of his head and the lights went out.

Tyvig's and Edward's assailants left the scene quickly, knowing Kurad would return soon and time was against them. Leaving the campsite nearly as quickly as they had attacked, the intruders disappeared back into the woods.

Blue's call had receded into the distance and the campsite was quiet now. Tyvig lay motionless, the snow around him becoming an ever deeper shade of red. Edward's tracks led to the wagon and the blood in the snow marked the spot where he had taken refuge and ultimately been discovered. This was how Kurad would find it. He would see the scene play out in his mind and he would know exactly what had happened. Then, the chase would be on. Kurad would be in full pursuit, revenge in the forefront of his mind. That would be his plan, but plans rarely follow the path first envisioned.

Troy A. Skog

Chapter Twenty Four

The gnomes left the scene of the attack as quickly as they had come. They took no time to disable the wagons or chase off the horses. This had been a target of opportunity. Use the element of surprise to take down their defenses, get in rapidly, and grab only what was needed. When their scout reported back to the captain that Kurad left the campsite to backtrack on the road, they knew that this was their chance. The attack had been thrown together quickly and executed perfectly. Now they were on the run with their prisoner slumped over the back of Yancik, the biggest brute in the gnome band.

It wasn't long before Edward regained his senses and became aware of several things nearly simultaneously. First, he was aware that he had been captured, and secondly, that he was being transported on the back of what he presumed was a gnome. From his angle he could see little but the back of his captor and his legs churning through the snow with a ragged uniform covering his legs. Then the smell of the creature permeated Edward's nostrils, leaving no doubt that he had fallen into the hands of those they had been trying to avoid. The third thing he became aware of was the pounding headache that seemed to throb to the beat of the runner's legs as he was jostled uncomfortably on the shoulder of the gnome. His hands were bound tightly together. Edward was pretty sure his legs were also trussed but he couldn't tell for certain and didn't want to give away the fact that he was conscious.

He was going to need some time to develop a plan to escape and the longer they weren't paying close attention to him the better his plan could be assembled. Additionally, the longer he was carried, the slower his captors could travel. His size and weight were going to start wearing down his transport and they would have to slow the pace.

He had no way of knowing how long he had been knocked out, but it couldn't have been too long because they were still moving as if they expected to be caught at any moment. Edward had to assume that this was the band that Kurad had scouted out and determined to be following them, but how many gnomes had Kurad counted in the group? Take better notes, Edward admonished himself. Now he would have to wait until they stopped to rest or he would have to risk giving away his level of consciousness to take a head count of those around him.

If only his head would stop pounding. He could hardly think straight. All of a sudden the band came to a halt and Edward found himself dumped into the snow, flat on his back. Edward stole a quick glance up at the gnome that had been carrying him. He was bent over at the waist, breathing hard, trying to catch his breath from the effort. In a moment, Edward was surrounded and prodded with a boot in the ribs. The time had come to open his eyes.

Kurad slowed his pace as he neared the clearing. It was quiet around the wagons but he had underestimated the gnomes and he feared that it had cost them dearly. There could be no more mistakes. He crept in slowly using the surrounding brush to conceal his approach. There was sign that the gnomes had been through there but it became clear to Kurad that they had left the area. When he worked his way clear of the tree line, he saw Tyvig's body lying in the snow. An arrow protruded from his back and there was enough blood to expect the worst. He cautiously worked his way across the small clearing looking for any sign of Edward.

The story played out before his skilled tracker's eyes. The men had been ambushed from the rear. The initial alarm had been sounded by Blue, and then they had struck, catching Tyvig with his attention diverted. Blue's tracks showed the direction of the archer as he had reacted to his master being felled. There was no sign of Blue in the clearing so he'd eluded the attacker for at least the initial charge. His attention swung back to the tracks in the snow. Although there was much confusion between the tracks of the gnomes and the men as they had set up camp, he picked up Edward's flight path to the cover of the wagon. Clearly they had encircled the clearing and left no place to hide. They struck quickly, and Edward had been dropped where he took cover, without a chance to defend himself. The small amount of blood in the snow told Kurad the boy was still alive, but now he was a prisoner in the hands of those that meant him great harm. At least he was alive. That kept the door at least cracked open for a chance at redemption.

Kurad could do nothing at this moment for Edward. His fate would be decided in the future and he would have to keep himself alive until Kurad could run this troop to the ground. Tyvig was here and his fate appeared sealed but Kurad knew him to be strong willed. If any could cling to life against odds, this was the man to do it. He hurried to his side now. The immediate danger had passed so Kurad was able to focus on his friend and his injuries. He knelt and carefully lifted Tyvig's body from his face down position, rolling him back so as to not break the arrow off and cause more injury. As he did so, Tyvig's eyes cracked open and a wry grin crossed his face.

"What took you so long, old man? I thought I was going to freeze to death waitin' fer ya." He was clearly hurting, but he had lived this long and it gave Kurad hope. The man hadn't been mortally wounded despite all the blood and the arrow still imbedded in his back, protruding through his chest.

He was in need of immediate medical attention and the side of a mountain wasn't the most ideal place to administer to his wounds.

"How far to these dwarf friends of yours? If we ditch the armor from one of these wagons and hitch an extra set of horses, could we make it within a day and night?" Kurad asked.

"You've clearly picked up some dwarven stubbornness, but you're in need of some healing and mine aren't the hands of a surgeon." He knew he needed to try and remove the arrow or at least cut it off so that Tyvig could lie on his back in the wagon. Also, tearing up some cloth and packing the wound would help to stop the bleeding and would buy Tyvig some time until proper doctoring could be done.

Kurad went to work cutting up Edward's bedroll. He would have to thank him for the donation later. Once the packing material was set aside, Kurad went about clipping off the end of the arrow. Tyvig grunted heavily when Kurad snapped off the feathered end and began dressing the wound as fresh blood flowed. It took a little time to pack the wound sufficiently to stop the blood from seeping through and then he laid him back down on the cold snow.

"The cold should help slow the blood loss, but it's packed pretty well. I'm going to unload one of the wagons and add another team to the rig and see if we can't make some better time." Kurad patted his patient lightly on his shoulder, trying to reassure Tyvig that he was going to be okay and they would get to the dwarf doctors shortly.

"You know you never answered my question, old man," he returned the jab he had gotten upon his arrival at the campsite.

"How long until we find your dwarves?" Tyvig didn't answer. He had lost consciousness. The injury and pain from breaking off the arrow had taken its toll and he couldn't fight off the darkness any longer. His friend nodded at his still form and noted his steady breathing. Kurad had work to do.

With the weapons and armor unloaded, he moved Tyvig's sleeping form to the buckboard wagon bed. Tyvig stirred only slightly as Kurad settled him in and tried as much as possible to pack bedrolls around him so as not to jostle him too much. The wagon was considerably lighter now and with extra horses pulling, and reserves tied off at the rear, Kurad figured to make good time. He was hopeful Tyvig would regain consciousness and help guide him to the meeting place because without Tyvig it was going to be difficult to find the elusive dwarves. For now though, all he could do was push on. He knew it was at least a day's travel even at the pace he intended to travel and Tyvig was going to need medical attention soon.

It was a haggard looking crew of gnomes that stared down at Edward. Clearly they had been on the road for many weeks, but the glint in their eyes showed him that they had found the prize they'd been searching for and it was him.

"So you decide to wake up, boy prince," stated Barmes in his choppy version of the common tongue, prodding Edward with Edward's own battleaxe. "It was good of you to shake off your little bump on the head. We have to get you home in a hurry now." His leering face was just inches from Edward's. Barmes was in charge of this ragtag troop and he knew exactly what he now possessed.

"You thought you could hide forever? I knew different. I tracked your whispers. I was a step ahead of you the entire time and I waited until the time was right." Barmes was proud of his accomplishment and knew that a reward beyond his comprehension awaited him when he delivered his catch to Orgle.

"It is time the boy prince made himself useful and started running. I hope you can keep up without me having Yancik motivate you." He nodded at the brute who had been carrying Edward and smiled knowingly.

Edward looked up at Yancik, sizing him up from his new vantage point flat on his back. He had to admit he didn't think he wanted to antagonize him, especially bound as he was.

"Let loose my arms and legs and we can make better time. Trussed up as a hog, I won't be going anywhere, no matter the motivation," he stated matter of factly.

"You think me a foolish gnome, but you underestimate me. I already tracked you across mountains and through forests and you should know that you only got as far as you did because it fit my needs and you were being watched over by the man Kurad. Best if you remember these truths until we get you home to Orgle." Barmes said with bluster, clearly confident that Edward would remain in his possession and none too modest about his abilities.

"Clearly you have me where you want me. I realize an escape attempt would be futile. You have my word that I will follow you willingly until I get my audience with this Orgle. I'm sure he's a reasonable individual and will be open to negotiations for my immediate release." He knew Orgle wasn't any of those things, and given the chuckles from the gnomes, they knew it too. Edward's curiosity about Barmes's comment concerning Kurad was great enough maybe his time with Barmes was not going to be entirely for naught.

"Orgle will not release you no matter how much you beg and plead. He has planned your execution for all your years, ever since he did away with the rest of your family. And just maybe he'll use your own axe to take care of you." Barmes laughed loudly along with the gnomes of his patrol at this proclamation. He hefted the axe overhead with both hands, knowing he had stung the boy prince.

Edward shut his eyes, unwilling to allow them to see the anger and the frustration. At last he regained his composure and opened his eyes once more to look up at Barmes.

"We'll see what he says when we get there. Release my bonds and we can get moving. I'm sure you don't want me to tell him that you tarried overly long in bringing me in," a jab for a jab in Edward's mind. From all he knew, Orgle wasn't of sound mind and anything could set him off. Maybe he could get Orgle to separate Barmes's head from his shoulders for him. It would save him a swing of his battleaxe. He would go to meet Orgle willingly, but there was nothing promised after that. Edward smiled as he raised his arms up so that the ropes could be removed, telling himself to remember to thank Barmes for carrying his axe home for him.

Chapter Twenty Five

The road to the dwarf stronghold stretched out before him as Kurad pushed the horses, rotating them regularly to keep them fresh. The hours passed quickly as he guided them through the growing darkness. He was unwilling to stop and rest for the night for fear Tyvig wouldn't survive the delay. The pace slowed with the onset of full dark, but the sky was clear and there was a bit of moonlight to show the way so he pushed onward, only stopping to rotate horses and check on his patient periodically. It was a tired Kurad that greeted the growing light as dawn crept closer. He had been awake for a complete day and then some, and was pushing the limits of his endurance.

"Old friend," Kurad said to the still unconscious Tyvig as he pulled off the road into a small windswept alcove, "I fear I must stop and take a rest lest I run these animals into the ground or worse yet, kill us all by piloting them off the edge of the road by my own inattentiveness. We won't tarry long, just enough to catch a wink of sleep and feed the horses so they can keep us rolling. I had hoped you would awaken soon to give some direction because I truly don't know our destination." He hoped Tyvig would hear him and shake off his slumber. His concern for missing his destination was genuine. If the dwarves didn't want to be found it would be impossible, even for an accomplished woodsman and tracker of Kurad's ability, to locate their home.

He got to work immediately, letting the horses loose from their trappings and tossing down feed to replenish depleted muscles. After a quick bite to eat himself and one last check on Tyvig, he found room in the back of the wagon to lie down to rest his eyes. Just a moment or two, he told himself as he settled in and let his eyes shut out the coming dawn.

It seemed but a moment before his eyes snapped open to the midday glare and he instinctively reached for his long blade. It was the cold touch of metal pressing against his throat that had awoken him from his slumber. His long blade wasn't in its sheath where it should have been. Looking up into the sun, he had no way to get a clear look at whomever it was that held the blade to his neck. His attacker had the drop on him and he needed to buy some time.

"I'm looking for medical help for my friend," Kurad began. "He's been wounded by an arrow in his back and I've no way to treat him." He didn't want to call out the gnomes as his probable attacker for he didn't know yet if it was the gnome party coming back to finish the task.

"What are you and your friend doing out here? This road doesn't get much use at this time of year," the gruff voice asked. "Is that lump of blankets your friend?" The blade didn't leave his neck, though the pressure eased ever so slightly.

"Yes, that is Tyvig. We are delivering blacksmith goods to his customer and it is imperative that they receive the shipment immediately." The blade remained poised to dispatch Kurad should he make any move, the attention diverted to Tyvig lying next to him.

"Check the wagon," Kurad's captor called out to his companions. "This man says that Tyvig is wounded and needin' doctorin'. Blosen, get up here and check him out. If your story checks out I'll apologize. For the moment, you just sit tight." The speaker with the gruff voice instructed Kurad.

Kurad felt the weight of the wagon shift as Blosen climbed over the side and began to pull back blankets.

"It was a gnome arrow that caught him in the back and found its way clear through." Kurad suspected the dwarves he was looking for had found him, so it was time to disclose who had attacked them. "Be careful not to disturb the dressing. The blood has stopped for now, but I think he needs some sewing."

"Tis Tyvig and true to his word he's been shot through by an arrow. He's still breathing but we should get him to the healer as soon as we can." Blosen gave his report and covered Tyvig back up before jumping back down from the wagon.

"Gnomes, you say," the gruff voice rumbled as the blade lifted away from Kurad. "As I said I would apologize, so I will. I regret drawing steel on you, but we've been crossing paths with a band of gnomes and we can't be too careful. Climb out if you can and we can meet proper."

Kurad was stiff and cramped from sleep. He unfolded slowly as he dropped his legs off the back of the wagon, still unsure of those who had found him.

"My name is Kurad. I am in service to the King," he paused. "King Samuel Ellingstone." He stopped to let the name hang in the air as all four members of the dwarf scouting party turned from their doings to regard him.

"Careful throwing that name out there, Kurad. I am Willos and would consider it a grave insult for someone to be misusing the Ellingstone name. There's still lots of pain and anger associated with King Samuel's defeat and his family's murder. Was I hasty in my apology about drawing steel against you?" The grip on his battleaxe tightened, as he shifted his weight ever so slightly, and eyed Kurad suspiciously.

"I have my answer, and I apologize for catching you off guard when I spoke the Ellingstone name, but, time is short and I had no time to try and gather your allegiances in casual conversation." Kurad focused on Willos, clearly the high-ranking dwarf in the scouting party.

"Tyvig and I, along with another, were bringing a load of armor and weapons to your doorstep when we were attacked by the party of gnomes whose path you've crossed. They attacked when I was scouting our back trail so I wasn't a witness. Tyvig was shot in the back while our companion was subdued and taken captive."

"Why did you not chase after the gnomes when they were at hand?" Willos asked. "You left your companion to the devices of the gnomes? He will most certainly be tortured and killed to gain information or merely for sport. Most likely, he is already dead." Willos's expression was of contempt now, clearly disapproving of Kurad's decision to abandon his companion.

"I'm positive that he is alive and will be kept as such for as long as they travel to meet Orgle. I was outnumbered and my friend was injured and unable to fight; I decided it was more important that I get Tyvig to you while there was life left in him. Our focus should be on Tyvig and the weapons he crafted for your people's hands." Kurad needed their help but they were demonstrating why dwarves were known as a stubborn race.

"We need to make a decision," Kurad said. Drawing them in and getting them to engage was vital. "Do we stay together and drive Tyvig to your doctor or do we split up and some of us go back for the weapons?"

"Let's send Pepper and Glip to get Tyvig to the doc and us three can go back and gather up the weapons." Willos stated as he took ownership of the situation. "You'll need to rig up a frame to carry Tyvig. I'm figuring we'll need the wagon and horses to retrieve Tyvig's works." He looked to Kurad who nodded in agreement.

The dwarves got to work immediately, constructing a crude frame from pine branches and unloading Tyvig. Before long, the two parties were heading in opposite directions, intent on completing their tasks. Kurad took the reins and guided the team back up the road, the horses working now to pull the wagon.

They rode in silence for a while. Willos was sitting next to Kurad on the wagon seat, it was Willos who finally broke the silence.

"How is that you know Tyvig and came to travel with him to the doorstep of our home? He would not bring anyone with him that did not have a very specific need to speak with us. This detail has me curious."

"Tyvig and I have known each other for many seasons," Kurad began, not taking his eyes from the mountain road. "We met when he was an apprentice blacksmith studying under some of Pendar's best weapons craftsman. As I stated earlier, I was in service to Samuel." He paused and reflected on their relationship and began again. "In truth, we were friends. An unlikely pair to be sure, him the king with wealth and power, and me just a drifter living alone on the road with naught more than the clothes on my back and my sword on my hip. Nonetheless we struck up a friendship, and though it's been some dozen years now, I still miss him." His voice cracked as he trailed off. He hadn't spoken of Samuel except recently with Edward and Tyvig, it was therapeutic, somewhat.

"I can tell from your voice that you speak honestly of your friendship with my king, and I'm sure if he were here today he would claim you as a friend also."

"A man of the road surely has few close friends, and certainly Tyvig is one of those, so don't worry about his wellbeing. We've got good surgeons back at our stronghold and he's probably already under their care. Truth be told, we weren't very far from the checkpoint where Tyvig usually delivers his wares."

They rode on in silence for a good share of the day, trust having been tentatively established between the man and dwarf. The focus turned to making the trip up the mountain and retrieving the weapons and armor so they could get them back to the stronghold. Kurad didn't want to tell Willos too much about Edward. He would rather wait until he had an audience with whomever was now in charge of the remnants. It was after they stopped and got off the wagons to have a bite to eat for dinner that the three of them began to talk again.

"Do you have many problems with gnomes coming through your mountain passes?" Kurad asked, attempting to get a feel for the movements of Orgle's troops.

"Not typically," Willos began, "but then again, this past year hasn't been typical. We keep our heads down and practice strict avoidance if we can. If Orgle knew we were living not more than a few weeks forced march from our old city, he might make an effort to dig us out. Someday we'll make some noise, but until then we'll sit quiet and resist the urge to confront his patrols." His clenched fists spoke stronger than his diplomatic words.

"We have three wagons worth of armor and weapons just ahead on the mountain. I have to think that would help." Kurad was prying around the edges, trying to get an idea of the army Edward would have at his back, or more likely coming to his rescue, as was the case now.

"The armor and weapons will help for sure. Tyvig has been an important source for us. He is a skilled blacksmith. If it weren't for our absolute need for secrecy, we would have invited Tyvig into our underground home years ago. He has access to resources we don't, or at least not the quantity we require. I know he understands our situation, but the slight has to make the man think we don't value him as a member of our clan." Willos was visibly distraught; clearly it pained him to exclude Tyvig.

"He might feel snubbed if he thought like a human, but he's as much a dwarf as yourself though he shares not your blood." Kurad reassured Willos who nodded in agreement.

"Let's get back on the wagons so we can get to the camp by nightfall. I like the idea of coming in under cover of darkness should the gnomes have circled back and laid claim to the treasure, although I doubt they are focusing on anything else but getting back to Orgle."

Willos looked to Kurad, curious about the reason that the gnomes would be in such a hurry to get back to the castle. He didn't ask the question, assuming the answer had something to do with the companion that had been taken captive. They were back in the wagon in short order and pushing on up the road. Kurad had broken the trail on his way down just yesterday so they made good time traveling along as the light began to fade and the sun was beginning to set behind them.

Kurad stopped the wagon about a mile out from where the gnomes had ambushed Tyvig and Edward. The three travelers hopped down from the wagon and quietly discussed their plan. At the end of the discussion Willos and Kurad headed up the road leaving Blosen to guard the wagon.

The two trotted up the road, glad to be off the wagon and moving again, generating a little body heat. The night air had cooled considerably in the absence of the warming power of the sun. Kurad was in the lead with Willos close behind as they closed in on the abandoned wagons. They left the roadway and came up to the camp through the trees and brush. Kurad squatted down and sat still with Willos at his side once they reached the perimeter of the camp. The scene was quiet, devoid of any sign anybody had been there since Kurad had loaded up Tyvig and headed down the road. Still they waited. The pair of them would be no match for a band of gnomes lying in wait to ambush them. In the moonlight, he could discern the wagons and the off-loaded weapons, but not much else, so he waited.

At last he saw what he was looking for and whistled low as he stood up and stepped into the clearing. Blue raised his head from his position next to the burned out campfire and looked up at Kurad, wagging his tail, not gaining his feet though he tried. His heart asked him to, but he was injured the same as his master. A couple of gnome arrows showed in the moonlight. Kurad ran to his side and bent low over his quivering form, rubbing his ears and talking quietly.

By morning they had loaded the last of the weapons back onto the wagon and were headed back down the mountain. Blue rode on the seat next to Kurad, his head on Kurad's lap and his wounds bandaged, waiting for the same healing hands his master had found.

Chapter Twenty Six

Edward trudged along in the middle of the pack of gnomes, a rope securely tied about his neck and then tied off at the other end around Yancik's waist. The prospect of escape seemed slim at best. If he tried to make a break for it, he would surely choke himself long before Yancik toppled to the ground. No, he decided, unless an opportunity presented itself he would remain tethered to his guardian for the duration of the trek.

The group had traveled for several days now and wasn't slowing their pace. They were focused on getting back to Orgle as fast as they could. Edward did what he could to delay the squad by running slower at times, although trussed as he was, there wasn't much opportunity. His efforts to engage Yancik in conversation were mostly for naught. His curiosity for where they were going and how long it would take went unanswered except that "he would know when he got there," according to Yancik.

Realizing as he jogged along that it had been more than a dozen years since he'd walked the halls of his family's castle. Was he going to remember his time there? At the moment, any details eluded him. He had been so young when Kurad spirited him away in the dead of night. Was there anything of theirs left in the castle? A painting perhaps, so that he could look upon their faces to help his lost memories come to the surface?

It saddened him to think about his losses, or maybe it was just the thought of what he missed or what could have been. It was best not to dwell on it too long. It was a completely different path than the life he had now. No, he had to amend that thought, as it was not entirely true. It would be best if he called it a slight detour. And now, after all these years, he was headed back towards the road he was always meant to travel. His had been a different life than what it would have been like growing up as the heir to the throne, but it was an experience that would surely help him if he regained his father's city and became king.

The miles disappeared under their feet and the days clicked by in Edward's head. Day followed night and night followed day as they jogged through the forests and down game trails, steadily making their way back to Edward's first home.

His count was seventeen days when they woke from the night's rest. The camp had a different feel on this morning. Barmes was excited and he barked his orders to break camp even louder than previous days. He came over to check on Edward first thing upon waking, making sure his prize was secured and ready for his unveiling to Orgle. Edward could only assume that today's march would be the last leg of the journey. He would finally get to meet his father's murderer, and if Kurad was right, he would also find Jessica and Helen.

These past days with no one to talk to while he ran, he had spent a fair amount of time thinking about the possibility of Kurad having misread the worth of the two women taken away so many months ago. It seemed like an extremely long time to have been held captive. Even if Orgle hadn't executed them, would they have had the strength to hold on? Edward could only hope they had found the strength within themselves to keep the flame of hope lit.

He was finally coming home and he was sure it was going to be quite an event. It wasn't exactly how he and Kurad had planned. It was to have been with an army of dwarves and men at his back, with Edward rallying his troops to conquer those who had unjustly taken what his people worked so hard to build. Edward realized he was still going to need an army, but just as important, he needed to figure out a way to stay alive long enough for Kurad to find the dwarves and convince them to attack a city defended by the very usurpers that had driven them out. He had to stop and wonder at the odds against them. It was then that the doubts he had been keeping at bay these past weeks surged up and took hold.

He replayed the scene of the attack in his mind. The last he had seen of Tyvig was him lying still in the snow, shot through with an arrow, and Kurad wasn't even in the vicinity. Kurad was an excellent tracker as Edward could personally attest, but how was he going to find an army of dwarves that were hidden in the mountains not wanting to be found? Tyvig was the key to finding them and now he was gone. For that matter, maybe Kurad had already come up against the gnomes who captured Edward and quite possibly been slain himself. Could that be why he had not received any sign from Kurad while they traveled through the mountains?

Without hope of finding the dwarves, he must surely be shadowing the band of gnomes, waiting for an opportunity to free Edward. Yet there had been nothing. No sign at all. How could he have not put the clues together? These revelations now creeping into his mind did little to lift his spirits and his confidence was eroding fast. By day's end he was, in all likelihood, going to be standing in front of Orgle, awaiting his own execution. Yancik yanked on Edward's rope to get him up and moving, tugging him from his thoughts realizing that he was terrified.

The day passed by quickly for Kurad, Willos, and Blosen as they drove the wagons down the mountain. By nightfall they made it back to the point where they split with Tyvig and the other dwarves. Willos took the lead and guided the wagons down a partially concealed trail that branched off from the main road. To the casual observer it would appear a game trail, but once through the brush at the entrance it widened out enough to accommodate the horse-drawn wagons. They went an hour further before Willos pulled up his team and began to clamber down.

"Leave the teams as they are. The others will watch over them and we will send help to care for them and unload the wagons." Willos instructed as he came over to stand next to Kurad's wagon. "Pass Blue down to me and please follow us." Even as tired as they were, Willos bore Blue's substantial weight with little effort as he headed down the trail.

Kurad hadn't seen any others as he pulled up on his team asking them to stop, yet he assumed he was being watched. Outsiders would be viewed with great skepticism until they were vetted and deemed trustworthy. The remnants of Pendar had been hiding for over a dozen years and their continued existence demanded strict adherence to the rules. Kurad would tread lightly.

Blosen fell in behind Kurad as the trio headed down the trail towards, what Kurad could only assume, was the entrance to the underground city. It wasn't long before they were challenged by the sentry guarding the entrance. Willos was recognized shortly and he vouched for Kurad before they were allowed to continue down into the caverns. The guards eyed Kurad in the torchlight as best they could as he went past, whispering amongst themselves after his passage. Kurad took note and quickly realized Willos was more than just a squad leader on patrol.

The pathways through the caves were well-lit by torches. Once they cleared the main entrance, word seemed to have spread quickly ahead of them as many inquisitive faces peered out at him from side passages. Kurad figured he must have been the only outsider, other than the incapacitated Tyvig, to travel these halls since the remnants had moved in. Kurad nodded to some, acknowledging their curiosity, but didn't attempt to speak to any of the curious on-lookers. Willos still led the trio though he had handed Blue off to another pair of dwarves as they entered the caverns. Kurad held his position ahead of Blosen and, though he never felt as if he was a prisoner being escorted, he understood their reservations. They continued through a maze of tunnels for nearly an hour before they came to a large assembly hall carved out of the rock. Ranking members were beginning to filter in and seat themselves.

Kurad had never spent any amount of time below the surface and his amazement at the size of the room was evident on his face.

"Welcome to our meeting hall," Willos turned and spoke directly to Kurad before turning back to the room and spreading his arms wide before him. "Our dwarf ancestors lived in this underground city many generations before we joined forces with our brothers from the surface. This city was my great-great-great, oh there's too many to count, but my many times over, great grandfather's boyhood home. They stayed here until the mines down below gave up the last of the ore and then they moved to the fortress that many believed was our last home before joining the Ellingstone nation. That is why Orgle could never find us even though we are still living less than a fortnight from his doorstep." He paused to let Kurad continue has scan of the room, his eyes finally coming to rest on Tyvig, propped up in a chair close to the center of the room.

"Do you mind if I go to speak with my friend Tyvig?" Kurad asked, not wanting to go against protocol.

"Follow me," Willos responded. "You are my guest here and I will vouch for you, but there may be many questions about your presence here." With that said he led Kurad to where Tyvig was sitting.

"You're looking good, old man," Tyvig said as Kurad came around the back of his chair to stand next to him. "What took you so long?" he said with a grimace, his wound causing him to wince.

"I was busy carting that mutt of yours to the doc." Kurad smiled as Tyvig's eyes lit up.

"His hide is no worse off than yours. Seems those gnome arrows aren't very lethal, but he'll be moving slow for a while. Probably perfect for you to take on walks." Kurad chuckled at his friend. He would recover just fine, though it would be a while before he was hammering out steel at his forge. They continued to talk until Willos came over and escorted Kurad to a seat in the front row of the meeting hall before climbing the few steps leading from the floor to the raised platform.

"Please be seated everyone," Willos called out. "We have much to discuss and a couple of guests with whom we need to speak. Not many of you had met Tyvig before his arrival and I believe he has spent most of his visit under the care of our doctors, but most assembled here today have used his weapons and armor. Tyvig," he said as he walked down the steps and over to the blacksmith extending a hand, "let me welcome you and extend a thank you from the entire nation for your fine work over the years. We are eternally grateful. Please, from this day forward, consider yourself one of us." There were shouts of approval as the two clasped one another's forearms in a clear sign of respect. When the room died down and Willos had returned to the platform he began to speak again.

"I would also like to introduce another to you all. He is a traveling companion and friend of Tyvig's. He was instrumental in getting Tyvig to us in time for our doctors to apply their healing hands. That, in part, was why I allowed him to enter our home." He stopped and motioned for Kurad to step forward and come up to stand next to him.

"I would like you to acknowledge Kurad, who makes the claim that he comes in service to Samuel Ellingstone." A low hum of whispers and mutterings went through the gathering as Kurad mounted the steps to stand next to Willos. Willos held up his hands asking for silence.

"Thank you for allowing me an audience, Willos." Kurad spoke directly to Willos. "And thanks to you all for accepting me into your home. I will get right to the point, as there is no time to waste.

"I know that it's been naught more than a dozen years since Orgle, with the aid of the trolls, breached your walls and forced you from Pendar. I look around and I remember some of your faces from his court and those that guarded his castle." There were a few more whispers, he continued on.

"My duties to Samuel required me to be invisible and to come and go as a shadow, to be seen yet unnoticed to even the most keen observer. It is the reason Samuel called me into service on the eve of that fateful day. The day so many years ago now when Orgle's army broke down the walls and murdered the royal family. It is the reason I stand before you today asking for your help by joining with me in battle against Orgle."

The crowd began to openly question Kurad at this juncture and even Willos standing next to him had a questioning look on his face. He held up his hands demanding silence, knowing Kurad had more to tell.

"It is not for me that I ask your help," Kurad continued after the voices in the room died down. "I ask it for Samuel. He left me with one task to accomplish should the worst befall him, as we now know that it did. There was one other in my party who traveled with Tyvig and me on our way to your home. The plan to bring him here was thrown off track when our group was attacked by a band of gnomes and he was taken captive." Kurad paused. The room was silent now.

"Kurad, you have spoken of this mysterious third person." Willos cut in, breaking the silence of the room. "Who is this man that we should come forth from hiding and engage in a battle we would be hard pressed to win?"

"Samuel's request was one of supreme sacrifice." Kurad began anew. "He feared what might happen when Orgle's army reached his walls, though they had never been breached. It was a different army than any he had faced. He asked me for one thing only, and that has been my singular focus leading to this day. It's why I came to the castle under cover of darkness that night and into Prince Edward's room. And why I had to make it appear as if he had been slain and his body taken away by enemies of the king." The tension was growing in the room, whispers gaining volume now, waiting for the fissure that would bust the dam open.

"The third person in our party, now in the hands of gnome raiders, is Prince Edward Ellingstone," he said, delivering the final blow. The room erupted, voices washing over anything else that Kurad could say. Kurad stood quietly next to Willos as the dwarf attempted to regain control of the room. Kurad was sure of only one thing at that moment: the remnants of Pendar would be going to war.

Chapter Twenty Seven

Apparently the whole city found out the prince was returning home, for there were more gnomes lining the streets than Edward believed to exist. He took it all in as he was brought in through the main gate, the gate still in disrepair from the day the trolls broke through. Though he was still tied to Yancik, he trailed Barmes and walked at the center of a protective phalanx. Barmes was taking no risk that Edward would escape and too that no power-seeking gnome would attempt to steal his prize. Orgle wanted the prince at his best and that meant he needed to be alive.

Barmes's patrol pushed through the crowd, spears lowered to keep the curious at a distance. The members of the patrol stood to gain nearly as much as Barmes and lashed out at more than a few who got too close. A few bloodied onlookers served well as warnings to others, the path to the castle opened before them.

They were met at the gates to the castle by Orgle's elite troops who, with the exception of Barmes and Yancik who both held Edward's rope, took over the escorting details. The rest of the patrol dropped back, following in the wake of Edward's new guardians. Edward remembered little of his time at the castle as a young boy, but the hallways they entered had a familiar feel to them. He could tell by looking at Barmes and Yancik that those two were now in unfamiliar territory. Much of their bravado on display out on the mountain was tempered as they looked about nervously.

The procession rolled on through the once majestic hallways leading to the throne room. As they continued on, fleeting memories flickered at his consciousness, only Edward remembered the hallways differently than what he saw now. Tapestries hung at odd angles on the walls and statues leaned precariously or had toppled and broken, the pieces pushed towards the wall only enough to clear a walking path. The scene convinced Edward that Orgle knew deep down this throne wasn't rightfully his and that his stay here was only temporary, until the rightful heir showed up to reclaim it.

It made sense now to Edward why Orgle had patrols combing the countryside searching for him. His own insecurities didn't allow him to take ownership. Edward would have to find a way to use this against Orgle, though his goal at the moment was to stay alive long enough to come up with a plan to escape with Jessica and Helen. Time was fleeting though. As they rounded a corner in the hall and marched through the throng of gnomes, he could make out the entrance to the throne room.

Barmes and Yancik held tight to Edward's rope. They would not relinquish their prize until Orgle knew exactly who it was that had brought the missing heir back home. The three were ushered to the foot of the steps leading to the throne and stood waiting for Orgle's arrival. All of them had very different thoughts going through their minds.

Yancik was on high alert, his muscles tense. It was his job to make sure Edward did not break free and attempt to escape, which was exactly what Edward was thinking while standing between his two captors. Still trussed as he had been for all those days on the trail, he calculated his odds of escape as he took in his surroundings. Barmes was on display with his chest puffed out, making sure everyone saw him. In one hand he held the end of Edward's rope, though it was all for show. Yancik was there to be the enforcer. In his other hand, he held Edward's battleaxe upright with the head resting on the floor, too heavy for him to hold aloft.

The room was buzzing with activity and speculation, the gnomes all jockeying for the best view and wanting to align themselves with Barmes. They knew he would be showered with praise and riches, his status in the room rose higher the longer they waited.

After what seemed an eternity to those gathered, especially the three up front, there was movement behind the throne. A gnome stepped out from behind the curtains to announce the imminent arrival of Orgle. The room settled down immediately. The long awaited hour of Prince Edward's reckoning was upon them. A grand spectacle was expected by all those gathered and Orgle was sure to impress the bloodthirsty throng.

Edward's attention was drawn to the throne. His family's murderer was about to reveal himself, and though he didn't have a good plan for escape, he welcomed the opportunity to look him in the eye and take his full measure. However, he wasn't prepared to see Helen and Jessica being ushered in ahead of Orgle. They were tied similarly as himself to an oversized gnome who grasped the rope and restricted them from running forward upon seeing Edward. He held his emotions in check though his fists clenched and his blood boiled seeing them trussed, wearing rags, and covered in filth. Before Edward could say anything to the women, Orgle strutted forth from behind the throne and stood glaring at the boy prince.

"So you have come home," Orgle began. "I knew someday you would return to pay your respects to your family and bemoan their most unfortunate accident." He smiled at his own mistruth, the audience of gnomes snickering at their leader's callousness.

"Accident you say?" Edward spoke through gritted teeth, staring directly into Orgle's eyes. "I'll remember that when I accidently remove your head from your shoulders."

"Young and foolish," Orgle chided. "You speak as if your fate has not already been determined. You evaded my blade the first time, but trust me when I tell you that that won't happen again. There will be no rescue in the middle of the night this time. No one will spirit you away and make me wait for my faithful to bring you back to face me again." Orgle was pacing back and forth in front of the women, his voice rising, forcing them to back up as he passed, fearing that he might lash out at them. His animated movements causing their guards to step back too.

"You should know your place, boy, and right now that should be on your knees bowing to the king!" He shouted the last word, clearly on the verge of losing control.

Edward suddenly found himself pitching forward onto his knees, feeling a sharp jab in the small of his back. Looking back from his kneeling position he saw Barmes pulling Edward's axe back to his side, a snarl on his lips. Edward snarled back, eliciting another jab from Barmes who was feeling pretty good about himself now that he had Orgle's attention. The axe caught Orgle's eye and Barmes's status was quickly knocked down a notch.

"Is that the boy's weapon?" Orgle asked, a gleam in his eye, as he motioned for Barmes to bring the axe to him. Barmes quickly stepped forward, extending the axe before him, its heaviness causing him to struggle with it at arm's length. Orgle grabbed it from Barmes and gave him a dismissing look as he turned back towards his throne attempting to disguise the effort required to handle it.

Climbing the steps to the throne, his back to the gathered mob, he admired the craftsmanship and the detail on the impressive piece of steel. Turning, he sat on the throne, cradling the axe on his lap, still unable to take his eyes away from the weapon. As he studied the axe, he noticed a space between the blades in the center of the crest that decorated the head. It appeared as if it had housed a stone at one time or maybe waited for one to be mated to it. The shape reminded him of a stone that he held in his possession. He would have to find it and get it reset by one of his dwarf slaves. He would never trust it to one of his gnomes. This would be his new scepter, the symbol of his power and position.

"Take him to the dungeons and keep him guarded day and night. I'll call for him when I've got all the arrangements made." He did not take his eyes from the axe. He would spill the boy's blood with this very blade. The bloodline would finally be severed, but not until the axe was properly adorned.

Edward realized he had been granted more time, but his odds weren't increasing by much. He still hoped that through some miracle Kurad would come to his aid, even if that seemed as unlikely as him surviving his next encounter with Orgle. Edward was alone and he would have to put all of Kurad's lessons into action to come up with a way out.

Yancik and Barmes finally surrendered Edward's tether to the gnome king's guards. They didn't want to get anywhere near the dungeons where their charge was going, too many of their own never came back from there. Orgle's personal attendant Kropett came forward to lead Edward and his new keepers into the depths of the dungeons. Edward watched his cautious approach. He was treating Edward as if he were a wild animal, not wanting to get to near at first but then suddenly stepping in close, touching Edward lightly on the forearm.

Very curious behavior was Edward's first thought, being touched by this gnome who was clearly afraid of him. He looked again at the gnome, trying to see his hand. The gnome must have been wearing a ring or something on its hand. It felt like he had been scratched in that brief touch.

It was then that Edward felt the warmth spreading up his arm. He pulled back reflexively, trying to avoid the heat as it climbed toward his shoulder. His guards thought he was trying to escape their grasp and grabbed his ropes tighter, yanking him off balance. He stumbled, regaining his footing after a couple faltering steps. Edward looked over to Orgle's lackey who once again walked at a safe distance off to the side. He was smiling at Edward's reaction to the poison he had just injected him with.

In moments his entire body was engulfed in this internal fire coursing through his veins. His vision began to blur as he stumbled on shaky legs, unable to see where they were taking him. For a moment he thought he heard either Jessica or Helen call out to him. It was a female's voice, though he couldn't make out what was said before he collapsed into the darkness, the poison taking away his ability to remain upright.

Jessica and Helen watched as Edward was carried away by the arms, slumping between his guards as they struggled to keep him from sprawling on the floor. They were confused initially, settling down after Kropett talked to them, then he disappeared from sight down the hall leading to the dungeons. Jessica knew that hall by heart, walking it every day for months.

She couldn't believe her eyes when she first saw him standing there. After all these months of waiting and hoping for him to come to their rescue, seeing him in the flesh had nearly caused her to collapse. Then, just as suddenly, she watched him being dragged away, stumbling and shaking his head as if possessed, only to collapse himself. Poisoned she deduced. He had to have been given a drug to make him act so erratic. Just then the women's guard prodded them to start moving and soon they too were following the path Edward had taken. He was gone from view as they headed towards their cell, but Jessica took comfort that he was here with them now. She was sure that the news of his arrival had already spread throughout the city and the army she had assembled right under Orgle's watchful eye would be mobilizing.

Troy A. Skog

Chapter Twenty Eight

Although Kurad pushed the pace, it was still difficult to move a small army through caverns and underground trails with anything resembling speed. The pace allowing him extra time to plan the invasion of Orgle's castle. The army of remnants he led was smaller than he had hoped. Many women, children, and the elderly had escaped from Pendar a dozen years ago, but the number of warriors that had fled was disheartening.

It didn't take him long to determine that the best way to slay the beast was to remove its head and that meant he was going to have to confront Orgle. He was outnumbered, or at least he assumed he would be, so it was going to have to be a precise attack. Get to Orgle, remove him from power, and hope his army would collapse and scatter enough for Kurad to battle small pockets instead of a unified front. He had a plan, but he needed to talk to Willos tonight when they stopped to rest the army.

The army of remnants pushed on through the tunnels by torchlight. Soon they would surface from the underground trails and then they would have to conceal their presence from gnome outposts and scouts. The element of surprise was Kurad's only hope. Reports of an army comprised of Pendar's remnants moving on the city would be cause for alarm.

At the end of the day's march, the army came into a large cavern. They were met by advance scouts who reported the entrance portal was just ahead and they would emerge from the tunnels on their next march. Kurad found Willos and together they rounded up the squad leaders to begin the next phase of the trek.

Once the squad leaders settled into a smaller chamber off to the side of the greater entry cavern, Kurad began to lay out his plans.

"The first thing I need to know is if it's night or day," he began, looking around the room for a little help.

"The sun is just now setting," was the response from a dwarf seated at the back of the group.

"Thanks. I'm not sure how you know these things when we haven't been above ground for longer than I care to think about." His tone was relaxed, but inside he was growing anxious from lack of sun and open spaces.

"I've done a lot of thinking on our trek so far, and Willos and I have come up with a plan that hopefully will find us successful." He needed to include Willos so that he could further build his trust level with this army. They would not follow where he needed to go unless they bought in.

"I will lead an advance scouting party that will leave here in six hours, enough time to get a bite to eat and rest our legs." He didn't know yet who Willos had tapped for this assignment, but pushed on explaining the plan with all the squad leaders listening attentively.

"We're going to blaze the trail to the castle. Our goal is threefold. The first is to eliminate any gnome patrols that the army, under Willos's command, may encounter. Moving an army of this size on the surface will draw attention, but if we can reduce the number of patrols we will allow ourselves to get a lot closer before we're detected. The less time Orgle has to prepare, the better off we'll be when we arrive at his front door.

The second goal of the advance team is to locate Edward wherever he is being kept and secure him. Lastly, and I don't want to put less importance on this aspect, I want to sever the head of the gnome army. We need to remove Orgle as the sitting king in the castle. I'm convinced the rest of the gnomes will scatter if he's eliminated." He wasn't ready for the cheer that went up from the squad leaders at the end of his plan, but he smiled inside.

"I have a question, Sir Kurad," spoke a voice from up front. The man stood to be recognized.

"I am Christopher, leader of the Fox Company. How is it that you believe the prince is still alive and that we can rescue him? His captors could surely travel faster than our army has navigated the halls of our dwarf brother's ancestors. He will have been in Orgle's clutches for at least a handful of days." There were murmurs of agreement amongst those assembled.

"To tell you the truth," he paused and looked around at those assembled. "I don't know for sure. I just have a feeling in my heart that he has to be still alive. From the day he was born, and I believe from even before his birth, he was destined to lead this nation. I can't explain it other than that.

We have been through much together and have grown to know each other's thoughts and feel each other's emotions. I believe I would know if he had been slain, and until that feeling of doom washes over me, I will presume no other possibility." The chamber was quiet. Many nodded, accepting the answer. They were a very spiritual people and believed strongly in the bond that developed between individuals who worked and trained together.

Willos broke the silence. "Christopher, you'll be taking your squad of men and accompanying Kurad when he leaves before first light. Have your men pack light because you'll be moving fast and we will be bringing the rest of your gear with the main body. Standard weapon issues: swords, bows with plenty of arrows. You'll be on your own for several days and I guarantee you will meet resistance. Kurad is in command of this operation, but he will be leaning on you to have your men ready at all times. Take leave now from this meeting and go prepare your men for what's to come. I'm picking your squad because I'm expecting them to deliver on their namesake, the Fox Company; speed, stealth and just a little bite." He smiled at Christopher. It was a proud unit and they were just as skilled as he declared.

Christopher nodded his acceptance and bowed as he turned and left the assembly, more than a little proud of his unit's reputation. He had just the right amount of nervousness about the task ahead to push his men to meet and exceed those expectations.

The remaining squad leaders listened as Willos and Kurad laid out the plans to attack the city. This would be the last time Kurad would have their ear to communicate what he anticipated they would find. He needed to know as precisely as possible when to expect them to arrive at the city and what they planned to be doing at all times. His plans, along with Fox Company's, however would be an exercise in adjustments and reactions to what they encountered once they infiltrated the castle. The meeting adjourned and they all scattered back to their troops to brief them on the plan and let them know their assignments.

Kurad headed towards the entrance to the labyrinth, settling in to get some shut-eye before he led his men to the surface to begin the last leg of this journey to bring Edward's army home.

He fell asleep remembering bits and pieces of the journey. There had not been a shortage of good times. And then Christopher was nudging him gently, asking that he wake from his slumber.

"Sir Kurad, it is the time you requested. We should go now if we want to use the darkness. My men are ready." Christopher spoke softly as he knelt next to Kurad.

Kurad nodded and thanked him for waking him. He stood slowly, gathering up his gear as he rose, everything settling into its place by the time he stood. The Fox Company was already up and out of the cavern, deployed in a defensive alignment, eyes probing the darkness that surrounded them, when Kurad emerged. He nodded his approval as they moved off ahead of him into the night.

Edward shook his head. The cobwebs were refusing to let go and he was drifting in and out of consciousness. He wasn't sure if it was dark wherever he was or if he was still in some sort of dreamscape; in the darkness between the scenes that played out in his mind. The cycle had been repeating itself for untold hours or even days. Confusion was his only constant. There were glimpses in his mind of Orgle standing above him, leering down at him, with Edward's axe ready to fall. Then running through the castle hallways as a child, a little friend in tow, looking for the Black Knight. There was even a brief appearance of a rock that moved and talked though he couldn't understand what the rock was saying. Always a period of darkness would take over and he would lose all awareness around him only to stubbornly drag himself once again towards coherence before he toppled off the ledge into the abyss to begin the cycle anew.

It was during a brief period of awareness that a voice spoke to him from somewhere behind him. The sound was different, and after questioning whether he was dreaming again, he responded tentatively.

"I'm awake or at least I think I am. Who am I speaking to?" He asked, turning slowly, reaching out into the darkness to feel for whoever had spoken his name. He expected to make contact, but only touched cold, damp stone.

"King Edward," the speaker began. "I am pleased that you are awake and aware. It has been nearly a week since you were taken below ground to your cell. My name is Konterra and I am a dwarf in your army. Well, until you arrived, it was your wife's army."

"Wait a minute," Edward interrupted. "Do you speak of Jessica? She is not yet my wife, but I can think of no other within the city who would fit that description. Is she alright?"

"Yes, Your Highness. She is being held in her cell with her mother though now they are not brought out every day to work in the fields or the kitchen. Orgle is taking extra precautions to keep her isolated from the rest of her army. We must not talk long. Your guard is only away from your door momentarily, responding to a diversion in the next corridor. My only word of caution to you is this: you must no longer eat the food that your guard provides you. They continue to drug your meals. Those in service to you will supply you with your food and drink. Prepare yourself for escape, we are only days away now."

The voice went quiet and Edward heard shuffling in the hall outside his cell. There was a brief moment of muted light that spilled into his world as the guard peered through the meal slot to check on his charge. Edward held still, scanning the cell quickly with his eyes to learn as much as he could about his current surroundings before it all went black again. It wasn't a big cell so it was easy to see the extent of the space he had in which to move about. In that brief moment of light, he spotted a raised pallet in front of him, immediately moving to climb onto it. The floor was beyond filthy and the thought that he had been laying on it for days nearly made him retch. There was a waste bucket near the door and a pile of half eaten meals just inside the door.

Now that he regained his faculties and had some knowledge of his immediate surroundings, he took a moment to consider what he knew of his situation. Jessica and Helen were still alive and, from what he could tell, still in good health. Konterra's statement about her army was both encouraging and confusing, and the comment about Jessica being his wife had caught him completely off guard. The army and the upcoming battle was the immediate concern. Everything else could wait until he regained his father's throne.

Regaining his father's throne suddenly seemed more plausible. Of course, he had no idea of the size and ability of Jessica's army, but that there was organization amongst those here within the very walls of the castle gave him hope. Kurad's unknown status gave him pause. The man had not shown himself during Edward's entire journey under Barmes's escort. It was unlike him to have abandoned Edward after all these years. Something must have befallen him, though in his heart he felt no sense of loss like he thought he would. He didn't want to dwell on Kurad's fate for long, for the thought of him being injured or even slain was more than he could consider. No matter the situation, Edward could only plan on using the resources he had at hand within the castle. He would find Kurad and do right by him no matter what, after he settled things with Orgle.

The food slot opened and more food was dumped through the opening, landing on the ever-growing pile below. He would wait until Konterra provided him a meal he could safely eat. Until then he would wait, rest, and plan for that which came next.

Chapter Twenty Nine

A tap at the back wall of his cell woke Edward from his slumber. He must have dozed off while awaiting contact from Konterra. He sat up, rubbing at the cramped muscles, aching from lying on the hard wooden pallet. It was better than the floor but still bone chilling. Moving cautiously, he slid off the pallet and felt blindly for the source of the tapping. It took a moment of feeling about, moving closer to the tapping noise, before his fingers felt the opening in the wall.

"Good day, your Highness," the voice spoke softly. "This is Konterra again. I hope your rest was more peaceful now that your mind has cleared from Orgle's taint. I am going to reach your meal through this hole. Be careful not to drop it, we are sharing my rations and I would rather not go hungry tonight."

Edward felt a piece of hard bread being pressed into his waiting hand from beyond the wall.

"Thank you for being so generous with your already sparse fare." Edward spoke as he took a bite of the stale bread. Even though it was tough he ripped off a piece, chewing and swallowing it quickly, realizing for the first time just how hungry he was. Apparently he hadn't eaten many of the drugged meals Orgle had supplied.

"When you have finished, I have a small cup with water for you to wash it down." Konterra spoke from the far side of the wall.

"Again, I thank you for sharing your drink and bread." Edward drank the cup dry and returned it to the hole in the wall.

"It is an honor to be able to aid the king in these last days before you follow your father's path and take your rightful place upon the throne." Konterra spoke with respect.

"I am not really used to all this 'King' talk," Edward said, feeling truly awkward about how to speak to Konterra. "I am just a man, though I still feel no more than a boy. Please though, let's not worry about all the 'Your Highnesses' and King talk. I will not feel disrespected. Agreed?" Stating, not asking, Edward didn't wait for an answer.

"I expect there is a plan to free me from my cell so we can remove Orgle from the throne and you can reunite me with Jessica and Helen."

"There is a plan, Your High... I mean Edward," Konterra spoke, catching and correcting himself. "We are all set to disrupt your execution."

"Hey, wait a minute," Edward interrupted. "I would rather not be anywhere near an execution. How about we just break me out now and not wait until Orgle has me trussed up with my head on the chopping block?" Edward got a little loud before he reined himself in. The guard outside his door heard him and banged a couple times, shouting for him to quiet down and quit talking to imaginary creatures again.

"Sorry, Konterra," Edward whispered. "It's just not what I was expecting. I envisioned a scenario where, I don't know, I would be marching up to Orgle with an army of dwarves and men at my back and...." his voice trailed off. Upon speaking his plan aloud, he realized it was probably no more likely to succeed than what Konterra was proposing. "Again, I apologize. I'm sure your plan has been well thought through."

"I do not doubt that you are nervous about our plan. I would rather expect you to be. We have considered many options, including breaking you free from your cell. However, we would not be able to bring enough warriors into the dungeons to protect you. As soon as we started breaking out of our cells the guards would fall back to secure you and we would never get enough of us close to you to succeed. I am only one of a handful of prisoners in this part of the dungeon. It was not easy getting this close to you this time, but I gave Orgle a reason to separate me from the rest of my brethren." Konterra stopped speaking abruptly, something clearly left unsaid.

Edward was curious and waited for Konterra to continue, but when he didn't explain, Edward chose not to push him on the matter. He figured that if it was crucial to the escape, it would come out before tomorrow. There were other details Edward needed to know and he focused his attention on those.

"So we've established that I will be the centerpiece to the ceremony. At what point in time will I be whisked away to safety?" Edward was still uncomfortable with the portion of the plan he knew so far and hoped more details would put his mind at ease.

"Orgle is planning quite a spectacle with all his high-ranking officers and many of his troops in attendance. He wants everyone to see him bring the Ellingstone name to an end. Bringing everyone out will be his undoing, for he has also mandated that all those enslaved to the crown be there to witness the event." Konterra paused to let that sink in and Edward immediately put it together, his hopes rising. He continued on, giving Edward the basics of the plan and how they hoped it would play out. There was risk to them all, but they were willing.

They talked for quite a while. Konterra growing concerned that they would be found out if they talked much longer, brought the conversation to an end. "The time for talking and planning has passed. I will tell you to sleep well, my King. Tomorrow is the ceremony and you must be in top form."

It went quiet in the cell except for a slight scraping noise as the block that Konterra used to conceal the hole in the wall slid back into place. Edward sat back on his pallet pondering what Konterra had outlined. He'd hoped he would be free from his cell already. The waiting was the worst part. He felt he would burst if he were to spend much more time sitting around, pondering his fate.

Edward figured it would be morning before Konterra reached out again. Doing as Konterra suggested, he lay down to rest. His residual questions about the plan kept him awake for quite some time until he fell asleep eventually, unanswered questions still floating about in his mind.

"Have they heard any news about Edward?" Helen asked Jessica when she came back from speaking quietly with someone through the window in the door and sat back down next to her on the pallet.

"Konterra has made contact with him," Jessica whispered to her mother. "Edward is no longer under the spell of Orgle's poison and for that we can be most grateful. I was beginning to worry he would not regain his senses until it was too late." She didn't need to explain what that meant. Everyone in the castle was aware of the plan to execute Edward along with several other criminals deemed a danger to Orgle's rule.

"I can only hope Konterra will not forfeit his life for positioning himself so close to Edward." She paused for a moment before continuing. "Of course, if the plan doesn't work Edward will have given his life as well. It is going to require a herculean effort by our army, even then, success or failure will rest in the hands of fate."

Success was a long shot at best and she suspected she and her mother would have front row seats to the spectacle at the very least, and more than likely, an honored spot alongside Edward, Konterra, and any others slated for execution. It wasn't what she wanted to think about as the two laid down next to one another to sleep on the pallet as they had done for countless nights before.

"We shall only have tonight here in our cell, Mother. After that, I cannot say what fate has in store for us. I do know that I won't miss this place."

Helen was quiet. The whole experience of being in captivity had completely exhausted her and left her with limited reserves. Jessica hoped her mother would sleep well, though she knew sleep would be hard to find for any of them tonight.

That night, as the sun was beginning to set, Kurad and his band of scouts began to reassemble. They spread out after spending the afternoon hours resting, hidden in the brush. Now they gathered around Kurad and Christopher as the two made the plans for the night. Christopher did a quick head count and nodded to Kurad to begin the briefing.

Kurad spoke in hushed tones. "We have not encountered any resistance up until this point, but I have to believe that will change very soon. Our plans have us moving within the city walls tonight and Orgle will have scouting parties out in full strength. He has a valuable asset in his grasp and will not risk losing him to an attempt such as the one we are undertaking. It is my belief that we have not run into any far-ranging patrols because he is concentrating his forces in a tight ring around the city; a ring he hopes is so tight none can slip through." Kurad paused, watching his words sink in. "I'm going to take point from here on in. We want to avoid any contact with outposts that could raise an alarm. We will move as a group around any obstacles we come across. However, if we accidently come into contact with the enemy, it is imperative that we silence their alarm instantly."

He looked around at the assembled squad. They were excellent trackers and moved across the landscape without stirring a leaf better than any he had seen. Now he was asking, demanding, that should the need arise they engage and kill the enemy. They were effectively declaring war on Orgle and it was imperative that the men move forward only after they had the proper mindset.

Looking into the eyes of each and every one of them the men nodded their acknowledgement. Kurad hoped they would not encounter resistance tonight and that dawn would find them within striking distance of Orgle but he was also keenly aware that what one hoped for and what actually happened could be entirely different. The odds of avoiding detection were not in their favor tonight. There was a good chance of bloodshed before dawn and it pained him to think that some of those gathered about him now might not see the morning sun. Kurad knew he wasn't the first commander to fret about the wellbeing and fate of the men they led into battle, yet those assembled before him were his responsibility and he wasn't taking that lightly. Kurad dismissed them, announcing that they would leave at dusk and should reassemble at that time prepared for a long tough, run to the castle.

Christopher stayed behind as the men briefly dispersed to tend to their personal needs. "How far behind us do you think Willos and the rest of the army are tonight?"

"Once above ground, I'm sure they will pick up the pace. We have marked the route well and there has been no sign of any gnome patrols. Willos will surely have scouts probing the route just in case any gnomes cross their path but I know he will be pressing them to make good time. I would say probably no more than three," Kurad responded confidently.

"We are on our own then," Christopher stated somewhat apprehensively. "The Fox Company will be hard pressed to hold out for three days should we get pinned down rescuing Edward."

"Our goal is to strike fast and move quickly once we have Edward free from his captors. I'm not sure how much I should be counting on for help from within. Hopefully there will be some sort of an uprising amongst those who remain enslaved to add to the confusion. We just need to get clear of the castle, away from Orgle's troops, and find a place to hole up until Willos arrives with the army."

Kurad remembered back to his reconnaissance soon after the fall of Samuel. Was the message he delivered in the dark of night to the lone dwarf passed on? He wasn't sure anymore if the count was right, twelve years and seventy-three days. That was less important than having the army within the city walls and ready. Kurad left it at that. He didn't have details to share with Christopher, and the leader of Fox Company needed to believe they were completely on their own and make decisions independently.

It wasn't long before the men had gathered about again so Christopher was able to pass on the last of Kurad's instructions. Kurad was the picture of calm as he gave them the signal to head out and proceeded to lead them into the growing darkness, though inside he knew that there were too many unanswered questions about this last bit of his mission. The morning would provide him with a clearer picture of the obstacles stacked against him in his effort to free Edward. Right now his focus was on watching over the men of Fox Company, a wave of shadows passing through the night following in his lethal wake.

There was a reason King Samuel had called upon his friend and entrusted the wellbeing of his son to this man. It was a skill set; an ability to survive that had kept him alive living alone in a hostile environment on the open road. Samuel had known no other man as dangerous as Kurad and in his mind that meant no harm could ever befall Edward. It was this Kurad, dormant these past twelve years while he raised Edward to manhood, which was now unleashed. Orgle had reason to fear losing Edward. He needed to fear his rescuer even more.

Chapter Thirty

Kurad led the Fox Company towards the city, all the members falling into line, keeping their gaps, not lagging, Kurad wanting to move fast until he got in close to the city. Orgle would have the majority of his soldiers located in tight groups around the perimeter. That meant fewer troops out patrolling the woods. Kurad intended to turn Orgle's tactics against him. They were all running now, keeping to Kurad's trail as he sped through the woods. Kurad had crossed a game trail that trended toward the city and he put it to use to help speed up his band of men.

Three miles passed beneath their feet as they cruised along the game trail when Kurad suddenly came to stop. The men behind him ducked off the trail to find cover as the message was passed backward. Kurad crouched silently at the side of the trail. A noise, a branch breaking ahead of him, had reached his ears. He needed to determine its source before he led his men forward. He signaled Christopher, who was next in line, to remain where he was and began to work his way up the trail. It was the most exposed route, also be the quietest. He knew there was something ahead in the woods, although whatever it was wasn't concerned with him at the moment. The rustling of branches continued.

He crept forward in the nearly complete darkness. It was a clear night. Only a crescent moon overhead provided him with light. The sounds were louder as he got closer. He couldn't have gone more than fifty yards, though it felt like an eternity as he crawled along the trail. He froze in place when he finally identified a voice amongst the sounds of movement through the brush. He couldn't understand what was being said although he was confident the speaker was a gnome. Kurad sat motionless as the sounds increased in volume, his senses reaching out, trying to determine their path.

There was definitely more than a few and his guess would put it closer to twenty than a dozen by the amount of noise they were making. In the open, he carefully slid over to find concealment in the brush. The sounds of their passing indicated that were still coming towards him. Kurad crouched in the shadows; he was running out of time. He had to decide if their course would bring them up against the Fox Company. Another series of sounds told him what he needed to know. It was time to go. They were on the same path as his men and would cross in front of him in no more than a twenty count.

Kurad rose from his position. Christopher and his men needed to clear the trail. It was the slightest swish of a leaf that froze him in place. An advance scout for the gnomes, the sound of his movements masked by the others behind, was no more than three paces from Kurad and bearing down on his position. There was no time for thought as Kurad reacted, his weapon drawn as he slid from his position of concealment. The eyes of the gnome grew large at the suddenness of the confrontation. Though the gnome tried to call out a warning, Kurad clamped a hand over his mouth as he simultaneously spun around behind him, driving his knife into the scout's chest. The scout was still fighting against Kurad's grasp as he was pulled from the trail into the darkness, his life blood flowing freely over the handle of the weapon. Kurad left the body a handful of paces off to the side of the trail, and after a quick check for signs of alarm, rushed back toward Christopher and the men awaiting his return.

He covered the ground quickly, slowing as he approached Christopher's last known position and finally stopped, calling quietly for him to reveal himself.

"We need to get off the trail," Kurad spoke through labored breaths as soon as Christopher stepped out. "There is a squad of gnomes coming towards us on this very trail, their numbers likely higher than our own. I've eliminated their scout. I didn't have a choice, hopefully they won't realize his absence until they are past."

"I will pass the word. You said 'until they are past' so the order should be not to engage unless we are discovered?" It was a question from Christopher, mostly so that there was no confusion on Kurad's intent. A quick nod from Kurad sent Christopher down the trail to pass along the message to the rest of the men.

Kurad turned and looked back the direction he had come. There were no calls of alarm so the scout's absence had gone undetected. He moved off to the side of the trail. They would have to wait this out.

If the gnomes passed, oblivious to the presence of Fox Company, they would be able to move forward with greater speed. However, if they were discovered, a skirmish was unavoidable. Kurad had to trust that the men would use their woodcraft to disappear into the brush and hold their positions until the threat was passed. They were too far away from the city to engage the gnomes. Secrecy was his best chance of gaining the city walls by the morning light.

He knew that he'd had to kill the scout to avoid having him sound the alarm, but he second-guessed his actions leading up to the moment of discovery. Should he have moved back to the men sooner so that they could have hidden from the gnome patrol? Would the risk of discovery have been reduced? No, he thought, he couldn't change what had happened, so he had to wait and hope the gnomes moved passed and beyond before they discovered that their scout was missing.

The main body of gnomes was soon passing Kurad's position as he sat motionless, deep in the shadows of the concealing foliage. He counted twenty-five gnomes spaced no more than a step or two apart and clearly not disciplined in the type of duty they were supposed to be performing. There was no apparent concern for stealth as they talked amongst themselves, not loudly, yet in the relative quiet of the surrounding forest, they might as well have been shouting. He knew these next moments would be most critical. Kurad needed the last gnome to pass all of his men so they could put distance between them and the patrol. He sat in silence, ears straining to gauge the distance they had covered. Were they clear of his men yet?

The answer came almost immediately. Calls from the squad leader brought the gnomes to a quick halt. There was a commotion as they bunched up and orders were barked out. Kurad's men hadn't been found yet but that discovery was imminent. Kurad moved quickly back down the trail, drawing his sword as he went. He would be needed at the point of attack the moment the alarm was sounded. As he moved down the trail he began to collect men of the Fox Company coming out from their positions to fall in behind him. He wouldn't be alone when he caught up to the gnomes.

Kurad and his men slowed as they approached the noise ahead. The gnomes had stopped moving forward, bunched up on the trail and squatting in an attempt to hide their presence, but not looking for cover. The gnome in charge barked out some orders, incomprehensible to Kurad and his men, sending several gnomes at the back of the line to retrace their steps in an effort to locate the missing scout.

His hand was being forced and Kurad responded by arranging his men on both sides of the trail. He ordered the men to let the gnomes pass if they weren't detected and then a few of the men were to follow and dispatch them, letting no gnome rejoin the main group or escape back toward the city. The rest of Fox Company would move on the main body of gnomes and attack once the alarm was sounded from behind.

Kurad had no way to communicate with the handful of men that were now isolated beyond the gnome squad. He could only hope that they were interpreting the situation as he was and would be in a position to attack. The gnomes missed Kurad and his men as they went past and were quickly followed by the men Kurad had tasked to take care of them. The remaining men followed in Kurad's wake, closing on the main body of gnomes, hoping to catch them off guard and confused as they reacted to the noises coming from the skirmish back down the trail.

Shouts of alarm from the five that had gone in search of the missing scout were the cue Kurad and his men had been waiting for. They immediately charged the main body of gnomes, who were frozen in place as they tried to interpret the cries of alarm. Kurad had only a handful of men to bring against them from his side, but they quickly began to even the playing field as the element of surprise tipped the initial battle in their favor.

The tight quarters of the game trail meant gnomes could not react in force against their attackers, but it also limited the number of men who could engage the enemy. The challenge of the confines of the terrain quickly became evident and several of the men moved to position themselves in order to loose arrows into the confused throng. It was a disjointed attack and the men had to take care not to hit one of their own. By shifting into the woods to flank the gnomes bottled up on the trail, they caught them in a devastating crossfire. From the sounds of it, the men trapped on the far side of the gnome squad had joined in the melee, effectively pinning the enemy down and forcing them to fight where they stood. Kurad directed his makeshift archer detail to make sure that none escaped into the brush. They would be difficult to track once they got clear of his men.

The attack continued for several chaotic minutes before the majority of the overmatched gnomes had been cut down by sword or arrow. Kurad shouted orders for his men to give chase of the few that had eluded them. Hopefully he could account for them all, but without an accurate count prior to the skirmish it was difficult to know with certainty that none had escaped. When the men that had given chase returned to the scene, Christopher helped him to get a head count of the members of the Fox Company. All were accounted for, though some had suffered cuts and scrapes.

Kurad was impressed with the results. The men had effectively engaged and eliminated a force twice their size with no more than a makeshift plan thrown together moments before they attacked. The only wild card now was whether or not any gnomes had escaped to carry word of their whereabouts back to Orgle. They had lost valuable time by standing and fighting. Luckily Kurad had not lost any men and because of that, felt it was a fair trade. The schedule had just gotten tighter and if they hoped to reach the city by dawn he was going to have to push the pace. He had to hope that they had eliminated the only patrol in this area and that the way was clear for at least the immediate future. It was with these thoughts on his mind that Kurad called the men together and quickly briefed them on the rapidly evolving situation before moving out.

The Fox Company followed Kurad off into the night. He pushed the pace as fast as he thought they could maintain. A few of the men wore bandages though none lagged or caused the others to be burdened by their injuries, and not one complaint crossed any of their lips. Kurad had had his reservations before they engaged the gnomes. Their woodcraft left him without any worries about their ability to reach the city if they encountered resistance, and flush from the rush of battle, he also had confidence that they would more than hold their own in battle.

The ground disappeared beneath their feet as they maintained the pace Kurad set and every step they took got them closer to the city. The moon was moving across the sky as the time slipped away. Would they make it before the sun started to rise? The pace quickened. If they didn't reach the city before the sun rose they would have to camp outside the city, losing an entire day. They pushed hard into the night. There was no sign of gnomes on the trail and Kurad began to regain his confidence in the mission. They needed a rest so when he came across a small clearing he pulled up and waited for the men to gather about.

"Take a few moments to catch your breath and sip some water from your water skins. We still have a little ways to go but we're getting close." Kurad was encouraged now that they had closed the gap to the city.

"We're going to slow the pace. The area will become more populated with gnomes the closer we get. After you catch your breath, we'll get moving again. Stay on high alert; we're not going to want to make contact at this point. That would bring the entire gnome army out from the city." He paused, a thought crossing his mind, briefly entertaining the idea of creating a diversion or making a small group of themselves known to draw the enemy away from the prince.

"What if we did get the army out of the city, or we created a diversion that would get them looking to the East as we approached from the West?" His sixth sense kicked in as he considered the change in plan and he stopped immediately. He wasn't sure what it was, but he knew that ignoring the warning was dangerous. There was no way to explain the feeling he had in the pit of his stomach or the hair raising on the back of his neck. All he knew was that it was never a good idea to ignore the signs. He could figure out the reason later.

"Get your gear ready. We need to push off in a candle mark. We go in as a group to secure Prince Edward."

Once again the men followed Kurad into the night, though now the pace was slower and the all their senses were on the highest alert. These next few miles would determine their success or failure on this night. There was plenty of cover for the men to use as concealment as they quickly reached the edge of the forest just outside the city walls. Kurad had chosen this route from his last visit and knew he was on target when they passed the little barn in the woods that he had used to hide Edward when he last scaled the city walls.

The wall was a short distance from the woods and the position of the guard towers would enable his team to reach the wall undetected. The defense of the city depended upon dedicated soldiers patrolling the walkways atop the outer walls, watching the dark for shadows. Orgle had precious few of those soldiers.

Kurad brought them to a halt just within the border of the trees. They had seen a squad of gnomes just past the old barn but the gnomes had not noticed their passing and no alarm had been sounded. Squatting in the shadows they watched the pattern of the patrols atop the walls as they walked to and fro. Orgle must have ordered more soldiers to walk the walls. There were fewer gaps now compared to years ago. The task of getting a dozen men into the city just became more difficult. Kurad instructed two men to continue watching the walls and brought the remaining men back a short distance into the woods.

"We have a slight problem," he began in a quiet whisper. "Orgle has increased his patrols. It's time for some diversionary tactics."

"I need a couple archers to position themselves at the forest edge a hundred yards down from us. As soon as you set up, we'll be waiting on your signal. Begin targeting gnomes walking the parapet. You'll have a moment or two before the alarm sounds and then you'll have to take flight. My hope is to draw those watching our stretch of wall towards you, effectively clearing a path for the rest of us to cross the open ground between the trees and the wall and get us into the city." Time was running short before the sky would start to lighten as dawn approached, so there wasn't much time for discussion.

Christopher pointed to two men. "Austin, James, take care of yourselves. Get clear as soon as you can and meet up with Willos and the army as soon as you can." The pair turned and were gone without another word. Christopher nodded to Kurad, confident the deed would be done as Kurad had instructed.

The remaining men adjusted their gear. They would need to be quick across the clearing to get up and over the wall. There would not be another chance after Austin and James had to take flight and there would be a large number of gnomes searching the woods for the assassins. Initially, the thought was that Austin and James had been assigned a suicide mission, but

245

those remaining with Kurad soon came to the realization that it could actually be they who faced the longest odds.

They quickly made their way back to the men positioned at the edge of the woods who had been left to keep watch of the gnomes on the wall, briefing them of the plan so that they too were prepared to scale the stones as soon as Kurad gave the signal to go. And there they waited. Austin and James would need a minute or two to get into position and determine the best targets that would cause the others around them to react and sound the alarm. Then they would take a couple more targets of opportunity for good measure.

The men were growing nervous as the minutes slipped by, anxious to get across the open space undetected. More so about whether or not the two archers would be able to safely slip away into the night avoiding capture. All of a sudden, the time for being nervous was gone as gnomes atop the wall began to shout. Though the members of Fox Company had no idea what was said, they were confident of what or rather who had caused the alarm. Together they watched expectantly as gnome soldiers began to react to the calls of those under attack, streaming down towards the fallen sentries, leaving their posts unmanned and the walls unguarded.

Kurad barely waited until the guards began to run towards their comrades before he rushed out across the open field, leading Christopher and the rest towards the wall. Reaching the base of the wall, the four men assigned the task of using their ropes to reach the top went to work securing them so they could all ascend rapidly. Soon they were walking up the side of the city wall. There was a brief window for them to get to the top, over, and beyond without being detected. It was going to be tight.

The first men up, Kurad among them, positioned themselves to hold the parapet while they waited for the next two waves to clamber up behind them. The walkway was clear. The diversion was working, but Kurad knew that every extra second atop the wall increased the chances of discovery. The men standing on the parapet with him unstrapped their bows and stood at the ready to defend those still climbing. Four more men topped the wall leaving just two on the ground. Kurad instructed the rest of the men to drop down the inner wall to the rooftops of the buildings ten feet below, to wait there and he would follow with the last two as soon as they were over.

The last of the men already on top dropped down to the rooftop below just as a lone gnome emerged from the guard tower not more than twenty paces away. Kurad spied the gnome before he realized that there was an intruder in front of him. Kurad had two men who were moments away from reaching the top and vulnerable, the rest of Fox Company was just out of sight.

He reacted instantly. Kurad drew his sword and rushed toward the gnome who was all too aware of the danger in front of him and was spinning around to run the other way, calling for help as he ducked into the guard tower.

Kurad needed to silence the alarm before the gnome could pass along the message that the walls had been breached. Sprinting towards the guard tower, unsure of the number of gnomes within, knowing the mission would fail if any knew that the Fox Company was in the city.

He skidded through the darkened doorway, tripping and catching himself as he nearly tumbled over the form of the sentry lying on the floor just inside the door, an arrow protruding from his back, apparently silenced by a member of Kurad's squad. Kurad took a moment to check to see if there was any response from any of the gnomes farther down the wall, and saw no movement coming his direction. He spun around to make his way back, finding the last two men waiting atop the wall. They were slightly confused at the absence of the rest of the members until they saw Kurad gliding towards them. Kurad helped them gather up the climbing gear and quickly led them down from the wall to rejoin the rest of the men waiting below. After identifying and thanking the archer that had cut down the escaping gnome in the guard tower, he led them down to the street below.

They were in the city now, hiding in an alley deep in the shadows of the surrounding buildings. They stopped to listen to the sounds of the city. There were still voices coming from the area on the wall where Austin and James had flung their arrows, but the commotion among the sentries was dying down. After confirming that no one was searching the streets for them, they began to move off into the city. There was still some distance to cover tonight and they needed to find a place to hole up out of sight and get some much needed rest, but they were much closer to their goal than they had been when the sun set last night. The rising sun in the morning would reveal an entirely new landscape for the men and begin an entirely new phase of Prince Edward's rescue.

Chapter Thirty One

There was a commotion in the hall outside Edward's cell bringing him instantly awake. Apparently he had been able to get some sleep, he realized, as he made his way over to the door to hear better. It sounded like Konterra was out of his cell and the guards were struggling to get him to fall into line with some of the other prisoners. Edward knew they were being brought up with everyone else to watch the ceremony scheduled for today. He crouched down in front of the meal slot in the door, hoping to catch a glimpse of the scuffle going on outside, but there wasn't an angle that would allow him a view. He shifted a bit to the left and pressed his face firmly to the door. If the crack was just a smidge wider, he thought, and then he found himself tumbling into the hall as his door was yanked open. He lay where he fell, a gnome sword hovering in front of his face as he blinked furiously at the brighter light in the hallway, trying to recover from his unexpected release.

"Don't move, young prince," the guard sneered at him. "If the boss wasn't so sure he wanted you alive for your execution, I would take care of you right now and we could just get on with the feast. Find your feet and show me your hands so we can get you shackled proper for the parade."

Edward looked away from the sword pointing at his face. The threat was meant merely to keep him in line, so he turned his focus to those around him and took a quick inventory of the hall's occupants. There were a handful of dwarves shackled in a line, staring at him sprawled out on his back. Not the most kingly position, Edward decided, but they did not look to be judgmental. Surrounding them were a dozen gnomes, all brandishing either swords or spears, and beyond them were twice again as many lining the walls, ready to lead them to the festival. Orgle wasn't taking any chances. Konterra had been right in his assessment of the dim possibility of breaking Edward loose down in the dungeons. The last dwarf in line gave Edward the slightest of head nods and Edward presumed that this was Konterra. He climbed to his feet, adjusting his clothes on his thick frame.

"Stick out your arms so that you can be shackled to your brothers," ordered the gnome, now with the sword pointed at Edward's midsection.

Edward hesitated, staring directly at the gnome and feeling belligerent, challenging him to force the issue. On his feet Edward was a much more intimidating presence compared to the spindly gnome, and though the gnome held the sword out in front of him, he shrank back as he tentatively jabbed at Edward, barking orders to those around him. Though the orders weren't spoken in the common tongue, he apparently called for reinforcements as several gnomes raised their weapons, bringing them to bear. Metal-tipped spears and swords pointed menacingly at Edward. He had proved his point to the gnome in charge, he wasn't afraid of him nor was he bowing to his authority. Should he decide to put up a fight, it was going to take more than a handful of gnomes to bring him down.

That thought gave him pause. Disarming the gnome nearest him would be a small matter of catching him flat-footed and then he would be armed. Not his first choice of weapon, given the choice between his axe and the cheap steel blade pointed at him, but he felt he was more than proficient for the crew that surrounded him now. He stepped forward, his decision made, raising his hands in front of him to receive his shackles. Edward had to trust the plan that Konterra had for escape. Risking an injury at this time was not worth proving a point, and so he fell in line behind Konterra. Orgle was the only gnome that mattered and he hoped he would deal with him shortly.

Orgle stood from the plush chair in his chamber and received the axe from the dwarf artisan, nearly dropping it as the weight transferred from the sturdy dwarf to his thin arms. He recovered as best he could, trying to disguise the effort it took to lift the axe high enough to admire the new black stone that adorned the head. Setting the stone had taken longer than he anticipated. The dwarf claimed unforeseen delays but that mattered no more. The ceremony was this very day and now that he had the weapon, he was overjoyed that it was finally ready and immediately forgot his previous dismay. He stared deep into the black stone, its near translucent composition allowing his eyes to delve beneath the surface, quickly becoming mesmerized.

The stone seemed to come to life now that it was paired with Edward's axe. No, he corrected himself, his axe. Even after he pulled his eyes away, Orgle couldn't remember the stone being quite so brilliant when mounted on his old scepter. It was clear to him that it had finally found its true home.

Orgle looked around the room. He was alone now. The dwarf and his guard had apparently let themselves out while he was entranced with the axe. There was much to do today and it was just as well that they had gone from his chambers. Their usefulness had expired.

"Kropett, come in here immediately," he called towards the closed doorway and was rewarded with sounds of movement from the next room as Kropett scurried to respond to his call.

"Yes, Your Highness?" Kropett called even as he pushed his way into the room.

"I need to know the schedule for the day. When will everything be in place?" Orgle asked. He'd left all the details to Kropett. The little gnome was very effective when it came to making things happen and Orgle was more than willing to let him do the bulk of the planning.

"Your Highness," Kropett began. He was always careful to make sure Orgle believed he was sufficiently respected. It allowed him to do the things that he felt needed to be done to run the country. More importantly, it kept him alive when so many of his successors had met an untimely end.

"The prince and his companions," he said with a smirk, "are being gathered up as we speak. They will be delivered to the stage in the courtyard before you have given your speech to the gathered slaves, just as you have requested. Your troops will have them locked down and the show of force should be more than intimidating. All of your troops, other than a few patrols out chasing some riff raff, will be in attendance. This is the moment you have been waiting for all these years; one and all will witness the end of King Samuel's line." Kropett was excited too. He had aspirations of his own and once Orgle completed his dirty work, it would allow him to move on and expand the empire beyond where they were stuck now.

Orgle nodded. He had waited many years for this day. He instructed Kropett to bring him his breakfast though he wasn't sure he could make himself eat. His head was spinning and his nerves were on edge. The realization of all his dreams was just hours away.

"Kurad," Christopher spoke quickly in hushed tones, "my scouts report activity in the courtyard. A gathering of dwarves and men are milling about, seemingly not by their own choice. Lots of gnome soldiers guard the captives. They outnumber them nearly five to one. More importantly, the scouts speak of a stage that has been erected outside the castle gate, possibly equipped for executions."

"We need to intercept the delivery," Kurad responded, his tone leaving no room for question or debate. "Edward is possibly mere moments away from being the guest of honor at his own execution. Get your men ready to move out, now!" Kurad spoke with intensity, and Christopher responded instantly, the message passing among his men like a wildfire. They all gathered their gear from around them in the abandoned apartment that they had found to rest overnight and began to shoulder backpacks and supplies. As soon as Kurad saw the men shouldering their packs, he quickly intervened.

"Men, we need little else but speed for this last rush. Bring only that which you need to wage battle. We either succeed in rescuing Edward, or we die in our attempt. None of the gear in our packs will matter at all at the end of this day." He left his own pack where it lay and headed for the door while the men scrambled behind him to shed unnecessary gear.

The streets were quiet in the neighborhood where they had settled in last night. The gnomes did not occupy this section of the city and now, with the gathering going on by the castle, the streets were completely void of any foot traffic. Kurad and his crew used the quiet to their advantage, running from building to building and alley to alley, using caution as time allowed, knowing that every minute they lost now could mean the difference between life and death for Edward.

It amazed Kurad as he led the Fox Company through the deserted streets of the city where they once lived, that these men were racing towards near certain doom for a young man they had never met. It was the embodiment of an ideal, of hope, that he would lead them to victory over the gnomes who chased them from their homes a dozen years ago. The allure of coming home was powerful. The anger at Orgle defeating Samuel's army and forcing them to leave everything behind as they escaped into the mountains still burned within them. Kurad could only hope that, should they rescue Edward and force Orgle from the throne, his young charge was up to the task of leading these men and all those others that marched towards the city.

They came to an intersection and Kurad halted them. He could hear more noise ahead and though he knew the city well, those in the Fox Company were coming home and they knew these streets better than him. Sensing his hesitation, Christopher came up alongside of him.

"The Square is just ahead; two more cross streets and then one block to the right. We'll be right in the middle of everything. If we want to intercept his escort we need to jog left right now and then circle out and around the gathering so we can get between the castle and the stage." He supplied Kurad with the information he needed and looked to Kurad for his plan of action.

"Our intention was never to take on the whole of Orgle's army, the majority of which is in that Square. I think we need to stick to our strengths and try to keep to the plan of breaking him free before he ever meets his executioner." Kurad paused, and though Christopher wasn't sure if he was done laying out the plan, a loud cheer from the gnome army gathered in the square interrupted him from continuing. Christopher knew without Kurad speaking another word that the plan had just changed and then they were all racing after Kurad as he sprinted towards the growing din.

Helen and Jessica turned around from their position on the stage to see what the gnomes in the crowd were cheering about. It took a moment for the gnomes escorting Edward and the dwarves he was shackled in line with to clear away so that the two women had a line of sight to Edward and could see the reason for the cheering mob. Jessica knew it was necessary to get Edward out of the dungeons. Still, it was disheartening to watch him being led through the throng, towards the steps leading up to the stage where she herself now stood. It had been a tough morning. They were awakened and pulled from their cell early in preparation of the day's ceremony. The two women had been surprised at the timing of their delivery to the stage.

Jessica hadn't had a moment to talk to her mother in private, though maybe it didn't matter if her mom was aware of the details of what was to happen. Jessica wished she was able to reassure her mother that things were going as they thought it would, but the time was past as she saw that Edward was mounting the steps leading up to where she was standing.

Edward fought the urge to make a break for freedom as he followed Konterra through the hallways of his father's castle. The idea of walking to his own execution screamed 'wrong' to him and yet he continued on without a fight, or any further protest towards Orgle's macabre ceremony. The dungeon was behind him now and the sunlight seemed bright as he emerged from the castle. He was still blinking his eyes, trying to accustom them to the glare, as he cleared the outer wall of the castle grounds when he heard the cheer from the gnome army. Edward was disoriented as he entered the square. His senses overloaded from the noise of the crowd, the bright sun glaring in his eyes, and the shackles throwing off his balance. He stumbled as the dwarves in line before him struggled to get their bearings too. His struggle to gather his feet underneath himself and his apparent disorientation only fueled the crowd in their bloodthirsty cries for his death.

The hatred that bombarded Edward as he approached the stage was nearly as disorienting as the sun and noise he'd encountered upon leaving the castle. It was hard to imagine that these gnomes could be so unified behind their leader and that his death was going to cause them such ecstasy. Edward could sense that he was reacting to the crowd and being bent to their collective will. He knew he needed to find his own strength, his own lifeline to grab onto, and pull himself through the haze that surrounded him.

The dwarves in front of him began to climb the stairs of the stage. Edward followed behind, the shackles giving him no other option. He made his way up the half dozen steps to the platform in an off-balance, halting gait as the string of dwarves worked together to navigate the stairs as one. As he cleared the last step and his foot was planted atop the stage, he saw Jessica and Helen through the bodies in front of him. His heart surged and he felt his body responding to the rush of emotions. They were here for him. They had endured months of captivity and living in the dark, dank dungeons just waiting for his return. The clarity he sought returned to him.

Jessica. She had organized an army to rescue him. The realization jumped to the forefront of his thinking, pushing all other thoughts to the side, his head turning about so he could take in the entire crowd gathered before him. It was then for the first time that Edward, looked past the gnomes spitting their hatred at him, saw amongst them the slaves of Orgle. They stood now and watched him as he surveyed the crowd. These were his people, the very dwarves and men that had served his father and had lost their freedom defending the city against Orgle's hordes. Edward couldn't know what they were thinking, but he could only assume they were taking his measure. Was it possible that there were those in the crowd that remembered him from his childhood? Would they fight for his freedom? Were they willing to give their lives to overthrow Orgle and raise him to the throne?

He knew he must send them a signal, a sign to let them know that he was the son of their fallen king, that he was Edward Ellingstone. It flashed in his mind.

His tattoo. It marked him as it had his father and the kings for generations before him. Kurad hadn't explained the mark on the inside of his forearm when he was younger, but he'd seen on his axe, and it was in the castle; carved into the granite of every column and decorating the stonework around the castle walls. Edward tried to lift his arm only the shackles held his arm firmly. Without the shackles removed, it would be impossible to get the message to even those closest to the stage. He knew that any extra motivation would help those who had given up hope, and he could see there were many in the crowd that had done just that. It could encourage them to revolt against their captors because he needed them all. His thinking had cleared and he knew his purpose this day. He would have to wait for his opportunity and hope that it presented itself in time to make a difference.

His chains yanked him back to the stage and the immediate situation. Konterra was being pushed forward by the guards and Edward had to either move too, or he was going to be pulled from his feet. A show of strength against the odds facing him was one more way to pull everyone to his side, so he moved as purposefully as his restraints allowed. The act was quickly met with force as Orgle, who had stood silently watching his enemy's arrival, barked out an order to strike Edward down and show him his place.

The blow from Kropett's staff caught him in the small of his back, pitching him forward into Konterra and upsetting the line as they shuffled forward. Konterra and the dwarves in front of him used their thick bodies, setting themselves as they absorbed the impact from behind. Edward righted himself, glowering at the smiling Kropett, hoping that he would have the opportunity to deal with the evil little gnome when this was all over.

Edward stood in line next to Konterra now as Orgle praised his assistant and then turned to the gathered assembly. He began his speech about his exploits, at which point Edward turned his attention to the rest of the individuals on the stage. Helen and Jessica stood off to the side. Though they didn't appear to be bound, it was hard for him to imagine that they wouldn't be restrained, leaving them free to interfere with the proceedings. He saw Jessica looking at him and flashed a reassuring smile which she returned, though with less enthusiasm.

There was a full contingent of gnome soldiers. It included all those who had escorted them from their cells. More than a dozen stood at the ready to the rear and three times that number below the stage with spears in hand. He wasn't sure if they were there to protect Orgle from the slaves in the crowd or to keep Edward from escaping. Because of where he was positioned, off to the side, Edward could see the execution block in front of Orgle's podium and there, leaning against it, Edward's axe. So that was the plan, he thought. Use his own axe to behead the rightful heir to the throne. Edward could see the irony in the situation and had to silently applaud Orgle for his theatrics, though Edward prayed that the event wouldn't play out as Orgle had it scripted.

Once he'd taken inventory of all the key players on the stage, his attention shifted to the crowd. He could see the stirrings of select groupings of dwarves and others of men and he could only assume that Konterra's plan was being set in motion.

Konterra was risking the most by putting himself so close to the prince. Edward had not realized until they were being led out from the castle that Konterra had been similarly sentenced to death. Konterra was an integral part of the plan to free Edward. He felt it was necessary to be at the point of attack, though if the plan failed he would be one of the first to fall to the spears of the gnomes surrounding the platform. It was a huge risk he was taking, but it spoke of the conviction he had in the need to overthrow Orgle and remove him from power.

Around the perimeter, beyond the men and dwarves positioned in the center of the courtyard, was the bulk of Orgle's army. Edward couldn't get an accurate count but the gnomes most certainly outnumbered their slaves by a wide margin. That caused him more than a little concern. The gnomes were also armed with either spears or swords, which meant that his secret army with weapons constructed from scrap materials, were sorely overmatched. It was clear why the focus had to be on taking Orgle out of the picture. 'Cut the head off the snake' was how Konterra had put it and, after surveying the situation, Edward had to agree that that would be their best chance.

Another jab into Edward's back from Kropett brought his focus back to the immediate proceedings on the stage and he realized that Orgle was coming to the climax of his rousing speech. The gnomes were getting whipped into a frenzy from the rhetoric Orgle was spouting and Edward knew that the time was growing near for Konterra's plan to be put into action.

In order for the plan to work, the timing needed to be just right. Edward and the others were to surprise the guards as the first prisoner was being brought to the executioner. Then, while they were distracted, they would launch their attack on Orgle. Simultaneously, the army hidden amongst the slaves would surge forward and attack those protecting the stage from below. The goal was to keep Edward protected by the dwarves surrounding him, his de facto bodyguards, until there was a clear path off the stage.

As the moment of truth approached, Edward grew apprehensive. The plan seemed more plausible when it was discussed in the bowels of the dungeon. In the bright sunshine of the day, the possibility of flaws was brought to light.

Kropett prodded him from behind more forcefully than before as his jailer fumbled with the keys to release him from his leg irons, freeing him to step forward and away from his companions. It became suddenly clear to Edward that the plan wasn't going to go as it expected. He was to be the first to meet his fate and not the grand finale as had been the assumption. He hoped the others had picked up on this detail and were making the necessary adjustments.

"I want to introduce some special guests to the stage," Orgle barked out as the cheering subsided at the behest of Orgle's raised hands, asking for quiet.

"Please welcome Barmes, who our nation owes so much, for running this criminal to ground and bringing him back so that he could be properly sentenced." At this point Barmes came running up the steps to the cheers of the gathered gnomes. He bowed profusely as he accepted their adulation before resuming his previous position off to the side.

"Next I would like to introduce our honorary executioner. Yancik, too, was vital in the capture of the criminal and will assist in carrying out the verdict rendered." Orgle motioned the oversized gnome to make his way up the steps to stand by him. It hadn't taken Orgle long to determine that he wouldn't be able to heft Edward's axe high enough to accomplish his goal so he had invented a way to bring Yancik into the proceedings.

Edward had no illusions of any verdict other than a death sentence so there was no change in his demeanor as he moved to where Orgle, accompanied now by Yancik, stood. He waited to receive his sentencing and Orgle wasted no time in delivering it.

"For the crimes committed against my throne, I condemn you, Edward Ellingstone, to death by my verdict of Guilty," he yelled out the last. It was met with howls and cheers from the gnomes in attendance and a hastening of the actions by the army of slaves as they moved to stop the proceedings.

Four gnome guards grabbed Edward's shackled arms and manhandled him to the execution block. Edward was struggling to get loose, but with so many hanging on, he had no way to break free. He could see Konterra and the other two dwarves being subdued, hearing a cry for help from Jessica above the scuffles going on as she too was held back. The contingent of gnomes guarding the platform turned their spears on the crowd and slowed the push from Edward's rescuers. Edward saw all this in brief snippets as he was being pushed towards the block before being bodily slammed down on top of it by Yancik. Once Edward was positioned, Yancik grabbed hold of the axe that had been placed there so he could accomplish his grisly assignment. Kurad skidded to the edge of the flat rooftop of the building his men had climbed. Their path had unwittingly been blocked by a cluster of gnomes on the street; they needed to see a way through to Edward. They arrived at the edge of the rooftop in time to look across the courtyard to see Edward being positioned on the block and the executioner reaching for the axe. The axe had been meant for Edward to take back his father's castle, not for taking his own life. Kurad called for his archers. It would be a long shot with an arrow but at the moment, it was all he could do for his friend. Several men of Fox Company reached for arrows and nearly simultaneously loosed their shots. There hadn't been time to pick separate targets. Instead, they all instinctively aimed for Yancik.

The arrows were speeding away and Kurad could only wait and watch to see if they found their target in time. He held his breath as they began the arc down from the height of their flight towards the axe-wielding Yancik. As the leading arrows closed on the target, Kurad gripped his sword, willing them to find the flesh of the big gnome as he raised the axe overhead, and praying that none would hit Edward. The proximity to one another made it a nearly impossible at this range to not endanger him. Yet the risk of doing nothing meant his death, so the risky shots were warranted. He could tell the aim of at least a couple of the archers seemed true as his eyes strained to track the slivers of wood through the air, waiting to see if they found their mark.

Instead, at what would have been the moment of impact, he and his men were reflexively covering their eyes and ducking for cover. A blinding flash of light engulfed the stage and all the actors in this life and death drama.

Troy A. Skog

Chapter Thirty Two

Edward pulled himself up from the wood planks of the stage, climbing to his hands and knees. He looked around at the others who had been with him on the stage as they too picked themselves up. All seemed as bewildered as he at the pulse of light. His first thought was that the axe had separated his head from his shoulders, the flash of light the end of his existence. Now he realized that they had all experienced it and were similarly trying to collect their bearings, deciding if they should flee for their own safety. Through the din he heard a gravelly voice that sounded vaguely familiar, yet he couldn't place it. It calmed him and pushed the fear away, giving him a sense of peace. Edward raised himself up from all fours so that he was kneeling and slowly turned his head to see who spoke.

The sight that awaited him was truly unexpected and, by the looks on the faces of those gathered on the stage, they were equally surprised and confused.

"My dear little Orgle," called the deep voice of the troll, "I can tell from your speechlessness that you thought you had seen the last of me." Wilgar wore what Edward could only assume was a smile on his stony face as he stifled a low chuckle. Orgle squirmed helplessly in the firm grasp of the giant rock troll as he held him by his neck, his feet dangling. Yancik, held in Wilgar's other hand, was not quite so incapacitated. He attempted to fight his way free, kicking and striking Wilgar with Edward's battleaxe. It had no effect against the skin of the troll, the blade harmlessly bouncing off the stone hide of his captor. Yancik was at least annoying, or too distracting for the monstrous creature; Wilgar shook Yancik violently, breaking him up inside and snapping his neck before summarily dropping the limp gnome to the wooden platform and turning his attention back to Orgle.

The sight of Yancik, the biggest gnome they knew, being tossed about like a doll, deeply affected the remaining gnomes on the stage. They were clearly torn. Should they go to the aide of their king or run for their lives? Wilgar had clearly shown he was impervious to physical attacks and was more than willing to dispatch any that opposed him without a thought. Fear of the giant creature overrode their loyalty to Orgle and sent a few gnomes scrambling off the back of the stage only to be followed shortly after by the remaining gnomes, hot on their heels, and quickly disappearing into the crowd below. The sight of Orgle's guards abandoning their king and running for safety caused Wilgar to laugh loudly, his voice booming across the courtyard.

"I've been waiting a long time for you to show up, young man." Wilgar spoke again, causing Edward to look about to make sure he was the one being addressed.

"I can tell by your expression that you don't remember my visit to your dungeon cell. You were incoherent at the time, so I will forgive you your incredulous stare." Wilgar reached down and picked up Edward's axe from next to Yancik's still form and extended it out to Edward. He continued to speak while Edward gathered the nerve to step forward and receive the weapon from him.

"I was able to access your dreams from the stone you see mounted in the blade, but I couldn't materialize until you were near the stone. There are limitations to each stone's powers." He turned his attention back to Orgle who had gone deathly still.

"When you released me from the Starrock and demanded I tear down King Samuel's walls, I was obligated to fulfill your orders. However, I swore that if the opportunity presented itself to put a descendant of Samuel's back on the throne, I would make amends for the atrocity my people were forced to commit." He turned his attention to Edward as the young man stepped forward and reached up to take the battleaxe from his apparent rescuer. As Edward grasped the handle, Wilgar bent forward, bowing deeply.

"I wish to apologize for the pain and heartache the trolls have caused you, and for the loss of your family. Your loss was in large part due to the actions of my people. I realize there is nothing I can do to bring them back to you, but I do take great satisfaction that I was able to return your bloodline to the throne." His head turned back to Orgle now.

"And to you, Orgle, I want to thank you for keeping my stone so close at hand. Its purpose was to provide me with a looking glass into the castle to watch for any who would present himself as the rightful king. You thought it another powerful stone you could use against your enemies, but it would not respond to your manipulations. In truth, it is very powerful, only not in the way that you had hoped." Another chuckle emanated from deep within his body. "I have watched you from a distance. I have seen all the atrocities you committed against the people of Pendar, and your own gnomes for that matter, and now I'm here to sentence you for all your crimes."

Orgle's eyes got even wider as Wilgar's grip tightened around his neck. He frantically looked about for help and found the platform devoid of any gnomes and those in the crowd were beginning to back away from the stage. Many more were running to get away, afraid of what the troll would do once he had dealt with Orgle. The only people on the stage left to witness Orgle's reckoning were Edward, Jessica, Helen, Konterra, and the other two shackled dwarves. Kropett had apparently made his exit with the other gnomes and was most likely putting distance between himself and his king.

Edward, standing in front of Wilgar now, held up his hand, begging Wilgar to ease his grip on Orgle's neck so the gnome could breathe.

"Kind troll, I do believe we have met. At least, I remember you from my dreams. My memory fails me though, I do not know your name nor your reputation."

"My apologies, I am Wilgar, High Priest of the Stone Trolls. Let me tell you of my history and hopefully it will shed some light on my reluctant relationship with Orgle." He gave his captive a little shake to emphasize the fact that he was still harboring anger over Orgle's abuses.

"I was imprisoned in the Starrock by a powerful wizard many years ago. When the trolls were driven from their home by his pet dragon, the Starrock, with me imprisoned within, was left behind and ultimately found by Orgle. You are all aware of what resulted from that discovery. After we helped Orgle take the castle, I left. Since then, I have used the looking glass to look for an opportunity to come back and atone for my transgressions." He was clearly distraught about his actions while under Orgle's control and seemed anxious to deal with the little gnome so his conscience could be cleared.

"This looking glass is a very powerful gem." Edward lifted the battleaxe to admire the stone set in the blade.

"I am very thankful that you had the foresight to give this gift to Orgle, and in the end, to come back and help me in my quest to liberate my people from a tyrant." He paused for a second to gather himself.

"Just so you know, we had a plan, though I think this turned out maybe a little better." A smile broke out on his face as he looked about at the others standing around him. He felt lighter at the release of the bottled-up tension leading up to this. He turned to look at the crowd. The gnomes in attendance were all gone and the dwarves and men held captive by Orgle all cheered as Edward instinctively reached upward, the family crest on his forearm matching the blade on the axe he held overhead.

It was a familiar voice that separated itself from the crowd and drew Edward's eyes to find the man to whom it belonged. Edward nearly jumped from the stage when Kurad broke through the crowd pressing against the stage. He hurried over to the edge and offered a hand to his teacher and friend, grasping his hand firmly. With help from the Fox Company that had followed in his wake, Kurad was hoisted up to stand next to Edward. The two men hugged. Both had had doubts that the other had survived the journey and now they were reunited, victorious on the very stage they'd feared would be the site of Edward's execution. They were quickly joined by Helen and Jessica, the scene was turning into a grand reunion as the four embraced with more than a few tears of joy and relief shared by all.

It was the booming voice of Wilgar that finally broke up the reunion.

"I hate to bring the festivities to a halt, but I must take my leave soon and we still have the little issue of punishing Orgle for his crimes." He gave Orgle another shake to make sure he knew that they had not forgotten about him.

"Wilgar, I feel as if I should defer to you to carry out the sentence," Edward said, composed now after his tearful reunion. "You have even more cause to carry out retribution than I do. The acts you were forced to do against your will, in a way, outweigh the evil done to my family and my father's people."

"There is more than enough blood on Orgle's head to warrant an execution by my hand or that of the King of Pendar." Wilgar stopped. Before he came back, he hadn't considered an alternative to settling the debts of Orgle himself, for his anger had brewed these past twelve years. Now though, as he looked down upon this young man, he reconsidered the cost of Orgle's actions on Edward compared to his own. The power of the Starrock had been abused and Wilgar had been made a slave to Orgle, but he was just a lone troll. Edward, however, represented an entire country. His decision was made as he stepped forward, holding Orgle out in front him as he approached the executioner's block. He slammed the kicking and clawing Orgle down, the impact disorienting him and knocking the air from his lungs. Wilgar nodded towards Edward.

Edward hesitated momentarily as he stepped into position, a flood of emotions taking him on a wild ride. Anger for all the pain Orgle had inflicted on his people welled up inside him. Years of slavery for those captured within the city when the trolls breached the gate and months of captivity for Helen and Jessica. And, as he brought the pain back full circle to himself, to the murder of his parents. His memories barely reached back that far, back to the time before Kurad had rescued him from sharing a fate similar to that of his loved ones.

As his anger reached its boiling point, the reality of taking another's life, no matter how evil the individual. The roles were reversed now. Would Orgle have afforded him a chance at freedom if Wilgar hadn't appeared to stay his hand? The grip on his battleaxe eased just slightly as he looked upon Orgle's pathetic form prostrate before him, a broken ruler who had been seduced by greed and stretched the definition of sanity to the extreme. He didn't take his eyes off the broken gnome before him. He knew those around him expected him to finish the execution, but he couldn't be swayed by their desire for revenge. This was his first decision as the King of Pendar and bowing to the pressure of his people would not serve him well when he finally sat upon his father's throne.

He weighed the decision made by Wilgar, and then asked the question of himself. Did Wilgar's dreams of vengeance truly mirror his own? Was this the right thing to do given the situation? He weighed all the crimes Orgle had committed against the fact that now he had been deserted by his people and seemed to be no more of a threat to anyone. Would locking him away in the dungeon and throwing away the key be the proper punishment for someone with so much blood on his hands? In that moment he knew in his heart what needed to happen and instantly felt at peace, knowing his own decision would stand the test of time when he looked back upon this day. His father's foresight had made this moment possible and it was Edward's belief that his father's decision would have been the same as his own. His feet shifted, and his hands gripped the handle just as Kurad had taught him. The axe blade rose and fell quickly. Orgle's reign of terror was over and Orgle was now relegated to the history books.

The cheers by those in the crowd reinforced his decision. Shouts of praise rained down on him from dwarves and men alike. He had accomplished the mission that his father had mapped out. Samuel's heir had assumed his rightful position on the throne of the country he had loved and ultimately died in service to. Edward felt the weight of the moment and knew the burden of responsibility would be great, he hoped he would be up to the task. The cheering quickly subsided and the crowd's attention was drawn to Wilgar as he moved to stand beside him. Edward turned to face the stone troll, craning his neck as he looked up at his immense height.

"I must take leave of you now, King Edward Ellingstone. I am impressed with the consideration you put into the decision concerning Orgle's fate. I see great things for this country under your rule. I wish you well in the years to come. You have much to do to erase Orgle's taint, but looking around, I see that you will have much help." He finished speaking and bowed deeply once more, acknowledging Edward's position, and then slowly straightened back to his full height.

Though Edward could not understand what Wilgar spoke next in his native tongue, there was no doubt as to its meaning. His words were followed by the same brilliant flash of light that had preceded his arrival and, when all those that had once again witnessed the flash lifted their heads, Wilgar was gone. The stone mounted in the handle was no longer translucent but rather a dark opaque. Edward could only assume it was no longer a looking glass between Wilgar's lands and his own.

The next couple of days passed rapidly as those enslaved to Orgle began the transformation back to soldiers. Edward had called them all to fall back to the castle grounds to regroup and allow the gnomes and their families a chance to evacuate the city that they had called home for the past dozen years. He didn't want the blood of the innocent on his hands. They were frantically packing all that they could carry, and though they weren't being harassed, they left much behind in their haste to go home.

There was plenty to do in the castle to erase the years of neglect and it was here that Edward turned the attention of his people. Kurad was at his side often, suggesting and guiding Edward as he began his reign. Jessica knew many of those who had been slaves from her time working in the castle and the gardens and organizing the army. She spent much of her time helping Edward learn the names and positions of those in her army. Though there wasn't much time for the two of them to be alone together, they enjoyed each other's company as they worked to pull everyone together.

It was on the third day after the fall of Orgle that a messenger came from the city gate. An army approached and the king's presence was needed immediately. Flanked by a small army himself, Edward set out to the gate at a brisk pace, nervous as to what challenge awaited his fledgling rule. It was his first time outside the castle walls. General Reylsis, assuming his role as the leader of the army and instrumental in organizing the troops, was adamant that until a complete sweep of the city had taken place Edward could not afford to be out in the open. Kurad had agreed. But now, in light of the reports from the city gate, they were forced to make a concession. Though as evidenced by the size of his company, they were still taking no chances.

He arrived at the gate and looked out upon the army assembling on the green space outside the city walls. "Your Highness," spoke a voice at his elbow, "their emissary has asked for your audience."

"Then let's grant their wish. Kurad and Relysis, would you please accompany me?" Edward asked as he prepared to walk out through the gate still in tatters from when the troll army had broken through so many years ago. He was quickly ringed by Christopher and the members of the Fox Company, who had assumed the role of his personal bodyguards, and began to move out onto the field. There was a stirring across the way as ranking members of the army responded to the sight of Edward's detail leading him from the city. By the time Edward had covered half the distance to the army he was met by their leader.

It was Kurad that began speaking as the two faced one another. "King Edward, I would like to introduce you to General Willos."

As soon as Kurad introduced Edward, Willos bowed deeply. "I am honored to meet you, Your Highness. I bring to your service the army of remnants."

"Thank you, General Willos. Your service is without measure. Kurad has told me much about your efforts to lead our people in the absence of my family. I hope you will accept an honored position within my council to assist in the rebuilding and governing of our city." Edward was aware of the sacrifices that had been made to keep the dream of reclaiming their home alive. Willos extended his hand to Edward who readily clasped it to seal his pledge to serve. As soon as the two released their grasp, Willos motioned for the bearers to come forward calling for them to bring the gift. When the two approached the group, Edward smiled disbelievingly as he recognized one of the young men that labored to carry the gift between them. His little friend Bernard had survived the exodus from Pendar and was right there in front of him. The emotions of the moment overtaking him as he rushed forward to envelop his lost friend in a bear hug, forcing Bernard to let go of his side of the gift.

"Your friend Tyvig sends his best, and I don't mean his regards." Willos motioned to the polished black suit of armor that had been gathered back up after the reunion of the two boyhood friends.

"I have never seen its equal. The man must have some dwarf in him," he said with a smile on his gruff face.

After several more introductions and a close inspection of his new armor, it was decided that they should move the army within the city walls to reunite them with those who had been left behind all those years ago. It was going to be quite a celebration.

As he walked back to the city, he thought of the armor Tyvig had given him and from somewhere far back in his memory, a line from the story his father would tell him came to the surface. A smile broke out on his face as he leaned over to whisper to Bernard, "Do you think that, after all this time, I'm the Black Knight?" The two men laughing between themselves as those around looked on curiously.

Epilogue

Several years later he stood on the balcony of the castle enjoying the view of the setting sun when his wife, Jessica, sought him out.

"Look what I found in the library." She held out an old leather bound book with the Ellingstone family crest emblazoned on its dusty cover.

"I have been reading it and I have to believe that it's your story written here. I'm not sure of the meaning of the part after this line that reads...." she handed the book to Edward, pointing to the line.

"The conquerors from the south had never rebuilt the city gates..." The pages began to glow in his hands as he read. Clearly there was magic at work within this old tome, he thought, holding it away from him as they were engulfed in the light emanating from the book.

ABOUT THE AUTHOR

The directions on how to write a biography suggest telling my readers interesting details about myself. That left me scratching my mostly bald head trying to think of what folks would find interesting. I guess I'm a product of my Minnesota upbringing; I like to say "my lack of flare is my flare".

After high school and a couple of years at the local community college I spent an enlistment in the United States Air Force providing security for the air base where I was stationed before finishing up my B.S. in Engineering Technology and Geography at St. Cloud State University.

In my free time I enjoy a long run, nothing cures writers block like an early morning run on the weekend. Sunrises really are inspiring!

My beautiful wife, who is one of my biggest cheerleaders, calls me her man-child for my goofy sense of humor and how I act like one of our kids most of the time. I try to bring all these values and traits that I find to be so important in my own life, to my characters in hopes that my readers can relate to them and immerse themselves into the story.

Hopefully this biography helps you, the reader, to get to know me just a little bit and gives you some background. Thanks for taking the time to let me tell you about myself.

Welcome to The Kings of Pendar, enjoy the adventure!